Little Shop
in
Cornwall

BOOKS BY HELEN POLLARD

The
Little Shop
in
Cornwall

helen pollard

bookouture

Published by Bookouture in 2020

An imprint of Storyfire Ltd.
Carmelite House
50 Victoria Embankment
London EC4Y 0DZ

www.bookouture.com

ISBN: 978-1-83888-892-3
eBook ISBN: 978-1-83888-891-6

In memory of Patricia

Prologue

Claudia sat stiffly in an armchair, waiting for Lee to get home from his Friday after-work drinks. She had declined to go. She'd had plenty to do.

At the sound of his key in the lock, she took a deep breath. Since she'd made her decision, she felt remarkably calm.

Lee stepped into the lounge, a frown on his handsome face. 'Why are the cases in the hall? You didn't tell me you had a conference this weekend.'

'I don't. I'm leaving you.'

Lee's frown morphed into confusion, then anger. '*What?*'

'You heard me.'

'I wasn't sure I heard right, with you just sitting there like that! You've already packed? We haven't even talked about this. What the hell are you saying?'

'I don't see how I can put it any plainer, Lee. I'm leaving. We're done.'

Lee threw his arms in the air. 'Is this about the other day? Because if it is, you're overreacting.'

Claudia could have lost her cool at that point, but somehow, she kept her voice steady. 'I don't think it's overreacting to end a marriage in which it turns out you've been lied to the entire time.'

'For crying out loud, Claudia. We went through this. Call it a misunderstanding, a change of heart, if you like.'

'No, Lee, I don't like. It may have started out that way, a long time ago. Now? Outright lies.' She sighed. 'You knew all along that I wanted a family. You said you wanted the same. You kept putting it off. I went along with that. But overhearing you telling those oafish poker-playing friends of yours that you'd never had any intention, that I'd come around to it once time ran out…' Her voice hitched, and she fought to control it. 'I'd say that was the trump card, wouldn't you?'

'I told you, I was drunk. I told you…'

'You told me a lot of things, but for the first time, I listened to my gut instinct. This marriage might have been working for you, but I've come to realise it isn't working for me.'

'And what exactly do you think you're going to do with yourself?'

Claudia ignored the derision in his voice; the assumption that she couldn't go it alone. 'I'm going to listen to my gut instinct more often, for a start.'

Lee snorted. 'You and your gut instinct. That's not the only skill you need in our business, Claudia. All your promotions at that firm are down to *me*. When I get promoted, you get promoted, because people know you go hand in hand with me. See how that works?'

Claudia shook her head. 'It doesn't matter. I handed in my notice today.' Lee's eyes widened as she pushed on. 'I'll be filing for divorce. I *don't* expect you to contest it.' When he opened his mouth, no doubt to tell her where she could stick her divorce papers, with quiet threat in her voice she said, 'I know your secrets at work, Lee. The way you operate. Nothing illegal but certainly morally underhanded. So I suggest you're civil to me while I work out my notice, and that you play nice with the divorce.' She cocked her head to one side. 'I don't suppose it occurred to you it's the other way around, by the way? That *you* get promoted because *I* get promoted?' The blank look on his face almost made her smile. Let him think *that* through at his leisure. 'As for the flat? You can buy me out, or we can sell and split. I don't care, but I do want my share as soon as possible. I have a life to live.'

Lee's features betrayed his struggle to process the turn of events since he'd walked through the door after a pleasant couple of hours in a wine bar. His eyes narrowed. 'Is there someone else?'

'No. Just most definitely not you.'

'Charming! You don't want to talk this through?'

His question was half-hearted at best – the final proof Claudia needed that he simply didn't care enough to fight for her.

'Do we have anything to talk about?'

Lee remained silent for the longest moment, then finally sighed. 'Truthfully? No.'

Claudia stood. 'Then I'll go.'

'Go where?'

'Debbie offered me a room. I'll work out my notice while I look for another job. I only intend to stay in London until the divorce is settled and I have my share of the flat. Then I'll live the life I want to live.'

'Which is?'

'Honestly? I don't know yet. But I do know it will be as far away from London as I can go. I do know I will wear what I like, eat what I like, never go near another gym again, never spend every morning battling with hair straighteners, just to please you. Never have to keep my mouth shut at work for the benefit of you blundering your way up that precious career ladder of yours. Most important of all, I won't be spending my life with a man who promised we wanted the same things, promised me a family – the one thing I knew I *did* want – but had no intention of delivering on that promise. A man willing to sacrifice his wife's wishes and happiness for his own selfishness and who could lie for years to do so.' She moved into the hall and hefted a case in each hand. 'Goodbye, Lee.'

Three years later...

Chapter One

Claudia looked up as the doorbell jangled and peered at her potential customers. A teenager in substantial biker boots and a purple tie-dye dress over black leggings clomped across the threshold, her long, black hair streaked with purple, an air of sadness and anger advancing with her into the shop. Trailing behind, a man perhaps in his mid-thirties glanced warily at the goods on display.

Claudia went back to the friendship bracelet she was weaving. She didn't believe in approaching customers. They would stay awhile or not; buy or not. If something was meant for them, it would catch their eye. Their purchase may only bring them fleeting pleasure, but Claudia always hoped it would bring them something more.

Surreptitiously, she watched as they browsed her Aladdin's cave of crystals, beads, jewellery, textiles; scented candles, handmade soaps, essential oils; coastal wall art.

The teenager was antsy, picking everything up as though she would only know what she wanted once she held it in her hand. As that was often true in life, Claudia didn't mind her handling the goods. Healing Waves was intended as a sensory space.

The girl's reluctant companion remained a few paces behind, his facial expressions alternating between puzzlement and outright disapproval. His appearance – short, sandy-brown hair; conventionally dressed in jeans and collared T-shirt – was the opposite of the teenager, but their shared lean height and startlingly-pale blue eyes told Claudia they were father and daughter.

Claudia got the impression the man would rather have waited outside but didn't dare, in case his offspring bought something unsuitable. Glaring at the small selection of fantasy figures she stocked, he picked up a mermaid embracing a dragon and stared at it as though he'd never seen the like. When he reached the shelf of self-help books and read the blurb on a pack of shamanic-themed oracle cards, she thought he might spontaneously combust with disapproval.

The girl gravitated to the counter to browse a stand draped with pendants of crystals and tumblestones.

'What's this one?' she asked, holding up a smooth circlet of purple on a black leather lace, her Scottish accent suggesting she was an early-season tourist.

'Amethyst.' Claudia nodded her approval. 'Good choice.'

'Why?'

'It's an all-rounder. Calming and peaceful.' Taking a chance, she added, 'Good for anxiety.'

The father narrowed his eyes in cynicism, but the girl gave an unconscious jolt.

Smoothly, Claudia said, 'And it matches your hair.'

'I'll take it.' The girl gave her a tentative smile, but Claudia sensed it was a struggle, as though she hadn't tried it for a while. As she handed over her money, the girl spotted Claudia's cat curled in his basket at the back of the counter. 'Oh, he's lovely! Can I stroke him? Is it a he?'

Claudia smiled. 'Yes, he's a he. This is Pudding. He's safe to stroke.'

The girl reached out black-painted nails to carefully stroke between the cat's ears. Pudding opened one eye, decided she was acceptable, and closed it again.

'He's an unusual colour,' the girl pronounced.

Claudia chuckled. 'That's the understatement of the year!'

Pudding was a mottled character, his fur a mishmash of ginger and black and brown and white. Depending in which light he languished, he could look like a tortoiseshell or a tabby, or sometimes, just a mongrelly mess. His half-ginger, half-black nose gave him a quizzical expression, and his white bib made him look like he was always ready for his next meal – which he usually was, and he could be quite vocal about it. His yellow-green eyes were, as with all cats' eyes, rather mesmerising. Claudia could spend hours returning his steady gaze, lulled by his engine-loud purr, if she allowed herself to.

The girl took her change, and Claudia watched as they left, the father clearly relieved to be on his way out, taking his frown lines and pervading sense of weariness with him. She could have suggested something for him, too, but she doubted he'd be willing to wear a crystal in *any* shape or form.

Ah, well. You win some, you lose some.

*

Strolling back along the beach road towards the harbour, Jason already knew he would come to love the setting for their new home on the south coast of Cornwall.

On their left, the beach was uncrowded – for now – and inviting, the sea still and sparkling and undoubtedly too cold to toy with. On their right, grey stone or whitewashed buildings lined the opposite side of the road that ran alongside the beach, old and characterful, with tasteful shops and cafés interspersed among the houses.

As they walked, Jason tried to engage his daughter in conversation. 'Do you like your new necklace?'

'Wouldn't have bought it otherwise, would I?'

'Do you believe what that woman told you? About it having… abilities?'

Millie shrugged. 'Dunno. I like the colour, anyway.'

Another sparkling exchange. Jason had been making allowances for Millie for a year now. Her mother's death, her teenage angst… He'd thought that if he was patient things would improve, but it seemed to get worse rather than better. Over the past few months, Millie had got into some kind of goth mode he wasn't keen on – dyeing her hair; wearing clumpy boots and dark clothes that either clung tight, emphasising her skinny frame, or dangled off her like rags.

Shops like the one they'd just been in didn't help. Whenever they passed one of those hippie-dippy places, in she wandered like a moth drawn to a flame. Incense that made him feel nauseous, colourful garments from exotic places, statues of Buddha everywhere… He often took to waiting for her outside.

To be fair, Healing Waves wasn't like that – it had a light and airy atmosphere – but Jason still wasn't keen on the merchandise. What he *was* keen on was his daughter growing out of this weird phase of hers as soon as possible, before they both lost their sanity.

'She's pretty, don't you think?'

Startled that Millie had initiated a topic of conversation with him, he asked, 'Who?'

'The lady in the shop where I got my necklace.'

His daughter was giving him a curious sideways look, and Jason wondered what to say. 'Pretty' wasn't the word he'd use. Striking, maybe? Wild curls in every colour from gold to red around an attractive face; a floaty turquoise top to match the sea outside her shop.

Not keen on having an awkward discussion with his fourteen-year-old daughter about which aspects of women he found attractive, all he said was, 'I suppose so.'

They reached the harbour, its boats bobbing with the tide almost in. Narrow side roads led uphill towards the wooded hillside that acted as a deep green backdrop to the bay.

Porthsteren was enough to serve their needs, Jason reckoned, with the Smugglers' Inn at the harbourside, the General Store opposite, a cluster of other small shops here, and the few dotted along the beach road.

Leaving Millie sitting on a bench to watch the boats, he crossed the road to the General Store, low and white and long – presumably two or three cottages knocked into one at some stage.

They'd had fish and chips for supper the previous night, after waving the removals men off, and they had bought pasties for tonight. He would do a proper shop tomorrow, but for now, they needed bread and milk.

Plucking a carton of milk from the fridge, he headed to the counter where fresh bread sat on the shelves behind – slim pickings, so late in the day.

'You must be our newbie,' the woman at the counter said, holding out her hand. 'I'm Libby.'

Jason took in the stout, middle-aged woman with greying hair and a friendly face.

He shook her hand. 'Jason Craig.' *How does she know I'm not a tourist?*

'I saw the moving van puffing its way up the hill yesterday,' Libby said in answer to his unspoken question. 'The men popped in for snacks after, so I interrogated them.' She winked, as though this were perfectly acceptable. 'Is that your daughter over there?'

'Er. Yes. Millie.'

'You're both very welcome here in Porthsteren. It's always good to have permanent residents to swell our numbers, and not just second-homers. Settling in alright, are you, my lover?'

Telling himself he would have to get used to this overfamiliar – to him, anyway – Cornish greeting, Jason said, 'Yes, thanks. The house is still topsy-turvy, though. Boxes to unpack. But we'll get there.'

'Where have you moved from?'

'Edinburgh.'

'You don't sound Scottish.'

'No, but we lived in Edinburgh for the past ten years.' *Why am I telling her all this?*

'Millie will be starting school after the Easter holidays, I take it?'

'Yes. She's looking forward to it.' *About as much as if I were pushing her into the fiery pits of hell in a uniform.*

Libby gave his hand a reassuring pat. 'She'll be fine. Kids are resilient.' At that, she looked stricken. 'Oh dear. That wasn't the best thing to say, was it? We're all so sorry to hear about your loss.'

Jason wasn't sure who she meant by 'we all'. Presumably the entire population of Porthsteren. He had no idea how these things got around without you imparting them. Had he mentioned it to the movers? Had his solicitor mentioned it to the sellers' solicitor?

With Libby waiting for a suitable reply, he said, 'Don't worry. We've had time to come to terms with it.'

'Ah well. A new start will do you both good.'

'Yes, I'm sure.' *I'm also sure I only came in for bread and milk, but it seems I have to endure the Spanish Inquisition to get it.*

'Have you explored today? Been in any of our little shops yet?'

Knowing it would be wise to show that he was making an effort, Jason told her, 'We walked along the beach road. Bought pasties. Had a quick peek in the bookshop.'

'Oh, I could spend hours there, if I had the time. Sarah and Evelyn have run that place for *years*. How about next door to them? Healing Waves?'

Jason tried not to make a face. 'My daughter wanted to go in.'

'You've met Claudia, then. She's newish, too. Well, she's been here a couple of years now, but that's new to an old-timer like me. We all love her to *bits*,' Libby gushed.

Jason's cynical side kicked in – not that it was ever too far away. He didn't believe in people who were as bright and shiny on the inside as they appeared on the outside. Everyone had their weaknesses, their flaws, their demons. Some were just better at putting on a front than others.

'Claudia was like a breath of fresh air to this place, I can tell you,' Libby went on. 'And her shop is *lovely*.'

'I imagine it appeals to the tourists,' Jason conceded.

'Yes, but the locals love it, too. Her soaps are to *die* for. She makes them herself, you know.'

'No, I didn't know,' Jason murmured, wondering if he was expected to have some input or whether this was just a one-woman Claudia Fan Club monologue.

'She runs her weekly meditation sessions in the upstairs room above The Porthsteren Page Turner. You could try those. Sarah and Evelyn run their monthly book club there, too. Leave the men to their pints at the Smugglers' Inn, that's what I say, and grab yourself a bit of peace at the other end of the village. Claudia runs the odd workshop, too. Crystals, oracle cards… They're really interesting.'

'I bet.' *If you're gullible.* Jason glanced at his watch. 'Well, I should get on.'

'Oh, of course. Just the milk, is it?'

He paid and fled.

The only downside to their new house was the steep climb up the road past the harbour. Jason's calf muscles weren't up to it, frankly, but he supposed they would toughen up. The spacious house, with trees providing privacy from the road and a sea view from the back garden, was ample reward – and not something he could have afforded, if it hadn't been for… Well. Every very large cloud must have an infinitesimally small silver lining, he supposed.

He and Millie had trudged halfway up the hill before Jason remembered he'd never picked up bread.

They'd just have to do without toast in the morning. He couldn't face Libby for a second time in one day. Jason felt like he'd left half his brain behind on the counter, and a chewed-off ear with it.

*

'The season's hotting up, and I don't just mean weather-wise.' Claudia squinted at the lowering April sun as she flopped into a chair on the terrace outside The Porthsteren Page Turner, a large mug of tea in front of her.

Sarah and Evelyn, proprietors of the bookshop and her very good friends, did the same.

Beyond the whitewashed stone wall that surrounded their café terrace lay the varying blue of the sea, the low sun sparkling across it like diamonds. A stiff evening breeze blew wisps of white cloud across the sky, but Claudia didn't mind. Huddled in her fleece, she warmed her hands on her mug. It was good to be outside after a day indoors.

To her left as she looked out to sea, the sand led to rocks which gradually increased in size and number until they blocked the beach. There was no access to the bay beyond without going around by road. To the right, the beach stretched in a long, beige swathe to the harbour, where boats huddled in their walled shelter from the elements.

Paradise.

'Best Saturday of the year so far,' Sarah declared in her light American drawl mixed with an interesting West Country burr after decades of living in Cornwall. Running her hands through her short crop of bullet-grey hair, she lifted her feet onto the bench opposite so that Evelyn would take them onto her lap to massage.

'It's good to feel we're coming out of the slow season,' Evelyn agreed, her white-blonde plait loosening in the breeze. She obliged her partner by kneading the soles of her feet. 'Been a slow winter.'

'You won't be saying that when the tourist hordes are baying for coffee and carrot cake,' Sarah reminded her.

'Have you heard about the new shop, Claudia?' Evelyn asked.

Evelyn acted as a conduit for Porthsteren gossip, and although Claudia didn't care for gossip herself, she accepted that it was unavoidable in a close-knit community like this.

'What new shop?'

'On Chapel Hill.'

Claudia frowned. 'How come I haven't heard about it?'

'They've only just taken it on.'

Claudia was intrigued. 'What's it going to be?'

'Even Libby doesn't know,' Evelyn admitted, looking so disappointed at this lack of information, Claudia smiled. 'But there'll be builders' vans there as of Monday.'

'Chapel Hill?' Leading off from the harbour, Chapel Hill was a steep, narrow road of fishermen's cottages, most now holiday rentals. The old chapel the road was named after, long since converted into holiday flats, stood at the top. A few of the cottages nearest the harbour had been converted into shops – Jenny's hair salon, Yvonne's card and gift shop, Ian's holiday lets agency. That only left… 'You don't mean Hester Moon's old cottage?'

Despite housing a newsagent for the past thirty years, that building was still better known as the cottage of a local legend – and purported witch – from the seventeenth century.

'The very same.' Evelyn held her face up to the last of the sunshine. 'But it's a wreck!'

'It's not as bad as it looks, apparently,' Sarah declared. When Claudia and Evelyn stared at her, she said, 'What, I can't have my own lines of enquiry? I bumped into Ian this morning. He knows the agent who let it. It *looks* a mess, but it's structurally sound. It only needs tarting up – new window frames, doors and all – and the inside completely doing out.'

Claudia laughed. 'Is *that* all? Who's taken it on?'

'Ian couldn't say. All he knows is, they've negotiated only paying rent for six months a year, April through October. I guess that means they're after the tourist trade.' There was an element of disdain in Sarah's tone.

'We all make a chunk of our living from tourists,' Claudia reminded her.

'I suppose you're right. I'm surprised the agent agreed to that, though,' Evelyn said.

'That place has been empty for three years now,' Sarah said. 'Between the way it got run down and the superstition people have about it, the agent must be grateful for anything they can get. The building's owners will do repairs and bring plumbing and electrics up to scratch, and the new tenants will do up the inside to suit them. Both sides gain. Remember how Claudia turned next door around.'

Claudia's half of the white clapboard building they shared had certainly been run down when she first saw it, forlorn next to the thriving Page Turner, but she'd loved its position at the far end of the village, away from the bustling harbour. The walk along the beach appealed to plenty of people, and the Page Turner's ongoing popularity drew them there. Once she'd seen it, then met Sarah and Evelyn, she knew it was where she wanted to be. And two years ago – almost a year to the day since she'd left Lee – she had opened the doors of Healing Waves.

'An empty shop spruced up is a good thing for Porthsteren,' Claudia said.

'But what if it's another café?' Evelyn wondered.

'Porthsteren can take another café,' Sarah reassured her. 'Especially if it's only open in the summer months.'

'It couldn't take another bookshop, though.'

Sarah only grunted. 'They're welcome. Then we could think about retiring!'

Sarah and Evelyn didn't live above their shop, as Claudia did, but in a lovely cottage ten minutes inland – the perfect place to consider retirement when the time came… although Claudia hoped that wouldn't be any time soon.

Claudia glanced back at her own flat over Healing Waves, set back a little so that it didn't sit quite flush with the shop frontage. It may be small, but she and Pudding didn't have far to walk to work, and she couldn't complain about the view.

'Well. Time for home.' Sarah reluctantly lifted her aching feet from Evelyn's capable hands. 'See you tomorrow, honey.'

Claudia stood, too. Retrieving her cat from the shop, she climbed the outdoor metal stairs to her flat, Pudding loudly demanding to know where his dinner was. That dealt with, she poured herself a glass of Saturday-night wine and decided everything else could wait, including her evening yoga.

Barely waiting until she'd sunk onto her squashy sofa amidst blue and green cushions, Pudding jumped onto her lap, circled, then flopped in his chosen position. Sipping wine, Claudia closed her eyes and concentrated on centring herself to his rhythmic purr.

This was the life she wanted, the life she worked hard for, and she was grateful every day that she'd had the courage to make it happen.

What she wasn't grateful for were her aching feet and the fact that she had to make her own dinner.

Chapter Two

Claudia took advantage of her shorter Sunday hours to spend the morning reading on the beach, wrapped in a shawl, a warm, flat rock at her back.

The sea drew Claudia like a magnet, and she rarely missed her daily fix – a read, a walk, even just five minutes watching the waves. This morning, the spring sun was a bonus.

Hearing the playful bark of a dog let off its leash, she glanced up to see it heading like a bullet for the water. It launched itself into the sea, fetched its ball, came back out and shook itself thoroughly, drenching its owner and making Claudia smile. Dogs were the kings of mindfulness, Claudia thought – the present was all that mattered to them. Joy in the moment. Humans could learn a lot from their canine friends.

Further along, she spotted the girl with vivid hair who'd bought the amethyst the day before, standing morosely at the water's edge. Unable to ignore the sadness that the girl wore like a cloak, she left her book on a rock and strolled over.

'Hi there. Enjoying your amethyst?'

The girl turned, startled, her hand at her throat where the purple stone lay flat and smooth. 'Yes. Thanks.'

'My name's Claudia.' She held out a hand.

The girl shook it awkwardly. 'I'm Millie.'

'Not with your dad today?'

'He has stuff to do.'

'Ah.' Claudia noticed how much Millie stood out, black and purple and defiant amidst the muted beiges and blues of the beach. 'I love to paddle, don't you?' She slipped off her canvas pumps and allowed the cold water to slide over her toes and then her ankles, watching out of the corner of her eye as Millie weighed up temptation against the hassle of removing her laced-up boots. Temptation won.

'Your mum's not here with you, either?' Claudia asked. *Nothing ventured, nothing gained.*

Millie's eyes became shuttered. 'No. She died last year.'

Claudia's heart sank. 'I'm so sorry.'

Millie shrugged, a deliberately casual gesture. 'We're used to it, pretty much.' She eyed Claudia from beneath mascara-laden lashes, and when Claudia didn't press for more information, she added, 'She got cancer.'

'That must have been hard for you,' Claudia said with heartfelt sincerity. 'For your dad, too.'

Another shrug. 'They were getting divorced. Before the diagnosis, anyway.' There was a hitch in Millie's voice which Claudia tactfully ignored.

What could you say about a wretched situation like that? But say something she must. She'd intruded on the girl's solitude and unwittingly opened a can of worms in the process.

'I know it sounds corny, and you must have heard it from every well-meaning person since your mother died, but it is surprising what time can do. Eventually.'

'How do *you* know? Did *your* mother die when you were thirteen?'

'No. My mother's alive and well and onto her third marriage in the south of France. But I do know people who've suffered loss.'

'Not you, though,' Millie said stubbornly.

Claudia sighed. She'd led herself down this very difficult cul-de-sac, and now she would have to offer up a small part of herself to get out of it.

Serves you right for interfering.

'No, but I have been through a painful divorce.' She looked Millie in the eye. 'That can't *begin* to compare with what you're going through, but I was very hurt, and I did have to start all over again. With time, the pain got less. The loss of a mother must be a million times worse, but I truly believe the principle's the same.'

'Do you have children?' Millie asked curiously.

'No.' And that was as much personal information as Claudia was willing to give, even if she was responsible for starting this conversation. Picking up a flat pebble, she skimmed it across the water. Three bounces. She tried again. Four this time.

'How do you do that?'

Claudia showed Millie how to choose a round, flat stone; the sideways stance; the throw.

Millie tried to copy, and Claudia was struck by how pretty she was when she concentrated and forgot to scowl. Just as she was getting frustrated, she managed a single bounce, then a double. Then she complained her arm was aching, and the scowl came back.

Claudia began to stroll along the shoreline, pumps in hand, and Millie fell in beside her. Two strangers with nothing to say to each other.

Claudia didn't mind the silence. Sometimes it was best not to try to fill it. Silence might help Millie enjoy the sensation of the breeze playing across her skin, the feel of sand between her toes. The sound of the waves, dogs barking, kids laughing, spades digging.

At the end of the bay, nearing the harbour, Claudia glanced at her watch. 'I should get back. I open at one on a Sunday.' She smiled. 'Until the summer season gets going, then I'll change it to eleven.'

'You don't get a day off?'

Claudia began the walk back, Millie at her side. 'There's an informal consensus here in Porthsteren that if we want to close, we do it on Wednesdays. Some take a half-day, but I take the full day. And I don't open on Sundays at all in the winter, and only Sunday afternoons in the spring and autumn. Even in the summer, Sunday hours are shorter.' She stopped. Millie wouldn't be interested in that level of detail.

But Millie didn't seem bored. Shyly, she mumbled, 'I really like your shop.'

'Thank you.' *Let's go out on a limb.* 'Your dad didn't, though.'

Millie laughed. It was brief, but genuine. 'Nah. He doesn't believe in all that. Calls it mumbo-jumbo.'

Claudia smiled, unoffended. She'd met plenty of people who felt that way. 'How long are you here on holiday for?'

'We're not. We've moved here.'

'Oh! I assumed, with the accent…'

'We came down from Edinburgh. Mum and Dad aren't Scottish, but we lived there since I was four, so…'

'When did you move?'

'Friday. Dad wanted to do it in the school holidays so we could settle in before I start my new school.'

Claudia's sympathy soared. Grieving for her mother. Moving to a new place. A new school. But she sensed that sympathy wouldn't be wanted.

'Whereabouts is your new house?' she asked. 'Is there a lot of work to do on it?'

Millie waved her arm towards the wooded promontory above the harbour. 'Up on Cliff Road. There's not much to do. Dad didn't want a fixer-upper. He said that'd be like a busman's holiday, whatever *that* means.'

'What does your dad do?'

'He's an architect.'

They reached the rock where Claudia had abandoned her book. As she picked it up, Millie tugged at her sleeve, a worried look on her face.

'I probably wasn't supposed to tell you about the divorce thing. Only friends and family knew, back home. It's easier not to complicate things, Dad says.'

Claudia gave her a reassuring smile. 'Your dad's right. Porthsteren's a small place. Everyone learns about everyone's business around here, sooner or later. But don't worry, I'm good at keeping confidences. If you fancy a chat, pop by the shop any time.' She grinned. 'Maybe without your dad next time' – a comment which elicited a brief but delighted laugh from Millie as they parted.

Barely a chapter of her book read – but if Claudia had helped Millie settle into her new environment just a little, then it was a morning well spent.

*

Jason was delving into a box of wrapped crockery when his phone rang. Grumbling, he fumbled in his back pocket – empty – then hauled himself off his knees to grab it from the breakfast counter.

His mother-in-law. *Great.*

'Morning, Jennifer. How are you?'

'Fine. More to the point, how are you both? How did the move go?'

Jason dutifully filled her in. He'd always got on well enough with his in-laws, but the last couple of years had been… Awkward didn't cover it. Jennifer and Harry had known about the impending divorce, but not the details. And naturally, as Gemma's parents, they blamed him. Then came Gemma's illness and passing. It was unbearable for them, to lose their daughter like that. Relations had been strained ever since – a polite gloss over unspoken recrimination.

'Is Millie around?' Jennifer asked as soon as the civilities petered out.

'No, sorry. She went for a walk.'

'On her own?'

'She's fourteen, Jennifer. She only went down the hill to the beach. I have to let her do these things.'

'Yes. I know.'

Jason pictured her pursed lips and sighed. He would never be an adequate parent in her eyes, not now her beloved Gemma had gone. Still, wouldn't he feel the same way in her shoes?

'I'll tell Millie you called and ask her to phone you back.'

'That would be good. And Jason?'

'Yes?'

'I just want to say…' Jennifer's voice hitched. 'Harry and I are so pleased that you've moved down south. It means a lot to us that Millie will be nearer, after Gemma…' Her voice tailed off.

Jason's heart went out to her. 'It'll be good for Millie, too. We'll see you some time soon, when we've got organised. Take care.'

Clicking off his phone, he let out a breath. They were good people who missed their daughter, and Millie was all they had left. Besides, Millie needed her grandparents. Jason's own parents were in New Zealand. Jennifer and Harry were a darned sight nearer in Devon. Another good reason for this move.

*

'Who was that on the beach?' Evelyn asked Claudia over coffee before opening. 'The girl with the only hair in Porthsteren more colourful than yours?'

Claudia ran her fingers through her curls and chuckled. 'Millie. She and her father are new to Porthsteren. They've moved down from Scotland, although he's English, apparently. I assumed they were tourists when they looked round Healing Waves yesterday. Well, Millie looked round. Her father was only along in a supervisory capacity. I don't think he's into New Age.'

'I'd heard we had newcomers,' Sarah admitted. 'Libby mentioned it last night when I called in the General Store for tortilla chips.' She shot an accusing look at Evelyn. 'We ran out, *somehow*. Libby said he's a widower?'

Claudia hesitated, but word would get around sooner or later. Better it came accurately from her than through the Porthsteren version of Chinese Whispers. 'Yes. Millie's mother died of cancer last year.'

'Poor man,' Evelyn murmured. 'Losing your wife and bringing up a teenager on your own. And so hard for the girl.'

'Indeed,' Claudia agreed. 'But I do hope they'll be able to move on with their lives.'

'Is that a hint that we shouldn't be speculating about their past when they're trying to create a new future?' Sarah cast a pointed glance at her partner.

Claudia maintained an innocent expression as she sipped her decaff latte. 'It's not for me to dictate what people talk about. All I'm saying – and I speak from personal experience – is that if you're trying to make a new start, it's not helpful when people keep on delving into your past. I'm sure Millie and her dad will expect curious questions along the lines of "What brings you so far south?" and the like, but I'm equally sure they might prefer to keep the more painful details to themselves.'

'Evie and I promise not to fuel the gossip,' Sarah said sincerely, reaching her arm around Evelyn's shoulders. '*Don't* we, Evie?'

'Of course!'

'You know I don't mean you two, specifically.' Claudia was mindful that Sarah and Evelyn had never delved too far into *her* past, for which she was grateful. Sarah had accepted that Claudia had shared as much as she was willing to – a painful divorce, a career that no longer meant anything to her, a desire to start afresh – and had tactfully persuaded Evelyn to do the same. 'But The Porthsteren Page Turner does seem to be a hub of gossip.'

'Is it our fault we offer the best view *and* the best coffee?' Evelyn said.

Claudia glanced at the turquoise sea and smiled. 'No. Can't be helped.' She tapped a finger against her cup. 'I might take a housewarming gift to our newcomers this evening. A suitable crystal, perhaps.'

Sarah frowned. 'I thought you said the father was unimpressed by your wares?'

'He was. But there's Millie to consider.' As Sarah and Evelyn gathered their cups, Claudia sighed. 'Two more minutes, then I'll open up.'

Once alone, she sat quietly, feasting on the view before her. Two minutes could never be enough. She would sit here all day, if she could. There was always something to see. Serene sailboats floating by, sails crisp white against the blue of the sea and sky. Speedboats zipping past. Paddle-boarders hugging the coastline. Claudia envied them their leg muscles – no amount of yoga would allow her to do that. Kayakers edging their way around the rocks. Kites adding dots of colour to the sky. Dogs chasing madly along the sand, barking, plunging into the water, mad as hatters.

In those two minutes of blissful solitude, Claudia gave her daily thanks to whoever or whatever was responsible for guiding her here.

*

Not knowing Millie's address was no obstacle in Porthsteren. All Claudia had to do was phone Libby at the General Store who provided her with the information she needed, including the father's name – Jason Craig. There wasn't much you couldn't find out in this place.

It was such a nice evening, Claudia decided to walk – along the beach road, past the crowded fishermen's cottages by the harbour, and steeply on past the surprising variety of larger housing up Cliff Road.

The Craig house was a modern concoction of wood and glass and balconies, situated on the flat after Cliff Road's incline evened out.

As Claudia paused to catch her breath after the climb, she studied the house, hidden away from the road by a screen of trees. She imagined it would have fantastic views from the other side.

Taking a deep breath, she walked down the path and knocked, keeping her fingers crossed that Millie would answer.

No such luck. Millie's father opened the door, his jeans shabby, his T-shirt a little grubby. Perhaps he'd been unpacking.

'Hi.' She flashed him her brightest smile.

He stared at her. 'Er. Hi?'

Claudia held out a hand. 'Claudia Bennett. Healing Waves.'

'Yes. I remember.' He shook her hand – reluctantly, she felt. 'Jason Craig.'

'Good to meet you properly. Is Millie in?'

He frowned. 'She's in the bath.'

Great timing, Claudia. 'That's a shame. I brought a welcome gift to say I hope you'll both be happy here in Porthsteren.' She handed over the tissue-wrapped package, although she herself felt about as welcome on his doorstep as something the cat had dragged in.

His eyebrows shot up. 'A gift?' Taking it, he managed a curt 'Thank you', and then an awkward moment followed while he decided what to do with it. Finally, he unwrapped it, revealing a long, smooth black crystal on a stout chain. He stared at it, at a loss.

Oh, Millie, why did you have to have a bath now? 'It's black tourmaline,' Claudia explained. 'The best place for it is near your door. It protects, and it blocks negative energies.'

'Uh-huh.' Millie's father held the crystal as though she'd presented him with a spider dangling from a thread, clearly torn between being polite and wanting to say what he really thought.

Claudia hid a smile. 'Look at it this way – it can't do any harm, can it? And by hanging it, you'll have made a local shopkeeper very happy.'

'Do you bring these to everyone who moves to Porthsteren?' he asked, his tone cynical. He obviously thought she was only after more of his daughter's business.

Her hackles rose. 'If I've met someone, or if they've been into Healing Waves, then yes, I do.'

'That's very *welcoming* of you.'

'Or a cynical ploy to get people into my shop?'

He merely raised an eyebrow.

Her voice colder, Claudia said, 'It's primarily a welcome. People welcomed me when I moved here, and I like to pay it forward. If it has a knock-on effect by tempting people into Healing Waves, then I'm not complaining.' With a sigh, she said, 'Just hang the wretched crystal, Mr Craig. It won't kill you.' She turned to leave.

'It's Jason,' he said. 'No need for formalities.' When she turned back, he managed a small – very small – smile. 'After all, you did bring us a housewarming gift.'

It was a concession of sorts, Claudia supposed, but she had no intention of pushing her luck. She nodded and scarpered.

*

'What's that?' Millie asked as she came downstairs, her face pink from the heat of her bath.

'Our local, friendly shopkeeper brought us a housewarming present.'

Millie inspected the crystal. 'Hmm. Black. Not very pretty. But it has interesting markings.'

Jason could have pointed out that nearly everything Millie wore nowadays was black, but he refrained. 'She said it should go by the door. Apparently, it'll protect us or some other nonsense.'

'That's thoughtful. What is it?'

'I… er.' He'd already forgotten, probably because it was information he attached no importance to.

Millie delved into the tissue and found a label. 'Black tourmaline.' Her pale blue eyes met his own. 'You are going to put it up, aren't you?'

'I wasn't going to, no.'

'Dad, you have to! What if she calls again?'

Jason couldn't imagine why Claudia Bennett would have any reason to call again. 'Look, Millie, it was good of her to bring it, I suppose, but we hardly know the woman.'

The mutinous expression his daughter wore so well – and Jason had come to know so well – appeared. 'Actually, I do know her a bit. We chatted on the beach this morning. She's nice.'

Jason's desire for his daughter to make friends and become comfortable chatting with the locals warred with irritation that she'd chosen a woman who peddled crystals for a living.

'What did you talk about?'

'Just that we moved here. She thought we were on holiday.'

Jason knew not to push any further. Millie only ever said as much as she wanted to, if anything at all.

'So, are you going to hang it up or not?' she asked.

Jason glared at the crystal. 'Fine. We'll hang the blasted thing.'

As he teetered on a stepladder, screwing a hook into his pristine ceiling, he cursed Claudia Bennett… Although, judging by some of the goods she stocked, she might have a thing or two over him when it came to curses.

*

'How did your welcome gift go down with the newcomers?' Sarah asked Claudia over coffee the next morning.

'Millie was in the bath, so I didn't see her. But her father looked at me like I'd handed him a shrunken head.'

Sarah laughed. 'You knew he would, so why bother? For Millie? Or to piss off her father?'

'It's my traditional housewarming gift.' Claudia cocked her head to one side, her eyes glinting with mischief. 'But in answer to your question? Both, I suppose.'

'So, what's their house like?' Evelyn asked, keen as ever for details.

Claudia obliged. 'Fancy. All wood and glass. The kind of thing you might expect an architect to choose. And it must have a fantastic sea view. Everything seems so spacious up there on Cliff Road.'

'Hmmph. Unlike Chapel Hill,' Evelyn grumbled. 'We drove down it on our way in this morning. There were vans everywhere, ready to start renovating the newsagent's. That road's narrow enough as it is. They're causing chaos.'

'It shouldn't last too long,' Claudia said. 'If the new people have only got a six-month season, they'll want to be up and running ASAP. No word about what it'll be yet?'

'None.' Sarah gave Claudia a considered look. 'Are you worried, honey?'

'Me? No. Someone taking on that mess of a place and turning it into another thriving business should boost trade for all of us. Besides, there may be room in Porthsteren for more cafés or souvenir shops, but I reckon there's a limit to how many essential oils and crystals one village can sell.'

Sarah smiled. 'Healing Waves *is* pretty unique. As is its owner. I can't see anyone trying to replicate either of you!'

Claudia was pleased at Sarah's compliment as she went to open up. Healing Waves *was* unique in Porthsteren, beautifully positioned and complementing the Page Turner next door. Both shops attracted tourists, but just as importantly, they were popular with the locals, too, giving them enough off-season custom to justify all-year-round opening.

Still, by the time she closed that evening, her curiosity was piqued enough to make her take an after-work stroll to the harbour. As she walked, Claudia tried to view the village with a visitor's eye. The buildings all along the beach road were picturesque, but it was the harbour to which people gravitated to admire the boats, browse the shops, sample the cafés and wander up the side streets for a sense of what the place was like in days gone by.

At the harbour, she turned back to look at the white wooden building that was Healing Waves and The Porthsteren Page Turner – the only building on the beach side of the road, just before the rocks signalled the end of the bay. Anyone who fancied a walk and had an ounce of curiosity would aim for it.

Past the General Store, Claudia turned up Chapel Hill. The builders' vans were packing up for the day, causing problems on the narrow street.

Claudia squeezed past to the new shop window, but she couldn't see any clues – it was covered from the inside.

Ah, well. She may be none the wiser, but keeping one business eye and one tourist eye open on her walk had reminded her that her own shop was in a great location.

As she was about to turn away, one of the workmen slid a large chipboard sign in the window:

Coming soon! Exciting new store for Porthsteren!

Claudia would hardly call it a store, but she supposed 'Exciting new shop in a small, possibly haunted, poky old building' didn't have quite the same ring to it, did it?

Chapter Three

Jason had timed their move so they had a week to settle in before Millie started her new school and he his new job. It had seemed like a good idea at the time, but by Tuesday, the house was already pretty much in order. They still had Millie's uniform to buy, and Jason needed to get to grips with information his new firm had sent him – policy documents that would have you pull out your own eyeballs with boredom; minutes of meetings pertaining to projects he'd been allocated – but they deserved a break.

'Fancy going out?' he suggested after breakfast. 'We could walk around the harbour again, and along the beach. I wouldn't mind a proper look in that bookshop. Have a coffee.'

Millie shrugged. He took it as enthusiasm.

They walked down the hill in near-silence, although that was sometimes better than chatting. Chatting often led to arguments, and it was too nice a day for that. At the harbour, they took another look at the shops, then walked round the harbour walls. All the while, Millie took selfies to post on social media – yet another bone of contention between them. Jason hated social media. Millie swore blind that it was necessary if you wanted to fit in. Did he *want* her to be a social outcast?

On the beach, Millie picked up a stone and skimmed it across the waves.

Surprised, he said, 'I didn't know you could do that.'

'Claudia showed me how.'

A bubble of resentment rose in Jason's throat. That was something a father did with his daughter, wasn't it? Not some random hippie shop owner.

Then why haven't you taught her yourself?

Because she wasn't interested when she was little. And I always thought there'd be more time. Then there was the thing with Gemma. And suddenly my daughter's too old to want anything to do with me.

Millie took a quick peek in the bookshop with him but soon declared that she wanted a 'proper' look in Healing Waves.

'Okay.' *If you must.* 'Meet me outside for a coffee when you're done, if you like?'

He watched her clomp off, then returned his attention to the non-fiction shelves. Breathing deeply, he allowed that special paper smell mingled with the wonderful aroma of coffee to calm his senses.

Jason loved all things digital, but there was something about the physical book, and The Porthsteren Page Turner was as perfect an environment as he could wish for. Books *and* coffee – what was not to love?

Polished wooden shelves divided into subject sections filled the back and left walls of the store; lower shelves and tables at the front of the store were given over to fiction. The coffee counter was to the back and right, with just a few tables for seating. The owners presumably expected customers to prefer to sit outside – and no wonder, with that view.

Too tempted by the aroma, he gave up on the books and ordered a coffee, choosing a table outside and taking his jacket off to feel the sun on his arms. *Fabulous.* He couldn't remember ever being in just a T-shirt in April in Edinburgh. Looking around, he sighed with satisfaction. Porthsteren had cafés aplenty, but the coffee the short-haired woman served him was good, and as he looked out at the sparkling sea and endless sky, he couldn't see the need to try anywhere else. In fact, the only downside to the location was that it was joined at the hip to Healing Waves.

Millie had obviously taken a shine to Claudia Bennett. Jason supposed that if it wasn't for the nature of the woman's business, he *might* have taken to her himself. She was bubbly; attractive, if you went for wild hair and golden eyes and floaty clothes. As a plus point, she hadn't been nosy about his house – not that he'd invited her in. Perhaps he should have, since she'd brought a gift?

Jason sighed. It was difficult, walking that tightrope between wanting to keep his business private, yet not wanting to come across as stand-offish. If he expected his daughter to make an effort, he should expect the same of himself. They'd been welcomed wherever they had shown their faces, but Claudia had gone a step further, turning up on their doorstep like that.

Had he been frosty? He must have been, because she'd turned rather frosty herself. Even though he was sure Millie was bound to have thanked Claudia for her gift while she looked round Healing Waves, perhaps he should make more effort next time he bumped into her; show that he could be polite.

Taking another sip of coffee, Jason looked around, taking in the eclectic nature of the outdoor space. Every piece of furniture was different. The seat of an old bench propped on two-foot-high slices of tree trunks; trestle tables; an old church pew. A couple of steps down from the terrace, the wall that surrounded it was whitewashed. A long shelf had been fitted all along its length, window boxes of herbs dotted here and there, with an eclectic selection of old bar stools pushed up to it, affording a view out to sea. The difference in height meant that the terrace tables still had a view of the sea or the rocks or the harbour, depending on which way you faced. The place was a mishmash, but it worked, the second-hand nature of it fitting in well with the second-hand books.

He said as much to the woman who collected his empty cup, a woman perhaps in her late fifties, her white-blonde hair in a thick plait draped over one shoulder.

She smiled at the compliment and perched on the bench opposite him. 'I'd love to tell you it was by deliberate design, but it was more a case of needs must,' she said, her soft Cornish accent as friendly as her face. 'Adding the café cost so much more than we'd expected! Fancy coffee machine, cutlery, crockery, cake stands, fridges… Posh outdoor furniture was a step too far. But Sarah's a whizz with DIY. We had a garage full of old stuff she'd kept "meaning to do something with" one day.' She made quotation marks in the air as she spoke. 'So, she started drilling and sanding and painting. Word got around that we were resurrecting a wooden graveyard, and people donated, too.'

Jason smiled. 'It's friendly and unpretentious. I love it.'

'Happy to please. I'm Evelyn, by the way.' She jerked her thumb at the short-haired woman heading their way. 'This is Sarah.'

'Jason Craig.' They shook hands. 'How long have you been here?'

'Thirty years, as a bookshop,' Sarah said, with a look of surprise that time had passed so quickly. 'We added the café five years ago.'

Jason noted her hint of American accent combined with something local.

'Is your daughter not joining you?' Evelyn indicated the empty seat beside him.

Jason mentally rolled his eyes. Of course they would know he had a daughter. No doubt Claudia had told them all about her. 'She's next door.'

He did his best to hide his distaste, but Sarah gave him a look that told him he was hiding nothing.

'I can't tell you how grateful we were when Claudia moved in next door,' she said with apparent nonchalance. 'That place was a *mess*. It had been empty for a year, and the previous owner had let it go to wrack and ruin long before that. It was bringing our own business down.'

'Let's face it, we'd've been grateful if *anyone* had moved in,' Evelyn pointed out. 'But Claudia was a happy bonus. We couldn't ask for a better neighbour.'

Jason managed a tight smile. 'She was kind enough to bring a housewarming gift round.' Perhaps *that* would get back to their perfect next-door neighbour, thereby mitigating his rudeness the other night. 'Well, I'll get back to the books. Good to meet you both.'

*

'Are these tarot cards?' Millie asked.

Claudia came over to her. 'No, they're oracle cards. Tarot cards are a traditional deck, very specific in structure, but I don't stock them.'

'Why not?'

Claudia thought how best to explain. 'Tarot cards aren't something I've studied properly. I don't stock anything I don't understand or have personal experience of. I prefer to leave that to the experts.'

'But you stock oracle cards?'

'Yes. I use them myself. They're more accessible, I think. Some are spiritual, some based on nature, some just have positive messages.'

Millie turned the pack over in her hands. 'What are they for, exactly?'

Claudia thought about how to word her explanation. She didn't want to influence a vulnerable teen. 'You can use them for something simple – to inspire you at the start of your day, for example. Or you can use them for guidance – ask them a question, perhaps about a problem, and they give you an answer.'

Millie looked incredulous. 'Like magic?'

Claudia smiled. 'It depends on your own beliefs. Those who believe in angels might believe they're channelling the angels' wisdom through an angel-themed deck. In my case, I think it's more about how you interpret the answer. Often, the cards flag up what you already know in your subconscious but haven't acknowledged yet.'

'How do you make them do that?'

'Let me show you.' Claudia took the pack from Millie, unwrapped the cellophane and shuffled the cards. 'The guide explains all the different layouts you can do, but I'll use just one card for now.' Claudia held the cards to her chest and closed her eyes. 'Concentrate on your problem or question. I like to spread the cards.' She fanned them across the counter, her hands hovering above them. 'Look for the card that's speaking to you. That one, see?' She picked one that had fallen free of the semi-circle. 'Take in the image and words, then look up possible meanings in the book.' She leafed to the correct page and showed it to Millie.

Millie gave her a curious look. 'Did it answer your question?'

Claudia smiled. Millie hadn't asked her what her question was, which was grown-up of her, she thought. 'No, but it posed another question, which is interesting. I'll mull it over. There are other layouts you can try – three cards to represent your problem, its solution and the way forward. Or the past, present and future.' She reined in her enthusiasm. 'They're not a magic wand, but they can be a useful tool.'

Millie leafed through the pack. 'I love the artwork.'

'Beautiful, aren't they? I have that deck at home. I like the nature-based packs best.'

'You have more than one pack?'

Claudia shrugged. 'Can't help myself. And I like to have a selection at hand.'

'I'll take these,' Millie said. 'I really like them.'

'If they spoke to you, then they're a good choice.' Claudia put them back in their box. 'Don't forget to cleanse them before you use them.'

Millie looked at her, askance. 'Do what?'

Claudia laughed at her expression. 'You should clear the cards of negative energy from the manufacturing process and other people handling them – and that includes me. Make the pack yours.'

'How?'

Claudia reached for a small, rough-edged pink crystal. 'You could store them with a rose quartz crystal. Here. On the house.'

'Thanks!' Millie paid for the cards and took the package with obvious pleasure.

'Let me know how you get on.'

'I will.'

*

Claudia always looked forward to the Tuesday meditation sessions she ran. Pudding was less keen, since he wasn't allowed to accompany her – a cat jumping onto someone's lap when they were in a relaxed state tended to have rather a startling effect.

Letting herself into the space above the bookshop, she set out a range of floor cushions and placed chairs for those who preferred them, making a guess at numbers.

The equivalent of her own flat next door, Sarah and Evelyn had never lived here, since they had the cottage that Evelyn's great-aunt had left her. At first, they'd used it for storage, but when they started up their monthly book club, they'd converted it into a meeting room. When Claudia had arrived, she'd been offered the use of it for anything she wanted to run.

Her weekly meditation group had slowly grown, and now she had a good base of locals keen for their weekly dose of Zen, followed by a cuppa.

'Hi, Alice. How are you this week?' she asked the first arrival.

'Oh. You know. Fine. Thanks.' Alice managed a small smile, and not for the first time Claudia wondered if she had ever seen this frumpy, middle-aged woman manage a heartfelt one. A regular customer at Healing Waves – sometimes for the company, Claudia suspected, more than to buy anything – Alice wore a permanent look of worry and caution, only mildly alleviated by her hour's meditation each week.

Alice fidgeted in her chair as Sarah and Evelyn arrived, followed by the other regulars. Libby cut it fine, arriving just before eight.

Five minutes of stretches, five minutes of breathing exercises, then Claudia would play a guided meditation from the internet – whatever she had come across that she thought might suit everyone. When she'd first begun holding these sessions, she'd thought about writing and delivering her own, but she simply didn't have the time to do that every week. Besides, she enjoyed relaxing along with the others. At the end, she would play ten minutes of calming music or nature sounds, and then Claudia would gently bring everyone back to themselves. Afterwards, there was the opportunity for a quick cuppa and a chat for those who wanted to stay a little longer.

This evening, the new shop was the prime topic over decaff tea.

'They're keeping it all very close to their chest,' Evelyn grumbled.

'That's the way publicity goes nowadays,' Claudia said. 'Build up a frenzy of speculation, then "Ta-dah!"'

'Well, I for one could do without the suspense,' Jenny, Porthsteren's only hairdresser, declared. 'It's right opposite me. I keep peering through my window when they're carrying stuff in from the vans. Nearly took a customer's eye out with my scissors!' She sighed. 'I hope it won't be another salon.'

Claudia felt for her. Another hairdresser so nearby could easily tread on Jenny's toes, especially since Jenny's salon wasn't as up-to-date as it could be.

'It might be something that would complement your salon,' she suggested in an attempt to reassure. 'A nail bar, maybe?'

At that, Jenny looked crestfallen. 'Hope not. I was thinking about adding nails to boost business. I've just been on a course.'

'Ah.' So much for trying to cheer her up. 'Well, I guess we'll all just have to wait and see.'

Claudia hoped that would put an end to the discussion. Much as she felt for those who were worried, obsessive speculation was pointless, as far as she could see. But Evelyn and Jenny were in full flow, so she drifted off to refill her tea.

Libby collared her at the kettle. 'Did you find the house?' When Claudia gave her a blank look, Libby said impatiently, 'Your gift for the widower. The address was right, wasn't it?'

'Yes, thanks.' Claudia couldn't help but smile. Libby would hate to give out incorrect information… although she wasn't above embellishing it on occasion. And Claudia wasn't sure that Jason would appreciate being labelled 'the widower'.

'Did they love it?' Libby pressed.

Claudia wasn't sure how to answer, but Libby went on before she had a chance to.

'What's the daughter like? She looked a little odd to me.'

'She's nice. Quiet. I hope she'll settle in okay.'

Libby took no heed of Claudia's loaded tone, instead giving her a speculative look. 'The father's quite handsome, don't you think?'

'Well, I…'

'Claudia, any chance of a quick word?' Sarah appeared at Claudia's side.

'Of course. Excuse me, Libby.' She allowed Sarah to lead her away. 'What's up?'

'Nothing whatsoever. I just thought you needed rescuing.'

Claudia kissed Sarah's cheek. 'I did. Thank you.'

Sarah looked over at Alice. 'Do you think Alice is okay? She looks a little down.'

'She always looks a little down, Sarah.'

'I know, but she was in the Page Turner yesterday, and she spent an awful long time at the self-help section. Got me kinda worried.'

Claudia smiled. 'On that basis, you'd've worried yourself sick over me three years ago!'

'Did they help you? Books like that?' Sarah asked her curiously.

'Some, yes. Some, no. Depends on what you need at the time, and if the book answers your call, I suppose.' Claudia yawned. 'Right now, my bed is calling me. Let's wrap this up, shall we?'

As she and Sarah tidied away and waved everyone off, Claudia was acutely aware that it wasn't only Alice who looked down. People like Jenny – generally chirpy – looked down, too. It was all that new shop's fault for winding everyone into a frenzy of speculation and worry, she thought as she headed for her own flat. Claudia didn't like to see her friends get worked up like that.

*

By Wednesday afternoon, Jason and Millie had ticked off most of Millie's school requirements, which had only put her in a worse mood – the new items festooning the lounge were a reminder that she had a new school to start next week, and her anxiety was palpable.

Jason felt much the same about his own impending Monday.

'Fancy a walk?' he asked.

Millie shook her head. 'Nah. I'll stay here. You go.'

Whether she didn't want a walk or whether she just preferred him elsewhere, he wasn't sure.

'Okay. I won't be long.'

'No rush. Take your time.'

The latter, then. 'Get name labels in some of those things while I'm out, will you?'

A grunt in reply.

Ten minutes after leaving the house, Jason was out on the coastal path – the advantage of living at the top of the hill. He breathed in fresh air, felt the spring breeze in his hair; admired the sea on his left, rocks jutting out from inaccessible coves, a boat on the horizon, white clouds in the sky. To his right, tall grasses waved in the breeze, backed by thorny shrubs. Beyond lay fields for crops – he had no idea what yet. Wheat? Barley? Oats? He was no expert. Wildflowers nodded among the green, but Jason guessed it wasn't time for the full display yet.

This was a long way from the city, he thought as his long stride ate up the path. He'd loved Edinburgh, but he'd done his stint there. It was time for somewhere new.

After twenty minutes, he felt better. After forty minutes, he felt great. Choosing a flat spot, he moved away from the path – but not too close to the edge – and sat, his arms around his knees, to look out over a tiny cove below.

'Hi.'

Jason jumped and turned his head.

'Sorry, I didn't mean to startle you. But I thought it would be rude just to pass by.'

The woman from Healing Waves. Claudia. Her hair was tied back, although the breeze was doing its best to play havoc with it, and she was dressed in jeans and a multicoloured sweater with an *interesting* design, probably from her own shop.

Remembering his rudeness the other night, he forced himself to smile. 'Hi. Not at the shop today?'

'Day off. Mind if I take a pew?'

'Help yourself.' Jason indicated the patch of grass beside him. He could hardly say 'No, bugger off', could he?

As though she could read his mind, she said, 'I won't intrude for long. It's just that these boots are rubbing.' She winced. 'New. Wearing them in.' She tugged them off, her socks too, wiggled her toes, then inspected a sore patch on her heel. Delving into her backpack, she brought out a strip of plasters. 'Out for a breather? Millie didn't want to come?'

He shook his head. 'We're out of sorts, kicking our heels, waiting for Monday – her new school, my new job.' He didn't want to share more than that, but sitting in awkward silence didn't seem a much better prospect. 'I think I made a mistake, giving us a week to settle in.'

'That doesn't sound unreasonable to me.' She smiled, her golden eyes warm. 'You must have had loads to do.' Her plasters applied, she curled her toes into the long, rough grass. 'It's the waiting, though, isn't it?'

'Yes.' *Come on, Jason, get it over with.* 'Listen, Claudia, I want to thank you for your gift. I wasn't very welcoming, and I apologise.

You… the gift… It was unexpected. Millie didn't tell me she'd already spoken to you on the beach until after you came by.'

'Don't worry. You're welcome.' She hesitated. 'Millie told me about her mother. I'm sorry for your loss.'

'Thank you.' Jason's mind raced. *What else did Millie tell her?*

Claudia was looking straight at him. Straight through him, maybe. 'She also mentioned that you'd been planning to divorce.'

Jason couldn't hide his dismay. 'I wish she hadn't.'

'Please don't be mad at her. She realised she shouldn't have – that you're worried about gossip.' She smiled. 'I won't say anything to anyone. I only wanted you to know that I know, in case Millie mentions it to you. And I'm sorry. That must have been a difficult situation for you all.'

'Yes.' Silence fell between them as Jason tried not to be angry at his daughter for divulging such information to a stranger.

Claudia pulled a flask from her bag. 'Coffee? I have a spare cup with me. Although it is decaff.'

'Thanks.' *Why would she carry a spare cup?*

'You never know who you'll bump into along here,' she explained – which was weird, since he was sure he hadn't voiced the question. 'Oh, and it's goats' milk, so double sorry.'

Dubious, he took the cup and sipped. 'It's not too bad.'

Hiding a smile, she said, 'I gather you were in the Page Turner yesterday.'

Jason made a face. 'I need to get used to this continuous monitoring of my every move, don't I?'

Her lips twitched. 'You knew that when you moved here, surely?'

'I did.' He sighed. 'But it'll be good for Millie, being in a smaller community. Give her a sense of belonging. A change from the city.'

Claudia smiled encouragement. 'I'm sure it will. That's what I did – made the switch from London to here. I haven't regretted it for a minute.'

Jason was surprised at that. He wouldn't have had her down as a city girl. 'Did you have a shop like Healing Waves there?'

'No. I…' Claudia hesitated. 'I worked for a business development consultancy.'

Jason's jaw would have hit the floor if he'd let it. 'That's quite a change!'

'Yes. But, as I say, no regrets. Porthsteren's a good place for you and Millie to make new memories together.'

Jason wasn't sure how to respond. Swapping a city career to sell crystals in a coastal village wasn't within his realm of understanding, but she didn't elaborate.

Deftly changing the subject, she pointed to the cove below. 'You know what amazes me? The colours. The water's so clear, you can see the sand beneath it; the individual pebbles and shells if you get closer. But the blue of the sea and the sky change all the time, with the weather and the seasons. I never get bored with it.'

'How long have you been in Porthsteren?' Might as well be polite, since she showed no sign of moving on.

'Two years.'

Jason would have asked more, out of courtesy, but he suddenly wondered how long he'd been sitting here.

'I have to get back – I don't want to leave Millie on her own for too long. Thanks for the coffee. I hope your feet survive the walk.'

She shrugged. 'Sometimes you just have to go through the pain till you come out the other side, don't you?'

Walking away, Jason glanced back at the figure sitting at the edge of the cliff, her escaped hair flying around her face. He'd promised himself he'd be polite, less stand-offish, next time he saw her, and he had. More than that – he'd shared coffee; had a conversation.

Retracing his steps along the path, Jason sighed. He didn't *want* to like this purveyor of New Age rubbish, but it was quite hard not to.

Chapter Four

A couple of days later, it was the other member of the Craig family that Claudia bumped into when she went down to the beach after locking up – she needed fresh air before thinking about yoga and dinner. This wasn't something that Pudding approved of, since it delayed *his* dinner… but he thought any time was mealtime.

Sitting on a rock, staring out to sea, it wasn't long before Claudia heard the scuffling of boots in the sand.

She smiled at Millie. 'Hi.' Sensing her awkwardness, Claudia patted the rock next to her. 'Take a seat. Your dad not with you?'

'He's at home, glaring at his laptop, trying to get himself up to speed before Monday. He keeps shoving his hands in his hair, making it stick out on end. I decided to give him some space.'

'Very wise.'

Claudia's encounter with Jason earlier that week had left her feeling that although they had broken the ice a little, there was still a distinct layer of frost underneath. She wasn't sure whether that was down to his natural reserve, his disapproval of her shop, or that he simply didn't like her. It *could* be all three, she supposed. But he'd tried to be polite, which was better than nothing.

'Is there anything you have to do before school on Monday?' she asked Millie.

'Nope, just turn up and hope for the best, I suppose.'

'At least it's not an exam year.'

'Hmmph.' Millie wrapped her arms around her knees. 'You're at the beach a lot.'

Claudia noted the not-so-subtle change of subject. 'I think it would be more accurate to say I'm in my shop a lot and squeeze the beach into every other spare moment. I find it therapeutic.'

Millie gave her a curious look. 'You mean like if you're ill?'

Claudia smiled. 'A lungful of sea air and negative ions never go amiss if you're not feeling well. But I mean mentally. If I'm tired or upset or unhappy, I let the waves lull me into a kind of trance. I always feel calm and centred afterwards.' She glanced sideways at her companion. 'Want to try it?'

Millie shrugged her indifference. 'Okay.'

'Keep your eyes on the waves,' Claudia directed her quietly. 'Follow their white tips as they come in, as they crest; watch them foam as they fizzle out then swoop back to start all over again. Be aware of their rhythm. Listen to it. Try to block out anything else.'

Claudia didn't hold out much hope – this was hardly an exciting pastime for a fourteen-year-old.

But, as with the stone-skimming, Millie persevered, and it was a good few minutes before she shifted uncomfortably on her rock and complained, 'My bum's getting sore.'

'Mine too, and I've got more padding than you! Did you enjoy the waves?'

Millie allowed her a small, grudging nod.

'I'm lucky,' Claudia said. 'I can hear the sea from my flat. Maybe you could download the sound onto your phone? It might help you sleep.'

'Maybe.' Millie stood. 'I'd better get back to Dad. He'll worry if I stay out too long.'

'It's a pity he's stuck inside working on a lovely evening like this.'

'Yeah. I suppose it's not easy for him, starting at a new company.'

It was good that Millie had *some* sympathy for her father, Claudia thought, but she sensed their relationship wasn't easy. It must have been hard, adjusting to being just the two of them.

'It's a long way from Edinburgh,' Claudia said carefully. 'Did you fancy somewhere new as much as your dad?'

'Yes. Things weren't good at school. I… I didn't behave very well after Mum died, and my friends got fed up with me being weird. Gran and Grandad – Mum's parents – live in Devon, so Dad suggested we move south to be nearer to them.'

Claudia's respect for Jason went up a notch. He was putting himself through a lot of upheaval and self-sacrifice for his daughter's sake.

'I was glad to get away,' Millie mumbled. 'Only now we're here, it's a bit…'

'Daunting?'

'Yeah. Dad wants me to make friends and do well at school.'

Not unreasonable wishes. 'But?'

'But I might let him down, mightn't I? Anyway, see you later.'

Claudia watched Millie retreat in the fading light, a thin figure in black skinny jeans, the heavy boots looking ginormous in comparison, and sighed. But as she brushed off sand, she reminded herself that she didn't know these people, and she shouldn't interfere.

*

'I've been asking around,' Evelyn said over Sunday coffee. 'But it's got me nowhere.'

Claudia smiled. Evelyn was not one to be thwarted when it came to knowing what was going on in Porthsteren. Between her and Libby, who needed social media?

'About what in particular?' Claudia asked, since Evelyn inevitably had her gossip finger in several pies.

'The new shop. I asked Ian again. All he's heard is that it's retail.'

'Not a café, then.' Claudia breathed a sigh of relief on her neighbours' behalf.

Sarah patted her partner's hand. 'It's driving Evie nuts. I've told her to put her energies into keeping our own business afloat, but…'

Claudia frowned at this seemingly throwaway line. 'Is the Page Turner struggling?'

Sarah played with a button on her shirt. '*Struggling* is too strong a word, but I'd be lying if I said things were buoyant. Takings are down from the same time last year.' She sighed. 'Let's face it, the second-hand book trade isn't what it was. We had a thriving business for years, but then digital came in, and people prefer new over old. We've been in this position before, only this time we don't have another rabbit in our hats.'

'Rabbit?'

'Opening the café to draw people in,' Evelyn explained.

'The trend for recycling's helped the book side a bit,' Sarah admitted. 'But not enough. It's the café that keeps us going nowadays, and we're rather weather-dependent for that.' She gestured around the terrace.

Claudia thought about the mystery surrounding the new shop. What if it was an independent bookstore? Somewhere selling shiny *new* books wouldn't bode well for Sarah and Evelyn… although Claudia would have thought a shop like that would get enough business all year round, so why the six-month lease?

'Could you increase the indoor café area? Decrease the books?' Claudia asked, her heart sinking at the thought.

'Then we'd be running a café and not a bookshop any more. It was our love of books that brought Evie and me together.'

Claudia remembered them telling her how they'd met at university, when Sarah was an exchange student. Love at first sight over the library stacks.

'Is Healing Waves doing okay?' Evelyn asked her.

'I make enough to get by. I'm looking forward to the summer trade, though.' Claudia smiled. 'And no doubt by the time summer's over, I'll be grateful for a chance to catch up, clear out, restock.'

Sarah frowned. 'You work long hours, running it on your own.'

'Yes, but I'll do whatever it takes, because I can't imagine things not working out for me here.'

*

'Hi. What've you got there?'

It was Sunday night, and Jason had decided that Millie had been holed up in her room for too long. He needed to know that she was okay before her big day tomorrow.

She was sitting cross-legged on her bed, a spread of cards across the duvet. 'Nothing.' Casting him a guilty look, she scooped them up.

'I can't take an interest?'

'You'll only be sarcastic.'

'Why don't you try me?' He stepped closer, frowning. 'You bought *tarot* cards?'

'They're not tarot cards.' His daughter was immediately on the defensive. Actually, she was always on the defensive – it was just a question of degrees.

'Look like it to me.' He picked up the box. 'Oracle cards. Same thing.'

'No, they're not. Claudia explained.'

Claudia Bennett. Healing Waves. I might have known. 'Oh, she did, did she?'

'Yes. *Not* that there's any harm in tarot cards, but these are different.' Millie glared at him. 'You know I could have hidden these from you, right? I could have only used them when you're out, or in bed.'

Jason sighed. She was right. 'I don't want you hiding things from me, Millie, but you know I hate this kind of thing.' He took a deep breath. 'Alright. Tell me about oracle cards.' Perching on the bed, he prepared to listen. Opening his mind was a step too far, but you couldn't have everything.

When Millie had finished, Jason couldn't say he felt any better about it. Okay, they weren't tarot cards, but all this drivel about the cards sending you messages and answering your questions?

He reached out to pick one up, but Millie slapped his hand away.

'You can't touch them. I already cleansed them.'

The image of his daughter running a pack of cards under a tap flitted across his brain. 'You *what?*'

'You have to cleanse them, so they're attuned to your energies. That's what this is for.' She waved a pink crystal at him.

'I see. Well. I'll leave you to it.'

Her expression betraying relief that her father wasn't going to blow a gasket, Millie turned back to her new acquisition, picking up the little book that came with the cards and leafing through it.

Jason managed to get all the way down the stairs and out onto the decking before he released the breath he'd been holding, and a squawk of suppressed rage with it.

What the hell did that woman think she was playing at, spouting this kind of crap to his daughter – a bereaved young girl in desperate need of comfort – and taking her pocket money into the bargain?

Millie might have thought he'd taken it lying down, but Claudia was going to find out *exactly* what he thought about it.

*

Jason's first day at work did not go well. It would have helped if people realised that, as he was new and not psychic, they should pass vital information on to him so he didn't look totally incompetent in front of the client. Since he couldn't take his bad mood out on his new colleagues – yet – he'd built up a shed-load of pent-up anger by the end of the day.

Getting away from a site meeting earlier than expected, he figured he could finish his working day at home, where he couldn't kill anyone with a look or by any other means. Driving along the Porthsteren beach road, he had to pass Healing Waves, and having already planned to tackle Claudia…

He'd parked up and barged through the door before he could stop himself. Thwarted by the presence of another customer, he reined in his impatience, hovering by the oracle cards, frowning with deep disapproval, then moving on to pick up the mermaid hugging the dragon again. *For pity's sake*.

The minute the customer left, he approached the counter. 'I'd like a word.'

Claudia's mouth turned down at the corners, presumably in response to his tone of voice. 'How can I help?'

'You can help by keeping your bizarre ideas away from my daughter. Stop trying to influence her, and stop selling her weird stuff. That child has been through a traumatic time, and she's still struggling to find her way through it. I don't want her head filled with mumbo-jumbo.' He swept his arm around the shop to make his point. 'Do I make myself clear?'

'Crystal clear.' Claudia returned his gaze, her golden eyes cooling. 'Have you quite finished?'

'That depends on whether you'll do as I ask.'

He could see it on her face – whether to remain polite or whether to let him have it.

She opted for the latter.

'Then let *me* be clear. I don't do the bidding of someone I barely know. I don't do the bidding of anyone *at all* unless their request is reasonable and polite. And I *don't* do the bidding of a person who is on my property, insulting my business. If you don't like Healing Waves, feel free to stay away. As for Millie, all I've sold her is an inexpensive necklace and a pack of oracle cards. *She* asked *me* about them, so I explained. That's what one does with customers. I wouldn't call it influencing her.' She jerked a thumb sideways. 'Are you going to have a go at next door's for selling paperbacks to her, or are you reserving all your obnoxious disapproval just for me?'

Taken aback by the vehemence of her defensive outburst, Jason muttered, 'I'd hardly call paperbacks the same as this stuff.'

'Depends on the subject matter, doesn't it? And what you mean by "this stuff", I'm not sure. Have you had a proper look around before shooting your mouth off?'

'I've seen enough.'

'You've been in here twice, for a couple of minutes, and you've only seen what you want to see, to prove the opinion you hold.'

She was making him sound like some prehistoric, small-minded bigot, when he was only looking out for his daughter. Jason didn't like it.

'I don't call it unreasonable to not want Millie involved with tarot cards or believing rocks have magic powers.'

Claudia gave him an exasperated look. 'I don't sell tarot cards, but not for the reasons *you* think. They're oracle cards. As for the amethyst, would you complain if Millie had bought a necklace with wooden beads instead? Can't you just see it as jewellery?'

'It's what you're telling her about them. Filling her head with all this spiritual healing nonsense. It's irresponsible. Can't you find a better way to earn a living?'

Jason knew he'd gone too far with that. He should never have come in here after the rubbish day he'd had. His legs wanted him to leave it there – he'd delivered the perfect line to stalk out on.

But Claudia's eyes, now a very cool amber, held him like a fish on a hook.

'Mr Craig. I don't sell anything I haven't personally experienced as helpful. Nothing "dark", nothing "occult". Open your eyes and take a look at the ordinary things I sell. Soap, candles, wall art. Bags, tunics. Ornaments – because that's all they are, those fantasy figures you keep glaring at. Would you complain if they were squirrels or flowers? As for spouting spiritual healing nonsense, you are *way* off base.' She took her strident tone down a notch. 'I'm genuinely sorry for your and Millie's loss. But Millie seems able to talk to me, and I have no intention of telling her she isn't welcome at Healing Waves. I'll leave that to you.' She let out a long breath. 'Before you rescue us both from this miserable conversation by leaving, let me ask you this. If Millie buys a necklace that I tell her might help with anxiety, and she wears it and believes it and feels less anxious – about her new school, say – then why, as her father, wouldn't you be happy about that, whether *you* believe it or not?'

Jason opened his mouth, but a clever comeback escaped him. He was saved by the jangling of the doorbell heralding another customer.

Claudia stood her ground for a brief moment, then turned to the woman approaching the counter, giving him the opportunity to leave.

Safely back in his car, he allowed his head to drop down onto the steering wheel. *Well done, Jason.*

*

A moment after Jason had left, Sarah came into Healing Waves and waited patiently while Claudia served her customer, then said, 'What was *that* all about?'

'You have to ask? I'd've thought you and your customers heard every word!'

'No customers this late in the day. Evie's closing up. We heard a racket through the wall, then Evie saw Millie's dad stomping off. Are you okay? Do you need tea?'

'No, I'm not. And yes, please. Although it'll take more than tea to rid myself of *that* conversation.'

Claudia flipped the 'Closed' sign, then followed Sarah to the Page Turner, plonking herself down on a stool at the counter and murmuring her thanks as Evelyn pushed Earl Grey towards her. Her hands were shaking, causing Jason Craig to go down another notch in her estimation. Claudia didn't like *anybody* having that effect on her.

'What did the shouty man have a bee in his bonnet about?' Evelyn asked.

'Apparently, I'm a bad influence on his daughter.'

'Why? What did you do?'

'Sold her goods he didn't approve of. Oracle cards.'

'Ah.'

'She asked me about them,' Claudia said, defensive. 'I was very careful, but she was drawn to the pack. There's no age censorship on them. How was I to know her father would go mad about it?'

'He seemed so nice when he came in here,' Evelyn said sadly.

'You sell books,' Claudia pointed out. 'Which are harmless, in Jason Craig's world.'

'For all he knows, Millie could have been studying satanic rites back there!' Sarah jerked her head towards the rear of the shop.

'But she didn't spend her money on them and take them home, did she?'

'What's he got against oracle cards?' Evelyn wondered aloud. 'I don't understand.'

Claudia shook her head. 'Neither does he. That's the problem. He thinks they're tarot cards, for a start, and he has a thing about *those* because he doesn't understand them, either.' She sighed. 'He hates my shop. I don't think he likes me much, either. He tried to be polite when I bumped into him last week on my walk, but I could tell it was a strain. Anyway, *that* veneer's worn off.'

'Nobody calls you a bad influence and gets away with it,' Sarah said crossly. 'Just wait till he sets foot in here again. I'll—'

'No, Sarah.' Claudia's voice was gentle but firm. 'I appreciate the support, but I can handle this myself.'

'How?'

Claudia took a sip of tea as she thought about it. 'Maybe he'll let me explain my stock?'

'Doubt it,' Sarah said. 'Some people are just closed-minded.'

'But if Millie keeps wanting to visit Healing Waves, he'll have to deal with it, won't he?'

'By shouting at you every time you sell her a bar of voodoo-cursed soap?'

Claudia laughed despite her misery.

'You could tell Millie she's not welcome,' Evelyn suggested.

'Not an option.'

'Or tell her that her dad's not happy about it?'

'No. I get the impression those two are on a knife-edge as it is. I don't want to be responsible for making it worse.' Claudia sighed. 'Well, thanks for the tea and sympathy. I'd better go – I'm due at Tanya's tonight. Staying over. I'll leave Pudding some food in his timer dish, so don't worry about him.'

Sarah smiled. 'Don't go cooking up any dark spells or sticking pins in Jason Craig effigies while you're over there, will you?'

Claudia gave her a long look. 'I'm making no promises.'

*

Claudia loved the drive to Tanya's, even though she lived over an hour away in Falmouth. Tanya ran her own business developing websites, so a busy town was a must for her, although she still did a lot of driving to meet clients.

It had often occurred to Claudia that the distance between them might not be such a bad thing. If they lived nearer, they would drink far too much wine and eat far more pizza than was good for them. And staying over meant a relaxed evening. The early alarm for the drive back was worth it.

She and Tanya had become firm friends from the moment they met soon after Claudia moved south. Tanya was the only person in Cornwall who knew how disappointed life and love had left Claudia, and how hard she'd worked to discover the Claudia she wanted to be, a woman who didn't answer to anyone. Claudia didn't regret that. It was healthy that one person in her new life understood her completely.

An evening of wine and chatter and laughter with Tanya was just what she needed after the afternoon she'd had.

Negotiating her way through Falmouth, she found a parking spot in the street outside Tanya's pale blue terraced cottage – not always possible in high season – and let herself in.

Tanya hadn't opened out the small 'two-up, two-down', but had left it with its original low-ceilinged rooms, cosy and cluttered with the paraphernalia that was unique to Tanya's… *natural talents.*

She greeted Claudia with a kiss, a glass of wine and a colourful veggie supper. An hour later, Claudia had caught up with Tanya's new website commission for a local restaurant and had commiserated over her latest dating flop.

'He was so into me when I met him at yoga,' Tanya lamented. 'Couldn't keep his eyes off me.'

This, Claudia could well believe. Tanya was petite, lithe, and had a short blonde haircut that rarely misbehaved (and if it did, it only made her look cute). She looked darned good in her yoga gear.

'But?'

'The usual. More interested in my body than my mind. And…'

Claudia gave her a knowing look. 'Did you tell him?'

'I always do. Easier to come clean at the start. No point investing time and energy in a lost cause.'

'He didn't want to date a witch?'

Tanya's alter-ego didn't always go down well with her dates. But it was who she was. She believed in the Craft wholeheartedly. Claudia wished her friend could find a soulmate who could accept that.

Tanya made a face. 'I got the impression he was thinking about going along with it just so he could get me into bed – you know, see if it was more exciting with a witch. But he bottled out.' She poured more wine. 'Enough about me. Tell me about you.'

A sinful slice of rich chocolate cake later, Tanya was up-to-date with Claudia's week. They made sleep-inducing herbal tea and sat cross-legged on the floor to drink it.

'So, to sum up.' Tanya counted off on her fingers. 'A new shop's due to open in Porthsteren and nobody knows anything about it. And you have newcomers – one a lonely, bereaved teenager, and the other her hostile, unreasonably angry, bereaved dad who has impressively managed to send your trademark serenity on a holiday to destinations unknown.'

Claudia laughed. Tanya always made her laugh. It was one of the many reasons she loved her. 'That's about the size of it.'

Tanya sipped her tea. 'Millie's straightforward enough. If she wants to chat, you'll chat to her. You've never been one to turn anyone away. If her dad doesn't like her coming to your shop, let *him* lay the lay down the law and take the blame.'

Claudia winced. 'I resent that he made me lose my temper – I haven't done that in ages – but I don't want to be the cause of friction between them.'

'You're not the cause of anything. You merely exist. Healing Waves merely exists. What they do about you and the shop is their problem. Whatever they've been through, he had no right to shout at you on your own premises. Narrow-minded idiot.'

Claudia sighed. 'The thing is, I don't know if he's narrow-minded so much as over-protective of his daughter – understandably, under the circumstances.'

'You may well be right, but don't be *too* soft. Don't let him walk all over you.'

At that, Claudia's eyes became steely. 'I won't.'

'I know you won't. You learned that lesson the hard way.' Tanya jumped up and started rummaging through her supplies cupboard in the corner of the lounge. 'How about a spell for staying strong in the face of obstacles? We need red candles, incense, something metal…'

Of course we do. Claudia smiled. She would never perform a spell herself – she didn't have the knowledge or the inclination to learn – but she trusted Tanya and didn't object to the occasional one being performed on her behalf.

As the incense (home-made and blessed at the correct phase of the moon and time of year) filled the room, Claudia slowed her breathing and concentrated on Tanya's words as she lit candles and drew metal through flame. Tanya had taught her that intention was paramount for a spell's success, and although Claudia wouldn't call Jason Craig an obstacle, as such, a little courage to handle him might not go amiss.

She couldn't deny the rain against the window and the rumble of thunder in the distance added to the atmosphere.

*

Jason couldn't sleep. The driving rain and loud thunderclaps didn't help, but primarily, it was the knowledge that he'd behaved so badly that kept him awake.

His intention had been to have a 'quiet word', not deliver a rant full of insults and abuse. He didn't see himself as a dinosaur about these things. He merely hoped that Millie's love of 'alternative' shops was just a phase, albeit a fairly harmless one as far as teenage phases went.

Jason also liked to think he was a fair man, and the truth was, Claudia was right in almost everything she'd said. He'd been unconscionably rude about her livelihood, even though her shop was light and bright and positive. He hadn't seen anything menacing in there, only things he didn't care for or believe in. She hadn't pried Millie's pocket money out of her hand. And Claudia *had* taken time to chat to his daughter and bring a welcome present to their home.

He'd behaved like a prize arse. And he'd put himself in a difficult position, because although he knew he should apologise for his behaviour, he still stood by not wanting Millie embroiled with all that woo-woo crap. He would rather his daughter worked through her grief in a more proven, traditional manner. Not that that had worked for her.

Jason turned over, tugging the sheets higher. As if grief for her mother weren't enough, he knew that Millie blamed him for the divorce that had been planned before fate changed the direction of all their lives. He'd allowed her to. There was no point in suggesting she might blame her mum, too. Gemma wasn't here to give her side of the story, and Jason couldn't bear the thought of altering Millie's perception of her mother. And so he'd let it lie, hoping time would lessen his daughter's anger towards him. Instead, time and hormones and all things teenage – he remembered his own teenage years all too well – had seen Millie retreating into her defensive armour, her grief and anger directed, more often than not, at him.

Jason hoped their move to Cornwall might release this stranglehold on their relationship. He was enjoying the coastal scenery and sea air. He also appreciated the change of faces. Even though it was common knowledge among the locals that he was a widower, they assumed he was moving on with his life. Jason liked that.

And yet he'd already managed to alienate one of those locals, a usually calm and pleasant woman who had turned pretty darned feisty, those eyes flashing fiery gold before cooling to amber ice, and that wild hair framing her livid, rather beautiful face. And who could blame her? Her empathy with Millie was evident, and Millie obviously felt able to chat to her in more than monosyllabic grunts. For that, he should be grateful.

Jason thumped his pillow into submission. Parenting could be seriously rubbish at times.

Chapter Five

Claudia's ringtone jolted her out of a deep sleep. She glanced at the time. Six o'clock. *What the…?*

'Sarah. Is everything okay?'

'Not really, honey.' Sarah's voice hitched, and a slow panic curled in Claudia's stomach. Sarah rarely got emotional.

'Is it Pudding?'

'Pudding's fine. It's the storm last night. Didn't you get it over there?'

'We had rain. A little thunder.' Realisation crept in. 'Why? Was it bad in Porthsteren?'

'Yes. It hit us hard, Claudia – the Page Turner and Healing Waves. A few other places. There's damage.'

Claudia's heart sank. 'How much damage?'

'It's not irreparable, but it is a bit of a mess. You need to come and see for yourself. Sort it all out.'

'Okay. I'll be there as soon as I can.'

Tanya came through from her bedroom. 'Problem?'

Claudia told her.

'Oh no.' Tanya folded her into a tight hug, stroking ineffectually at Claudia's morning mess of hair. 'I'm *so* sorry. I'll come with you.'

Claudia gave her a wobbly smile. 'Thank you, but no. You have a meeting at that restaurant for the website. They won't thank you for cancelling.'

'Friends are more important than work.'

'You need to make a living, Tanya. It would only make me feel guilty. Sarah and Evelyn are there. I'll be fine.'

It was a long moment before Tanya relented. 'Okay. But please drive safely. And let me know what's happened as soon as you get a chance.'

*

From where Claudia parked on the beach road, she could have thought everything was normal if she hadn't known. Walking around to the front of the building was another matter.

The Porthsteren Page Turner's large display window was boarded over. Healing Waves' glass was, remarkably, intact, but a tarpaulin had been fixed over part of her roof and window, and smashed roof tiles littered the ground beneath. She could see at a glance that her window display was ruined, and she was scared to imagine what might be damaged inside.

'I'm so sorry, Claudia.' Evelyn rushed out, pulling her into a distressed embrace. 'We would've done more, if we could. All we've managed so far is to get our window boarded and that tarp put up for you. Libby's son-in-law did it for us.'

'Thank you. I appreciate it.'

'We had no idea until Libby called us around five thirty. We're sheltered over at the cottage – the storm didn't seem too bad there.' Evelyn sighed. 'I think we've been unlucky with the direction of the wind here – it looks like it caught us head-on. Most of the businesses along the beach road are alright because they're set back. But the beach is a mess.' She gestured at the sand, covered in debris. 'A couple of boats in the harbour were damaged – tossed against each other. The Smugglers' Inn has roof damage and a broken window. Anywhere that juts out has caught the worst.'

'Being in prime position has its downside,' Claudia commented dully. 'You haven't been inside mine yet?'

'No. Sorry. We were busy protecting the outside, in case it rains again. But Sarah checked on your flat and Pudding, and she fed him.'

'Thank you. I should go and see.'

But Claudia's hand was shaking, and Evelyn had to unlock the door for her.

Claudia stepped inside, her eyes roaming the front end of her shop. All the goods in the window display were ruined by water or wind. The wall at a right angle to the window had taken the most damage. That was where she stocked her textiles, and the handmade soaps she left unwrapped – she didn't believe in unnecessary packaging and plastics. The wooden shelves, left untreated for a natural look, appeared water-logged. The water would turn the wood black and mouldy.

Claudia viewed the damage with dismay. That this had happened at all was bad enough, but at this time of year, just as things were gearing up… Panic gnawed at her insides at the thought of all the things that must be done, and done quickly.

Remembering Evelyn, she tried to smile but failed. 'How bad is yours?'

'Some of the outdoor furniture was damaged.' Evelyn pointed at a jumble of broken wood piled in a corner of the terrace as Claudia followed her out. 'But not all of it. It's sturdier than you'd think, and the wall protected it to some degree.' They stepped over the bookshop's threshold. Everything near the window was wet through and sprinkled with glass.

'All the books on the tables and shelves nearest the window will have to go.' Evelyn's words were matter-of-fact, but her voice shook. 'Even those that didn't get sodden might have slivers of glass between the pages. We can't risk it.'

'Are they replaceable?'

'Oh, heavens, yes.' Evelyn crossed her arms over her chest, hugging herself. 'Those at the front are the blockbusters, the holiday reads, the thrillers. Nothing too specialist.'

'But they're at the front because they bring in your trade,' Claudia said, realising as soon as it was out of her mouth that it wasn't tactful.

'Yes. We'll need to clean up and restock as quickly as we can. One of us will get off to a few car boot sales, I suppose.' Evelyn wafted a hand towards the rear of the store. 'Let's face it, we can hardly rely on people desperate to purchase books on the history of the traction engine or how to build your own greenhouse. But it could have been worse. Structurally, it's only the window.' Evelyn sighed. 'We should have had it fixed sooner. That crack in the corner, the one caused by the marble, you know?'

Looking like a bullet hole with cracks radiating outwards, it had appeared overnight a couple of months ago, and Sarah had found a marble beneath, they assumed tossed by a bored youth.

'But we weren't sure how much longer we'd carry on,' Evelyn went on. 'And money's been tight over the winter. We were putting off repairs until we had summer season money in the bank and the prospect of winter weather on the way. Who'd've guessed that nature would be so contrary and send the storms *now*?'

Claudia wasn't feeling too fond of nature herself right now. 'Is Sarah alright?'

'Yes. She's on the phone to the insurance company.' Evelyn pointed at the mess. 'Apart from having the window boarded, we haven't done anything, in case they want to inspect. Sarah doubts they'll bother if she sends the photos she's taken, but you never know.'

Claudia hadn't thought it through yet, like they had. Her first instinct would have been to clear up, but she realised now that that wasn't necessarily the right thing to do.

Back outside, she stared out over the sand. 'The beach is a mess.'

'The council'll do something, but I've heard talk about volunteers chipping in to get it done faster.'

'I should help.'

'Absolutely not. Nobody who has their own damage to worry about is expected to help.'

Claudia looked back at their shambles of a building and sighed. 'Well, I can't say I feel up to arguing.'

'Workmen'll be busy with all this damage,' Evelyn warned her. 'You'll have to act fast to stand a chance of quick repairs.' She placed a hand on her arm. 'I can't even make you a coffee. The machine isn't fired up.'

'Don't be ridiculous, Evelyn! You have your own problems.' Claudia straightened her spine. 'And I should get on with mine. Thank you for everything you've done.' She slapped a hand across her forehead, making Evelyn jump. 'Meditation!'

'You can't be considering running that tonight! You have to cancel.'

'That means letting everyone down.'

'Claudia, you have enough to cope with. People will assume it's cancelled, anyway.'

'But it's at times of stress that people need it the most.'

'And it's at times of stress that you should listen to your old friend Evelyn. I'll put a notice on the door upstairs. You put a notice on your website. I'll be checking up on you.'

Claudia couldn't help but smile. Sarah was usually the strident one, but Evelyn could show a streak of feistiness now and again. 'Okay.'

First, she went up to her flat to double-check there was no damage there, breathing a huge sigh of relief to see everything intact. Because it was set back a little and not flush with the shop front, it had escaped the full force of the wind.

Pudding wound around her legs as she made some herbal tea. When he tried to follow her to the door, she fixed him with a steely glare.

'You can't come with me today. It's too messy down there.'

He watched her leave with a melancholy look, but she knew he'd soon accept his fate and take a nap.

Back downstairs, clutching the bamboo takeaway cup in her hands, she eyed the front of her premises. The tarpaulin would have to stay in place until she got the roof sorted. Inside, she would have to assess and clear up. There was her window display to recreate, the ruined textile goods to reorder. As for the soap, she could buy some in, but that wasn't what her regular customers expected… and yet handmaking it meant a lot of hard work.

Claudia had no idea how long all this would take. What she *did* know was that she couldn't afford to close for long.

*

By late afternoon, Claudia had taken photos, spoken to the insurance company and got permission to clear up, reassured Tanya that there was no need for her to rush over, had a visit from Ted the roofing contractor… and virtually had a nervous breakdown while she was at it.

So many people had stopped by to commiserate, especially those volunteering on beach clean-up duty. All were well-meaning, but each had their own tale of how the storm had affected them. It was understandable, but exhausting.

When Millie showed up on her way home from school, Claudia was on the verge of screaming.

The teen looked crestfallen at the damage, but instead of the usual platitudes, what popped out of her mouth was, 'Ironic, don't you think?'

'What is?'

'Healing Waves.' Millie pointed to the shop's sign, half-obscured by the tarpaulin, then jerked her thumb in the direction of the sea. 'Not very healing, in this case.'

Claudia had to smile a little. 'Nature can be cruel as well as kind, I suppose.' The sight of Millie's uniform reminded her to ask, 'How were your first couple of days at school?'

Millie scuffed her feet on the ground. 'Okay, I guess. Everyone stares at me.'

'Bound to happen.' Claudia tried to sound bright and breezy. 'You're a novelty. It'll wear off.'

'S'ppose.' Millie tugged at her hair. 'I'm not allowed to have purple. They're giving me till Monday to sort it out.'

Claudia felt sad at that. The purple streaks in Millie's hair seemed a part of her, somehow. But rules were rules, she supposed. 'What will you do about it?'

'I usually do it myself, but it drives Dad mad 'cause I make a mess of the bathroom and stain the shower curtain.'

Claudia opened her mouth to offer to help, then closed it again. Jason Craig had made himself quite clear.

'I'm sure he'll understand, since it's school rules,' she said instead. 'But you might need an expert to cover the purple.'

'What's the place by the harbour like?'

'A little old-fashioned, maybe.' Claudia sent a silent apology to Jenny for that. 'But you'd be in safe hands.'

Millie refocused her attention on the shop. 'When can you reopen?'

'There's a lot to do. A few days, at least.'

'Shame about that horrible cover thingy.'

'Can't be helped. It'll be there till the roofer can get to me.'

Millie studied it. 'Your window display's a mess, so why not let the cover hang down properly rather than being half-tucked up like that, then paint something on it? It might make people smile instead of just feeling sorry for you.'

The wisdom of youth. Claudia eyed her cautiously. 'Do you have an idea? Do you want to have a go?'

'Can I?' Millie's shoulders sagged. 'But I might make a mess of it.'

'It can't look any worse, Millie! And if it covers the window, it could be like I'm waiting to do a grand reveal.' *Like the new shop. Two can play at that game.* She eyed Millie's hopeful face. 'It'll only be there a few days, so it doesn't have to be a masterpiece. When could you do it?'

'Now?'

Ah. Claudia realised she should have thought this through. Jason had made it plain he didn't want his daughter hanging around Healing Waves… but Claudia had told him she wouldn't turn her away. She wasn't sure where she stood with an endeavour like this.

'Won't your dad expect you home?'

'He's got a late meeting.'

'No homework?'

'Only a stupid maths sheet. And it doesn't have to be in tomorrow.'

Claudia hesitated. It was good to see Millie looking enthusiastic about *something*, and it might take her mind off school. Surely Jason couldn't object to her cheering his daughter up?

'Okay. But only if you text your dad to let him know you're here. Do it now. Then let's see what supplies I've got.'

Claudia ducked under the outside metal staircase, opened the cupboard there, took a torch from a shelf and flashed it around. 'Two different blues from when I did my flat,' she reported to the teen waiting at her shoulder. 'A deeper blue gloss from the door. And white from the ceiling.'

Claudia passed the cans out to Millie, found a screwdriver to prise the lids off, then rummaged for brushes. While Millie ferried it all to the front, Claudia fetched a stepladder from the back of the shop. Clambering up, she looked at how the tarp was fixed.

'I don't want to take it down,' she called to Millie. 'I might never get it back up again!'

'Just pull it so it hangs down. Then maybe you could hold it tight while I paint?'

'Okay. But be careful on the stepladder. Your dad'll kill me if you fall.' Claudia eyed Millie's brand-new school uniform. 'And you can't do it in that.' When Millie scowled, she gave her a steely look. 'Come with me.'

She led Millie up to her flat and went into the bedroom to hunt for something suitable. When she came back out with a pair of old jogging bottoms and a T-shirt, Millie was looking around with undisguised interest, idly stroking Pudding in his chair. 'I *love* this place!'

'Thank you. Here, put these on. The bottoms'll be too big, but they have a drawstring. I'll wait for you downstairs.'

Claudia tried not to laugh when Millie came back down. She was skinny and tall – what Claudia's mother would call a string bean – and Claudia was not. But Millie was too keen to get started on her impromptu project to mind much.

Just as when they'd skimmed pebbles, Millie was transformed when she was concentrating. Focused, she studied the colours, then slowly but surely transformed the dull, grubby tarpaulin while Claudia held it taut or steadied the stepladder or passed her paints and brushes as requested.

When they eventually stood back to admire her handiwork, a cheerful mural stared back at them – a simple but effective design of two-tone waves tipped with white crests. White Ws were dotted above to look like seagulls in a stormy sky, which was where the grey of the tarpaulin came into its own.

At the bottom, Millie had printed in blue gloss:

HEALING WAVES
REOPENING SOON

'It's fantastic! Thank you.' Spontaneously giving her a hug, Claudia quickly backed off in case it annoyed her, but Millie seemed pleased with the praise. 'Come with me.' Inside Healing Waves, she pointed at the laced crystals. 'Pick any you like.'

'Really?'

'Yes. Just a small token for a huge favour.'

Millie rotated the stand, undecided.

'So how *is* school going?' Claudia asked, her gut instinct kicking in.

Millie scowled. 'People are either all over you or don't want anything to do with you when you're new.' Her shoulders slumped.

Nodding understanding, Claudia fingered a wand-shaped, marbled crystal. 'Do you like blue? How about this sodalite?'

Millie read the small, handwritten label attached to the lace. 'Emotional balance. Self-acceptance. Self-esteem.'

'It's good for panic attacks,' Claudia added. 'And it can help with judgement, so it might help you work out who might be a good friend and who might not.' Too late, she remembered Jason's warning not to fill his daughter's head with rubbish.

'A crystal can do all that?'

Claudia could have laughed at the way Millie's eyebrow arched in the same way her father's did.

She tempered her response. 'So they say. But if not, it's a lovely colour. What have you got to lose?'

'Thanks.' Millie smiled. 'I love my oracle cards, by the way.'

If you had any idea what trouble they caused me… Claudia forced a smile. 'I'm glad.'

'Dad saw them. He wasn't keen, but I explained they're not tarot cards and he seemed okay with that.'

And again, if you had any idea…

At least Jason hadn't had a go at his daughter and made her feel bad. That was one small point in his favour, Claudia supposed. It didn't make her feel any better about the way he'd treated her, though.

*

Jason had caught the local headlines about storm damage in the village that morning, so he'd driven the long way to work, inland and along country roads through farmland. No point in getting snagged up. They'd had no damage at home, thank goodness, perhaps because the house was set back from the cliff and the gentle slope of trees below afforded a buffer.

There was a call out for volunteers to help clean up the beach. He would have liked to offer to lend a hand, but as this was his first week at a new job, it wasn't an option.

Only one of his company's projects, along the coast towards Penzance, had been affected, but that wasn't one of his, for which he was grateful.

To his relief, his second day was better than his first – not that *that* would be hard. Only one short (he hoped) meeting to go, and then he could get back home to subtly – or not so subtly – interrogate Millie about school.

His phone buzzed as he made his way to the partners' office. A text from Millie.

Hi. In case you get home before me, I'm at Healing Waves, helping Claudia after the storm. She said to text you.

Jason's initial reaction was anger. Hadn't he told the damned woman yesterday that he didn't want his daughter there?

Then he remembered how awful he'd felt about that afterwards. Rereading Millie's text, he registered that Claudia had insisted Millie text him. She wasn't trying to hide it from him.

He allowed a smidgen of sympathy to come to the fore. It sounded like the storm had caused her problems, and he wouldn't wish that on her.

As he seated himself at the conference table, he stifled a sigh. Millie should be hanging out with new friends after school, not loitering at unsuitable shops and being roped into sweeping up or whatever it was she was doing. He couldn't say he was happy about his daughter being used as free labour. Then again, he couldn't complain about her being public-spirited, could he? And he could hardly have a go at Claudia Bennett when he'd spent the past twenty-four hours feeling guilty about his previous outburst. Best to let it lie... this time, anyway.

Chapter Six

'Very nice!' Sarah said as she stood side by side with Evelyn the next morning, studying the newly decorated tarpaulin.

Claudia smiled. '*Something* had to be done. It was so dreary!'

'It's fun,' Evelyn agreed.

Sarah frowned. 'You know if Millie's father finds out you let her go up a ladder, he'll sue you from here to Sunday on health and safety?'

'Only a *step*ladder,' Claudia said, defensive. 'That's why we left the top part grey for the sky, see? And I made her change out of her school uniform.' She sighed. 'I can't see why letting her paint an old tarpaulin should aggravate him, but who knows? Anyway, I've already weathered two storms this week – one from him and one from Mother Nature. If he wants to whip up another, I'll be ready for him.'

'He seems a nice enough bloke,' Sarah mused. 'Just over the top when it comes to his daughter.'

'*And* the company she keeps,' Claudia said. '*And* the establishments she frequents. *And* the purchases she makes.' *Time for a change of subject.* 'What's with the rubbish bags in your doorway?'

'Don't you just love Porthsteren?' Sarah declared as she untied a black plastic bin bag to show Claudia what was inside – a selection of second-hand books.

'We got a couple of bags yesterday, too,' Evelyn told her. 'Word got around that we've lost our popular paperbacks, so people have had clear-outs at home.' Her eyes welled with tears. 'People are very kind when the chips are down, aren't they?'

Claudia smiled. 'Yes. We're in a good community here.'

She thought about her old life, the ruthless nature of the work environment she'd been so caught up in; people treading on each other to clamber up their own career ladders. She didn't miss it for one single moment.

'When will you get your window replaced?' she asked them.

'Tomorrow,' Sarah told her. 'Hopefully, we can reopen the day after that, if we finish cleaning up. Have you got a schedule yet?'

'The insurance company want to send an assessor out. They've accepted the storm damage – thank goodness I didn't stint with a cheap policy! But they want to see the damaged goods and have me explain the costs involved. I guess some people exaggerate that kind of thing. They said I can clear up, though.'

'Will they insist on using their choice of company for repairs?'

'No. They want me back in business, otherwise they'll have to cough up for more loss of earnings, but they'll need to approve Ted's quote.'

'You're lucky to get Ted at all,' Evelyn pointed out. 'He's booked up at the best of times.'

'He's prioritising storm-affected businesses. He knows how important seasonal trade is.'

'Like I said, don't you just love Porthsteren?' Sarah sighed. 'Still, not much of a day off for our "Wednesday closing" this week, huh?'

They parted ways, and Claudia steeled herself to open her shop door. Despite it being as depressing as the day before, she had a sense of purpose now. The repairs would take their course. The insurance would take its course. Those were things she couldn't influence. Best to concentrate on what she *could* do.

*

Jason's evening stroll took him down the hill and past the harbour. Millie was doing homework, and since he'd been stuck in interminable meetings all day, he needed to stretch his legs.

Avoiding the beach – a mess of seaweed and rubbish, still in the process of being cleaned up – he walked along the road to Healing Waves. He was under strict instruction from his daughter to admire her handiwork and report back.

Jason had mixed feelings about Millie's mission of mercy. He was proud of her for being independent enough to volunteer without asking him first. He was also fed up that she'd volunteered without asking him first. He was pleased that she knew a local well enough to want to help. He wasn't pleased that the local was a woman whose ethos he didn't care for. He was still embarrassed about his over-the-top treatment of Claudia the other day. He was sorry she'd been affected by the storm, just as he would be sorry for any business in the same boat.

Yup. Mixed feelings.

He took in The Porthsteren Page Turner's boarded-up window and winced. A pile of broken wood on the terrace suggested some outdoor furniture had taken a battering, but there was still plenty intact, presumably protected by the sturdy wall surrounding the terrace. The wind and rain must have gone right over it to hit the building.

His gaze turned to Healing Waves and the cheery tarpaulin covering the window and half the roof. It would make anyone smile, with its blue waves, a boat's sail, and seagulls in the sky. He loved that his daughter had created it.

His smile dropped when Claudia came out of the store with an armful of wood. *Damn.* He'd assumed she would have finished for the day by now.

Wearing grubby cut-off jeans and an oversized shirt and with her hair gathered into an untidy knot on top of her head, curls escaping everywhere, she should have looked a mess, but she didn't.

As she came nearer, adding her planks to the pile on the bookshop's terrace, what she mostly looked, he realised, was exhausted. The animosity he'd felt towards her the other day melted away and sympathy kicked in.

'Hi. I was sorry to hear about the damage,' he said lamely.

'Yeah, I bet you were.' Before he could speak, she held up a hand. 'Sorry. Uncalled for. I'm knackered.'

Jason pulled out one of the Page Turner's benches that had survived, and Claudia landed heavily on it, her shoulders drooping.

'Damaged shelving,' she explained, pointing to the wood she'd thrown down.

'How bad is it?'

She hesitated, as though unsure whether to have a conversation with him at all – hardly surprising, after the last one they'd had.

But she shrugged and said, 'The window display was ruined. Some shelving. A lot of stock. One wall needs to dry out and be repainted. No electrical damage, thankfully, but the roof needs repairing – the wind took off some tiles, and some of the pointing was past its best. Hope the insurance company doesn't realise how much past its best.'

'If you have a good policy, the small print probably only states reasonable maintenance. You can't legislate for a major storm like that. Besides, I presume you had the place surveyed when you bought it?'

'Yes.'

Claudia looked comforted by his words, and that pleased him. A small repayment for his bad behaviour the other day, perhaps. He surprised himself by wishing he could do something about the shadows under her eyes so easily.

'Anything I can do to help?'

She looked startled at the notion. 'Thanks, but I've had it for the day.'

'Have you taken a break?'

She thought about it. 'A cuppa with Ted the roofer when he brought the quote. A salad sandwich that Libby brought over from the General Store.' She smiled. 'People are telepathic in Porthsteren. She guessed I hadn't stopped for food.'

'Then you need to eat now. I could take you for a pub meal?'

Good grief, Jason. Where the hell did that come from?

Claudia looked as shocked as he was. 'Ah. That's kind of you, but no thanks. I just need to get upstairs and take a shower.' She made a face. 'I would say I'd love a soak in a hot bath, but since my bathroom's too small to contain one, a shower will have to do.'

Jason managed to refrain from inviting her to enjoy a hot bath back at his house. The poor woman *so* looked like she needed one, but he didn't think either she or his daughter would take the invitation in the right spirit.

What popped out instead was, 'Why don't you let me fix you something to eat while you shower?'

And again, Jason, what on earth…?

When her eyes widened in surprise, he held his hands out, palms up. 'If I don't, you won't eat. You'll just fall into bed. Call it a peace offering for the other day.'

'Is that the nearest you'll get to an apology?' She shook her head. 'You know what? I'm too tired to argue, so I'll take it as one. Come on up.'

Jason wasn't sure he was happy for her to accept an apology he hadn't proffered, but he followed her up the stairs. 'Was your flat damaged?'

'No.' She unlocked the door. 'Maybe the roof's sounder? Anyway, I'm not complaining.'

Her flat was as small on the inside as it looked from the outside. The door opened directly onto the living area. At the back was a small kitchen space and then a stretch of bead curtains which he assumed hid the bedroom. A door in the far corner presumably led to a bathroom.

But Claudia had made the best of it. Hues of sea blues and sand beige – lamps, throws, cushions, curtains – made it appear more spacious than it was. Soft textiles, fairy lights strung here and there, unusual ceramics and ornaments, all added a personal touch. Knowing she'd come from London made it all the more intriguing. This was about as far from urban as she could get without being in the sea.

Jason could hear the suck and whoosh of the waves from in here and imagined it was soothing; that it might lull you to sleep. He could hear the sea from his own house, but they were so high up, it was a distant sound, muffled by the trees on the clifftop.

'I know it's tiny.' Claudia's tone was defensive. 'But it suits me. And look – not a sacrificial altar in sight.'

Jason winced. 'I may have come on a bit strong the other day…'

'*May* have?'

'…for which I'm sorry. Millie's vulnerable, and I can be over-protective.' He didn't want to start another argument, but he didn't want her to misunderstand his apology, either. 'I suppose I'm apologising for *how* I said it, but not necessarily *what* I said.' If that had her pushing him back out the door, then so be it.

She merely gave him a weary nod. 'I need my shower before I fall over.'

Grateful for the opportunity to allow the practical to take over from the awkward, Jason made a beeline for the kitchen area. 'Anything in particular?'

Claudia pulled her hair out of its fastenings, allowing it to tumble around her face. She looked like some wild – and dusty – goddess.

'No. I'll be grateful for anything you throw together, but keep it light, okay? I'm too tired to digest much.' She went through the bathroom door, then stuck her head back around it. 'And thanks. Peace offering accepted.'

After texting Millie to say he'd been waylaid – but not why – Jason hunted through the fridge with misgiving. He wasn't the best cook in the world, but 'keep it light' might be his saviour there. He dug out salad and found a shallow bowl to mix it in. The lack of meat didn't surprise him – he had a feeling Claudia would be a vegetarian. He grated cheese, added olives, found slightly stale sourdough bread which he lightly toasted. That would have to do.

By the time Claudia came back out, swaddled in an oversized cotton robe, her hair damp, it was laid out for her on the coffee table.

She sent a grateful smile his way, and his pulse stuttered. That smile, unguarded and heartfelt, was quite something.

'You're a star.' She slumped onto the sofa and took a bite of toast.

Did that mean he was forgiven?

'I wouldn't have eaten *anything*. I would've just fallen into bed.' Claudia tugged at her curls. 'And going to bed with my hair wet is never a bright idea. I'd look like I'd plugged myself into a live socket by morning.' She fingered the robe. 'Sorry. I couldn't be bothered to get dressed.'

'Understandable. Don't worry on my account.' He went to put the kettle on. 'Tea?' But when he opened a cupboard looking for teabags, he was confronted with numerous jars of leaf teas instead. 'Ah. Which one?'

'Chamomile, please.' Claudia yawned. 'Just put two heaped spoonfuls in the pot and let it steep. Bring the honey. You'll have some too, won't you?'

Jason grimaced as he sniffed the contents of the jar. 'Er. Hmm. Thanks.' He couldn't imagine anything he'd rather drink less, but he didn't want to offend her. Again.

He brought the tea to the coffee table and took the armchair, jumping when something soft brushed against his leg. The large and indescribably coloured cat Millie had seen on their first visit to Healing Waves leapt onto the chair arm next to him and sniffed.

'*There* you are!' Claudia crooned. 'I can't believe you didn't make an appearance when the fridge door opened. Have you been hiding from the nasty newcomer? Jason won't bite.'

Jason might not, but he wasn't sure about the cat. Feeling obliged to make an effort, he cautiously reached out to tickle between its ears.

The cat leaned into his hand and then, without a by-your-leave, stepped onto his jean-clad thighs, twirled around in a circle and plopped down in a warm, furry heap.

'They always gravitate to the person who likes them the least,' Claudia told him with a knowing look. 'You're honoured. Pudding's put you before food.' When Jason rolled his eyes at the name, she said, 'The name's not my doing, but it's not inappropriate.'

Jason reached over the cat's head for his tea and took a sip. *Yuk.*

Claudia laughed. 'You know you're making a face, right?'

'Sorry. I was trying not to.' *But at least I made her laugh.* 'I spend a lot of time on building sites. You can stand a spoon upright in most of the tea I drink.'

'That would keep you awake at this time of night. This will help you sleep.'

She added a teaspoon of honey for him, but it only made it sweet as well as disgusting.

He chuckled when she yawned. 'Looks like *you* won't need any help sleeping tonight.' But because they still had the tea to drink – heaven help him – he didn't feel that he could leave yet. 'So, you've been clearing out today?' he asked.

'Yep. I took out the whole window display – ruined – then removed the damaged shelves. I've sorted through and boxed up all the goods I can't save because the insurance assessor wants to see them. Then I mopped and cleaned the whole shop, because the wind blew sand and dirt and water everywhere.'

'No wonder you're exhausted.'

'Yes, but it felt good. Yesterday was so frustrating – although your daughter cheered me up.'

'I'm glad.' And he was, he realised. 'What's next?'

'If I can clear the roofer's quote with the insurance company, he can get going, then there's the stock to replace.' She sighed. 'All the textiles are unsaleable. I stock fair trade, organic, so they'll take a while to reorder and get delivered. As for the soap, I make it myself. I *usually* find it relaxing.'

'You don't have any staff?'

'No. I'm a one-man band.'

'You work hard.' Jason had been so caught up with not liking her shop, he hadn't thought about that before. Six long days a week for most of the year. Evenings spent replenishing stock.

'Yes. But I can catch up in the winter, when it's quiet.' She sipped her tea. 'Millie said you're an architect. How's your new job going?'

Jason had to admire her for trying to make polite conversation between stifled yawns, especially after the way he'd treated her the other day.

'It's hard, getting the measure of the people I'm working with and getting up to speed with everything. But I'm optimistic.'

'What kind of work do they do?'

'They specialise in upmarket homes, holiday homes, second homes. Extensions, conversions. Sometimes people buy a property, tear it down and start again because the land's worth more than the modest home that's on it. Whatever we do, it has to fit into the locality, the landscape. And people like to go in an eco-direction nowadays.'

Claudia started to ask another question, but it was overtaken by a long yawn she couldn't control.

Jason smiled. 'You need to get to bed.'

'I do. Sorry.'

Extricating himself from the cat wasn't easy. The animal mewed his protest, and in the end, Claudia had to come over and lift the cat off him.

'Come on, sweetie. Let's get you some supper.'

But the cat seemed more interested in being petted – he lay like a baby in his mistress's arms, purring contentedly.

Shaking his head, Jason took the crockery over to the sink, then made for the door.

'Thanks for supper,' she said as he opened it.

'You're welcome. I owed you.'

'Does that mean you're not going to yell at me next time Millie buys a trinket?'

'Trinkets, I can live with. As for the rest, I'm making no promises,' he said gruffly. 'Get some rest.'

As Jason went down the steps, he heard the windchimes that dangled outside her shop jangling in the strong breeze that had blown up. The sound of the sea, he loved, but they would drive him mad.

As he walked home against the wind, cold now, he tried to process the surprising turn his evening had taken.

Claudia was alright, after all. Hardworking and independent. Kind-hearted. It was hard not to feel sorry for her troubles with the storm. He told himself that was no different to how he felt for the bookshop owners or anybody else in Porthsteren who'd been affected, but... Claudia had that extra pull, somehow. He wasn't attracted to her, was he? Jason pushed *that* idea right out of his train of thoughts before it could stop at the station. Wild, colourful curls and floaty clothes were one thing, but the two of them had absolutely nothing in common. How could a man who dealt in structure and practicality be attracted to someone who believed in all that airy-fairy crap?

At least he'd had the chance to make up for his bad behaviour the other day. As he climbed the tree-lined hill to his house, he bet Claudia was sound asleep already, that strange-looking cat of hers curled up at the foot of the bed. The way she couldn't stop yawning, he could have scooped her up and placed her on the bed himself.

For pity's sake, Jason. What the hell?

Chapter Seven

Claudia slept long and heavy, and her head was fuzzy when she woke soon after dawn. Usually, an early morning walk along the beach would do the trick, but since the beach was still a mess, she settled for the road alongside it.

When she'd first woken, she'd thought Jason making her supper had been a bizarre dream. Once she'd realised it had actually happened, she'd wanted to ask who'd snatched the old Jason Craig and put that one in his place. She supposed his better nature had been unable to ignore the opportunity to apologise by doing something practical, and that was all there was to it. Whatever it was, there was no denying she preferred last night's Jason Craig – kind and personable – to the versions she'd met so far.

Depressed by the sight of the two wrecked boats in the harbour, Claudia was about to turn back when her feet pointed her in the direction of Chapel Hill instead.

The new shop now had a large purple fabric sign in the window, stating in scrolled gold letters:

Hester's Cauldron
Opening soon!

Claudia stared at it with her first unfurling of apprehension. Hester's Cauldron?

Her footsteps were quicker on her return journey to tell her neighbours. It made a change to be one up on Evelyn. Perhaps the storm had briefly interrupted Porthsteren's gossip communication lines.

With the bookshop still closed and no point in revving up the coffee machine, they sat with tea out on the terrace. It was still breezy enough to warrant the fleece Claudia had worn on her walk, and she used the mug to warm her hands.

'Hester's Cauldron?' Evelyn frowned. 'What do you think *that's* all about?'

'They're obviously playing on it being old Hester Moon's cottage,' Sarah mused. 'I'd've thought the name suits a café, but Ian said it's retail.' She turned to Claudia. 'What do you think?'

'I suppose "cauldron" could mean "melting pot" – a cornucopia of things. Gifts and the like? Or…' Claudia tapered off.

'You don't think it could be something like Healing Waves, do you?' Sarah asked.

'Like we said before, I wouldn't have thought Porthsteren could hold another New Age shop. But if they're capitalising on the witch theme…'

'You don't sell anything remotely "witchy"!' Evelyn said.

Claudia sipped her tea. 'No, but I suppose some people might see *some* of my goods that way.' An image of Jason Craig popped into her head, his face cynical.

Evelyn stood suddenly, knocking the table so their tea sloshed. 'Now we know the name, we can look for a website.' She shot indoors for her tablet, tapping away at it as she came back out.

The home page showed a replica of the message in the shop's window. The menu only allowed them to click on 'Gallery'. A 'Before' heading had photos of the store as it had been, run down and forlorn. Under the 'After' heading were shots of builders gutting the place, but no indication of what it would eventually look like.

'That's no use at all!' Evelyn squawked in frustration.

'No point in creating a mystery and then giving everyone the solution, is there?' Sarah said in her usual practical way.

Evelyn huffed. 'We don't even know what "opening soon" means. They can't take much longer or they'll miss out on some of this season's income.'

Privately, Claudia hoped 'soon' didn't mean *too* soon. How much would someone else's grand opening – no matter what kind of shop it was – affect her takings, if her own shop was still a mess and low on stock?

Sarah stood. 'Well, maybe we should concentrate on rebuilding our own businesses, not worrying about theirs. Shake your booty, Evie!'

*

Tanya arrived unexpectedly mid-afternoon, claiming a client had cancelled a meeting. Claudia suspected it was the other way around, but she wasn't about to call her best friend out for coming to check on her.

Ted and his apprentice were outside, battling with roof tiles and pointing and whatever other structural wonders were required to keep out the elements, and working their way through numerous cups of tea – *normal* tea that Claudia had pilfered from Sarah and Evelyn.

'Where's my man?' Tanya asked after she'd delivered much-needed hugs, referring to her favourite feline as she looked around the disordered shop.

'Firmly out of the way,' Claudia told her. 'I don't need him causing chaos on top of the storm.'

'Understandable. So, where are you at?'

Claudia sighed. 'I've been soap-making because I can't paint the wall until Ted's finished, and Sarah can't help me put up shelves until the wall's painted and dried, but Sarah and Evelyn reopen tomorrow so we'll have to wait till Sunday morning, then I'll need to do the window and shelf displays. So it looks like Monday before I could reopen.'

Tanya studied the wall. 'The shelves are the sticking point? Did you buy them yet?'

'No. I was going to go into Penzance before they close today.'

'Hmm. I saw something the other day that might work, if you fancy a change?'

Claudia shrugged. 'They say a change is as good as a rest. And since I'm not getting any rest…'

Two hours later, they were back at Healing Waves for a well-deserved cuppa after a long drive and some fearsome bartering on Tanya's part at a salvage and antique store she was currently designing a website for.

On the counter sat a box of assorted antique hooks and hat pegs for the textiles Claudia would hang at the end of the wall nearest the window. On the floor were a dozen metal wire baskets from some long-closed-down swimming pool, once used to put clothes in after swimmers had changed then hung on a long rail and looked after by an attendant… and now to be hung on Claudia's wall for soaps.

'They'll look brilliant,' Claudia decided as she studied the bare wall. 'The scents won't mingle that way, either.'

'So, if you paint the wall tonight, then fix up all the hooks and baskets and cut and arrange the soaps and redo the window display tomorrow…' Tanya suggested.

'Is *that* all?'

'…You can reopen on Saturday.'

Claudia sighed. 'That new shop's threatening to open soon, and I'm at such a disadvantage!'

'I'd forgotten about them.' Tanya frowned. 'Know what it is yet?'

'It's called Hester's Cauldron. Other than that, Evelyn has a gossip network like a spider's web stretched right across Porthsteren, but it's not caught a fly yet.'

'Hester's Cauldron?' Tanya mused. 'In a legendary witch's cottage?'

'You haven't heard anything, have you?'

'Do I have a direct line to old Hester Moon who might still be haunting the place and let me know what's going on in there? No, Claudia, I'm afraid my witchy skills fall short of that. Why, are you worried?'

Claudia sighed. 'I wasn't before. Now? Maybe a tiny bit.'

'Healing Waves is well-loved. The new place would have to be almost identical to affect you – which I doubt, with a name like that.' Tanya laid an arm across Claudia's shoulders. 'Just remember, until you *know* you've got a problem, you haven't got one. Schrödinger's cat and all that. Either way, the sooner you reopen, the better. Concentrate on your own business for now.'

'That's what Sarah said.'

'She's a sensible woman. Maybe you could run one of your workshops? Show you're back in the game and raring to go.'

Claudia gave her a look. 'I think "raring to go" might be overoptimistic. I'm knackered.'

'I know, my lovely.' Tanya wandered outside. 'Shame that tarpaulin'll have to come down. Millie did a great job. Her dad didn't play merry hell?'

'No. He…' Claudia stopped.

'He what?'

Knowing it was hopeless to keep anything from her, and feeling that Jason deserved *some* redemption in Tanya's eyes, Claudia told her about the previous evening.

Tanya gaped at her. 'He made you *supper*? While you were in the *shower*?'

Claudia winced. 'When you put it like that, it sounds kind of dodgy.'

'I'll say! But it wasn't?'

'No. He was trying to make up for his bad behaviour, partly.'

'And the other part?'

'I think he's a nice bloke, deep down, who saw a worn-out woman and wanted to help.'

'Hmmph. I'll go for your first theory and hold back on the second, for now,' Tanya said. 'Do you want me to do a little… investigating?'

'If, by that, you mean do I want you to ask the goddesses for intel, then no, I do not.'

'What if he tries to do something weird again?'

'It wasn't weird. It was… spontaneous.' Claudia smiled. 'And yeah, a bit weird. But I was too tired to care.'

Tanya cocked her head to one side. 'What does he look like, this Jason Craig?'

Claudia thought about it. It didn't take long. Jason's face, in all its incarnations – wary, furious, kindly – was right there at the forefront of her mind. 'Tallish. Sandy-brown hair. Seriously-pale blue eyes.'

'You noticed the colour of his eyes?'

'It's hard *not* to notice when they're boring into you, flashing ice-fire.'

'Point taken. He's not like Lee, then?'

Claudia thought about her ex-husband – gym-sculpted muscles, sharp suits and crisp shirts, dark hair slicked back, beard trimmed to within a micro-millimetre of perfection. In contrast, she had a feeling

Jason Craig didn't pay much attention to his appearance, something she *did* like about him. Hair often breeze-blown and a little unkempt; day-old stubble; the shirt and chinos combination he seemed to favour for work, T-shirt and jeans at other times.

'Not a jot,' she finally answered.

Tanya winked. 'That's in his favour, then. Better watch yourself!'

*

It had been a strange week, Jason decided as he drove home on Friday evening.

His new job had been… challenging. Millie's new school had *probably* been challenging, but how would he know? She told him bugger all, and the more he quizzed her, the less she said. He assumed he'd have heard about any major disasters.

And talking of major disasters… He was grateful the storm hadn't affected them, but it had affected plenty of others. Thinking of one local in particular, it had led to him coddling her with supper and tea.

What was *that* all about? One minute he was giving her a roasting about peddling her wares to vulnerable teens; the next he was making her salad and brewing her tea and worrying about how exhausted she looked.

His ringtone filled the car as he was pulling into the drive. His mother-in-law. Again.

'Jennifer. How are you?'

'We're fine, thank you, Jason. I'm ringing to find out how Millie's first week at school went. Oh, and yours at work, of course.'

Always an afterthought with you, aren't I?

Recognising unspoken recrimination that he hadn't reported back sooner, he started with, 'My week's been okay.' *No need to tell her you've been tearing your hair out.* 'Millie's week has been okay, too.' *Probably.* When she waited for more, he added, 'You know how teenagers are. She hasn't said much.'

'I was hoping to chat to her myself.'

You think you can do a better job than me at finding anything out? Good luck with that.

'Let me get inside, then I'll put her on the phone.'

'She's home alone?'

'Only for an hour after school, Jennifer. She is fourteen.'

A huff at the other end of the line. 'It'd be good to speak to her, but it'd be much nicer in person. We haven't even seen your new house yet.'

More thinly disguised recrimination. Just what I need on a Friday night.

Millie entered the hallway as he dumped his laptop case, saying, 'If you're free tomorrow, you could drive down, take a look around.'

Millie shot daggers at him. Jason kept his fingers crossed that it was too short notice.

No such luck.

'That would be perfect! What time?'

Arrangements made, he tossed his phone onto the hall table with a clatter and faced his daughter. 'Nothing I could do about it, kiddo. She's like a dog with a bone. Might as well get it over with.'

Millie's answer was a toss of her hair and a 'What's for dinner? I'm starving.'

*

Claudia did manage to reopen on Saturday, after all – by which time she was exhausted and emotional.

She'd taken on board what Tanya had suggested and advertised a crystal workshop. If nothing else, it would show her regulars that it was business as usual. She already had a few bookings via her website and expected more when customers saw the posters around the village, but it was less about numbers and more about promoting interest in her wares.

The noticeably low footfall in Healing Waves was a different matter, though, and when Sarah brought her a toasted panini at lunchtime, she said as much.

'We're the same.' Sarah petted Pudding, who was curled in his basket on the counter, looking as forlorn as his mistress. 'Could be that word hasn't got round yet that we're up and running, I suppose.'

Claudia sighed. '*And* we have Hester's Cauldron opening "soon", whatever that means.'

'It means next Saturday,' Sarah told her. 'Libby phoned Evie this morning to say that a new sign's gone up. "Hester's Cauldron. Grand opening. All will be revealed!" and next Saturday's date.'

'"All will be revealed"?' Claudia let out a breath. 'Well, at least the entire village will be put out of its misery.'

'You'll be put out of yours sooner if you don't eat that panini before you fade away,' Sarah said sternly.

Claudia dutifully took a bite. It oozed warm houmous and roasted veg – her favourite – but she was too tired to enjoy it.

'Have you seen Millie since she painted the tarpaulin?' Sarah asked.

'No. I saw her dad on Wednesday, but not Millie.' Before Sarah could ask about Jason – no way would she admit to her that he'd made her supper – Claudia went on, 'I hope she's okay after her first week at school.'

'Poor kid.' Sarah gave Claudia a knowing look. 'I presume you armed her with crystals?'

'She already had her amethyst, but I added sodalite.'

'Good girl. Well, I'd better get back. Not that we're snowed under.'

'Thanks for the sandwich, Sarah.'

'You're welcome. But I expect you to get it eaten!'

*

Sunday morning found Claudia on the beach, but it wasn't doing its usual job of calming her.

She was exhausted by all her hard work and the thought of what was still to do. She was angry at the storm that had been so disruptive. She was beginning to get a tad anxious about Hester's Cauldron's opening. She was worried about Millie. And she was confused by the girl's father – one minute, a raging torrent of prejudice against her; the next, a man who could show empathy and kindness. Claudia didn't have the time or energy to get her head around Jason Craig right now.

Time for a little sea therapy.

Picking out a stick from the debris still gathered at the tideline, Claudia chose a large patch of smooth sand and began to draw long, bold lines, her strokes fuelled by emotion.

'Hey.'

Absorbed in her task, Claudia hadn't noticed Millie approach. 'Hey yourself. How are you? How's school?'

'Okay.' But Millie didn't look okay. And there was something different about her.

Ah. No purple streaks. Claudia gestured at her hair. 'I like it.'

'Hmmph. Dad paid for Jenny at the salon to do it, so I wouldn't ruin the new bathroom. It's boring. So's school.'

'Even your first week?'

'They make fun of my accent. And everybody wants to know everything about me and they're all, like, "What about your dad?" and

"What about your mum?" and then I have to tell them Mum died and they don't know what to say and they talk about me behind my back.'

Claudia's heart went out to her. A new start, and already she was having to explain her past, bringing the pain back… not that it had ever left.

'Loads of kids have one-parent families,' Claudia said gently. 'But a bereavement is less common. I should think they're sympathetic but don't know how to say so.' She smiled encouragement. 'Dazzle them with just being you, and they won't care about it, after a while.'

Millie pointed to the sand. 'You're drawing?'

Drawing. Claudia's head told her to leave it at that. But Millie had that permanent air of grief and anger – such a maelstrom of feelings for a young girl.

Don't do it, Claudia, Jason won't thank you.

But it might help her. And it can't do any harm.

Jason doesn't want you meddling.

I won't be told what to do by any man, if I think something's right.

He's not just any man. He's the girl's father.

While Claudia's head and heart battled it out, Millie frowned at her silence.

Claudia's heart made a snap decision. 'It's a sort of therapy,' she said, cautiously. Her heart may have won, but her head warned her to be careful. 'I draw a picture representing something I'm upset or angry about, then I wait for the tide to come in and wash it away, imagining the negative emotion being dissolved and carried out to sea.' Millie looked curious enough for Claudia to break her stick in two and offer half to her. 'Want to try?'

With her usual indifference, Millie took it, saying, 'It's not like there's much else to do around here. What should I draw?'

'Maybe something you'd like to let go of, or lessen the pain of?'

You're leading her, Claudia.

Claudia turned back to her own efforts – clouds and jagged lightning strokes, a pictorial representation of the storm that had caused her so much trouble. From time to time, she looked over at Millie, who had started out uncertain but was now furiously dragging her stick through the sand. As the minutes ticked by and whatever idea she'd got in her head developed, she became almost manic. When she stood back, her face was fiercely angry – way beyond the sullen scowl Claudia was used to.

'All done?' Claudia moved to Millie's side, glancing at the angry monster before her – a devil's face with horns and evil intent in its eyes. For a sketch in the sand, it was petrifying.

Millie swallowed hard. 'Yes.'

'Okay. Now we let Nature do her work.'

They sat side by side, cross-legged, to wait.

'What's yours?' Millie asked. 'Or shouldn't I ask?'

'It's the storm.'

'You're still mad at it?'

'Yes, even though it was just an act of nature and it wasn't directed at me personally. I need to accept that and let it go.'

'Do you want to know about mine?' Millie murmured.

'Only if you want to tell me.'

There was a long pause, filled by the sound of the waves and the occasional screech from a seagull or dog barking.

'It's Mum's cancer,' Millie said, so softly that Claudia barely heard her.

Claudia looked sideways at her. 'That's how you see it?'

'Yes. Like a monster that swept into our lives and took her away.' Millie's voice hitched. 'I need to let go of my anger – that's what the counsellors said. But I can't, even though I know it's like your storm – just nature, something that couldn't be helped.'

Claudia struggled for what to say. 'I can understand you seeing it like this.' She pointed at the remarkable picture in front of them. 'But letting that anger go would be such a good thing, Millie. Your mum would understand you feeling this way, but she wouldn't want you to hold onto it for too long.'

The first wave licked at the far end of Claudia's drawing, smoothing out the top of the lightning strike. The next wave touched the tips of the devil's horns on Millie's.

A tear formed in the girl's eye.

Claudia shuffled closer until their crossed knees touched and took Millie's hand in hers. 'Let go, Millie. The monster did what it did. Let go now.'

And there they both sat as the tide came in, Millie's face streaming with tears, her hand squeezing Claudia's so tightly, it hurt. Claudia said nothing, struggling to concentrate on her own drawing while acutely aware of the terrible grief shaking through the young girl next to her.

Chapter Eight

Jason *should* have been seriously unhappy when he walked along the beach towards Millie and Claudia, only to find his daughter wracked with sobs.

He wasn't. He was relieved. Millie hadn't cried since the first few weeks after Gemma's death. He knew she kept it all inside, but he'd found no way to shift it.

It seemed Claudia had found a way, though. He expected to feel an element of jealousy over that, but all he felt was gratitude.

'Hey there,' he said lamely.

Millie looked up from her seated position, hugging her knees with her arms.

He dropped down to sit beside her and gently used his sleeve to wipe her face, a mess of mascara and goodness knew what else she insisted on hiding her pretty face with.

'Dad.' Only one word, but as she buried her face in his sweater and sobbed, it meant a great deal to him.

He cradled her head against his chest, looked at Claudia and mouthed, 'Thank you' – the sincerest thank you he'd ever said.

Claudia smiled in acknowledgement, silently stood and moved away along the beach, leaving him alone with his daughter.

When Millie's tears eventually dried up, he said, 'Do you want to talk to me about it?'

'Do I have to?'

He stroked her hair back from her face. 'Not if you don't want to.'

Relief flooded her features.

'Did you talk to Claudia about it?' he asked.

'She said I didn't have to, but I did, just a bit.'

Jason suppressed disappointment that Millie could talk to Claudia but not her own father. There wasn't much he could do about that, although it complicated his feelings about the woman even more.

He touched the blue crystal around Millie's neck. 'This is different to your purple one.'

'It's sodalite. Claudia gave it to me for doing the painting.'

'That was good of her.' Jason hid a frustrated smile. He'd ranted at the woman on Monday, and by Tuesday she'd already gone against everything he'd said by giving Millie another crystal.

Unfair, Jason. If she gave it to her as a pretty necklace, a thank you for a kind deed, that's not a problem, is it? If, on the other hand, she filled her head with…

'I've been wearing it under my shirt at school,' Millie confided. 'We're not allowed jewellery. But Claudia said it might help work out who'd be a good friend.'

Oh, for pity's sake. 'Has it worked?'

Millie gave him a look that only a fourteen-year-old daughter can give a father. 'Duh! I won't know yet, will I? I've only had it a few days. Give it a chance.'

She might as well have said, 'And give Claudia a chance, while you're at it.'

They walked home in silence. Millie was emotionally exhausted.

As they neared the house, she asked, 'Can I go to Claudia's meditation session on Tuesday evening?'

Jason could hardly object to meditation, could he? The counsellors had told them both to try it, but neither of them had got very far before Millie refused to attend any more and Jason quit in solidarity. After her breakthrough this afternoon, though, perhaps it might be helpful.

'You can try it, if you like. I could drive you down, then pick you up after.'

He worried that she might ask him to go with her. But all she said was, 'Okay. Thanks' – a response he accepted with relief.

*

The following evening, Claudia was flipping the sign to 'Closed' when Jason appeared.

'Hi. Sorry. I'm just closing. Did you want something?'

Despite his recent apology, Claudia thought that was highly unlikely, considering his attitude to her shop and the contents therein.

'I do, actually. Do you have time for a quick chat, maybe a stroll along the beach?'

Intrigued, she said, 'I could do with a little stroll.'

She locked the door and they made their way down to the sand, where Claudia immediately pulled off her sandals. Jason must have come straight from work – he was dressed in smart chinos and a shirt and tie. He loosened the tie, but he didn't go as far as taking off his shoes and socks. *Ah, well*, she thought. *Baby steps.*

'I wanted to thank you for yesterday,' he said. 'Whatever you did with Millie, I'm grateful.'

'I thought you might be furious,' Claudia admitted.

'Quite the opposite.' Jason sighed. 'I don't know if this had anything to do with it, but Millie's grandparents – Gemma's parents – came down from Devon on Saturday to see the new house.'

'Millie mentioned you'd moved to be nearer to them.'

'Let's say it was a *consideration* in the move. They're good people. Millie should have that connection with them. But they can be intense. Millie was really stressed by the time they left. Anyway, whatever it was, Millie's bottled things up for too long. I'm glad she let it out.'

'Then I'm glad I could help. I know you're not overly keen on my… interests.'

Jason scuffed his shoes through the sand. 'Usually, I'd say "Each to his own". But after what Millie's been through…'

'I understand.'

'Look, Claudia, I know Millie likes chatting with you, and since it'll take time for her to make friends and she's in a downright unsociable phase anyway, I'm happy with that. I also know she loves your shop, and while I can live with her wearing a lump of rock around her neck, and I know you say your stock is harmless, there are a few grey areas where I'm struggling with that "Each to his own" thing.'

'People are often afraid of what they don't understand.'

At this, he looked defensive. '"Afraid" is a strong word. "Cautious" might be more accurate. "Askance", possibly.'

He smiled – a lop-sided, self-deprecating smile that crinkled the lines at the corners of his eyes.

Claudia laughed at his choice of words. 'I'd be happy to explain anything in Healing Waves that you don't like the look of. Come back with me now, if you like.' *Although Pudding will resent the delayed dinner service.*

But he shook his head. 'Millie's expecting me back. I need to cook dinner before she takes it upon herself to make a start. That girl's like a human wrecking ball in the kitchen.'

'Do you think she's settling in at school?'

'She says it's okay, and she's been buckling down to homework, but who knows? Communication's limited.' He released a breath. 'I only hope all this upheaval will be worth it.'

Wanting to reassure him, Claudia laid a hand on his arm. 'I'm sure it will. Give it time.'

'Yeah.' He looked at her for a long time. 'I'm just so damned tired.'

Claudia tried not to show her surprise that he would confess this to her. 'You've already been through such a lot, Jason, and now you have a new life to get to grips with. That's exhausting, I know. But things will turn around, and you'll start to feel *energised* by your new environment, the new challenges.'

'I hope so.' He managed a small smile. 'Thanks.'

'What for?'

'For listening.'

This, too, surprised her. 'You don't have anyone? To listen?'

Jason hesitated, as though wondering how much to share. 'I had mates in Edinburgh. But I was married, I had a child, I was busy…' His excuses fizzled out. 'There was nobody close. I haven't stayed in touch. I feel guilty about that, but… It's hard to explain.'

'You're worried that staying in touch would keep you back in the same old place, emotionally?'

Jason stared at her, startled. 'I suppose so. How do you *know* things like that?'

'I spent a lot of time analysing my own emotions after I left my husband. I left behind all my friends, even the good ones. I didn't want to be *that* Claudia any more. I felt guilty about it, but the person I'd been with them wasn't the person I wanted to be. Does that make sense?'

'Yes. Perfect sense.'

By unspoken consent, they turned back, walking through their own outward footprints in the sand, silent for a while, listening only to the waves and the gulls.

Claudia wondered if he regretted sharing these things with her. She wondered if she regretted sharing what she'd said with him. She hadn't told him anything too revealing, but she had revealed more than she'd expected to.

'Did Millie see a counsellor after her mum died?' she asked. 'She mentioned it, but only in passing.'

'Yes, we tried counselling – Millie on her own, and together with me. But she hated it, so we stopped. She didn't want to talk to me about anything, either.'

The hurt in his voice was evident, and Claudia felt for him.

'Yesterday was the first time I've seen her cry in months,' he went on. 'What did you do with her?' He shrugged. 'I don't suppose you feel you can tell me.'

'I can, but within limits.' Claudia thought about how much she could say without betraying Millie's trust. 'I have a few ways I like to release anger, regrets, negative thoughts. I was on the beach using one when Millie joined me. You draw a picture, anything you like, even squiggles, representing the thing you want to let go. Then you concentrate on it – hopefully for the last time – as the tide comes in. The idea is that as the waves take it, you release it from own system and back into the universe.'

He nodded, seemingly not too disturbed by the idea. 'Any idea what she drew?'

'Yes, but it wouldn't be fair to tell you.' When he didn't push – something that pleased her – she said, 'Since you've probably already guessed, I *can* tell you it was connected to her grief. I could try to think of other things, if Millie wants to explore them. And if you don't mind.'

She saw his Adam's apple bob in his throat and suspected that his natural prejudice against all things 'weird' was warring with the beneficial effect of yesterday's impromptu exercise on his daughter.

'I appreciate what you did for her,' Jason said. 'It sounds straight-forward, and it can't do any harm. I wouldn't mind something along *those* lines, I suppose.'

'I'll bear that in mind.' Tired of treading on eggshells, Claudia decided it was time to have a little fun with him. 'If my friend Tanya had been with us, we could have woven a spell into it.'

His face was a priceless picture – well worth the danger. 'Did you just say "*spell*"?'

'I did. Tanya would argue that asking the universe, and whichever goddesses might be appropriate, for their intervention would improve the outcome.'

Jason's eyebrows were nearly up in his hair. 'And this Tanya is…?'

'My best friend. And a Wiccan.'

He curled his lip. 'You mean a witch.'

'No, I meant Wiccan. Technically, there's a difference, although the lines are blurred. And you can get the idea of warts and broomsticks and black hats out of your head. You're an intelligent man. You know that's just historical rot, right?'

'What about modern rot?'

She grinned. 'As you said, "Each to his own".'

Claudia wondered if she'd gone too far, but it was as good a way as any to test out how reticent he still was about anything outside of his comfort zone.

As they approached Healing Waves, he was still shaking his head and muttering, 'Friends with a witch, for crying out loud.' But his face wasn't *too* thunderous, and she knew he understood she'd been teasing him when he held his hands out wide and said, 'Claudia, we both know that I'm a practical bloke who wouldn't recognise an aura if it hit me in the face. My parents were science teachers – one Physics, one Chemistry. Have a heart.'

Smiling, she gave it one more shot. 'Why don't you tell Millie you'll be late tomorrow? Come by after work and ask anything you like about my goods.' When he hesitated, she said, 'Whether you like it or not, Millie's taken a shine to me and the shop. I can't do anything about that. But I *can* try to make you feel better about it.'

Jason nodded. 'Alright. Tomorrow, then.'

Pleased, Claudia added, 'Oh, and Jason? About not having anyone to listen? You know where I am if you need me.'

For anything, she thought as she walked away.

*

Jason struggled to concentrate at work the next day, still distracted by his daughter's tears at the weekend and by what Claudia had said about Millie taking a shine to her shop. Her words had brought on a dawning realisation that it might be less about her trying to influence Millie and more about Millie bothering Claudia… That Claudia, kind though she was, might not welcome being saddled with Millie. Perhaps he should bear that in mind.

And then there was the small matter of admitting more than he would have liked to her about not keeping in touch with old friends. After all, he hardly knew her. But she'd immediately understood, and that was freeing.

It was only after he had left her that Claudia's own admission had filtered through. She'd been married and left her husband. That wasn't something he'd expected her to tell him – although he suspected she'd only done so to make him feel better about his own situation.

Was she was involved with anyone now? If so, surely he would have heard about it? Nothing was private around here.

When he arrived promptly for his tour of her shop, Claudia greeted him with, 'You made it!'

'Did you think I wouldn't?'

'I wasn't sure,' she admitted.

'I like to keep my word, if I can.'

'I believe that about you. Flip the "Closed" sign, will you?'

Her navy tunic swirling around her as she moved, Claudia made tea using leaves that Jason would sooner decline but couldn't work out how to, despite silently begging that strange cat of hers for any bright ideas as he tickled between his ears.

The cat only gave him a baleful look.

Well, you're no help.

Claudia passed him a mug of steaming but indeterminate liquid, and he sniffed it dubiously.

'It's a vitality mix,' she explained.

'Why? Do I look like I'm lacking vitality?'

'You look like a man who's had a long day at work.'

He noted the way her lips curved, then took a sip of tea to distract himself. It distracted him alright. He managed to stop short of spitting it out, but it was a close call.

'I'll let it cool.' Placing it on the counter and hoping she'd forget about it, he glanced around. 'The repairs look good. You must be exhausted.'

'Yes, but most of it's done now. I'm just waiting on the textile orders. And I replaced some soap, but not all of it yet. That takes time and hard work. I need a breather.'

He jerked his thumb at her poster advertising a crystal workshop. 'You call that a breather?'

'I call it flagging up to my regulars that it's business as usual.' She shrugged. 'It'll be the last before the summer season gets going. I'll be too busy then.'

Only a week ago, Jason would have assumed that workshops were a marketing ploy to get the punters in and persuade them to buy whatever she was touting. Now, he thought she was brave to add to her workload after her traumas.

He crossed to the newly painted wall. 'I like the baskets.'

'They were Tanya's idea.'

'That's your witch friend?'

'Careful, Jason, you almost said that with a straight face! Rest assured, we obtained the baskets by the usual means and we travelled by car, not broomstick.'

Jason smiled. He liked it when she teased him.

'So. Where do you want to start?' she asked.

Since he couldn't quibble with home-made soap, he moved away. But as he wandered the shop, the cat following him as if daring him to find fault, Jason began to feel foolish. Claudia was right – fantasy figures were only ornaments. Dragons, mermaids, castles… He might not like them, but they weren't seedy like some he'd seen. The art on the walls was mostly coastal-themed. The jewellery revolved around natural materials – crystals, shells, wooden beads. No dubious symbols that might be of satanic origin. And then there was the long shelf with every type of crystal imaginable – large, glittering chunks; small, smooth stones – intriguing in their endless colours and variations.

He felt her watching him; felt he was expected to say something, ask *something*. In desperation, he plucked out a turquoise crystal and held it up. 'Why do you think they have healing properties?'

'Years of wisdom passed down. If you wouldn't deny that some herbs or natural supplements work, then crystals having properties is no different.'

'Hmmph.'

'I'm not asking you to believe it, Jason. I'm asking why the idea could be harmful to your daughter, even if it doesn't work.'

Defensive, he tried to explain. 'I just don't want her head filled with ideas that I…'

'That you don't personally subscribe to?'

'That makes me sound churlish.'

'It's natural for a parent to want to pass their own values on to a child. But it's equally natural for a child to want to push at boundaries and explore what interests *them*, what resonates with *them*.'

Her words were loaded, and as his hackles rose, his eye caught the shelf of oracle cards. 'As for those…'

It was a comment which bought him a ten-minute lecture on the damned things. And once more, he was disarmed. He might think they were rubbish, but he could find no fault with the pictures and words on the packs she showed him, and although he was incredulous at the idea of asking a pack of cards for guidance and them providing it, he had to concede that, at worst, it was harmless nonsense.

Claudia smiled at the way he put that, but she didn't argue, making him feel smaller by the minute.

'Anything else?' she asked.

He took a deep breath. 'No. But I do owe you an apology. Again. I misjudged your shop. I don't believe in some of what you sell, but there are worse places Millie could spend her time.'

Claudia arched a neat brow. 'Thank you. I think.'

Aware his apology had come out half-hearted and searching for something positive to say, Jason gravitated to a display of rock-like lamps, giving off a pleasing pinkish glow. As an architect who incorporated natural materials into his designs whenever he could, he liked that about them. In fact, closer inspection of Claudia's shop had shown him that most of what she sold was connected to the natural world.

'Himalayan salt lamps,' Claudia told him. 'They cleanse by releasing negative ions. They're especially good for bedrooms – they're calming and absorb negativity.'

Jason sure as hell doubted the science of that, but he couldn't deny that a little less negativity in their new home and a little more calm wouldn't go amiss.

'Millie likes them,' Claudia added. 'Why not start with one in her bedroom and see how you go?'

Jason pulled out his wallet, muttering, 'If they reduce my daughter's negativity in any way, shape or form, I'll take another dozen and put them in every last nook and cranny of the house!'

Claudia smiled. 'I'll hold you to that.'

Jason glanced at his watch. 'Sorry. I've kept you longer than I should have. I gather you have meditation tonight. Millie's going to try it.'

'Good. How about you?'

'Ah. No, thanks. I have work to do.'

She gave him a disbelieving look that made him squirm. 'Some other time?'

'Hmm. Yes, well, thanks for the tour. Better go.' And he scarpered.

Millie was in the kitchen when he got home, stirring something involving cans of chopped tomatoes. 'Where've you been?'

'Sorry I'm late.' Jason toyed with any number of work-related excuses, but he didn't lie to his only offspring. Bend the truth a little, maybe. 'I promised I'd nip into Healing Waves on the way home.'

At that, Millie lost interest in cooking. 'Huh? What? Why?'

Ah, the vocal dexterity of youth.

'I…' *Because I ranted at the poor owner last week over your sodding oracle cards and she thought I was the devil incarnate but then I cooked her supper which she ate in her bathrobe and then she made you hysterical on the beach but I thanked her for it and then she offered to educate me in the ways of her shop so I wouldn't shout at her any more.*

'She knew I had reservations about what she sells, so she invited me to ask questions.'

'And?'

Jason sighed. 'I don't hold with all of it, but it isn't as bad as I thought.'

Millie had 'I told you so' on the tip of her tongue, he could tell, but a flash of his eyes warned her not to voice it.

'I bought you a present,' he announced to deflect further questioning. 'It's in the hall.'

Abandoning her pans, Millie raced out, coming back in with the box and lifting out the salt lamp. 'I love it! Thank you!' She kissed his cheek, the nearest he got to affection nowadays.

'It's supposed to help with negative something-or-others,' he informed her knowledgeably.

She laughed, something else he didn't see very often. 'Yeah, I know. Can I put it in my room?'

'That's the idea. How was school?'

'Science was boring. French was okay. We had a sub for English, but she usually teaches Chemistry, so she let us do what we liked. Phoebe asked me to go to after-school drama on Wednesdays.'

'Great!' *Good old Phoebe, whoever she is.* Millie had mentioned a few people's names, but she hadn't yet fallen in with (or been admitted to) a proper group of friends.

'It means I'll miss the school bus, though, so…?'

'I can pick you up after drama.'

'Thanks.'

Millie served up pasta and, well, tinned chopped tomatoes, which she seemed to consider an adequate sauce. Jason knew she could do better, but since he wasn't home in time to cook, he daren't complain. Fetching sliced chorizo to top the sumptuous dish, he made a mental note to find out about any decent takeaways within a five-mile radius.

*

'How was meditation?' Jason asked as he drove Millie home later that night.

'Okay. My mind kept wandering, and I was a bit bored, but everyone else seemed chilled afterwards, so I'll try again.'

'Good for you. How much is it per week?'

'A quid.'

'A *quid?*

'Uh-huh. Just a donation for the tea and biscuits.'

'Claudia doesn't charge?' Jason shook his head, but he was getting to know Claudia now – enough to realise she didn't always operate for profit.

'No. Da-ad…'

Jason recognised that wheedling tone. His daughter wanted something. 'Yes, oh light of my life?'

'If I'm the light of your life, then you need to *get* a life.'

Very probably. 'You *are* my life.'

Millie made a puking noise. 'My point exactly.'

'May I remind you, Millie Craig, that you appear to want something and this might not be the best way to go about it?'

'Ah. Well. I-saw-a-poster-tonight-saying-Claudia's-holding-a-crystal-workshop-at-Healing-Waves-and-can-I-go?' She ran the words together as though saying them too fast might stop Jason absorbing the question too well – an old technique, and well-worn.

'Why are you interested?'

'Dad, you're always saying an inquisitive mind is a good thing. I'm being inquisitive. And I'll meet people, like I did tonight. You want that, too.'

She had him there. Except he meant making friends of her own age, and this workshop would probably be middle-aged women. Still, if they smiled at Millie in the street, that was better than nothing, wasn't it? He didn't like Millie believing this crystals-cure-all-ills crap, but since Claudia had gone out of her way to explain her stock to him, it would look churlish if he said no now.

Face it, Jason. You're cornered. 'When is it?'

'Thursday, seven thirty till nine thirty.'

Well, that clinched it, didn't it? Only that morning, Jeff, a partner at the firm, had invited Jason to dinner on Thursday. Jason didn't mind leaving Millie alone for a couple of hours in the daytime or after school, but he was less comfortable about leaving her for an entire evening in the new house yet. His mind raced as they parked up and went inside. Jeff knew Jason was a single parent. If he explained that his daughter had an invite too, but it meant he could only be at dinner a couple of hours, he was sure Jeff would be fine about that.

'Okay.'

'Aw, but Da-ad… Wait. Did you say "okay"? Thanks!'

Millie had obviously been expecting an argument. Jason *could* tell her it happened to fit with his own sparkling social agenda… or he could wait till tomorrow to tell her he'd been invited out and wasn't it good that it fit in so well? He felt guilty deciding on the latter, but it wasn't often his daughter threw her arms around his neck in gratitude.

*

Claudia spent the morning of her Wednesday "off" working. Again. Her soap stocks were still too low after the storm, and as the season got busier, soap was one of the things that appealed to idle browsers the most, practically flying off the shelves.

She only stopped when all her free moulds were filled, and by the time she'd cleared everything away, her arms ached, and her utility room – an add-on at the back of the building that Claudia had always been grateful for, needing the extra space as she did – felt like a prison cell.

Throwing off her apron, she went upstairs to feed and pet Pudding. After explaining to him that she needed fresh air – which, by the look of the way he was curled up in his armchair, he was *not* interested in, thank you very much – she went back downstairs, car keys in hand.

Half an hour and some narrow, winding roads later, she'd parked at Sennen Cove and was climbing up from the harbour area on the South West coastal path. The steep ascent had her huffing and puffing, and her leg muscles wanted to know why she was punishing them when she'd already done so much manual labour lately, but she told them the view would be worth it.

She was tempted to take a load off her feet when she reached the old coastguard lookout at the top, but she knew that if she did that, her calf muscles might seize up, so she ploughed on. The path levelled and opened out, providing unrivalled views of turquoise sea and grey, jagged rocks. This section of the route, leading as it did to Land's End, was always popular and already busy for late April, but it would only get busier as spring moved into summer. Now was a good time to enjoy it.

Past the rusting shipwreck at the base of the cliffs – more recent than its state might suggest, and a sight that fascinated her every time – Claudia eventually chose a large rock off the path and sat to admire the view and just *breathe*. The breeze was gentle, the sea calm.

'Why couldn't you have stayed this way *last* week?' Claudia said aloud. 'Why was a spring storm such a good idea?'

The only answer was the song of an unseen bird somewhere behind her. 'Hmmph. Pretty song, but it's a fat lot of use to me. I'm knackered.'

Pulling her collar tighter to block out the breeze now that she was stationary, she watched gulls circling around the cliffs.

This is why you're here, Claudia. It's all yours, whenever you find time for yourself.

'The storm put paid to that lately.'

Remember London.

Oh, Claudia remembered it well enough. It bewildered her that she'd ever thought it was what she wanted. Perhaps it had served her well at the time, but it was hard to see that now. What it had done was earn her a good salary. Her half of the flat, her savings, had enabled her to make this move, own her own business, be answerable to nobody but herself. To bring pleasure to people with the goods she chose so carefully. To integrate into a small, friendly community where nobody knew the old Claudia and so many accepted and liked the now-Claudia. For that, she was grateful to London.

The storm wasn't the end of the world. She could have done without it, but it had brought Porthsteren together, helping each other, prioritising repairs, cleaning up the beach. Community at its best. Claudia's community. The storm was only a blip. This was going to be a good season for her.

What about Hester's Cauldron?

'Let's cross that bridge on Saturday, shall we?'

Chapter Nine

'I need to stop at the General Store,' Jason told Millie as they drove down the hill on the way to her crystal workshop and his work dinner. 'I should take wine. Don't know if Jeff likes red or white. Better take one of each.'

'Are you nervous about dinner with your bosses?' Millie asked him – over-perceptively, in his view.

'A little,' he admitted. 'People act differently outside of work hours, let their guard down, but you need to be careful what you say when you don't know people well enough yet.' He glanced at his daughter. 'Like you at school, I imagine. It's different in class compared to social activities out-of-school.'

'I guess. But I enjoyed drama yesterday. Phoebe wants me to go again next week.'

'That's good.'

'Will everyone be couples at your dinner?' Millie asked.

'I assume so. Both the partners are married.'

'Won't that be awkward for you?'

'I hope not.' Pulling up outside the General Store, he winked at her. 'I could've taken you as my plus one.'

Millie made a scoffing noise and gestured at her deep purple tunic-thingy over black leggings. 'I don't think I look the part.'

'And I don't think middle-aged dinner parties are your thing.' *Not sure they're mine, either*. He took out his wallet. 'How much is the workshop?'

'A fiver.'

He happily handed the note over. 'Back in a mo.'

'These are fancy,' Libby commented as she put his bottles through the till. 'Going anywhere nice?'

'Just dinner with the bosses.'

'Is Millie going with you?'

'No. She's got Claudia's crystal thing.'

'Me too! She'll love it, I promise. Claudia knows so much, and she has a great way of explaining it all.' When Jason made a non-committal noise, Libby lowered her voice and said, 'Shall I let you into a little secret?' Taking his lack of comment as acquiescence, she went on, 'When Claudia first moved to Porthsteren, there were *rumours*.'

At this, Jason paid attention. 'What kind of rumours?'

'Rumours she might be a witch.'

Funny how Claudia didn't mention that *when she joked about being friends with a witch.*

'As in pointy hat, broomstick…?'

'No, silly.' Libby batted his arm. 'Just a modern witch, you know.'

Just a modern witch? No, Jason didn't know.

Sensing his distaste, Libby hurried on. 'It was only a case of everyone being bored by the end of winter, if you ask me. Claudia arrived in the spring, and what with her shop having all that New Agey stuff and her dressing so bohemian-like and making her own concoctions, and that strange-looking cat of hers, people let their imaginations run away with them.'

I should say they did. 'But you all came to your senses?'

'Oh, yes. Claudia *knows* things, like all about what she sells, and she's always ready to listen and help, but we soon found out she's not an *actual* witch.'

Jason had a mental picture of the villagers getting the old ducking stool out of storage. 'How?'

'She told us so.'

'She *knew* about the rumours?

'My 'ansum, *of course* she knew. You don't live here without hearing rumours, do you?' She winked. 'You'll find that out soon enough. Talking of witches, have you heard about the new shop opening around the corner? Hester's Cauldron?'

'No, I hadn't.' Jason needed to be on his way, not get embroiled in a new strand of speculation. 'Well, I'd better go. Thanks.' He lifted the bottles of wine to show he meant for the goods, not the free gossip that had come with them.

Libby glanced at her watch. 'Gosh, I ought to get a move on, too. Enjoy your dinner.'

She might as well have said, 'Enjoy your appointment with the firing squad'.

*

'Need a hand?'

Sarah came into the meeting space as Claudia placed folding chairs in a semi-circle. Crystals were laid out on small tables dotted in between, so people could easily access them.

'No, thanks. I'm good. What are you still doing here?'

'We were sorting out more book donations, but we're heading home now. How many are coming tonight?'

'Twelve. I'm happy with that. Any more would make it less personal.'

'You look tired, Claudia. Is this my fault for saying we should do something positive business-wise?'

'Not just you. Tanya suggested a workshop. I need to do it.'

'Worried about Hester's Cauldron opening on Saturday?'

'I'm trying not to. Tanya said there's no point in worrying until we know what it is, and she's right. But they know how to whip up a marketing frenzy, I'll give them that. They're the talk of the town.'

'I know. Everyone's speculating.' Sarah smiled. 'Well, I'll leave you to it. Evie's planned a movie and popcorn evening. How about you? Any fun on the agenda?'

'Tanya's coming tomorrow evening.'

'Good. Say hi from me.'

When Sarah had gone, Claudia filled the kettle, then went downstairs and up to her own flat to fetch a tin of home-made oat and raisin cookies she'd baked the night before while practically dead on her feet. She couldn't bring herself to buy them – she always served home-made cookies at her workshops.

Pudding tried to sidle through the door with her, almost tripping her up in the process.

Catching herself, she glared at him. 'Do you *have* to do that? One of these days, I'll break my neck, and then who'll indulge your every whim?'

The cat looked up at her with amber-green eyes, then rubbed against her legs.

'If that's your idea of an apology, it's accepted. You can come *if* you behave and don't spend the evening batting crystals around the floor.'

As she reached the foot of the steps, cat in tow, Millie appeared.

'Sorry I'm early,' she said, nervously chewing her bottom lip. 'Dad had to go to dinner with his bosses, so he dropped me off on the way.'

'No problem,' Claudia said brightly, anxious to put her at ease. Millie would be the youngest there this evening. 'Come on up.' When they were inside, she opened the tin. 'Want a preview of the cookies?'

Millie picked one and took a bite. 'Mmm. They're great!'

'Thanks.' Claudia put the lid back on. 'They'll have to stay in the tin for now, though, otherwise Pudding will have them.'

Millie bent to stroke the cat. 'He eats *cookies*?'

'Ha! I once left a batch cooling while I went out for an hour. When I came back, they looked different. I couldn't work it out for a minute, then I realised all the raisins were missing. The little so-and-so had nipped them all out with his teeth!' She glared at the cat. 'Yes, it's you I'm talking about. And very lucky you were, too. Raisins aren't good for you. Be thankful you're not a dog.'

'A dog?'

'Dried fruit damages dogs' kidneys, apparently. I looked it up when I realised what he'd done. It can affect cats, too, but he got away with it.' She wagged a finger at Pudding. 'That might have been one of your nine lives, mister, so watch it!'

Pudding gave her such an indignant look that Millie burst out laughing – still an unusual event, Claudia suspected.

Pudding, not remotely fazed by the chastisement, stalked across the room, jumped up on the front table, climbed into the box Claudia had used to bring her crystals up from Healing Waves, twirled three times and settled down for the evening.

*

'Stress? Gosh, that's a broad one.'

The evening had gone well, and they were near the end – Claudia hoped – of her question-and-answer session. 'There isn't really just one crystal for that. It's better to ask yourself *why* you're stressed.'

'Can you give us an example?' Libby asked.

'Okay. Do you need to feel more focused because stress has your mind all over the place?' Claudia held up a yellow crystal. 'Citrine. Would it help if you felt more organised? Do you need better sleep? Fluorite and howlite can help with aspects of stress. But when in doubt… Can anybody guess?'

'*Amethyst!*' The shout came back from several of the group.

'How well you know me!' Claudia noticed Millie touching her necklace. 'Yes, if you're not sure what you need, amethyst's my go-to crystal.' Claudia held a large, rough crystal up to the light. 'Look at that purple! For me, it instantly brings peace and calm.'

'Do we wear it?' Alice asked, her usual expression of worry back now the evening was drawing to a close. For a short while, she'd looked almost like she'd forgotten whatever troubled her.

'Yes, you can wear it, or carry one in your pocket to handle. If you meditate, try holding one in each hand. Don't forget we have meditation here every Tuesday.' Claudia smiled. 'Well, that's it. If anyone wants to come down to Healing Waves, the till's open for the next twenty minutes.'

Everyone followed Claudia downstairs and into her shop, making a beeline for the crystals, keen with their new knowledge. The group slowly trickled out, most with purchases – a bonus, not a given – until just two remained.

'Millie, is everything okay?' Claudia asked.

'Yes, thanks,' Millie said from her position near the door. 'I texted Dad to say we're finished. He's on his way.'

'Did you enjoy tonight?'

'Yeah. It was interesting. Thanks.'

'You're welcome.' Claudia turned to her remaining customer. 'Alice. Anything I can do for you?'

Hovering at the counter, ostensibly to pet Pudding who had followed them down, Alice glanced nervously over at Millie. Her shoulders visibly dropped with relief as the teenager left with a wave when a car horn beeped.

'I – er – couldn't decide which would serve the right purpose.'

Claudia drummed up an encouraging smile, even though all she could think about was her bed, and led Alice to the crystal shelves.

'Are you stressed? What do you feel you need?

'Well, I… Maybe courage?'

Courage for what? 'Hmm. Carnelian, perhaps?' Claudia indicated tumblestones in varying shades of red.

As Alice's hand hovered over them, waiting for one to speak to her as Claudia had instructed in the workshop, Claudia noticed the woman's hand was shaking – the tiniest tremor, but it was there.

'It depends what kind of courage,' Claudia added cautiously. 'Some stones offer protection, for example.'

Alice jolted. 'Protection? Why would I need protection?' She giggled nervously. 'No, courage is okay. Anyone would need courage with my mother-in-law coming for the weekend!' Her hand shot out and grabbed a stone near the top. 'This is fine.'

Claudia smiled, pretending to fall for the obvious cover-up. 'Okay. But there are others, if that doesn't do the trick.' She took Alice's money. 'Anything else you need?'

Alice shook her head, although Claudia got the impression there was. 'No. Thanks.'

Claudia walked her to the door. 'Did you enjoy the workshop?'

At that, Alice's face lit up. 'Oh, yes. I find it all so fascinating!'

'Good to hear.' *Let's fish a little.* 'It was all women again tonight. George didn't fancy coming?'

'Hardly! He thinks it's all utter rubbish.' Alice's hand flew to her mouth. 'No offence, Claudia.'

'None taken. I know plenty who agree with him.' *Jason Craig, for one.* Claudia let out her reel a little further. 'Did George take the mickey about you coming tonight?'

'No. I… I told him I was going for a drink with the girls from work. It's easier that way.'

'I understand.' Claudia made a zipping motion across her lips. 'Don't worry, he won't hear about your nefarious activities from me. Goodnight, Alice. Take care.'

*

There was no *need* for Jason to call at Healing Waves on his way home on Friday. He'd had a long week.

But Millie had phoned to ask if she could go to Phoebe's after school, to which he'd given his blessing… although it occurred to him he ought to meet this Phoebe some time, in case Millie was getting in with the 'wrong sort', as his mother-in-law would put it. Jennifer had an obsession about her granddaughter getting in with the wrong sort. He sometimes wondered whether she'd considered *him* the wrong sort when he'd married Gemma.

Anyway, he had a good reason to call in. Or was it an excuse? Well, it would only take two minutes.

'Jason! This is becoming a habit,' Claudia said as he entered.

She came around the counter to greet him, wearing a knitted cotton sweater in varying shades of blue over navy linen trousers that showed off her figure, without showing off her figure.

As if that makes sense.

Pudding lifted a lazy head from his basket, saw it was nobody of interest, and went back to sleep.

'To what do I owe the pleasure?'

Now he was here, Jason felt like an idiot. 'I – er – I was passing, so I thought I'd pop in to say how much Millie enjoyed the workshop.' *Pathetic, Jason.*

'I'm glad. Although I'm surprised you are.'

'Look, just because I think it's a load of… Just because I don't subscribe to it doesn't mean I'm not pleased that Millie enjoyed herself and met people.'

'Okay. How did your dinner go?'

'Ah, you know – everybody pussyfooting around under the pretence of getting to know each other better.'

Claudia nodded, and Jason shuffled from foot to foot as silence fell. Why had he come? It was as though he'd been drawn here, like someone bewitched.

Ah, yes. That reminds me…

'I heard rumours about you.' He blurted it out with no finesse whatsoever, but it was, after all, his main reason for stopping by.

'Oh?' Claudia looked both amused and wary. 'Since gossip's a way of life in Porthsteren, those rumours could be many and varied. Any in particular that you'd like me to debunk?'

'I was told that people thought you might be a witch when you first came here.'

Those rumours had niggled at him ever since he'd spoken to Libby yesterday – or she'd spoken to him, more like. Every time he thought he'd got Claudia pegged, he discovered another aspect to her – and he wasn't sure he liked this one. He *wanted* to dismiss it as idle gossip, but with Millie so keen on Claudia and Healing Waves, and Claudia already admitting she was friends with a witch…

Claudia sighed. 'Jason, you know as well as anyone that people speculate about newcomers. I suppose, many years ago, my shop and unconventional appearance might have raised a few eyebrows – but it's hardly anything out of the ordinary nowadays. Cornwall attracts free spirits like a magnet. But add to that a rich history of witchcraft in the area and yes, it set bored tongues wagging. Nothing more than that. The rumours were good-hearted, never malicious. I didn't encourage them.' She flashed a quick smile. 'I admit I didn't actively *discourage* them, at first – I had a newly opened business, and I was happy for any footfall I could get. But I played the rumours down, and they soon died of their own accord.' She studied his face. 'You're worried about Millie again.'

'When am I not?' He sighed, wanting to say something conciliatory. 'I knew it was only gossip, Claudia, but it's my job to make sure.'

Oh, Jason. Is that how you see fatherhood? As a job?

If Claudia thought the same, she let it slide. 'Jason, we all know that witches were just healers – wise women who supplied herbs and concoctions; an early version of complementary medicine. I don't even do that. I didn't ask for the label, it was way off base, and it's no longer a thing. I'm surprised anyone bothered to mention it to you.'

'It was only with idle amusement in mind, I think, but I was…' *Dubious. Worried for Millie's sake.* '…intrigued.'

Claudia smiled. 'Better that you're intrigued than furious with me, I suppose.'

Oh, I'm intrigued more than you could know.

The ping of the door interrupted this disturbing train of thought, for which Jason could only be grateful.

Claudia's face lit up. 'Tanya!' She embraced the woman who came in, and her hug was returned with the same affection.

'I finished my appointment sooner than I expected,' the woman said, then looked curiously across at him.

Claudia introduced them. 'Jason, meet Tanya. Tanya, this is Jason.'

As Jason walked over, his mind scrambled. *This* was the witch? She sure as hell didn't look like one, although Claudia had already told him off about hanging onto childhood images of warty hags on broomsticks.

Tanya was as far from that image as she could get. Petite with short blonde hair, wearing a jacket, T-shirt and jeans – no cloak, no dramatic colours – she had a friendly, elfin face and, in one small nod to the stereotype, green eyes.

She shook his hand. 'So *you're* Jason.'

'You've heard about me?'

Her lips twitched. 'A little.'

Jason wasn't sure what to say to that, but he did know that glances were being exchanged that were perhaps best left unexplained. 'Well, I should go.'

'Why don't you join us for a drink?' Claudia asked him.

Taken aback – as was Tanya, judging by her expression – he stuttered, 'Ah. Hmm. It's getting late…'

'Not even for half an hour?' Claudia turned to Tanya, mischief in her eyes. 'Jason and I have been having a very interesting discussion about witches, one which you're far better qualified to continue than I am.'

Bamboozled by the two wily women in his presence, Jason blushed a little.

'Phone Millie. Ask if she minds,' Claudia persisted.

Unable to come up with an excuse, he obediently fished out his phone, hoping his daughter was already back from Phoebe's and would demand his immediate return.

But Millie betrayed him. 'I'm staying late, if that's okay. We're going to watch a movie. Phoebe's mum'll drive me back.'

Defeated, Jason shoved his phone back in his pocket. 'Seems I'm not wanted at home yet.'

Claudia linked her arm in his. 'Then you're wanted with us. Smugglers' Inn?'

They walked along the beach road to the harbour, an odd threesome – Tanya and Claudia catching up on news, Jason shuffling awkwardly beside them.

At the harbourside, the Smugglers' Inn was a low, whitewashed building with a thatched roof and small, square windows, their frames painted pale blue. Trestle tables were set up outside, but the cool breeze drove them inside.

Jason looked around the cosy pub, taking in the flagstone floors and low-beamed ceilings. He was reminded how short people must have been when it was built. In more recent times, the beams nearest the bar had been padded with deep red leather to prevent concussion. A plaque by the bar stated there had been an inn on the site going back to the thirteenth century.

They placed their order, Jason gallantly paid, and the ladies gallantly let him. While they waited for their drinks, Claudia gave him a curious look.

'You've been in here already, surely?'

'Actually, no. I...' Jason didn't want her to think he was *too* unsociable. 'I've been meaning to pop in for a pint. But what with work, and I try to be home in the evenings for Millie… and at weekends, I got addicted to the coffee at the Page Turner.'

Tanya smiled at him. 'Easily done.' When they had their drinks, she led the way to a small table. 'So, Jason, what's all this about witches?'

'I was only asking Claudia about the rumours I'd heard,' he said defensively. 'About her being a witch.'

'Jason still has the storybook stereotype in his head,' Claudia said to Tanya. 'Feel free to try to shift it.'

Tanya took a sip of her drink, giving him a speculative look over the rim of her glass. 'Look, Jason. Witchcraft, Wicca – whatever you choose to call it – has been around for as long as humans have been alive. It wouldn't still be with us if there wasn't something to it. Potions for healing? Early medicine. Taking note of the stars? Early astronomy. All we do nowadays is combine ancient traditions with modern knowledge, to work with the seasons, the moon, nature. If we use it to try to heal or ward off harm or bring good luck, where's the harm in that?'

She paused, and he knew the two of them were waiting for him to find fault. The trouble was, the way Tanya had worded it meant that he couldn't – as much as he wanted to.

He picked up on the one thing he didn't understand. 'Witchcraft and Wicca aren't the same then?'

'In simple terms, Wicca's more of a spiritual path, with magic. Some Wiccans honour gods and goddesses, but that varies – it's all very individual.'

Jason didn't like things that couldn't be tied down. Nor was he sure why he was sitting in a perfectly good pub with a perfectly good pint, having a conversation like this.

'Please don't tell me you have a crystal ball,' he said.

'No, please don't,' Claudia warned her friend. 'His head may explode.'

Jason recognised delight in her eyes, presumably already knowing the answer.

'Yes, I do.'

Jason turned to Claudia. 'She's not teasing me?'

'No. Sorry.'

'And you tell the future with it?' The cynicism in his tone was blatant.

'No…'

Victory! 'Thought not.'

'Scrying isn't really about foretelling,' Tanya told him. 'It's…'

'But you perform spells?' he interrupted.

Claudia whispered, 'Have a sip of beer, Jason. You look like you need it.'

He did, but he scowled at her first. He didn't like that she could read him like a book.

Tanya cast an amused glance between them. 'I prefer "weave". "Perform" makes me sound like a stage magician.'

'And they work, do they?' Jason couldn't keep the incredulity out of his voice. He could try until doomsday and fail.

Tanya gave him a look which he probably deserved. 'It's not as simple as that.'

'Hmmph. Didn't think it would be.'

Tanya looked at Claudia, jerking a thumb in his direction. 'It's like trying to push a brick wall over. Can I stop now?'

Claudia smiled. 'The Craft takes years to learn, Jason. It takes dedication and skill and knowledge. You shouldn't dismiss that.'

Jason was defensive. 'You can't expect me to believe in spells and love potions, surely?'

Tanya shook her head. 'Love potions are unethical. But I could whip you up an aphrodisiac if you need one. Mint, thyme, rosemary, lemon zest, rose petals in black tea would probably do the trick. No eye of newt or powdered bat's wing whatsoever.'

Jason grinned. He liked this woman, even though she was teasing him and his head was telling him to finish his beer and get the hell out of there before he said something he might regret.

Still seemingly reading his mind, Claudia placed her hand lightly over his in sympathy. If he did believe any of this crap, he could have sworn his skin fizzed at the light touch.

Perhaps she, too, felt it, because she hastily drew away. 'Did you know we have our very own witch legend here in Porthsteren? Old Hester Moon. Back in the seventeenth century, when this was still just a tiny fishing village, she was the local wise woman.'

'She also had second sight and predicted a couple of disasters over the years,' Tanya chipped in. 'But as I'm sure you know, people became rather *paranoid* about witches around that time.'

Her emphasis wasn't lost on Jason, and he gave her a small smile.

'People began to view village healers with distrust,' Claudia went on. 'One night, Hester predicted a terrible storm. There were no indications in the sky or sea to back her up, as far as the fishermen could see. And because people had become suspicious of her ways, they were scathing of her prediction. The fishermen took their boats out.'

'I'm guessing Hester was right?' Jason asked, caught up in the tale.

Tanya nodded. 'The storm came out of nowhere, and a dozen men were killed. Hester was seen standing on the harbour wall, watching, the whole time. She was probably only waiting for the men to come home. But the villagers decided she'd used witchcraft to bring the storm about, to spite them for ignoring her warnings and to prove herself right.'

'She wasn't burned at the stake?' Jason asked.

'Actually, not many witches were in this country,' Tanya told him. 'Generally, they were hung or drowned. In Hester's case, the villagers couldn't quite bring themselves to do either, but in some ways, what they did was worse. She was hounded out of the village, up into the hills, without any belongings or food. There was a bitterly cold spell. Hester was an old woman. She was eventually found in a basic shelter she'd made of branches, starved and frozen to death.'

Jason paled. 'That's appalling!'

'Yes.' Tanya's tone was sad, reverent. 'She spent her life healing the sick, tried to warn them about a tragedy, and died a slow, lonely death for her pains.'

'As for the name Porthsteren?' Claudia said. '"Steren" is Cornish for star, and one of the meanings of Hester is "star". So poor Hester has immortality here, in a way.'

'Not much of a consolation,' Jason murmured.

They fell silent as he absorbed the local history lesson.

Jason remembered something Libby had told him – which was impressive, since he generally only took in half of what she said.

'Isn't there a new shop opening?' he asked. 'Hester's Cauldron or something?'

'Yes. It's in Hester's old cottage,' Claudia told him.

'What kind of shop?'

'Nobody knows. They're keeping everyone on tenterhooks until their grand opening tomorrow.'

Jason noticed Claudia's frown. 'Are you worried about it?'

'No. Not at all. Well. A bit, maybe.'

What could he say to cheer her up? 'Claudia, you have the weirdest shop in Porthsteren. I doubt anyone could beat you at that game!'

Chapter Ten

'You're attracted to him,' Tanya said after Jason had made his escape.

Claudia stared at her. 'Hardly! I spend half my time treading on eggshells in case he yells at me again. You saw the way he reacted to anything outside his comfort zone.'

'I also saw a man who listened. And he was *trying* to be polite.' Tanya paused. 'You don't deny he's attractive, then?'

Claudia shrugged. 'If that's your type.'

'What, a fit physique, fair hair, a sweet-if-underused smile? That sexy voice? Those *eyes*?'

'I suppose, if you put it that way…'

'No suppose about it,' Tanya said brightly, enjoying watching Claudia squirm. 'But you're in denial. So is he.'

'What *are* you on about?'

'He's bewitched by you.'

'I don't think so!'

'He doesn't *want* to be – that much is plain. But when he's talking to you, his eyes are on yours. When you speak, he watches your mouth. When you move away, his eyes linger on you.'

'You got all this from one drink in the pub? Or have you been reading the tea leaves again? Maybe even smoking them?'

'No tea leaves required. I used my eyes.' Tanya patted Claudia's hand. 'You wish you weren't attracted to each other?'

Claudia harrumphed. '*If* he's attracted to me – which I very much doubt – then I'm positive that, as you said, he doesn't want to be.'

'What about you?'

'It's a moot point, isn't it? We're incompatible – diametrically opposed in the way we approach life. He thinks in terms of logic and things that can be measured. I go by gut instinct and play with crystals and have a witch for a best friend.'

'Variety is the spice of life.' When Claudia said nothing, Tanya asked her, 'When was the last time you were truly attracted to a man? Ever since I've known you, you've rejected every single offer of a date!'

'I needed a break after Lee. I didn't want to become involved with someone local and be gossiped about. Besides, no one attracted me enough.'

'And Jason…?' When Claudia remained stubbornly silent, Tanya threw her hands in the air. 'Okay, I give up – for now. Did I tell you about my neighbour who asked me for a spell to make her husband enjoy washing up? I mean, honestly…'

*

Saturday began with a depressing lack of customers at Healing Waves. Since it was opening day for Hester's Cauldron, Claudia told herself it was inevitable – people were bound to be curious about the new shop. She reminded herself that it may have no bearing on her own business and she was probably worrying for nothing. But since she couldn't be in two places at once, she couldn't put her mind at rest.

Mid-morning, she phoned next door. Stopping short of barking, 'Well? Any news?', she asked Sarah, 'Any chance of you popping round with a coffee?'

'Just coffee? Or intel?'

Claudia sighed. 'Both.'

Sarah appeared five minutes later, along with the much-needed coffee, and glanced at Claudia's one customer browsing near the window. 'We're quiet, too.'

'They'll all be sussing out the new place.'

'I'm sure they are. That's fair enough. *We* hoped for plenty of interest on *our* opening days, didn't we?'

'You're right. Have you heard anything yet?'

Sarah gave her a look. 'I live and work with the queen of Porthsteren gossip, remember? Her phone's been buzzing all morning. Good job we *are* quiet.'

'And?' Claudia held her breath.

'Seems the clue was in the name, after all. Hester's Cauldron has a witch theme. You know – witchy ornaments, witchy jewellery, fantasy ornaments.' Sarah hesitated. 'Crystals, essential oils, soaps.'

Claudia dropped her head into her hands as her heart plummeted to her feet. Ever since she'd seen the sign revealing the name, she'd had a *feeling*. But she'd told herself, as had Tanya, that there was nothing to worry about until she *knew*.

Well, now she knew.

Sensing she was upset, Pudding climbed out of his basket and nudged his head against her, but Claudia was oblivious.

Sarah clucked in sympathy. 'Do you want me to look after Healing Waves while you go see? We're not exactly overworked. Evelyn could manage.'

Claudia thought about it. A quick recce wasn't good enough. She needed a proper look. 'No, but thanks for the offer.'

'Today's probably not the best day to go anyway. Apparently, it's heaving over there.' Sarah's face fell. 'And I wasn't going to tell you that.'

'I'd already guessed that much.' Claudia gestured at her almost-empty shop. 'What else aren't you telling me?'

Sarah heaved a sigh. 'Everyone's raving about it – great window, great layout, intriguing stock.'

Claudia managed a wobbly smile. 'Well. Another successful business around here is good, right?'

Sarah popped a kiss on her cheek. 'That's the spirit! They're doing full Sundays, so you could call in tomorrow before you open up here. Settle your mind.'

'I'll do that. Thanks, Sarah.'

But Claudia doubted a visit *would* settle her mind. She'd told herself the place was unlikely to be a competitor; thought that even if there was a small crossover of stock, it wouldn't matter too much. But from what Sarah had said, it was more than that. And if people could buy their essential oils, their soaps, their crystals by the harbour, why bother walking all the way along the beach to her?

*

The following morning, Claudia stood in front of Hester's Cauldron, taking in their window display with a practised eye.

It was bound to entice. Fairy lights in the form of stars and lanterns twinkled around the window and were threaded in and among the goods – a display method Claudia used frequently. She swallowed down the feeling that they'd copied her idea – she could hardly claim it was unique to her.

A deep purple velvet cloth had been draped over surfaces of different heights, upon which were placed a range of objects – a crystal ball on a stand; tarot cards spread in a fan with a skeleton hand hovering over them; cauldron-shaped mugs; decorated goblets.

Dangling above at different heights were pentagrams, mirror balls and witches on broomsticks.

Claudia took a deep breath and stepped inside.

Wow! They had taken full advantage of the building's layout. According to Evelyn, when it was a newsagent's only the small front room was used. The new people had opened out into the back room, and stairs led to the next floor.

The walls were painted dark purple – a surprising choice, since it made the space seem smaller, but that was obviously the idea. With the low ceiling and spot-lighted alcoves, it was like a secret cave, fairy lights strung everywhere, creating a grotto effect.

The front room held the counter and concentrated on less expensive items to tempt the casual browser who might not venture further into the shop – witch-themed jewellery (some of it rather macabre for Claudia's taste) and, to Claudia's dismay, the promised crystals and tumblestones.

An archway led to the back room, where an old fireplace suggested this might be where Hester Moon had brewed her healing potions for the village. Rows of essential oils arranged on a shelf made Claudia's heart sink further. Other shelves held an array of bath products – all chosen, no doubt, because their appearance fitted the shop's theme rather than for their quality. Dark-coloured bottles predominated, and soaps were only given space if they were purple, green or black. Even so, they were yet another crossover with her own stock.

A large framed poster on the wall next to the fireplace told the legend of Hester Moon. Reading it, Claudia couldn't quash her dismay that these women were exploiting a very real and tragic story.

Overhead throughout, goods dangled to tempt: pentagrams, witches' mirror balls and a myriad of puppets – some fun, others downright scary. Spotting a particularly hideous hag on a broomstick, Claudia stifled a sigh. What would poor Hester Moon have made of this? A good woman turned upon towards the end of her life; suspicion and superstition and intolerance to be perpetuated through the centuries by this sort of thing. Claudia knew it was seen as harmless fun by so many, and she could go along with it up to a point, but...

'Hi. Can I help?'

Claudia turned to the young woman at the counter. Young, tall, slim, in a figure-hugging purple velvet dress, her hair was long and jet-black, her nails the same, her lips purple, her eyes loaded with eyeliner and mascara. Claudia swallowed down a sigh at the modern-witch stereotype, then immediately pulled herself up short. After all, her own choice of attire and hair (not that *that* was a choice!) could also be deemed a stereotype to match her own place of business.

'No, thank you. I'm just browsing.' Had she seen this woman in Healing Waves recently, dressed differently? If so, she couldn't get away with pretending to be an anonymous browser. She held out her hand. 'Claudia Bennett. Healing Waves. Welcome to Porthsteren.'

'Thank you. I'm Raven.' The girl shook her hand, but her purple-painted smile didn't reach her eyes. 'Do you like what you see?'

There was a challenge in her voice that Claudia didn't appreciate in someone new to the village and younger than herself, but she forced a smile.

'You have an eye for a good layout,' she conceded.

'That's my partner's thing.' She gestured as another woman came down the stairs. 'Amber, this is Claudia from Healing Waves.'

Amber – another willowy young woman, this time in a black corset-style dress, with vivid hair that graduated from orange to deep red, and with the same proclivity for heavy make-up – pasted on a smile and shook Claudia's hand, while Claudia wondered at the coincidence of these two women having exotic names that matched their hair colour. Accident or design?

'Well. Nice to meet you.' Claudia saw the two women exchange a glance as she moved towards the stairs where a large arrow proclaimed, 'Mount the stair if you dare!'

She dared.

The upper floor had a dark theme, one that wouldn't please Tanya. In theory, Tanya should be thrilled to see somewhere selling witchcraft supplies, since she had to do most of her shopping online. In practice…

Cauldrons, crystal balls, spell candles, tarot cards and chalices were all well and good – but it was the way they were displayed that Claudia took exception to. Signs warned the faint-hearted not to meddle in dark magic. A big deal was made of the fact that the ceremonial blades could only be sold to over-eighteens. A bookshelf declared, 'For those who dare to learn more'. It was all very clever from a marketing point of view, but it made Claudia uncomfortable. Did these women know what they were doing? Were they witches themselves?

Back downstairs, Claudia took her time inspecting jewellery in a dark corner, near enough to the counter to listen in. And she did *not* like what she heard.

*

'Did you have a good afternoon?' Jason asked Millie as she clomped in, bags and boots scuffing the walls, making him wince.

'Yeah. Great!'

'Want some tea?'

'No thanks. We had a green smoothie at the café on the harbour.'

'Uh-huh.' *Smoothies. In my day, a milkshake was considered exotic fare for an afternoon out.* 'Who were you with? Phoebe?'

'Yep. And Jessica. They want to come again some time.'

'That's good.' The downside to a small place like Porthsteren was that any potential schoolfriends were scattered. And heaven forbid that Millie should manage to hook up with the ones who lived nearest. 'Did they get a bus back okay?' Those were few and far between, especially on a Sunday. 'I could've driven them.'

'The bus was okay.'

'What did you get up to?'

'The beach was a bit breezy. They said they might come more in the summer. We skimmed stones.'

'And did some shopping, I see. Did you go into Healing Waves?'

'Yeah. The girls liked it. They thought Claudia was cool. But they weren't bothered about the Page Turner, so we went to the harbour and spent ages in the new shop.'

'That Hester's Cauldron place?'

'Yep. It's all done out in purple and fairy lights, and they sell *loads* of cool stuff – jewellery and bath stuff like potions. The building's an old witch's cottage – there's a poster on the wall telling you about her. Part of it looks like a witch's kitchen, and there's a really interesting upstairs, too, with…' Millie's gushing stopped abruptly.

Jason's internal alarm system jangled. 'With what?' When his daughter hesitated, he said, 'I can look online, Millie. Or ask Libby at the General Store. Or do things the old-fashioned way and take a look for myself.'

Millie sighed. 'With tools and things for…' If her defeated shoulders sagged any more, they'd overtake her knees. 'For casting spells.'

'Casting spells. Here in Porthsteren.' Jason's voice was low and dangerous.

'It's just for fun, Dad. Everybody loves it.'

'Everybody meaning you and Phoebe and Jessica?'

'No – everyone. It was heaving in there.'

Jason let out a long breath. *For pity's sake.* He'd only just got to grips with one shop he hadn't cared for in Porthsteren, and now another had come along to plague him. 'What did you buy?'

'Nothing much.'

'Millie…'

'Okay.' Reluctantly, she lifted a purple carrier emblazoned with a black cauldron. Before pulling out her purchases, she narrowed her eyes in a perfect imitation of him. 'I *thought* about tarot cards,' she told him defiantly. 'But I knew you'd have a fit.'

'And you would have been right.'

'So, I settled for this.' She held up a star-shaped pendant on a lace. 'And this.' A purple bath bomb, covered in silver stars and glitter, wrapped in tissue. 'It's a witch's brew for relaxation.'

Jason rolled his eyes. He very much doubted a seventeenth-century witch would have heard of a bath bomb.

'And this.' Millie's final purchase was a shining silver ball on a wire.

Jason frowned. 'You bought a Christmas bauble? It's only just May.'

'It's not for the Christmas tree. It's a witch's ball.'

'You mean a crystal ball?'

'No, a witch's ball. Amber said it wards off evil.'

'Amber?'

'She's *so* cool. You should see her hair. Bright orange that changes to red at the ends!' Millie let out a sigh of envy as she fingered her own school-enforced brown hair. 'I'll hang this in my room.'

'You will do no such thing' was on the tip of Jason's tongue, but he bit his lip. He didn't like the sound of this shop. He certainly didn't like his daughter's enthusiasm for it. But if there was one thing he'd learned from his dealings with Claudia, it was that he should get his facts straight before he had a fit. As for Millie, he knew the minute he said, 'I don't want you going to Hester's Cauldron', she'd be in there every day after school. It was the way teenagers worked.

Sensing his hesitation, Millie quickly stuffed her purchases back in the bag, declared she was off to try out her bath bomb, and scarpered.

Jason looked at his watch. Too late. Hester's sodding Cauldron would be closed by now.

*

Spending so long at Hester's Cauldron gave Claudia no time to catch up with Sarah and Evelyn before opening up.

Sarah poked her head through the door mid-afternoon with a 'Well?' but had to settle for 'Tell you later', since Claudia had customers.

Tanya also texted to enquire, so Claudia texted back with a brief gist and referred her to the Hester's Cauldron website which was now up and running and full of photographs.

When she finally closed up and settled on the terrace for a cuppa with Sarah and Evelyn, all three of them were het up and tense.

'Well?' Evelyn was desperate for news. 'We were going to go and look this morning, too, but my nephew – the one on his gap year – wanted to chat online.'

They all looked up when Tanya appeared.

Claudia frowned. 'What are you doing here?'

'Hi to you, too. I couldn't stand the suspense. Had to see for myself. Got in there twenty minutes before they closed.'

'And?'

'You first.' Tanya took a sip of Claudia's tea and sat back to await the verdict.

Claudia's gaze settled on Evelyn. *Hmmm.* There would have to be some ground rules. She deliberately took her eyes from Evelyn's and switched to Tanya's before speaking. Tanya would understand.

'Before I say anything, you all have to know that this isn't for anyone else's ears. I can't give an opinion if I think it would get around.'

Evelyn wasn't fooled. 'You mean me.'

Claudia reached for her hand and said tactfully, 'Not you personally, Evelyn. But the bookshop *is* a hub for chit-chat and gossip. Wouldn't be much of a local café if it wasn't. But I can't say what I think if others might hear of it. It wouldn't be professional.'

'I promise.'

Claudia smiled. Evelyn might love the local buzz, but she'd kept her mouth shut before, when Claudia had asked her to. She trusted her.

'Thank you. Well, Hester's Cauldron is stunning. Exciting. Enticing. They'll attract a lot of business.' She sighed. 'Unfortunately, they do cross over some stock with Healing Waves: essential oils, soaps, jewellery, crystals. That could be a problem for me. But putting that aside...' Claudia lifted her hands, palms up. 'On the one hand, you *could* see it as a tourist trap exploiting the legend behind the building. No real harm in that, I suppose. Personally, I feel sorry for Hester, but that's me being soft. As for what they sell, witchcraft and Wicca are having a big resurgence lately, so there's a genuine market for it.'

'But…?' Sarah asked.

'*But* I'm not sure that Hester's is aimed at those who are knowledgeable; those who believe and practise. It's… schlocky. Their witch puppets and ornaments are mostly ugly – the usual stereotype. I know that's tradition, but it makes me sad. The toiletries they sell look like potions – everything's purple and black. Again, no harm done, but very theme-driven.'

'They're selling some things I wish they weren't,' Tanya said. 'Some of the jewellery, the symbols, head towards dark magics. I doubt a twelve-year-old wearing a cheap necklace without any intention behind it will summon up something they shouldn't, but out of principle, I'd rather they weren't given the opportunity. And as for upstairs? Don't get me started.'

'Upstairs?' Evelyn asked.

'They have signs suggesting it's not for the faint-hearted; that it's "darker". They're selling proper supplies, to be fair, but the signs dare you to dabble. The tarot cards they've chosen all have menacing illustrations. The fantasy ornaments are rather… erotic. As for their bookshelf, there are so many good books available, but theirs all seem to be there purely because the covers fit the shop's image.'

'The trouble is, I'm not sure they know what they're doing,' Claudia said.

Evelyn looked alarmed. 'What makes you say that?'

'I overheard some advice they gave someone about crystals and essential oils, and they weren't even close. I noticed they had laminated crib sheets under the till, but they were so busy, they didn't have time to check them. It felt like they were making it up as they went along.'

'You're worried they could do harm?' Sarah asked her, concerned.

'If someone buys the wrong crystal or uses the wrong oil, it won't kill them. But it won't do any good, either, will it?' Claudia was close to tears. 'I worked *so hard* to get to know my goods, and I keep on learning. I want to do my best for my customers.'

'If they can't even get those right, what are they doing selling specialised items?' Evelyn asked, dismayed. 'Are they witches themselves?'

'I wouldn't bet on it,' Tanya said. 'They don't know me, so I asked a few things. They had a basic beginners' grasp, but they came unstuck pretty quickly. I overheard them with a couple of customers, too. At worst, they were making it up.'

Claudia sighed. 'I suppose they're young and only just starting out. They can't know everything. I was once in their position.'

'No, you weren't,' Sarah insisted. 'You did your homework *before* opening Healing Waves.'

'I get the impression they decided on this business last-minute and set it up in a hurry, determined to open before the tourist season gets going,' Evelyn grumbled. 'They've concentrated on the layout, the visuals. Maybe they didn't expect to have to dole out much advice.'

'Then they should rethink what they're selling or get studying,' Tanya said crossly.

Sarah sighed. 'Maybe when the curiosity wears off and the crowds let up a bit, they'll up their game.'

'Did Claudia tell you what they were wearing?' Tanya asked. 'Slinky velvet dresses, spiky lace-up boots, long hair – they've got the "sexy witch look" down to a T.'

'Maybe they like dressing that way and always have done,' Claudia said, defending them.

'Maybe. But if they've only just started doing it to pull in the punters…'

'Sounds to me like they're out to make quick money,' Evelyn said with disdain. 'They'll close up in October and there's no guarantee they'll be back next year.'

Sarah shrugged and turned to Claudia. 'Don't worry about the crossover stock. People trust you. They'll still be drawn to Healing Waves.'

'I hope so, because I can't compete with the wonder of Hester's Cauldron.' Claudia made a face. 'And I can tell you now, I couldn't fit into those dresses, no matter how hard I tried!'

Chapter Eleven

Mondays were rarely busy, but this one saw the lowest footfall in Healing Waves for a long while. A few tourists. Very few locals… making Claudia inordinately pleased to see Alice, despite the woman's usual air of melancholy.

'Alice. Good to see you. After anything in particular today, or are you just browsing?'

As ever, Alice looked like a rabbit caught in the headlights. 'I – er – saw some notebooks last time I was in.'

'In the corner.' Claudia came out from behind the counter to accompany her.

Alice scanned the shelf, undecided.

'For a gift?' Claudia prompted.

After a moment's hesitation, Alice straightened her spine. 'No. For me. A treat.'

'How lovely! Well, why not do the same as you do for a crystal? Just keep looking until one speaks to you. I'll leave you in peace.'

A few minutes later, Alice came to the counter with her choice.

'I love that one.' Claudia ran her fingers over the embossed cover – a mermaid emerging from an undersea cave, the colours rich and jewel-like. 'Is it for anything special?'

Alice's nerves returned in a blink. 'I – er – thought I'd write up the notes I've made at your workshops. To help me remember things.'

Claudia slipped the book into a paper bag. 'Good idea.' As she rang up the purchase, she said, 'I read an article the other day about journaling. It's very therapeutic, apparently, getting your thoughts down on paper.' She winked. 'As long as nobody else reads it, I suppose.'

Alice gave a nervous chuckle. 'I heard that somewhere, too. But I'm not. I'm just writing up notes.'

Claudia nodded and reached under the counter. 'I got some new pens in the other day. This turquoise one goes with your notebook.' She slipped it into the bag. 'On the house.'

'Oh, no, I couldn't.'

'You'd be doing me a favour, Alice. I haven't stocked these before. Let me know if it writes nicely, will you?'

'Oh. Well. Thank you.' Alice blinked away a tear. 'You're very kind.'

'You're welcome. See you soon.'

As she watched Alice leave, Claudia wondered how much kindness that poor woman received, if she was moved by the small gift of a pen. George couldn't be a very demonstrative husband.

When Jason stormed in just before closing, Claudia was still depressed by Alice's gratitude and doubly depressed by the parlous state of her till drawer. She wasn't in the mood for one of his rants.

'I am *not* happy about that place, Claudia!' he exclaimed, exuding antagonism. The only saving grace was that it didn't appear to be directed at her.

'I can see that. Which place are you talking about?' *Bet I can guess, though.*

'Hester's bloody Cauldron.'

'Why don't we take this outside with a soothing hot drink? Those negative vibes of yours are pinging off the walls and stabbing me to death.'

Jason opened his mouth to retaliate, then closed it again, giving her that tiny wry smile he had. 'What are you going to poison me with this time?'

'Lemon verbena.' Claudia spooned leaves into her teapot.

'Don't you have a teabag?'

'The roofers used all the ones I pilfered from next door. Don't you trust me? You think this is desiccated frogs' innards?'

'How the hell would I know?'

Ignoring him, Claudia carried the tea out onto the now-empty terrace of the Page Turner, flipping her 'Closed' sign on the way. 'Drink. Tell me you're not dying from my brew. Then tell me what's got you so riled up.'

He drank. He didn't keel over. He even said of the tea, 'Hmmph. I can live with this, I suppose.' Then he looked at her, his pale eyes earnest. 'Hester's Cauldron. Have you been?'

'Yes.'

'Don't you have an opinion?'

'Oh, I have plenty of opinions,' Claudia assured him. 'But I'll listen to yours first. What's up?'

'I know I was hesitant about Healing Waves at first…'

'That's one word for it.'

'But I opened my mind. To a point,' he added, making her smile. 'Your shop is well-meaning, at least. But that new place screams tacky and tourist and everything I hate. And of course, Millie loves it. She went with her friends. She bought a *witch's* ball. She's got the blasted thing hanging from her bedroom ceiling!'

'It's harmless enough, Jason,' Claudia said patiently. 'The shiny surface is supposed to deflect negative spells; send them back to the source. That's all.'

'So, my daughter's expecting someone to curse her now?'

'I doubt it. Maybe she just likes the idea of it providing protection. Why's that any different to you hanging the black tourmaline I gave you?'

An unspoken 'It isn't' hung between them.

'Because it's a *witch's* ball,' Jason said stubbornly.

'You're hung up on the name. If Millie told you she bought it because it's pretty in lamplight, you wouldn't complain. You hang baubles on your Christmas tree, don't you?'

'Yes, but…'

'There's every likelihood they originated from witch's balls. You're not going to ban Christmas baubles, are you?'

Jason sighed. 'Millie and her friends are already planning on going back there.'

'I can imagine. That place is designed to appeal to their age group.'

'I went in first thing this morning to see for myself,' Jason told her. 'Told work I'd lost my car keys to buy some time.' When she raised an eyebrow, he held his hands out. 'I could hardly tell them I needed to visit the local witch shop, could I?'

Claudia's lips twitched. 'And?'

'Either those women have got a great flair for design or they've paid someone who has – all those nooks and crannies and alcoves; that narrow staircase; the colours and clever lighting.'

'I agree.'

'And did you see how they've done themselves up?'

'You don't like the sexy witch look?' When he stared at her, she shrugged. 'Tanya's words, not mine.'

'The truth? It does nothing for me.'

Claudia found herself surprisingly pleased with that. If Jason didn't go for their kind of thing, did he go for *her* kind of thing?

But he was still ranting. 'It's one thing Millie enjoying the novelty…'

'Millie has a good head on her shoulders, Jason. They won't sell her anything she shouldn't have.'

Jason studied her for a long moment, as though something had only just occurred to him. 'They stock quite a lot of things that you do. Aren't you worried?'

Yes. Very worried indeed. But Claudia lifted her chin in a show of bravado. 'No. I'm one up on them, because *they* don't know the first thing about half of what they sell!'

Jason's eyes narrowed. 'What do you mean?'

As the tea grew cold and the air grew cold along with it, Claudia summed up her visit just as she had with her girlfriends the previous day.

'You're saying they're frauds?' Jason asked when she'd finished.

'That's a strong word, Jason. If they sell something without comment, then no. If, however, they're passing themselves off as experts, as witches – and Tanya's certain they're not, in any serious way – then yes, I suppose they're frauds.' Hearing a scuffling noise from the direction of the beach, she glanced beyond the wall, but all she saw was a man walking by the edge of the incoming tide. His dog was no doubt digging through the seaweed at the top of the beach. Still, it occurred to her that a discussion like this would have been better held indoors, after all.

Time to outweigh the negative with a positive. 'But I'm sure they'll learn as they go along, and if people enjoy their purchases, who am I to quibble?'

'That's magnanimous of you, under the circumstances.' Jason frowned. 'Wait. Tanya's been in there? What did *she* think?'

His tone was earnest, surprising Claudia. Had he come to accept, if not condone, Tanya's beliefs?

'What did you think of Tanya?' Claudia probed, ignoring his question for now.

Jason shifted in his seat. 'She's nice.' When Claudia just waited – a technique she'd learned worked well in getting people to say more when further interrogation might make them clam up – he said, 'Okay, she's delightful.'

A laugh escaped from her throat. 'Oh, Jason. That hurt, didn't it?'

'Yes, it did.' He scowled. 'But just because I liked her doesn't mean I agree with anything she said.'

'And yet you're asking for her opinion about Hester's Cauldron?'

'Yes. I might not believe in that stuff, but she obviously does.'

'Okay, well, she thinks the same as me.' Worried by the grim expression on his face, Claudia said, 'We all have to make a living, Jason. They're just trying to make theirs. We might not like the way they're doing it, but they're entitled.'

'They're not entitled to sell my daughter any dark sorcery crap.'

'Worried she'll learn how to turn you into a grumpy toad? Because I'm telling you now, you're already halfway there.'

Jason glared at the dregs in his mug. 'Yeah, well, this'll probably finish the job.'

*

'I didn't expect to see you here' was Claudia's greeting when Jason turned up to meditation the following evening.

'My daughter was insistent.' When Millie scuttled off to bag a comfy floor cushion, he added in a low voice, 'She didn't find it easy last week, but she wants to persevere and she wanted me to come. So here I am.'

Claudia patted his arm. 'Good man.'

Jason chose a chair – he didn't think his body would thank him for an hour on a floor cushion. Millie grinned and whispered 'Oldie' before Claudia dimmed the lights and began the session.

An hour later, Jason was… well, quite relaxed. Like Millie, he'd struggled to stop turning over his worries, but he'd tried to concentrate on the guided meditation, and he'd drifted during the music at the end.

'Normal tea?' he asked hopefully when Claudia handed him a cuppa afterwards.

'Decaff, but you'll live. How did you find the meditation?'

'Last time I tried it, with Millie, I was told to empty my mind, but I couldn't. The guided meditation's easier – your thoughts get pushed to one side without trying too hard.'

'I agree. Emptying your mind's nigh on impossible, if you ask me! I'm glad you came.'

Jason looked around the room. Millie was chatting to Libby, Sarah and Evelyn.

'I know it's not the vibrant social circle you want for her,' Claudia said. 'But it means friendly faces to bump into. The meditation's good for her. And I have another idea. My soap stocks are still low, so I thought Millie could help me tomorrow evening. Take her mind off Hester's Cauldron.'

Jason let out a mental sigh of relief at the nature of Claudia's 'idea'. You could never tell what she might come up with.

'I'm sure she'd love to, but she does drama after school on a Wednesday now.'

'Thursday, then? And while she's still out of earshot, I have a favour to ask.' Claudia smiled when he couldn't keep the caution out of his expression. 'Don't worry, I won't ask you to dance naked with me under a full moon.'

Jason kept his face poker straight. 'That's a shame. I might have granted you that one.'

Jason Craig, are you flirting *with her now?*

Claudia spluttered out a delighted laugh, making his stomach flip. 'I bet! No. I was wondering if you could dig out some old photos for me.'

His brows knitted together. 'What kind of photos?'

'Shots of Millie and her mum looking close or having fun, from Millie as a baby through to the most recent, although preferably not with Gemma looking too ill. I'd need at least thirty, but I could work with up to fifty.'

'Why do you need them?'

Claudia became cagey. 'Something I want to do for Millie. Can you trust me?'

Jason could hardly say 'No', could he?

'Will it help if I tell you it might help her?' Claudia added, backing him further into a corner.

Jason managed a tentative smile while his emotions swirled. Claudia's sand-drawing exercise had been a success, but he still didn't like the idea of her experimenting on his daughter. As for photos? Other than those on the wall at home, he hadn't looked at any since he'd chosen some for Gemma's funeral. He wasn't sure how they would make him feel – a catalogue of a love that had slowly died; a reminder of a mother-daughter relationship that had ended too soon.

He saw recognition in Claudia's eyes, then sympathy. 'Jason, I'm so sorry. I was thinking about Millie, not about how painful this might be for you. If you don't want to…'

'No. It's fine,' he mumbled, embarrassed that his emotions were so transparent. 'If it'll help Millie, I'll do it. It might be good for me, too. I presume it's a secret for now?'

'If that's okay with you.'

When Millie re-joined them, her response to the soap-making invitation was an immediate 'Yes' – no indifferent shrug in sight. Jason was grateful for that rare flash of enthusiasm.

When Claudia asked Millie for her mobile number, Jason said, 'You'd better have mine, too. Just in case.'

On the drive home, he worried that Claudia might have taken that the wrong way. He'd only intended it as a safety net – for all he knew, soap-making could be a dangerous process and Millie might get hurt and Claudia would need to get hold of him, wouldn't she?

But it also meant their communications were no longer dictated by chance or engineered by him choosing to drop in at Healing Waves.

Jason wasn't sure how he felt about that.

*

Claudia enjoyed her Wednesday off – the first proper one since the storm. A walk along the coastal path, a scramble down a hidden path to a secluded cove, a read of her book, a doze on the sand under a sunny, cloudless May sky… Bliss. If she could bottle this and sell it at Healing Waves, she'd be a millionaire and make a lot of people very happy.

For now, she would settle for her own soul being happy. She'd weathered the storm, literally, and she was back in the game, ready for the summer season. She'd weathered the opening of Hester's Cauldron, too, although she could only hope there was profit enough for them both in Porthsteren. And after their rocky start, she was getting on well with Jason Craig, while helping Millie settle.

All in all, things were looking good... until she set foot in the General Store for a midweek tuna treat for Pudding.

'Claudia. Good day off?' Libby's greeting was unusually curt.

'Yes, thanks. Just had my usual fix of coastline. You know me.'

'I *thought* I did.' Libby's lips pursed as she zapped the barcode on the tuna, but no further conversation was forthcoming – a highly unusual state of affairs.

Claudia frowned. 'Anything wrong?'

'To be frank, Claudia, I'm surprised at you. I didn't think you went in for gossip at the best of times, but certainly not that sort.'

Claudia stared at her, bewildered. 'What gossip?'

'Bad-mouthing the new people. Not like you at all, I wouldn't have said. I'd think you'd be pleased to see new businesses here in Porthsteren – that's good for all of us. Hester's Cauldron might not be your cup of tea, but it appeals to plenty of others, locals and tourists alike. I wouldn't have thought you so quick to judge. I'm disappointed in you, if you want the truth.'

Her mind still foggy after her relaxed day, Claudia struggled to make sense of Libby's tirade. Gossip? Bad-mouthing? Her mind raced. Jason had asked her what she thought, but she was sure that if he'd said anything to anyone, it would have been to express his own strident opinion. Besides, who would he talk to about it? He was mostly either at work or with Millie. Then there was Tanya, Sarah and... Evelyn. *Surely not?* Evelyn lived and breathed gossip, but she'd never before passed on anything Claudia had asked her not to.

'Libby, what do you mean? Who said what?'

'How should I know? You know how things work around here. What I *do* know is that you called them frauds. That's a strong word, Claudia. Raven told me you went in last weekend and didn't seem keen. Now, don't get me wrong, a lot of us don't like that preferential rental deal they got, but we want them to succeed, just the same. You've said more than you should, I reckon.' Libby softened and patted her hand. 'You were a welcome change to Porthsteren, my lover, and we think the world of you. But you should extend the same courtesy to others, seems to me.'

Claudia fought back a tear. Tears might suggest guilt, and what had been reported was one-sided at best. She should clear that up right now, with the one person bound to pass it on.

'It's odd how the negative things flow fastest through the grapevine, isn't it?' she said firmly. 'I expressed *private* views to close friends in *private* conversations. I also expressed many positive sentiments – that new business is good for Porthsteren, as you say, and that they're as entitled to be here as any of us. That the shop looks impressive; that the women have a talent for design.' She paused for effect, picking up the tuna and slipping it into her bag. 'Perhaps you wouldn't mind passing *that* along.'

Don't make an enemy of Libby, Claudia. That wouldn't be wise.

She managed a tight smile. 'I know you like to be fair with everyone, Libby, after all.'

Claudia's walk home along the beach road felt like it took an age, until she was safe in her flat. Pudding was comically enthusiastic about his tuna and effusive in his gratitude, but Claudia could only manage to force down a slice of toast – a meal was beyond her. Miserable, she curled up on the sofa with a large mug of soothing tea at her side and her feline friend on her lap, willing his rhythmic purr to calm her, but this time, it failed miserably.

Even a phone call with Tanya couldn't soothe her. Tanya said all the right things – it was a private conversation; Claudia wasn't known as a gossip; it would soon blow over and, if it didn't, she had a right to her opinion (a valid one, in Tanya's view).

But Claudia did not sleep well that night.

*

The way Claudia was currently feeling about conversations on the terrace meant she didn't fancy her usual morning coffee with Sarah and Evelyn. But since it was drizzling and they would be inside, she took it as an opportunity to get to the bottom of things, much as she dreaded doing it.

'Peppermint tea? Not coffee? What's up?' Sarah asked her as they settled in a corner of the empty bookstore.

'I had a conversation with Libby last night. Word appears to have got around.'

'What about?' Evelyn asked, her tone cautious.

'What I think of Hester's Cauldron.'

Evelyn's shoulders sagged. 'And you think it was me.'

'I don't know what to think. I *am* concerned about how my private conversations seem to have become public.'

Tears formed in Evelyn's eyes, making Claudia feel awful. 'It wasn't me! I…' Evelyn shook her head and looked at Sarah.

'We heard that, too,' Sarah said briskly. 'I know Evie likes to… get involved, Claudia, but she knew you wanted to keep it between us, and that's exactly what we've done. We need to appear professional, just as you do. We've been asked what we think, even what *you* think, but we've been circumspect. I *knew* you'd think it was Evelyn…' Her steady gaze bore into Claudia like a drill, making her want to bolt for the sanctuary of her own shop. '…So I did some digging. Without boring you with the long chain of who said what to whom, I ascertained that it was a guy walking his dog on the beach who heard you call them frauds. Now, from what I remember, that specific term wasn't in the conversation you had with us, so I suggest you think about who you said that to and give Evie a little credit.'

Feeling like a child brought before the headmistress for a misdemeanour, Claudia squirmed in her seat.

'It was Jason, and it was his choice of word,' she said with a sigh. 'He was unhappy about Millie going into Hester's and wanted to know what I thought. When I said they lacked knowledge, he asked if I was saying they were frauds. I qualified that in my answer to him, but if someone only heard a snippet…' She took Evelyn's hand. 'I'm so sorry, Evelyn. I… I should go and open up.'

Feeling sick, Claudia left her peppermint tea and fled. In Healing Waves, she phoned the florist on the beach road and ordered a large bouquet to be delivered to Evelyn, telling the florist there was no message, thank you (the less gossip available to the residents of Porthsteren, the better). She could only hope her peace offering would be enough.

Worry over Libby's accusations and guilt over her own words to Evelyn, combined with the continuous drizzle outside, made for a long, miserable day. Claudia was thankful she had Millie coming to make soap that evening. Soap-making soothed her. With scents that calmed her soul, from fresh and zingy to warm and spicy; the satisfaction of putting together her own combinations; the excitement of inventing new ones… It was just what she needed after a day like this.

When Millie arrived, Claudia showed her through to her utility room at the back. Wide-eyed, Millie took in the catering-sized pan on the hob, the shelves filled with bottles of essential oils, jars of peel and dried flowers and bunches of dried herbs hanging from a wooden rack overhead, declaring, 'It's like a witch's kitchen!'

Claudia laughed. 'I wouldn't tell your father that, if I were you.' Handing her a vinyl apron, she directed her to wash her hands in the deep ceramic sink.

'First, we need to make colour for this batch because I've run out. You don't have to use colour, but yellow suits this one.' Claudia placed a small saucepan on the hob, had Millie measure turmeric and vegetable oil, simmer it until they got the right colour, then showed her how to strain and bottle it.

'Now for the exciting bit. You can make soap completely from scratch, but I use this vegan melt – it's much easier. We need to be careful, though – if we overheat it, it'll go cloudy, and if we overstir it, it'll get bubbles.'

Millie stared at her. 'It's trickier than you'd think!'

Claudia handed Millie the bottle of colouring to add a few drops. As with the stone-skimming and the sand-drawing, once Millie was concentrating, her attitude and scowls disappeared and contentment showed on her face.

'Time for a selfie?' Claudia pulled her phone from her pocket and snapped herself and Millie stirring the pot.

'Can you send it to me?'

'Of course! Okay. Scent next.' Claudia reached for two bottles of essential oil. 'Lemon and bergamot, I think.'

'How do you decide which goes with which?' Millie asked.

'Trial and error. There are recipes online, or books, but I rely on instinct nowadays. Although if I try something new, I make a small batch first, to be sure it works.' Claudia sprinkled lemon peel slivers into the pot, and Millie gently stirred them in. 'Don't heat it too long, or the scent will evaporate. Let's pour it into the moulds now.' Pulling large oblong pans from a cupboard, she said, 'You can get fancy shapes, but these are easiest for large batches – I can just slice it into bars. Sterilise them first, though, because we're not using preservatives.' She supervised Millie as she poured the mixture into the moulds, then said, 'Now for the washing up.' She laughed when Millie made a face. 'It's an important part – lingering scents can taint the next batch.'

Millie showed no sign of being bored, so when they'd cleared up, Claudia fetched two trays of olive oil and mint soap, carefully turned the blocks out onto a large chopping board and let Millie slice them.

'How's drama club?' Claudia asked.

'Okay.'

'It's a good way to make friends.' Claudia glanced sideways at her. 'Were you okay after the sand-drawing? I was worried about you.'

Millie's trademark shrug appeared. 'I needed to cry. Hadn't done it for a while. Felt better.'

'Your dad was pleased.'

'Well, that's twisted, isn't it? A dad pleased that his daughter couldn't stop crying?'

'That isn't the way it is, and you know it,' Claudia said gently.

Another shrug. 'Yeah, I know.'

'He worries about you. Maybe you could cut him a little slack sometimes?'

'Hmmph.'

Oh dear. 'You said something about counselling. That didn't help?' She knew it hadn't – Jason had said as much – but she wanted to hear it from Millie.

'I didn't like talking to a stranger about Mum and me. About Mum and Dad.'

'Perhaps you weren't ready. Maybe you could try again?'

Millie shook her head. 'I liked the sand-drawing. I did it again, on my own. It helps.'

'Good.' Claudia reached into a drawer for a small net bag. 'I put together a crystal combination for you. You could keep it in your pocket or put them in a dish in your bedroom.'

Millie poured the smooth crystal chips into her hand. 'What are they?'

'Rose quartz, amethyst and moonstone. A good mix for grief.'

'Thank you.'

'You're welcome. Let's carry these through and put them in the right basket.'

That done, Millie turned to Claudia, her eyes bright. 'Can I help again some time?'

'Yes, but I don't want your dad telling me off for taking up too much of your time or interfering with your homework.'

Millie curled her lip. 'Dad'll always find something to complain about.'

Claudia inwardly winced. 'I'm sure he has good reason *most* of the time. It's a parent's role, after all.'

'S'ppose.' And there she was again – the Millie that Claudia had first come to know, sullen and awkward. But for one whole evening, Claudia had seen the other side of her. Distraction was a great technique when it came to healing your troubles. Claudia knew that from her own experience. The problems and pain might not go away, but they could be forgotten for a while and were often a little less, somehow, when you came back to them.

Perhaps Millie could help more often. Claudia didn't mind the company.

Texting her dad for a lift as she walked to the door, Millie said, 'I went into the new shop.'

Not my favourite subject right now. 'Oh?' Best not let her know that Jason had already spoken to her about it. 'With your friends?'

'Yep. They like your shop, by the way. And they love Hester's Cauldron.'

Claudia tried not to take offence at them only liking her shop while loving Hester's. 'How about you?'

'I love the way it's done out, and they sell great stuff, and Amber and Raven are brilliant!'

Claudia's heart sank. 'Did you buy anything?' she asked, already knowing the answer.

'Just a bath bomb and a necklace.' Millie pulled the pentagram from under her T-shirt. 'And a witch's ball. Amber said they're for protection. I looked it up when I got home. There's *loads* on the internet.'

'Yes, there is.' Claudia hesitated. 'Be careful, though. Most sites are fine, but a few aren't. And some might be best taken with a pinch of salt.'

At that, Millie's face fell. 'You're just like Dad.'

Ouch! That hurts. 'Millie, I couldn't reach your dad's level of cynicism if I practised for a decade!' *Tone it down, Claudia.* 'Look around you.' She gestured at the oracle cards, the crystals.

'You're right. Sorry.' Millie stepped outside. 'But witch stuff's different. You don't do that at Healing Waves.'

'That's because I'm not an expert.'

'Have you even been to Hester's Cauldron?'

'Yes, I have.'

'Didn't you think it was cool?'

Be careful, Claudia. Your mouth has already got you into trouble this week. 'Like you said, it's… aesthetically appealing.'

'But?'

'It's not my cup of tea, that's all.' Claudia scanned the beach and saw no one. *This is Millie. Jason will never forgive you if you don't say something.* 'Just make sure you know what you're buying there. Amber and Raven are busy ladies, what with it being a new shop, so their advice… Just make sure you check for yourself, okay?'

Millie gave her a mutinous look. 'Are you saying they don't know stuff?'

'I'm only saying they might not know *everything* right off the bat.' Claudia gave a sigh of relief when she heard a car. 'That'll be your dad. Thanks for your help. I enjoyed tonight.'

Millie managed a smile. 'Thanks. I enjoyed it, too.'

She might as well have added, 'But not the lecture', Claudia thought as she watched her clomp around the building.

Deflated, Claudia headed upstairs to the comfort of a warm cat on her lap, a cat who asked no questions and didn't put her in difficult situations – other than demanding extra helpings. By trying to help Jason out, Claudia had spoiled the mood of the evening.

She just couldn't win.

Chapter Twelve

'Have fun soap-making last night?' Jason asked his daughter over breakfast, he with his trusty bacon butty and Millie with the grudging slice of toast he insisted she eat.

'Yup.' Millie gave him a look. She was very good at giving him looks. 'Stop pretending to take an interest in something you couldn't care less about.'

The old Jason might have snapped at her for that one. The lately-Jason was too worn down by interactions like these. He let it slide.

'I admit I have very little interest in the intricate process of soap-making. I'm more a chuck-it-in-the-supermarket-trolley-with-the-baked-beans man myself.' The twitch at Millie's mouth encouraged him. 'I am, however, interested in whether you enjoyed your evening. I'm your father. So sue me.'

At that, Millie did smile.

Hurrah for small results.

'Yeah, it was good,' she conceded. 'Claudia showed me the whole process.'

'You and Claudia get along well, don't you?'

'Yes. *She* doesn't treat me like a two-year-old.'

'Perhaps that's because she's not your parent,' Jason snapped, quickly adding, 'I'm glad you had a good time.'

'She said we can do it again. *If* you don't object.' With that, his daughter stalked off to get ready for school, leaving Jason with his half-eaten butty and an empty space where a conversation used to be.

If Millie had stayed, he could have told her he wouldn't object. He could also have told her that that was quite magnanimous of him, considering that after dropping her off at Healing Waves, he'd strolled to the harbour and back, only to see his daughter and Claudia silhouetted in a window, stirring a large pot, for all the world like a witch and her apprentice huddled over a cauldron. All they needed was for Tanya to join them, and it would have been like the opening scene from *Macbeth*.

Pushing his unfinished butty aside, he picked up his mug of strong tea to help him start his day. It was reputed that his Great-Uncle Douglas had been in the habit of pouring whisky over his breakfast cereal instead of milk. If Great-Uncle Douglas had had kids like Millie, Jason could understand why.

*

That evening, Jason strolled along the seafront, listening to the rhythmic swoosh of waves. Millie was at Phoebe's, and he needed fresh air and space to think.

Work was still a struggle. Millie had been difficult this week. He had the prospect of driving to Devon with her tomorrow to spend the day with his in-laws. *Oh joy.*

And he'd found Claudia's request for photos so much harder than he'd thought it would be.

Assuming she planned to make a photo album for Millie, he was both touched and annoyed. That was something *he* should have done. But there had been so many things to do after Gemma's death – paper-work and legal stuff; deciding on a new start and where; selling the old house; finding a job, a new house and Millie a school place. If Claudia wanted to do this, he shouldn't complain.

The past couple of evenings, after Millie had gone to bed, he'd stayed up late with his laptop. Even though Claudia only wanted mother-and-daughter photos, something had compelled him to start right back at when he'd first met Gemma and work his way through.

Memories had come flooding back – funny, painful, touching – charting his life with Gemma from their first date all the way through to the awkward years as they grew further apart.

Jason had laughed. He'd cried, even choked on sobs for a marriage that had become so broken, it could never be mended.

'Don't you wish we could be the way we used to be, Jason?' Gemma had asked him once at the beach, ostensibly on a happy family holiday in France, a ten-year-old Millie splashing like a three-year-old in the waves.

Jason had turned to look at his wife, but she was concentrating her gaze on their child. Her profile was stark. Rigid. A tear had escaped and run down her cheek.

Jason had touched her arm, and when that elicited no response, grasped her chin in his hand and turned her to face him. The sadness in her expression might have broken his heart, if it hadn't already been broken.

'Things change, Gemma. *We've* changed. We can't help that. We're doing our best.'

'Well, it's just not good enough!' she'd said, her voice fierce.

'I know. I'm sorry.'

She'd sighed. 'We both are. Should we… should we think about divorce?'

'Divorce?' He'd looked back to the shallows. 'What about Millie?'

After a long moment, Gemma had nodded sadly. 'Okay. But, you know, Jason, this is only like pulling the plaster off slowly, instead of ripping it off quickly and getting the pain over with.'

Gemma had been right. Jason knew that now.

At least the photos reminded him there had been good times. The unhappy years had dominated his memories so much, he'd almost forgotten the youthful joy of being in love; the wonder at the birth of their daughter; the blooming of their careers. Their shared pride as their child learned to walk, to talk; her first day at school, her first sports day medal.

As he walked, the insistent sound of the sea invaded his consciousness and his melancholy gradually quieted. The sound was hypnotic, the light breeze pleasant. For one mad moment, he considered walking barefoot… but he resisted.

At Healing Waves, the shop windows were dark, lit only by the twinkling of fairy lights strung through the display. His gaze drifted to the upstairs window, not quite in darkness but with a hint of light – knowing Claudia, candlelight – beyond the gauzy curtains. One of these days, she'd set off a conflagration with those things.

Just as he thought it, there was a flash of light, and Jason realised with horror that it was the yellow of flame and most definitely *not* from a candle. His feet were moving before his brain could register the fact, charging across the sand and up the steps to Claudia's flat.

Praying the door wouldn't be locked, he got his wish as he shouldered his way in to see flames rising from the coffee table. Grabbing a vase of flowers from the nearest shelf, he dumped the lot over the flames. They sizzled disappointedly for a moment, then died. His heart pumping, he looked for Claudia.

She was sitting cross-legged on the sofa, her eyes wide in the candlelight, staring at him as if he'd lost his mind. Pudding remained curled in his armchair, although he deigned to open an eye to observe proceedings.

Jason let out his breath in a whoosh. 'You're alright?' He rushed over and squeezed her tight, his heart pounding. When she squeaked in protest at being smothered, he pulled away and, dissatisfied by the candlelight, switched on a lamp.

Claudia might appear startled by his sudden entrance, but she didn't seem at all perturbed about the fire in her lounge.

He waved his arm at the coffee table. 'What the hell…?'

'I could say the same thing,' Claudia said calmly. 'What was that all about?'

She unfolded her legs from beneath her and stood, looking down at the detritus of ash and soggy flower stems and ruined petals. Water spread across the tiled surface and dripped onto her rug. With a tut, she trotted into the kitchen area and fetched a towel to mop up the worst of it.

Jason watched her in bewilderment, his legs – now like jelly – rooted to the spot. 'I saw the flames from the beach. I thought your flat was on fire!'

Claudia looked at him in astonishment, then shook her head. 'Only this bowl was on fire. Its contents, anyway.' Dismayed, she looked down at it, grumbling, 'I'll probably have to do that all over again some time.'

Jason ran an agitated hand through his hair, making it stand on end. 'This was *deliberate*?'

'Of course! You don't think I'd just sit there on the sofa while my flat was alight, do you?'

'You could have been asleep.'

'I wasn't. I was visualising.' Claudia carried the sopping towel to the sink, squeezed it out, shoved it in the washing machine, walked back to the coffee table for the bowl, poured what she could of the water down the sink, then unceremoniously tipped the rest of the contents, flowers and all, into the bin. Finally, she opened windows to let out the lingering smoke. 'Tea?'

Frustrated, Jason nodded. 'But I don't want any of that herbal crap.'

'I can do normal, too.'

Can you? Jason wondered. *Do you ever do normal?* But then it wouldn't be Claudia, would it?

'I sponged more teabags off Sarah and Evelyn, in case you popped by unexpectedly,' she admitted. 'Little did I know. Take a seat.'

Jason perched on the sofa and ran through the last five minutes in his head, but it didn't play back any other way.

When she placed his 'normal' tea in front of him, he almost sighed aloud with relief. 'Thanks.' He gestured around the flat. 'Care to explain? Just for my sanity?'

Claudia gave him a look. 'Firstly, for the health-and-safety part of your brain – which I know is screaming loudly inside your head – I was fully in control. The bowl's metal, and it only contained paper. I suppose, when I first set fire to it, there was a bit of a glow. You must have looked up at just the wrong time.'

'Rather me than the fire brigade. Why didn't your smoke alarm go off?'

At that, Claudia looked sheepish. 'I took the battery out.' When Jason's expression became thunderous, she added hastily, 'Only for a minute.'

Jason didn't trust himself to comment. 'Dare I ask *why* you were burning paper in a bowl? Have you never heard of a shredding machine? And why were you just sitting there?'

His heart had calmed now, settling into a slow but heavy thud as he took in the vision of Claudia in lamplight. The golds and reds of her hair shone. Soft, white yoga pants clung to her thighs, while an oversized green knitted cotton top draped across sculpted collarbone and curves, hinting at what might be beneath. Her golden eyes sparkled at him in amusement. It took all his willpower not to allow his gaze to drift down to her mouth. Alarmed, he tried to corral his thoughts. What had they just been saying?

'It was a ritual,' she told him.

'You mean a spell.'

'No. I said a ritual. A spell is different.' She sighed. 'Do you want an explanation or not?'

Jason nodded, curiosity overriding cynicism.

'It's a bit like the sand-drawing. If something's upset me and I can't let it go, I write it down. Fair enough? Writing down your thoughts to release stress?'

'I have no quibble with that.'

'Glad to hear it. When I'm done, I tear up the pages – a symbolic gesture.' She waited for him to say something as she sipped whatever disgusting tea she'd made for herself.

Jason didn't. He'd been known to tear up pieces of paper he didn't like.

'I set it alight then watch the flames, imagining those thoughts going up in smoke so I don't have to give them headspace any more. Do you have a quibble with *that*?'

'No, but I think your beach version's safer, unless you drown yourself.' A thought struck him. 'Did you manage to rid yourself of your unwanted thoughts before I threw a vase of perfectly good flowers over them?'

'I won't know until or if they come back, I suppose. But I can do it again.'

'Great. More fires.' Jason caught Pudding's eye. No wonder the cat wasn't ruffled. He was obviously used to minor blazes in the home. 'I'm sorry if I wrecked it.'

'Don't be. You were being a hero. A misguided one, maybe, but I am sorry for worrying you. Your heart was racing like mad when you hugged me.'

Ah. She'd noticed that, had she?

Jason wondered what she'd taken that fierce hug to mean. Only that he cared, he hoped.

'It wasn't me that upset you, was it?' he asked.

'You're not the only person who can upset me, Jason Craig.' Her brows drew together. 'Although you are quite good at it, and you do manage it on a frequent basis.' She sighed. 'It was to do with you, but only in an indirect way.'

By the time Claudia had told him her woes about overheard conversations and allegations of her bad-mouthing that wretched Hester's Cauldron, Jason was beginning to hanker after his old life in Edinburgh. There was an element of anonymity in a big city. There was no anonymity here in Porthsteren.

'I can't believe that the worst thing we said was the one bit that was overheard,' Claudia finished. 'And I have no idea how – that dog walker was right down by the water's edge.'

Jason shrugged. 'Maybe there was another one, nearer the wall,' he pointed out. 'Or the breeze had carried our words.'

Claudia sighed. 'Things are still stilted with Sarah and Evelyn. Evelyn thanked me for the flowers and said they weren't necessary, but we all know they were. I've always had such an easy relationship with them.'

'It'll come back,' Jason soothed, hoping it was true. 'I'm sorry our conversation caused you problems, but just so you know, I haven't said anything to anyone other than Millie – and she knows that came from me, not you.'

'Thanks. I cautioned her, too, last night. I could tell how much she likes the shop. I was careful about what I said – I just told her to double-check any advice on the internet.' Claudia's face fell. 'Which could be worse – but she's already been on there, anyway.'

Jason's gut flipped, and he wasn't sure whether it was because he didn't want Millie looking up inappropriate crap online or because this woman in front of him clearly cared so much about his daughter.

'She guessed that I didn't rate Amber and Raven's advice,' she added, 'but I played that down.'

'I appreciate you sticking your neck out. Thanks.' Talk of Hester's Cauldron led Jason's mind to witches and then Tanya. 'How on earth did you become friends with a witch, by the way?'

'We met when I contacted her about designing the website for Healing Waves.'

Jason realised he hadn't even thought about what job Tanya might do.

Claudia gave him a knowing look. 'Wicca's what she *is*, Jason, not what she does for a living. We clicked the moment we met, and the rest, as they say, is history. I wasn't *looking* for a best friend, and I had no intention of confiding in anyone about my old life – if I wanted to reinvent myself, I had to leave the past behind.' She sipped tea. 'But it was different with Tanya. It felt *right*, telling her. And it's good that one person in my new life understands my old one.'

Jason could understand that. He kept so much to himself. Having just one person who knew where you were coming from? There would be comfort in that.

He was itching to know about this past she'd mentioned. An ex-husband was all he knew so far. A career she no longer wanted. But she'd made it plain it wasn't open for discussion.

Pudding provided a timely change of subject by jumping onto his lap and pushing his head into Jason's hands. Jason cautiously stroked his head and ears, making him purr loudly. The sound was strangely hypnotic.

'How long have you had him?' he asked.

'Before I moved down here, I lived temporarily with a friend in London. Pudding was Debbie's cat. They didn't get along, but he took to me.'

Jason smiled at the way she said it, as though she couldn't imagine why. *He* could imagine why. She was calm and kind and warm and everything a cat might prize in a human.

'When I left, Debbie said she didn't have enough time for him and claimed the sea air would be good for him. So here he is.'

Pudding lifted his face in expectation of a tickle under the chin.

Jason provided it. 'He seems happy enough.'

'We're both well suited here, aren't we, Pudding?'

Perhaps due to Pudding's copious supply of fur, Jason sneezed without warning. A phalanx of claws dug deep into his thighs. Jason yelled. The cat shot off his lap.

'I have holes in my leg,' Jason announced, rubbing ineffectually at his jeans.

'Then you shouldn't sneeze unexpectedly,' came the mild reply. 'Want me to take a look? I have tea-tree oil.'

Jason stared at her, unsure whether she was teasing. 'Er. No. I can manage my own wounds, thank you.'

Claudia's lips twitched.

In response to his act of wanton vandalism on Jason's person, the cat moved onto Claudia's lap and curled into her midriff, one proprietorial paw across her arm. Watching, Jason was horrified to realise he felt… *Surely not. Jealousy?*

Disturbed, he distracted himself by gazing around the room, taking in the muted coastal colours and tasteful art.

'I do love your flat.'

'Thank you. When I came down here, I expected to lease retail premises and buy a little cottage. But I fell in love with this building, and it was purchase-only. I knew the downstairs could work for me, and the position's incredible. But it left me without the money for a home. Anyway, this suits me well enough. There's only me, after all.'

Why *was* she unattached? Jason wondered. Still scarred from a painful divorce? Not found the man of her dreams yet? She must surely have had plenty of offers.

Aware that she was waiting for him to say something, he brought himself back to the conversation. 'Sarah And Evelyn told me it was a mess. That they were grateful when you moved in.'

'Ha! I bet they didn't tell you how much they helped. It needed structural repairs, so by the time I got to the interior, money was running tight. They realised what was happening.' She laughed. 'My glum face every time a tradesman gave me a quote probably tipped them off. Sarah's a DIY queen and it was still off-season, so she helped with shelving and what have you. I don't know what I'd have done without her.'

Jason smiled. 'I think the businesses complement each other – both are places to browse, to relax, to not be rushed.' He glanced at his watch. 'Talking of which, I should go. Millie might be home soon.'

'Give her my love.' Picking up Pudding, Claudia followed Jason to the door.

Her necklace glinted in the soft light, and he'd lifted it to get a closer look before it occurred to him that that would mean brief contact with the soft skin at her throat. He examined the silver pendant – a full moon, with a waxing crescent moon on one side and a waning one on the other.

'Is this a Wiccan symbol?'

She arched an eyebrow. 'Yes, it is. Clever you.'

'I thought you said you aren't a Wiccan?'

'I'm not. Tanya bought me this. It represents the three phases of woman – maiden, mother and crone.' When he let it drop back against her throat, she gave him a wry smile. 'Not that I fit any of those at the moment.'

'What do you mean?'

'I wouldn't dare claim myself as a maiden any more. I'm not a mother. And I'm not quite ready to identify with crone. Although the word crone conjures up the wrong image – it only means an older, wiser woman. I might grow gracefully into that one.'

Jason touched a finger to the necklace again. 'Not yet. Not for a long time yet.' Trying to unscramble his brain, he muttered, 'I should go.'

She kissed him on the cheek. 'Thank you, Jason.' She waved a hand at the coffee table where the fire-bowl had been. 'For caring.'

Pudding, curled comfortably in her arms, gave him a smug smile as if to say, 'Bet you'd like to be in my place right now'.

Jason went down the steps, his skin humming where Claudia's lips had touched, shaking his head.

Jealous of a cat, for pity's sake! There is no hope.

Walking back towards the harbour, he wondered how many psychiatrists practised in the vicinity of Porthsteren.

And then he grinned. He'd been taking himself way too seriously lately. Claudia was a good influence on him. Lighter and dafter thoughts could only mean that better things were around the corner.

Chapter Thirteen

Claudia was run off her feet all Saturday. Locals enjoyed being out and about, catching up with friends over coffee and browsing the shops, but weekend visitors were increasing, from regular second-homers to one-off B&Bers taking advantage of the good weather. Claudia wouldn't have eaten if Evelyn hadn't brought her a falafel and salad wrap. She hoped the gesture meant that all was forgiven between them.

'Phew!' Evelyn mopped her face as the three of them collapsed outside the Page Turner at the end of the day, iced elderflower cordials in front of them. 'What a day!'

'A relief, though.' Claudia blew a curl off her face, grateful that any ill feeling seemed to have blown over. 'I was worried last weekend – barely a customer, what with Hester's Cauldron opening. But today was a good, solid Saturday.' She wiggled her toes. 'I'll get varicose veins at this rate.'

Sarah shot her a sympathetic smile. 'At least there's two of us to cope at ours.'

'So there should be. You run a bookshop *and* café.'

'And we have Kathy on a Saturday,' Evelyn said. 'I don't know what we'd do without her.'

'Could you lend her to me?'

'Not on your very sweet life, honey,' Sarah said. 'Couldn't you hire someone for summer Saturdays?'

'I'm thinking about asking Millie.'

Evelyn opened half-closed, sun-drowsy eyes. 'Isn't she too young?'

'Fourteen. There's a legal limit to how many hours she could do, but that suits me.'

Sarah gave Claudia a knowing look. 'You think it'll be good for her.'

'Yes, but I could do with the help too. She made soap with me this week, and she takes a real interest in the shop's stock.'

'It'll help her get to know the locals better,' Evelyn said. 'And you get quite a few school kids coming in.'

'Hmmph. They browse more than spend, bless them, especially on drizzly days – although they've been scarcer since Hester's Cauldron opened. Before that, I was the only "alternative" shop in Porthsteren for them.'

'Evie and I closed early yesterday and went for a look-see.' Sarah made a face. 'Let them have the teenagers. Like you said, teens don't spend much.'

'A few fivers are better than no fivers, Sarah.'

'We don't get many teens in our place nowadays,' Evelyn said. 'They prefer their screens. Millie's been in a few times, though. I think she'd enjoy working in Healing Waves.'

Claudia nodded. 'There's only one problem.'

'Her father?' Sarah guessed. 'He's been okay lately, hasn't he?'

'He's been better,' Claudia conceded. 'But Millie working at Healing Waves might be a step too far for him… although I might be helped by Hester's Cauldron in that regard.'

Evelyn's eyes widened. '*Helped?* By Hester's Cauldron? How?'

'Because Jason hates that place. He thinks it's a bad influence.'

'That's what he said about you at first.'

'Ah, but I am now a paragon of virtue in comparison to the Hester's Cauldron gang.'

They laughed, and then Evelyn dropped her voice to a whisper. 'I found out more about those Hester's girls.'

'Wait.' Sarah held up a hand, walked to the edge of the terrace, peered over the wall, then reported, 'Just two teenagers gossiping about boyfriends on the way back to the harbour.' She looked at Claudia. 'You were right. We should be more careful.'

'Let's go inside,' Evelyn mumbled. 'Safer that way.'

Claudia followed them in, hating that they felt the need to skulk around like this.

'They *are* young – early twenties,' Evelyn told her. 'From London, but their parents own second homes near St Ives. And when I say second homes, I'm talking villas with a view, if you get my drift. *Serious* money. Rumour has it that one of the girls dropped out of university under a cloud. Cheating, maybe? But I don't know for sure, so I wouldn't care to speculate.'

Claudia and Sarah grinned at each other. Lack of facts had never stopped Evelyn from speculating before.

'They could afford to set up Hester's because they're backed by their daddies' money.' Evelyn sniffed. 'Spoiled little rich kids, if you ask me.'

'Give them a chance, Evie,' Sarah chided. 'We all had to start somewhere. You seem to have forgotten your father loaned us five hundred pounds many moons ago when we set up this place.'

'And *you* seem to have forgotten that he demanded it back less than a year later when he realised we weren't just friends!' Evelyn shot back.

Claudia's eyes widened. 'Really?'

Sarah chuckled. 'He turned up at the cottage unexpectedly – the first time he'd visited since Evie's great-aunt left it to her. Took himself on a tour, saw the one bedroom with a double bed and the second bedroom which we'd turned into a study. Asked where the other bedroom was. We were caught on the hop. He twigged, we were in disgrace, and he wanted his money back.' She shrugged. 'It was the mid-eighties, bear in mind, and he was of a different generation.'

'That was a hard year,' Evelyn grumbled. 'We had to live off lentil broth and Sarah's economy stew.'

'Economy stew?'

'Swede and carrots, mainly.'

'Evie's had a thing against swede ever since.' Sarah smiled. 'Good thing the cottage was left to her and not her dad, or we'd've been sleeping on the beach! But the point is, we had help, however briefly.'

'There's a difference, though,' Evelyn insisted. 'We've made our home here. We've invested time and money and energy into Porthsteren. All year round. Just like Claudia has. Those girls only want to cash in on the tourist trade and run.'

Claudia shrugged. 'Locations like ours are seasonal, Evelyn. It's just the way it is. Not everyone can make it work all year round. It depends on the type of business, doesn't it? I guess we're lucky that we make enough in the summer to see us through the quieter months.'

Claudia reminded herself of that as she hauled her tired body up the stairs to her flat for a long shower. But as she allowed the warm water to run over her skin and the steam to envelop her senses, she could confess to herself, at least, that she didn't *feel* lucky right now.

*

When Jason called in at Healing Waves on his way home on Tuesday, Claudia said, 'Ooh, I'm glad you're here. I need to speak to you about Millie.'

'Oh?' What did Claudia have in mind now?

'I'd like to offer her a few hours in the shop on Saturdays, just for the summer. There are rules and regs because of her age, so maybe ten till three. And maybe the occasional evening helping me make soap, restock, that kind of thing. What do you think?'

Up until recently, Jason's reaction would have been, 'You must be joking!' But he didn't feel that way about Healing Waves any more. His healthy scepticism was still in place, but it had softened around the edges.

'I've been thinking about getting help for a while now,' Claudia went on. 'It might give Millie confidence. Regulars would get used to seeing her here, and I get a lot of her age group in at the weekends.'

'Okay.' It was out of his mouth before he knew it. What she'd said was persuasive, and any objections would seem petty.

'You're sure?'

He smiled at her worried expression. 'I'm not out to make Millie's life a misery just for the sake of it, Claudia. If it doesn't interfere with homework or building up a social life, it's fine by me. I appreciate you checking with me before asking her, though.' He dug into his pocket for a memory stick. 'The photos you asked for.'

'Thank you. I'm sorry I didn't think about how hard it would be for you to look through all of these.'

'That's okay. Actually, it was therapeutic. Reminded me of the good times. And it reminded me that Millie had her mum for those years, at least. That Gemma was a good mother, no matter what happened between us as a couple.'

Night after night this past week, studying the photos on his laptop, Jason had been reminded of that. And whatever Claudia was plotting to do with the photos would remind Millie, too.

He sighed at that thought. Millie already idolised her mother. It was *him* she had the problem with, *him* she blamed for their impending divorce. But Millie didn't know the full story… and she never would.

At his sigh, Claudia laid a hand on his cheek, her warm eyes sympathetic. 'So much sadness.'

The gesture seemed to surprise her as much as him – she quickly pulled her hand away. 'Okay. Well. You should ask Millie about Saturdays. Will you be at meditation tonight?'

'I thought I'd just drive Millie here and back. Have some time to myself. The photos… I'm feeling out of sorts, and I don't think meditation will do the trick.'

Claudia nodded. 'Good.'

He looked at her in surprise. 'You're not going to try and persuade me that meditation would be better for me?'

'Not at all.' Claudia gave him an encouraging smile. 'You're beginning to listen to your inner voice. That's good.'

He smiled. 'Well. See you some time.'

Back in his car, Jason sat for a moment without starting the engine. When Claudia had touched his face, so full of empathy, he'd felt… what? Caring? Attraction? Desire?

He *could* add irritation to that. Life was complicated enough. He didn't need Claudia and her hypnotic eyes making it worse.

*

Heavy showers on her Wednesday off would usually disappoint Claudia, but not today – it was a great excuse to get on with her project for Millie.

Going through the photos was harder than she'd thought it would be. After all, she'd never known Gemma – but to see a happy woman holding her baby, playing with her toddler, walking hand in hand with her soon-to-be-teen with no idea of what lay ahead… It was so sad, knowing the outcome.

It was fascinating to see how Millie had grown, yet painful to think that all these memories were for Millie to keep alive in her own head – no opportunity to chat with her mother over a coffee in years to come and say, 'Do you remember when…?'

It took Claudia all day and into the evening to choose the photos that best served her purpose, to think about the right words to match each image, then to put together her designs on her laptop. By the time she'd finished, Pudding was incandescent at the lack of attention, but he purred forgivingly when she carried him off to sleep at the bottom of the bed.

Still hyped up by working so late, Claudia's mind raced. Online printing options didn't suit what she was trying to do. She would have to go to the printing shop in Penzance that she'd used in the past for promotional material. A custom job like this wouldn't come cheap, but hopefully it would be worth it.

Even though Pudding had stealthily sneaked up from the bottom of the bed (where he was allowed) to her side (where he wasn't), it was a long while before his incessant purring and the feel of his soft fur against her arm lulled her to sleep.

In the morning, unable to bear the idea of waiting a whole week until her next day off, Claudia pinned a notice on her shop door declaring that she would be opening late, texted Sarah and Evelyn to say she was running an errand, so they wouldn't worry, and drove off to arrive at the printer's the moment they opened.

Recognising her, the owner took on her unusual project with assurances that it could be done. Beyond Claudia's wildest hopes, he told her that they were quiet and he could have it done by Friday evening. Claudia beamed at the thought that she could give the gift to Millie on Saturday… and took a deep breath as she handed over her credit card.

'I'm sure they'll love them,' the printer told her.

'They?'

He gestured to the uploaded images on his screen. 'The mother and daughter.'

Claudia didn't have the heart to dash the happy look on his face. 'I'm sure they will. Thank you.'

As she drove back to Healing Waves, she hoped she hadn't lost too many customers.

On that subject, Sarah wagged a finger at her when she popped in with Claudia's sandwich. 'One of us could have opened up for you. Why didn't you ask?

'I didn't decide till really late last night. I didn't want to trouble you.'

'It's no trouble, and you know it. Must've been important, whatever it was, for you to risk losing custom like that.'

'It was.' Even so, Claudia's shoulders sagged. She shouldn't have put a gift for Millie before her livelihood. But if she'd waited till next week to take them in, then the following week to collect… She thought about the printer's promise of Friday. It was obvious that Sarah was hurt about Claudia not asking for help. 'I need to close early tomorrow evening, too. Just half an hour. Could you…?'

'Consider it done.'

'Thank you. You're good neighbours.'

When Sarah had gone, Claudia looked at her sandwich without interest. She hated that she was still second-guessing their friendship like this.

*

Claudia tried her best to make sure that Millie's first Saturday at Healing Waves was varied, but if nothing else, it had kept her out of Hester's Cauldron.

At three o'clock, Millie's finishing time, Claudia asked, 'Was today okay?'

'It was great!' Her enthusiasm reassured Claudia – she still regretted their awkward ending to the soap-making, when Millie had looked so disappointed with Claudia's take on Amber and Raven.

'You're happy to do it every week?'

'Yeah. Especially as it means extra pocket money. Granny Jennifer isn't pleased about it, though.'

'Oh? Why not?'

'She said she thought the whole idea of us moving down here was so they'd see me more.'

Claudia remembered Jason saying that his in-laws could be emotionally intense because Millie was their closest connection to their late daughter.

'Do *you* want to see them more?' she asked.

'I suppose, but Gran wants me to go for whole weekends sometimes, and now I have this job, that scuppers it, so she's mad with Dad for allowing it.'

Poor Jason. He can't win. Gives way to his daughter and ends up alienating his in-laws.

'Well, you finish here at three, so on those weekends, your dad could drive you there straight after, then bring you back Sunday evening. Perhaps twenty-four hours is enough?'

Millie thought about it. 'You're right. Gran and Grandad can be a bit much. Especially after… you know, after Mum.'

Pleased – for once – that there were no customers in the shop, Claudia said, 'Listen, Millie, before you go, I want to say I'm sorry if I annoyed you the other night about Hester's Cauldron. I know it's fun in there. I just didn't want you buying…' *'Something you don't understand' is too patronising, Claudia.* '…something that isn't right for you. You know I like *my* customers to end up with the right thing.'

'I know. I told Jessica and Phoebe what you said so they'd be careful, too.'

Ah. Hmm. 'So we're good?'

'We're good.'

'I'm glad, because I have a present for you. Come through for a second.'

In the back room, Claudia handed her a purple velvet bag, its drawstring pulled tight.

'Thank you!' Loosening the drawstring, Millie reached inside. 'Oracle cards? I love the design on the back.' She traced a finger over the swirls of sea blues, a design that Claudia had created herself, then turned the cards over. At the sight of the first one, her lip quivered.

Praying she'd done the right thing, Claudia kept an eye through to the shop, waiting silently as Millie studied each photograph and its message. By the time she'd finished, tears were openly falling, making a mess of her mascara.

Claudia handed her a tissue. 'I'm sorry I made you cry.'

Millie shook her head. 'These are amazing. I can't believe you made them for me.'

'Well, I designed them, but I had a printer make them.'

'I can use them like ordinary oracle cards?'

'That's the idea. Maybe a card a day at first, each morning before you start your day or each evening before bed.' Claudia felt a little tearful herself. 'I wanted you to know that your mum didn't leave you, Millie. She's still with you. She always will be.'

The tissues couldn't keep up with Millie's tears. She reached for another. 'After Mum died, I tried looking at photos, but it was too hard. But maybe one a day… Thank you so much!' She flung her arms around Claudia's neck and clung tight. Claudia hugged her back, profound relief flooding her body that her gift had been well-received.

Until Jason finds out…

Claudia knew she should have spoken to him about her plans, but she couldn't bear the thought of him pouring cold water on the idea.

'I cleansed them for you,' she told Millie. 'But since I handled them to do that, you should do it again yourself, and then every so often.'

Millie looked guilty. 'I just stored the other set with the rose quartz.'

Claudia smiled. 'That's okay. You can put them on your windowsill when there's a full moon, too. Best not tell your dad about that one, though. Let me know how you get on with them.'

'I will. Bye.'

'Bye, Millie. See you next Saturday, if not before.'

Claudia was buoyed by Millie's reaction to the cards, but the rest of the afternoon's lack of customers gave her too much time to brood.

Would Jason be mad with her? That would be a shame, now they were getting on better.

And then there was the small matter of Millie telling her friends what Claudia had said about Hester's Cauldron. Had *they* said anything to anyone? She'd been as cautious as possible with Millie, but anything you said could be misconstrued around here.

When Alice came through the door, Claudia suppressed a sigh. She could do with someone to uplift her, but Alice tended to have the opposite effect.

'Hi, Claudia. I wanted to say thanks for the pen. It works fine. Writes nicely.'

For a moment, Claudia couldn't think what she meant. 'Oh. Glad you like it. How's the journal coming along?'

Alice frowned. 'The notes. I was writing up notes.'

Come on, Claudia, think before you speak. 'Sorry. I forgot. What can I do for you today?'

'I wanted to return the favour.' Alice looked more uncomfortable than usual, if that were possible. 'I thought you should know that people are saying things about you.'

Not this again. 'What things?'

'About how you don't like the new shop. That you don't like the women running it.'

Nothing new, then. 'That isn't quite true. You know what Porthsteren's like, Alice. Someone overheard something they shouldn't have, and they took it out of context.' *Although not much.* 'Then it gets passed around like Chinese Whispers.'

'You don't hate Hester's Cauldron?'

'Hate's a very strong word, so no, I don't hate it.' Claudia didn't want to have to explain her views to Alice. That would only mean yet another person who knew what she thought. She switched the emphasis. 'Have *you* been in there yet?'

'You must be joking! George already hates me coming in here. He'd have a *fit* if he heard I'd been in a *witch* shop!' Alice's cheeks flushed. 'No offence about Healing Waves, Claudia. You know *I* love it here.'

'Don't worry. George is like half the men in Porthsteren, I expect. Thanks for popping in, Alice.' *You've made my day, as usual.*

When Alice had left, Claudia let out a long sigh. *That poor, unhappy woman.* Claudia knew what it was like to not be your own person. Her heart went out to her.

*

'Did you buy something yesterday?' Jason asked when he went to Millie's room to check she'd packed for school and caught her putting something back in a velvet pouch.

'No. It's a gift from Claudia.'

She looked shifty, and for the thousandth time Jason regretted that his daughter felt she couldn't talk to him any more. It had been like pulling teeth trying to find out if she'd enjoyed her first Saturday at Healing Waves the day before.

He put on a positive tone. 'Oh? What is it?'

Millie hesitated. 'Oracle cards. Personalised ones, just for me.'

'Oracle cards?' Suspicion crept into his voice.

'Yes.' Millie narrowed her eyes. 'I thought Claudia explained all this to you?'

'She did.'

'So?'

Jason tried to lighten things. 'So, I could take you to a taxidermist and have him explain it to you, but I wouldn't expect you to agree with what he does or sells.'

'*Really?* You're comparing Claudia to someone who stuffs dead animals now?'

'Okay. Bad comparison. Especially for a vegetarian. You won't tell her, will you?'

Millie snorted out a laugh before she could stop herself.

Pleased with this small achievement, Jason ventured, 'Can I see them?'

'You're not supposed to handle them.' She shrugged. 'I suppose I can cleanse them again. But don't pass on too many bad vibes, okay?'

Jason grunted. *That* was an ask too far. Claudia may have talked him down on the evils of oracle cards, but she knew how he felt about them, so why had she given Millie a deck?

He started to flick through them, slowing down when he realised what they were. Gemma cuddling her baby girl. Gemma and Millie laughing uproariously together. Shots to remind Millie of a particular day – the beach, the funfair, the garden. And on each, a short caption that fitted the photo and might act as a mantra for Millie's day, from 'Remember to smile' to 'You are always loved' to 'Laughter is the best medicine'. The reverse of the cards was a soothing swirl of blues, presumably designed by Claudia, and they were printed on high quality, glossy card.

'Claudia designed them, then had them printed at a proper place,' Millie said proudly. Trepidation crept into her voice. 'Are you upset about them?'

Jason shook his head, still in awe. How could he possibly be upset? It must have cost Claudia a fortune to have these individually printed. And he couldn't imagine how many hours she'd spent designing them.

Maybe he should embrace Claudia's eccentricities more; see past them to the woman behind them. They were Claudia, and she was them. If you wanted her as a friend, you had to take the whole Claudia.

Jason *did* want Claudia as a friend. And with a rush that crept from his toes to his head, he knew with unnerving certainty that he might want her as something more than that.

Chapter Fourteen

Feeling guilty that he'd skipped the previous week, Jason allowed Millie to drag him to meditation on Tuesday.

'Any easier this time?' Claudia asked him as they drank tea afterwards.

'Yes, it was better.' Jason had enjoyed the guided meditation she'd chosen – a walk through a cool forest to a ruined temple – and he felt relaxed. It was certainly better than a night at home ploughing through the surveyor's report on his desk. 'How did Millie get on, on Saturday?'

'Really well. It helps that she's so enthusiastic about the stock.' Claudia's mouth twitched when Jason winced at that. 'She was polite with the customers, and we had a few kids her age coming in. Some of them with Hester's Cauldron bags, but that can't be helped. Anyway, Millie chatted with them all. I think it's going to work out.'

'Thank you for asking her.'

'Thank you for letting her.'

More importantly, Jason wanted to thank Claudia for Millie's oracle cards, but he was scuppered by Libby butting in, then Millie tugging at his sleeve because she had to get back to finish her homework, so he had no option but to leave it for now, which would mean contacting Claudia some other time. Whether that was a good or a bad thing, he wasn't sure.

As they left, he glanced back to see Claudia walking over to Evelyn, leaving him with the vision of her hips swaying under the loose linen tunic over her cotton trousers. Tight clothes left little to the imagination. Those floaty things Claudia wore only tempted the imagination.

Stop it, Jason.

'What do you think about asking Claudia for dinner some time?' he asked Millie as they drove home, keeping his voice as nonchalant as he could. He didn't want Millie reading anything into it that wasn't there.

'Claudia? For dinner?' A pause, then, 'Why? Do you *fancy* her?'

Jason almost snapped out a 'no', but that might seem like a case of protesting too much.

'It's not that,' he said carefully. 'Do grow up a bit, Millie.'

'Why, then?'

'You spend a lot of time with her, and now you're working for her. I thought it might be good for the three of us to spend an evening together. Get to know each other better.'

'Can you get through an evening without arguing about her shop or whatever else you don't agree with?'

Jason bit back a sharp rebuke. 'Claudia and I have come to an understanding. A social evening might build on that.'

'Okay. Do you want me to cook? I could make my veggie Bolognese.'

'No, thanks. Last time you cooked that, it looked like there'd been a tomato massacre in our kitchen.' He parked in the drive. 'Can you pop into Healing Waves tomorrow after school and ask her?'

Millie shook her head. 'Drama, remember? Then I'm off to Phoebe's.' She smirked. 'You'll have to do your own dirty work.'

*

Having spent her previous Wednesday off making Millie's oracle cards with rain drumming at the windows, Claudia was pleased to wake to sunshine this time. Salt air in her lungs, the feel of the sand beneath her toes… *Mmm.* Perhaps a mooch around a few shops and galleries? St Ives could deliver all those requirements. Afterwards, she could drive straight to Falmouth for her evening with Tanya.

St Ives was one of Claudia's favourite places. Yes, it was busy and yes, it attracted the tourists – a good reason to visit midweek in May rather than on an August weekend. But there was no denying its beauty. No wonder it had attracted so many artists across the years – the colours were uniquely exquisite.

Pleased to get a parking spot at the Porthgwidden end of town, Claudia enjoyed a coffee looking out over the beach before wending her way towards the harbour, dropping in at any shops or galleries that took her fancy. So many talented artists, so many things she loved that she had to promise herself she was only window-shopping.

Maybe I could learn ceramics or how to paint. One day…

Picking up a sandwich, she walked right to the other end of town and Porthminster beach. Sandals in hand, she had to go quite a way before finding a spot that would give her the peace and quiet she craved – given any decent weather at all, Porthminster was always busy. The view out to perfect blue sea and sky, the feel of the so-pale sand between her toes… *Bliss.* When she'd finished her sandwich, she rolled her sweatshirt into a pillow and lay back, closing her eyes.

Yes, bliss…

Her phone's ringtone startled her out of a light doze.

It was Sarah. 'Claudia, honey, I'm sorry to interrupt your day off…'

Claudia sat up, squinting against the sun. 'What's wrong? Are you alright?'

'Yes, honey, we're fine, but there's been a thing…'

'What kind of thing?'

'Evie popped into the General Store, and Libby had the radio on as usual, and the Hester's women were doing an interview with that Ollie somebody who does the local business news every Wednesday morning, and… It's not good, honey.'

Claudia's heart had sunk so low, it was threatening to be absorbed by the sand beneath her feet. 'What kind of not good?'

'They were touting their new business – free advertising, I guess – but the interview took a turn, and you were mentioned. You didn't come out of it well.'

Claudia's sandwich threatened to come back up as her stomach churned. 'What did they say?'

'Evie only heard a snippet. But Libby pointed out that we could listen to it on catch-up, which was what *she* was planning to do.'

I bet she was. 'Is it popular, that show?'

'I don't know, but businesses in Porthsteren often have the radio on in the background. And I suppose people might spot it later on social media and catch up. And if Libby tells everyone…'

Claudia tried to even out her breathing. 'Have you and Evelyn listened?'

There was a long pause. 'Yes. You need to listen to it yourself, Claudia, and work out how to deal with it. I didn't want to spoil your day off, but… Well.'

Only then did it filter through to Claudia's brain that it was the Page Turner's closing day, too. 'This has spoiled *your* day off,' she stated numbly.

'Not as much as yours, honey. I'm so sorry.'

'Thank you for letting me know. I'll head back.'

Claudia thought about listening to the broadcast on her phone, right there on the beach, but it sounded like it might be best done in the quiet of her home with her feline ally at her side. Sarah wasn't prone to exaggeration.

The trek back along the beach and through town took forever, and Claudia no longer drew any pleasure from her surroundings. Walking fast, her breathing laboured, her mind ran through a hundred scenarios.

As she drove back to Porthsteren, she told herself it might not be as bad as she imagined.

She was wrong.

With a pre-emptive soothing herbal tea at her side, Pudding on her lap and her laptop on the sofa, Claudia searched online for the interview, then listened impatiently to the pre-interview chatter and adverts until – finally – the show's presenter, Ollie Barton, introduced Amber and Raven as the owners of the most exciting thing to happen to Porthsteren for years.

Hmmph.

For the first ten minutes, the women chattered about their vision for the shop; how they had planned its décor and layout; the lack of a similar shop in nearby places leading people of all ages to flock to them. Claudia could live with that.

And then Ollie asked whether they had been welcomed by the other business owners in the village. They had, the women told him, with one exception – the owner of a New Age shop who had visited Hester's Cauldron once and denounced them to whoever would listen ever since.

Shocked, Claudia took deep breaths.

Ollie decided this was an avenue worth exploring. Amber and Raven did a sterling job of sounding affronted and hard done to, saying that all they wanted was to serve the local community…

What, for just six months of the year?

…and although they understood that not everyone would like Hester's Cauldron, they were surprised that someone who purported to be 'alternative' themselves would make such vicious attacks on their livelihood, warn teenage customers to steer clear and go so far as to say they were frauds.

Ollie had obviously been taken in by the two women and made no effort to keep the interview impartial. He could have asked, 'How do we know you're *not* frauds?' or, at the very least, 'How would you reassure your customers that you're not?' But he didn't bother – although, perhaps worried that the conversation was becoming one-track, he did stir himself enough to take it back to what they sold, their opening times and so on, before wishing them every success and sincerely hoping the odd *naysayer* wouldn't deter them in their new venture.

Claudia shut her laptop and closed her eyes, listening for the sound of the waves and the windchimes outside. She tried to breathe, long and deep. She couldn't. Everything she'd worked so hard for was crashing down around her ears, and she had no idea how to stop it.

She was hyperventilating, she knew, but she couldn't seem to stop it. Alarmed, Pudding hopped off her lap and sat beside her, staring. The knock at the door barely registered with her.

Pudding jumped off the sofa, ran to the door, leapt up onto the windowsill beside it and mewed, plaintively and very loudly. The door opened. In six strides, Jason was on his knees in front of her.

'What is it?'

'I can't… can't breathe.'

He held her by the arms. 'Yes, you can. You *are* breathing. You just need to do it slower.'

Claudia gasped, but it felt like none of the air reached her lungs.

Jason gripped her harder, his fingers digging in. 'Claudia, focus on my face. Breathe with me, okay? Slowly. In. Now out. Again. Slow down. With me.'

Five minutes later, he'd pushed a glass of water into her hands and was kneeling in front of her again, concern etched across his face.

'What the hell was that about?'

Shakily, Claudia brushed hair from her face. 'It was stupid. I *know* not to do that. I know *how* not to. But I wasn't expecting…' She sighed. 'It's been a long time. I used to have them, but I learned not to. I'm sorry.'

'Don't apologise. Millie used to have panic attacks when her mother was ill, and after she died.' He got to his feet. 'I'll make tea, then you can tell me about it.'

Jason made her chamomile tea. He listened to her incoherent rambling. He listened to the interview with her. He swore volubly and frequently.

'They make it sound like you've bad-mouthed them to *everyone*!' Jason said. 'And you spoke to, what, less than half a dozen people? In private.'

'It's so unfair,' Claudia complained. 'I *know* none of the people I spoke to said anything. How do they get from one overheard comment to everyone in Porthsteren thinking I don't approve?'

Jason's expression was grim. 'I wonder if mentioning you was planned?'

'Surely not. It's hardly to their advantage to have it broadcast that someone says they're frauds, is it?'

'No… But if they know that people have already heard that, it *is* to their advantage to shift the focus onto you. They come across as young, innocent victims; they portray you as older, bitter…'

Unable to sit still, Claudia got up and paced the room. 'What the hell am I supposed to do now? Porthsteren is my whole *world*, Jason. I worked so hard to build up my business, my place in the community. I can't watch that slide away. I just can't!' Her breathing quickened again.

'Stop that!' Jason waited while she slowed it down, then said, 'You need to work out how to respond.'

'But all I can do is reassure people that I meant no harm, that I *do* wish those women well, that I'm not saying they *are* frauds…'

'That's my fault,' Jason said quietly.

She shook her head. 'The choice of word was unfortunate, but they could've picked up on so much more of what I've said.'

'Claudia, what Ollie said about you warning off teenagers… You don't think that was Millie?'

'No.' That, at least, was something Claudia felt confident about. 'But she told Phoebe and Jessica what I said. They could've passed it on.'

'I'm sorry. You were only trying to do me a favour.'

'Not just you. Millie, too.' Claudia jumped as her mobile rang and looked at the caller ID. 'Tanya. Oh no! What time is it? I'm supposed to go over there this evening. But not yet. I…'

'Just breathe, for crying out loud, and give me the phone.'

Jason took it from her, answered it and stepped outside. Claudia heard him murmuring. She couldn't feel mad at his high-handedness – she was too drained to care.

It was five minutes before he came back in. 'Under no circumstances are you driving to Falmouth tonight. Tanya will come here. She heard some of the interview on her car radio, but she couldn't listen to the whole thing until she got home. She was ringing to see if you knew about it. I filled her in. She's setting off now. She'll be with you as soon as she can.'

Claudia smiled, grateful that he'd sorted it out for her. 'Thank you.'

'You're welcome. Well, I'll leave you to it. You need to get your equilibrium back before Tanya gets here. Maybe you could have a rest or a shower. Use some of those aromatherapy thingies.'

Claudia couldn't help but smile. 'I'll do that.' Following him to the door, she asked, 'Jason, why did you come? Don't tell me you're psychic and knew I was having a panic attack?'

'Ha. No. It was Pudding that alerted me to that. Good job, too. I would've assumed you were out and left.' He bent to stroke the cat winding around Claudia's ankles. 'I *would* have a go at you for leaving your door unlocked all the time, but I have a feeling that breaking through a solid door isn't as easy as the movies would have us think.' He smiled. 'It doesn't matter why I popped by. You're in no fit state. I'll catch you another time.'

She laid a hand on his arm. 'No. Tell me.'

'Okay, well, I came about the oracle cards you gave to Millie.'

Here we go again. Claudia steeled herself for a lashing of disapproval.

But Jason said, 'I came to thank you. They're beautiful and thoughtful. And time-consuming, I imagine.'

Claudia smiled with relief at being on the receiving end of his praise instead of his temper. 'We can always find time for something, if it's important to us.'

'Millie's important to you?'

Claudia hesitated. Jason worried about her influence over his daughter; about the amount of time they spent together. She didn't want him to think that she was trying to usurp him in Millie's affections. Nothing could be further from the truth.

Carefully, she said, 'Millie's welfare and happiness are on my priority list, yes.'

'That's good to know. And I… Millie and I were wondering if you'd like to come to dinner some time?'

Claudia's mind raced. A meal, a planned evening, instead of an impromptu bumping-into? 'Er. That would be lovely. Thank you.'

'Would Sunday be okay? Say, six thirty? You finish earlier, so you won't have to rush.'

'I'll be there. Should I bring anything?'

He gave her a reassuring smile. 'Don't worry, I won't serve you raw steak. Just bring yourself. No cat.'

With a smile, he turned and left, leaving Claudia with more questions than answers.

*

Jason had only dropped by Claudia's to issue his dinner invitation. He'd forgotten that Healing Waves closed on Wednesdays and had felt awkward about trying her flat – which was ridiculous, since he'd been there before. He would have left after he had knocked, if it hadn't been for the cat frightening him half to death by leaping onto the windowsill, a look of concern – was that possible? – in his amber eyes.

Claudia's panic attack hadn't worried Jason. What *had* worried him was that the Claudia he knew was usually calm, positive and occasionally steely. He didn't like that this thing with Hester's Cauldron had got to her so badly.

When Phoebe's mother dropped Millie home after dinner, Jason was hoping for a quiet evening with his daughter, maybe some TV. But Millie was in a difficult mood. Again. Her maths teacher was an idiot; Jessica had said something about her to Phoebe that she shouldn't have; school uniform rules were stupid… His brain hurt from listening to it all. By the time he'd battled his way through a desultory cup of tea with her, he needed air, and the fact that it was dark out made no difference to him.

Leaving Millie to sulk or muck about on her phone to well past an acceptable bedtime, Jason strolled down to the harbour, its lights twinkling on the dark water, then along the beach towards Healing Waves. He was still worried about Claudia.

Walking around to the road side of the building, he saw Tanya's car. Good. Claudia had support. Back on the beach side, he glanced up to see candlelight. Indistinct murmuring drifted through the open window, combining with the light jangle of the windchimes outside to create an unworldly kind of sound. For all he knew, those two were doing all sorts of weird spells up there.

Ah, well. As long as Claudia sticks to making just soap with Millie in that cauldron of hers.

*

Sarah and Evelyn were solicitous and kind over coffee the following morning. When Claudia had texted them after Jason left to say she'd listened to the interview, they'd offered to drive over, but she'd told them that Tanya was on the way.

'I couldn't believe it!' Sarah huffed as she handed Claudia her decaff latte. 'The nerve!'

Claudia shrugged. 'They were asked if they'd been welcomed in Porthsteren and they answered.'

'Yeah, in a totally loaded way. You're being very calm about it, I must say.'

'I wasn't yesterday. I had a panic attack,' Claudia admitted. 'The first in a long time. It was… disappointing.'

'Was Tanya with you?'

'No. She came by later. Jason happened to pop by. He was a godsend – he did all the right things.'

At this, Sarah and Evelyn both raised eyebrows. But when Evelyn opened her mouth, Sarah placed a quieting hand on her arm.

'That's good, honey. I'm glad someone was there. So, what are you going to do by way of a comeback? You have a right to reply. Those women have cast aspersions about you.'

'And so have I about them. I don't want to dig myself deeper. Best to let it lie and hope it goes away. People will get bored, soon enough.'

But none of them looked convinced about that.

Business was quiet at Healing Waves that day – and the next. Too quiet to be a coincidence. Oh, she had tourists browsing, but locals were sparse on the ground, and those that came only wanted to talk about the radio interview.

Claudia did her best to pour oil on troubled waters – it was a private conversation, overheard; it had been taken out of context; she welcomed new businesses to Porthsteren; she wished Amber and Raven every success. *Bla bla bla.*

But people wouldn't let it be. What did she think of what they sold at Hester's Cauldron? What did she think of Amber and Raven? *Why* did she think they were frauds?

What on earth was Claudia supposed to say? She tried saying that the shop looked great; she explained that she was pro-Wicca and her best friend was a Wiccan. But whenever someone pushed her on the 'fraud' comment – a strong word she would never have come up with if Jason hadn't – all she could say was that she felt they were a tad inexperienced. If that fanned the flames, then so be it. She *really* couldn't bring herself to say they were experts about everything they sold.

By Friday afternoon, Claudia could have wept. She'd moved to Cornwall to be true to herself, but with trying to smooth things over about Hester's, more or less lying about what she thought, justifying herself and her own store while trying not to malign theirs, she was drifting a long way from that.

A visit from Alice felt like the last straw.

'I heard the radio interview,' Alice said. 'You told me you didn't hate Hester's last time I was here.'

Accusatory *and* glum. *Great.*

'And that was the truth,' Claudia reassured her, following up with her usual spiel, so well-practised that she could have done it in her sleep.

'Well, George agreed with you, for a change,' Alice grunted. 'Said you were quite right. Purveyors of rubbish.'

That was all Claudia needed – Alice's George on her side. *When will this week ever end?*

'That isn't what I said at all,' she said, reining in her temper. 'As I just explained.' *Give me strength.*

But Alice was staring into the distance. 'I wish I could go in there,' she said, almost to herself. 'I'd love to see what all the fuss is about.'

'Then why don't you?' Claudia asked, already knowing the answer but past caring, her nerves frayed to breaking point.

'I told you before. George wouldn't like it.' Alice glared at Claudia. 'And now you've done a hatchet job on those women, he'd like it even less, wouldn't he?'

Hatchet job? Claudia could have lost her temper at that. But what concerned her more was that a woman she knew, a woman who regularly frequented her shop and came to meditation every week, daren't enter a shop without her husband's permission.

She reached for patience. 'Alice, you can tell me to mind my own business, but is everything okay between you and George?'

A panicked look came into Alice's eyes. 'Everything's fine. Why would you think it wasn't?' When Claudia said nothing, she hurried on. 'George has his ways, that's all. Has his views. Best to keep my own views to myself. Easier that way.' Her smile was brittle. 'You know what men are like.'

'Yes. All the same, aren't they?' Claudia swiftly changed the subject. 'How are your notes coming along?'

'Notes?' Alice looked puzzled, then shifty. 'Oh! Er. Good, thanks. Once I got started, I couldn't stop.'

'That's good.' *And odd.*

'Well. Must go. Bye.'

Claudia had never seen Alice move so fast as she scuttled out the door.

Oh, Claudia, why did you have to stick your nose in where it wasn't wanted?

Because I'm worried about her.

Have you seen anything concrete to make you worry, really? Bruises?

No. Nothing like that. But…

You don't know what goes on between two people.

But she's so unhappy!

Yes. But it's not your business.

How could the unhappiness of someone I know not be my business? I can at least keep my eye on her, can't I?

Chapter Fifteen

Sunday evening saw Jason well-prepared for their dinner with Claudia. He'd found a vegetarian recipe he thought he could pull off, bought the ingredients, chilled the wine, ironed a shirt. All was well. Until…

'Dad? Jessica's asking me to go to the cinema tonight with her and a couple of others. Her dad'll drive us. I told her we had someone coming for dinner, but…'

Jason's mind raced. He could see that Millie didn't want to let him down and land him in the proverbial soup, but she'd spent the day before with Claudia at her Saturday job, and she needed to cement these new friendships from school. He couldn't let her turn this down.

'We'll be fine. Tell them you can go.'

'Sure?'

'Sure.'

'Thanks. And Jessica says I can stay the night if I take my school stuff with me.'

Jason was less keen on that, but Millie hadn't been inundated with invitations, and this was the first for a sleepover.

'On a school night?'

'Don't worry. Jessica says her mum'll put her foot down.'

Good old Jessica's mum. 'Okay.'

'Thanks!' Millie shot off to make arrangements, leaving Jason to damp down panic.

As he began cooking, he noticed his hand was lightly shaking – not ideal, with a sharp knife in his grip – and recognised that he was nervous. Millie deserting him had suddenly turned a family threesome into a cosy twosome.

It's a simple dinner, Jason. How complicated can it be?

Who was he kidding? Everything about Claudia was complicated, including this attraction he was trying so hard to ignore.

It wasn't only the way she looked – although, heaven knew, she could knock him for six if he allowed her to. He found her tenacity attractive, too. Her quietly assertive manner, her empathy, her vivacity.

Jason had felt hemmed in for so long by his downward-spiralling marriage, the responsibility for bringing up a child, dealing with Gemma's death… Sometimes it felt like he could barely breathe. The sea air was helping. The challenge of his new job was (mostly) helping. But it was still there, that weight.

Claudia had been like a breath of fresh air in his confined existence.

As he stirred chilli powder into the pot, questioning how spicy she'd like it – *Stop right there, Jason. Don't allow* that *thought to wander* – he wondered if she'd always been that way, or whether she'd cultivated it.

If the latter, he sure as hell wished she'd tell him how.

*

When Claudia knocked on the door of the Craig house, she was less nervous than on the last occasion. At least she'd been invited this time. And she bore no unwanted gifts – merely wine and elderflower cordial.

Jason opened the door in his trademark off-duty jeans, faded and fitting familiarly to his thighs. A smart, grey shirt was a nod to expecting company.

'Claudia. Come on in. Thanks.' Jason took her offerings and glanced at the labels, presumably with relief that she hadn't brought any home-brewed concoctions, then led her through to the open-plan kitchen and lounge.

'Wow!' Claudia looked around in awe. It was a fabulous space, with vaulted ceilings and wood floors and swathes of glass letting in light.

'You like it?'

'Ha! You've seen my flat, Jason.'

'I like your flat. It's very you.'

'Thank you.' Claudia wandered the room, taking in the Scandinavian-style furniture; pieces of pottery and glass dotted here and there; muted rugs. No clutter, but she supposed that was the idea with a new start.

From the patio doors, she could see the incredible view she'd imagined this place would have.

'Would you like to take a look outside?' Jason asked.

'What kind of stupid question is that?' Claudia stepped out onto the decking. '*Oh*.' Her breath left her with a whoosh as she looked out over the sea, calm and turquoise, navy in places where seaweed darkened it, the white froth of the waves, a sail in the distance, gulls wheeling overhead. 'This is *perfect*.'

'I know. I couldn't believe my luck, finding this place.'

Claudia walked across the decking to the railing and peered over to where trees and shrubs stretched down in a gentle slope. The house was well away from the cliff edge – a good thing, she reckoned, after seeing a recent documentary about coastal erosion. Some of the houses she spotted on her walks looked like they might tumble into the sea at any moment.

'It's safe enough,' Jason said at her shoulder.

As though he can read my mind. 'I'm sure it is.' She turned to him. 'I shouldn't think an architect would take any risks.'

He smiled. 'Not that kind, anyway.'

Anxious not to concentrate on how Jason looked when he actually smiled, Claudia took in the rest of the outside space. On either side of the decking, large pots nestled in shimmering white gravel that stretched to border beds of shrubs, ferns and grasses.

'No lawn, I'm afraid. This was a holiday home – easy maintenance. Suits me for now.'

'This was only a *holiday* home?'

'You've lived down here for a while. You know how it works.'

She did, but Claudia could never get her head around people having enough money to own somewhere this size, in this position, done out in the excellent way it was, as a second home. It must have cost a fortune.

That thought brought her up short. How much did architects *make* nowadays? Not that it was any of her business.

But it seemed Jason was still reading her mind. 'It's not something I could have afforded,' he admitted. 'But Gemma's life insurance was left to me. You know how quickly properties get snapped up around here – I was struggling to find anywhere. Then my new boss told me a property they'd renovated was going up for sale and was I interested in taking a look?'

'Serendipity,' Claudia murmured.

'If you believe in that kind of thing. Anyway, I couldn't resist.'

'I can see why. It's glorious.'

'It's bigger than I'd've chosen, but Millie and I need space from each other. I fancied living right by the coast – I was done with city living. Millie loves it. Plus, it'll be easy to sell if things don't work out.'

Claudia saw the doubt and worry in his eyes. Jason had taken a huge leap of faith.

She touched his arm. 'I hope it does.'

'Thanks.' Jason cleared his throat. 'Millie told me she enjoyed working with you yesterday.'

'I enjoy having her with me.'

'Good. I hope she thanked you properly for those oracle cards. I still can't get over how much effort you made.'

'She told me yesterday that she uses them every morning before school and every night before bed. That's the only thanks I need.'

Jason nodded, a sad smile at his lips. 'That's more than she's told me, then. But I'm glad.' Another hesitation. 'She said Healing Waves was quiet yesterday.'

'Yes.' So quiet for a Saturday, Claudia had had Millie slicing the soap she'd spent her evenings making since the Hester's radio interview, too unsettled to relax.

'Do you think it's to do with the radio thing?' he asked.

'I'd love to say no, but the locals are staying away. Those that do come only want to interrogate me.'

'I told Millie about the interview,' Jason said. 'I hope you don't mind, but with her working there…'

'That's fine.' Claudia let out a long sigh. 'Jason, can I ask a favour? I know you were concerned about me the other night, and I'm grateful you were there, but can we ban all talk of Hester's Cauldron tonight? I need to think about something else.'

He smiled. 'No problem.'

Talk of Millie had made Claudia conscious of her absence. 'Where *is* Millie?'

'Ah.' Jason gave her a sheepish look. 'She got a last-minute invite to the cinema and a sleepover. I didn't want her to turn it down.'

'No. Of course not. She should go out with her friends.'

'I hope you don't mind.' Jason seemed suddenly nervous. 'Now that it's just the two of us, I mean.'

Still processing the idea that they'd gone from a trio to a couple, Claudia said, 'I'm sure we'll manage.'

Jason gave her a knowing look. 'Shall I get you a glass of wine before you bolt for the door?'

'Do I look like I might?'

He grinned. 'Yes, you do.'

*

Jason survived dinner alone with Claudia.

They had wine outside first, the breeze balmy, the decking sheltered, enjoying the colours of the sea, muted in the evening light. Suspecting that Claudia would need more than her one glass allowance now she knew that Millie was no longer acting as chaperone, Jason suggested that he walk her home and she could collect her car tomorrow. He stuck to his promise not to mention Hester's Cauldron, and instead they chatted about his job and Millie's school. Claudia claimed to enjoy his vegetarian offering of Mediterranean risotto, and when he refused to let her help with the dishes, they settled with more wine in the lounge.

He watched as she folded her legs beneath her, her long, pale blue skirt draping across the sofa. 'How on earth do you *do* that?'

'Yoga.'

Jason winced. 'Always looks painful to me – all that twisting into unnatural poses.'

'You should try it. It's the perfect excuse for me-time.'

'Is that important to you?'

'Yes. I believe it's important to do things for yourself and not for others all the time.'

'You do plenty for others, Claudia. You don't even charge for meditation.'

'I'm happy to give back to the locals. They welcomed me into their community and supported my shop. If I can help people relax, relieve their stress…'

'And what about that crystal workshop that Millie attended? A fiver each barely covers the cost of tea and biscuits.'

'Ah, but they could buy all the crystals they wanted – or as you'd probably have it, goods they were coerced into thinking they wanted – so it's a good business strategy.'

Jason shook his head. 'I don't think you coerce anyone into anything. I *do* think you're very persuasive about the things you believe in, but that's different.' He headed back to safer waters. 'What else do you do besides yoga? For yourself, that is?'

Claudia sipped her wine. 'I walk a lot. I can't get enough of the scenery down here. I like to cook fresh food. I enjoy the company of my friends. I love owning my own business, deciding how it might change and grow, knowing it earns me a modest living. I love handmaking the soap, some of the jewellery.' She frowned when he didn't say anything. 'Does that answer your question?'

Actually, it only throws up a million more.

She gave him a curious look. 'What do *you* do just for yourself?'

That had him stumped. 'I enjoy my work. The rest is all about…'

'Millie?'

'Yes.'

'Jason, you're spending all your energies on building a life for Millie, encouraging her social life and interests outside school. Shouldn't you do the same for yourself?'

'I'll get to myself eventually. Just being somewhere new is refreshing. It got so stifling in Edinburgh. People treated me with kid gloves after Gemma died. Only close friends and family knew about the impending divorce, and it was an odd situation for them, sympathising with a man who'd lost the wife he was about to separate from. Most people didn't know about the divorce but still had no idea what to say to a thirty-six-year-old widower with a teenage daughter to raise. Down here, it's a year on and pity is limited. I find it easier that way.'

It was freeing to be able to mention the divorce to Claudia. At first, he'd been upset that Millie had told her, but now…? Like Claudia had said of Tanya, perhaps it was good for *one* person in your new life to know about your old one.

'What about making new friends?' she asked.

'I'll make an effort. Some time. Soon.'

'Jason, it's so easy to put yourself last – to lose yourself in what others want or need.'

She knew, he thought. The look she gave him, her quiet encouragement. She *knew* he was still trapped inside himself and didn't know how to get out. How had *she* managed it?

'Why did you need a new start?' he asked, wanting to understand. 'Was it your divorce?'

She sipped her wine, the shoulder of her cream cotton top slipping off her shoulder as she shifted on the sofa. 'That was the catalyst. But it was more a sudden realisation that my marriage, my career weren't *me*. I couldn't see it when I was in the midst of it all, but one day something happened, and I knew with an amazing clarity that I couldn't do it any longer. I couldn't be that person any more. I wanted to find out who I really was and be *that* person.'

Jason was fascinated. It occurred to him that the wine might have loosened her tongue, but he wanted to know more about her. 'You had an unhappy marriage?'

'I didn't *think* I was unhappy. We both had impressive careers that bought us a swanky apartment, and we had a hectic social life, but I had no idea what was going on underneath.'

How far dare he dig? 'Which was…?'

Claudia hesitated. 'Lee liked me to be a certain way,' she said, her tone cautious.

Jason frowned. 'What do you mean?'

She shrugged. 'He liked to stay fit, and he liked me to be slim and fit, too. I never felt free to enjoy my food – it was like he was judging me whenever I put anything in my mouth. We had gym membership, and he made sure I used mine. I *hated* the gym. He had preferences about my appearance. He liked my hair straight, for example. He thought it was better for my image at work.'

Jason had been listening carefully, not wanting to interrupt now that she was opening up – but at that comment, he nearly dropped his glass.

Claudia laughed, jabbing her fingers into the wild curls haloed around her head. 'I know, right? Yes, it *was* hard work, and each hour I spent with the straighteners in my hand is an hour of my life I won't get back. I regret that *very* much.'

Jason stared at her. The riot of curls *was* Claudia. But he was beginning to get the picture.

'So now you let it do what it wants to do? Eat what you want to eat? Exercise the way that suits you – long walks along the coast and yoga?'

'You got it.'

Jason tried to envisage a skinnier, sleeker version of Claudia and failed. The Claudia in front of him was vibrant and energetic, while exuding calm and warmth. Why would that idiot Lee want a different version?

'Why was he worried about your image at work?'

She hesitated. 'We worked in the same firm and moved up the ladder together, as a team. Lee was highly ambitious, and he was keen that we maintained an attractive, professional image at all times to impress clients.'

Jason bristled. 'He used your attractiveness to get deals?'

'Anything goes in that world, Jason. Lee wanted to get onto the next rung of the ladder – he didn't worry about moral rights and wrongs when it came to his career. That didn't sit well with me.' Claudia sighed. 'And talk about arrogant! Lee thought *he* was the one sealing the deals, with me as an intelligent accessory, but he was too forceful. They could smell his ambition, and I'm not sure they trusted him. Mine was a quieter, perhaps more effective kind of persuasion. I certainly doubt it was all down to toned calf muscles or sleek hair.'

Jason took a sip of wine to quell the notion that he'd quite like to punch her ex-husband, but the alcohol only emboldened him to ask more.

'Was that why you broke up?' He made an apologetic face. 'Or shouldn't I ask?'

Claudia looked at him for the longest time, her cat's eyes penetrating, then said, 'It's okay. I want to tell you.' She sipped her wine. 'I wanted children. Lee knew that. We'd discussed it before we married, but we were busy with our careers, so it was put on hold. And that's where it stayed. He kept saying he wasn't ready. As time went by, I tried to pin him down. His excuses became thinner. And then…' Another sip of wine. 'Lee had friends over for poker once a month. They drank and behaved in a laddish manner which I hated, so I usually made sure I was out. That last time, I'd felt under the weather all day, so I cancelled my night out and stayed upstairs, out of their way. Later on, I went downstairs to boil the kettle, and as I passed the doorway…' She shook her head. 'They say you should never listen in, don't they? In case you hear something you don't like.'

'What did you hear?' Jason prompted softly.

'I heard one of his mates say, "No sprogs for you yet, Lee?" And Lee said, "Not bloody likely. She keeps nagging, but it won't get her anywhere." His pal said, "Can't avoid it forever, mate. She'll get her way in the end. Women always do."' Claudia's voice hitched. 'And Lee said, "No way. I'll keep her dangling. Keep her busy at work. She'll give up asking. Time'll run out."'

Jason couldn't believe the man's cold-heartedness. He could see the betrayal in Claudia's eyes, even now.

'You didn't ever consider…?' He stopped. *Unfair, Jason.*

'Did I consider getting pregnant deliberately? Yes, I considered it. And I dismissed it. Why would I choose to bring a child into the world knowing it wasn't wanted by its own father? Besides, Lee had that covered. Literally. He was always very careful. Anyway, three days later, I handed in my notice at work, packed my bags and left.'

'How did that go down with Lee?'

'He didn't care enough to make a fuss. And I had my freedom.'

Jason was beginning to see why Claudia prized her freedom so much. Stifled in her marriage, denied the family she wanted, persuaded to follow someone else's whims… No wonder she did her own thing now. Unable to picture her any other way, he found himself fiercely pleased that she'd escaped a man who didn't appreciate her and could be so dishonest, so selfish.

'How do you feel about him now?'

Claudia smiled sadly. 'He wasn't an abusive man, but I allowed him to have his own way; allowed his ambition to take over. I've forgiven him for not valuing who or what I was. But I am still struggling to forgive him for lying to me, for allowing me to stay with him for too long under false pretences – if he'd had his way, until I'd have little or no chance of a family. It was so calculated.'

'Did you move to Cornwall soon after?'

'No. I took a temporary job in London for a few months until the flat was sold. I used that time to think about what I wanted; tried a few different therapies.' She chuckled. 'A *lot* of different therapies. Some were helpful, some weren't. I spent so much time looking into everything, I figured I could help others with what I'd learned. And the sea was calling me. I didn't *have* to pick Cornwall, but I did want to be as far away from Lee and London as I could get. A stone's throw from Land's End seemed apt.'

Jason smiled. 'You've been through the wringer.'

'Not as badly as you. I can't imagine losing a spouse, but to have been on the verge of divorce…' Her eyes caught and held his, compelling. 'Tell me.'

Jason couldn't break the eye contact. 'Gemma and I met at the start of university. She found out she was pregnant just after graduation. I've no idea how that happened – end-of-exams drunken forgetfulness, probably. It wasn't the end of the world – we'd already been together three years, and we figured we'd've got married and had kids anyway.' He let out a breath. 'The first few years weren't easy. I had to continue studying to become a fully fledged architect, and Gemma had to establish her teaching career, both of us trying to bring in money while bringing up Millie. But we were happy enough.'

'What went wrong?'

'We were too young. People grow and mature, don't they? We might not have even got together if we'd met when we were thirty.' He sighed. 'We changed; the life we lived was too demanding. We grew apart, but we ignored it for Millie's sake.'

'But you finally decided to get a divorce?'

'Yes. We hadn't even started proceedings yet. We'd only just told Millie, close family, a couple of best friends. Then Gemma was diagnosed.' Jason stopped. The need to tell someone the *truth* of what had really happened between him and Gemma had been choked down for so long... and here was Claudia, so trusting in telling him her own painful details that he knew she'd only shared with Tanya.

What the hell, Jason. You need *to do this.*

'Gemma was having an affair,' he blurted out, watching surprise dawn on her face. 'I don't blame her. To all intents and purposes, we were finished, and she wanted something more. But nobody knew about that, not even her parents or Millie. Gemma had wanted to deliver the bad news in small doses – tell them we were planning a divorce, wait for them to absorb that, then explain about her new man. We only got as far as the first stage.' He swallowed. 'The pains Gemma had been having on and off became acute very quickly, and the doctor finally sent her for tests. It was late-stage bowel cancer.'

'Oh, Jason.' Tears pricked Claudia's eyes, golden in the lamplight.

'It was such a shock. And everything was already such a mess.' He took a moment. 'Gemma's new bloke scarpered.'

Claudia held his gaze. 'But you didn't.'

'How could I? I wouldn't have let her down like that. Millie and I coped with Gemma at home for as long as possible, but for the last few weeks, she was in a hospice. I thought Millie might break and never mend.' His voice hitched. 'But Gemma and I became friends again before she died. That was important for us, to get from where we'd been to that, at least.'

His mind drifted back to Gemma's room in the hospice. Holding hands with her for the first time in so long. The afternoon sun slanting through the window.

'Do you remember when we first met?' she'd asked him, her voice slurry from the drugs.

Jason had squeezed her hand. 'How could I forget? You had the prettiest smile in the student union that night.'

'You were pissed.'

'Guilty as charged. But I hadn't lost my eyesight.'

'When you asked me out, you stammered.'

'That was the beer. Or maybe nerves, because I was asking the hottest girl in the place out on a date.'

Gemma had smiled at that. 'You thought I was pretty *and* hot?'

'Oh yeah.'

She'd drifted back to sleep then, but the smile had stayed on her face.

Jason blinked away a tear as he brought Claudia back into focus. 'Gemma didn't deserve to die so young. Millie didn't deserve to lose her mother.'

Claudia moved to sit beside him, placing a hand against his chest. 'You never told *anyone* about Gemma's affair?'

'No. What good would it have served, other than putting Gemma in a bad light with her daughter, her parents, when she couldn't defend herself? I got enough sympathy as a grieving widower.'

'I'm betting her parents blame you for the divorce? Millie, too?'

'Yes. Her parents… Bound to happen. Isn't that the way it always works? As for Millie, we'd told her we'd grown apart, but when Gemma became ill…? Millie couldn't be angry with her mum. But she *could* be angry with me.' Claudia opened her mouth, but he cut her off before she could speak. 'And no, I won't tell her just to stop her being mad with me. I wouldn't do that to Gemma. Not ever.'

'I understand.'

'I'm not saying it isn't hard. I am saying I won't have it any other way.' Jason sighed, his chest sinking under her hand, relieved at having finally shared his burden.

Claudia squeezed him lightly, and it was only then that he truly registered her closeness. There was no danger of him taking it any other way than it was meant – the caring of an unexpected confidante. He was too emotionally exhausted. He placed his hand over hers, and they sat in understanding silence.

And for the first time in a very long while, Jason felt just a little at peace with himself.

*

By the time Jason had walked Claudia home, it was almost midnight. As they hovered at the base of her steps, he offered to come by in the morning and drive her back to her car at his house, but she said she'd walk. If she woke with a hangover, the fresh air would do her good.

As she got ready for bed, her emotions were in turmoil. A simple meal with Millie in attendance had ended up as an unchaperoned tête-à-tête with a man she had very mixed feelings about, one that gradually became an evening of revelations neither of them had seemed able to contain.

Claudia understood Jason more now. The way he was always so protective of Millie was understandable, if occasionally misguided – but knowing what he'd been through made a difference. She could only admire his self-sacrifice for the sake of Gemma's memory, and she wished Millie could see him in a kinder light. Even without the knowledge that her mother had had an affair, it was unreasonable for Millie to blame her father. But without Gemma there to take equal blame, it was understandable.

That Jason was willing to wear the villain's mantle for Millie's sake was remarkable. It made his relationship with his daughter so much harder, and he must have a will of iron not to lash out whenever Millie behaved badly towards him.

Jason had seemed better for telling Claudia, though. It had been too much for him to have carried alone, and he'd held onto it for too long.

As Claudia climbed between cool sheets, Pudding curling sleepily at her feet, she smiled at the progress she had made with Jason. With Millie moving forward, too, perhaps it wouldn't be long before father and daughter could finally understand each other. There was nothing Claudia would like to see more.

Chapter Sixteen

Jason woke with an ominous feeling of dread. At first, he couldn't put his finger on it. He'd had a successful evening with Claudia – a nice meal, a few glasses of wine. They hadn't fought once. In fact, they'd got on the whole time…

And there was the problem. As their conversation came back to him, he remembered how much he'd shared. *Too much.* He couldn't blame the wine. He'd *wanted* to tell her; to unburden himself. It was such a release to be with Claudia, willing to listen and empathise without suffocating him with pity.

But in the cold light of day, he seriously regretted that impulse to offload details that nobody could ever know. What if Claudia let something slip with Millie? What if she forgot what she was supposed to know or not know? Had he made it clear? He couldn't remember his exact words. He shouldn't have let his guard down.

By the time he'd choked down toast that tasted like cardboard, dressed and climbed into his car – noting that Claudia's was no longer parked outside – Jason had subtly managed to shift the blame onto her. She encouraged confidences, whether deliberately or not. She certainly had Millie doing the same.

Driving along the beach road, he braked sharply at Healing Waves. He needed to be sure she knew how important this was to him. How confidential.

*

Claudia was suppressing a yawn when there was a knock at the locked shop door.

'Just a minute!' *Not even opening time yet. Some people…*

She opened it to find Jason standing there, an agitated air about him, all trace of the relaxed state she'd left him in the night before gone. Claudia suppressed a sigh along with another yawn as she let him in.

'Claudia. About last night…' he began.

She couldn't help but smile.

Jason frowned. 'What's funny?'

'Think about it and be glad I don't have customers in here to spread the word.'

Claudia watched, delighted, as his cheeks reddened.

'Ah. I see. Sorry. Yes, well…'

'What about last night?'

He fidgeted, picking up a pale blue-green tumblestone from the tray nearby and rubbing it between his fingers. Claudia smiled to herself. If only he knew that amazonite could help with communication.

Jason took a deep breath and launched right in. 'Claudia, last night I shared things with you that I haven't spoken about to *anybody*. I want to reiterate that. I need to ask you to keep what I told you to yourself.'

Claudia felt like all the wind had been knocked out of her. She'd thought they'd made progress; that they'd built up a level of trust between them. Knowing he liked to keep his cards close to his chest, she'd felt safe telling him details of her own past. Didn't he feel as comfortable with her? Surely he knew that what he'd told her was safe?

And yet, here he stood.

'You don't need to ask, Jason.' She kept her voice as even as she could, although it still shook slightly with disappointment. 'I assumed the same over what I told you – things that nobody in Cornwall knows, apart from Tanya. I'm sure you'll respect my confidences, too.'

He stared at her, perhaps recognising the strain in her voice. An awkward moment passed between them.

'Of course. Thanks. Well. I should get to work.'

After he left, Claudia stared at the closed door for a long moment. She'd thought they'd taken great strides forward last night. But Jason was clearly full of regret.

*

'Claudia Bennett?'

'Yes?' The incoming call on her business mobile wasn't from a caller she recognised, but since she gave this number out on her website, that happened a lot.

'This is Ollie Barton from your local, friendly radio station. I don't know if you've heard of me?'

'Oh, I've heard of you.'

If Claudia could have heard him smirk at the other end of the line, she knew she would have.

'Did you hear the interview last week with Amber and Raven of Hester's Cauldron?'

'I heard it.' *And it feels like I've heard about nothing else since.*

'Then you may be interested in my proposition. I have a slot on our Wednesday local business news tomorrow morning. I'm offering you the right to reply. Will you take me up on it?' There was undisguised challenge in his voice.

Claudia's initial reaction was to tell him where to shove it. The thought of appearing on the radio made her feel sick with nerves. And she could make things a whole lot worse than they already were. But the logical part of her brain told her to hang fire. She needed to think it through.

'When do you need to know by?'

'First thing tomorrow morning. You'd have to be at the studio by eleven.'

'We couldn't do it by phone?'

'Sorry, Ms Bennett. I prefer to conduct my interviews face-to-face.' An unspoken 'take it or leave it' hung between them.

Claudia closed her eyes. 'I'll let you know by nine tomorrow.'

Clicking off, she dropped the phone onto the counter, glanced at her watch and flipped the 'closed' sign ten minutes early.

When she walked into the Page Turner, Evelyn looked at her in concern. 'Claudia, you're as pale as a ghost. What's the matter?'

Sarah rushed over and sat her down. Evelyn made peppermint tea and flipped their closed sign as soon as their one remaining customer left.

When Claudia had told them her tale of woe, Sarah said, 'I think you should do it.'

'But Sarah! A radio interview!'

'Claudia, you told us you used to work for some fancy firm in London. Didn't you give presentations to clients?'

'Yes.'

'This is no different.'

'But I left all that behind!'

'I know, honey, but sometimes we have to do things we don't want to, and at least you have the training and experience for it.'

Evelyn took Claudia's hand. 'If you don't go on, it'll look bad, and those girls will have won at whatever game they're playing.'

'Hmm. I'm still torn on that one,' Sarah said. 'We know they went on the radio to plug their new business. What we don't know is that they planned the verbal attack on Claudia. It might be that Ollie Wotsit happened to ask the question and they took advantage. Spontaneous, you know?'

'I'm not sure that matters any more,' Claudia pointed out. 'What matters is that all I can say on the radio is what I've been saying all week… which is at best lame and at worst barely true.'

Evelyn had been tapping at her phone. 'Claudia, I don't think you have any choice.' She turned the screen so they could see Ollie Barton's page on social media:

I invited Claudia Bennett of Healing Waves, Porthsteren to give her side of the story in the ongoing tale of rivalry between herself and Amber and Raven of newly opened Hester's Cauldron. She'll let me know. Running scared?

Claudia got up to pace around the tables of books. 'I hate that man.'

Sarah caught her hand as she went past. 'You don't hate anyone, honey. You don't have it in you.'

'I think I could cultivate the skill.' Claudia stopped and closed her eyes. 'Ugh! It's meditation tonight. People might have seen this. I'll have Libby on my back. And Alice.'

'You could cancel,' Evelyn suggested.

'That'll look worse.'

Sarah thought about it. 'Okay, here's what we'll do. Evie and I will set up. You'll walk in dead on eight, run the session, leave at nine. We'll do the tea and chat, then lock up.'

'That'll look like I'm avoiding people.'

'It would… if you didn't happen to have Tanya coming over to join in with meditation and want a glass of wine with you afterwards.'

'But she isn't.'

Sarah picked up Claudia's mobile and held it out. 'She is now.'

*

Jason was not having a good week.

He was still tired from staying up so late with Claudia on Sunday. Work had been a pain, from dealing with an incompetent sub-contractor to heated words with a colleague. And it would be an understatement to say that he and Millie were not enjoying each other's company.

He'd insisted it was time he met Phoebe and Jessica. Their parents had met Millie, so it wasn't unreasonable, was it? Millie had been damned awkward about it. Why did he want to inspect her friends? she'd asked him. Was he going to interrogate them?

Even though Jason insisted that he only wanted to say hi and provide pizza, it had taken negotiation worthy of an international peacekeeping organisation to arrange their presence at the house this evening.

Over pizza, he managed a cursory chat and ascertained that they were polite enough, if a little uncommunicative – but then again, so was half the teenage population. And they favoured a similar wardrobe to his daughter, all black and purple and heavy boots. Quite the trio.

After pizza, Millie shot him a glare, suggesting he was no longer required. When he didn't respond – he could be awkward, too, when he felt like it – she dragged her friends up to her room.

The girls' presence meant that both he and Millie were missing meditation – not a good idea soul-wise but certainly good for him embarrassment-wise, after Monday morning's shambles.

Jason could barely bring himself to think about that. He'd only meant to reiterate to Claudia that what he'd told her was confidential, in case he hadn't made it clear on the night. As usual, he'd bungled it – or she'd taken it the wrong way – and his wonderful experience of getting to know and understand her better, the relief of being with someone who seemed to want to know and understand *him* better, had gone up in smoke. He should apologise, but with his track record, he'd probably only make things worse.

Well, Millie wanted him out of the house, and he needed fresh air. His walk *could* take him towards Healing Waves. If Claudia was home from meditation early enough, he could get the damned thing done. At least it would be quick, since he had to give Jessica and Phoebe a lift home.

But when he got there, he spotted Tanya's car next to Claudia's. No way would he eat humble pie with her there. They were probably talking about him right now, dreaming up suitable hexes.

To make his evening complete, when Jason got home and knocked on Millie's bedroom door before poking his head in, he saw Phoebe shoving a book into her bag. A black book with purple lettering. A *spell* book, no doubt purchased from Hester's sodding Cauldron.

Barely able to contain his rage and disappointment, Jason forced a smile and declared it was time for them to go home. He drove without incident – no mean feat with blood pressure that high – and when he and Millie got back, he managed not to mention what he'd seen. It wasn't intended for his eyes, and he respected that.

That didn't mean he had to like it, though.

*

'Sarah and Evelyn are right,' Tanya said, a grim expression on her face as she and Claudia sipped their post-meditation Pinot Grigio in

Claudia's flat, Pudding curled on the sofa between them, lapping up Tanya's attentions. 'You have no choice.'

'I had a nasty feeling you'd say that.'

'I know you're all about *live and let live*, Claudia, but they're not doing that, are they? Nor is Ollie Barton. He's been sneaky, publicising it as a challenge so you'll look bad if you decline. Even his phone call to you was strategic.'

Claudia frowned. 'In what way?'

'You can't tell me that that slot only just came free. I reckon he's had it since last week but waited till the last minute to approach you – catching you on the back foot. Giving you less time to plan.'

'Hardly impartial, is it?'

'No, but it makes for drama and higher listener ratings. I doubt the local business news is usually the most-listened to show of the week.'

Claudia dropped her head in her hands. 'I don't want to do it.'

'I know.' Tanya stroked her hair. 'What does Jason think?'

'He doesn't know. I haven't seen him since Monday morning.' *And what a joy* that *was.*

'I thought you might have asked his advice. He seemed to be the man for a crisis last week, when you had that panic attack.'

'That was just accidental timing.'

'So how did dinner go on Sunday? Wait. You last saw him on *Monday morning*?' Tanya wiggled her eyebrows.

'It's not like that. Don't get excited.'

'But you are attracted to him, aren't you?'

'I suppose I am,' Claudia admitted with a resigned sigh.

'I can see why.' Tanya stroked Pudding's ears, sending him into a state of bliss. 'Interesting eyes. Doesn't smile much, but when he does? Gorgeous.'

'Yeah. That's what gets to me most – the smile. It's rare, and sometimes only a glimmer of one, but there's that upturn at one side of his mouth and his eyes crinkle so you know it's genuine.'

'That's quite descriptive from someone who only *supposes* they find him attractive.' Tanya frowned. 'Why doesn't he smile much? Apart from the fact that his wife died and he's a single parent to an awkward teenager?'

'Turns out there's more to it than that, but I'm not at liberty to say.'

Tanya raised a brow. 'He opened up to you?'

'Yes. On Sunday night. We opened up to each other.'

The second brow joined the first. 'How much did you tell him about Lee?'

'Everything.'

'Everything!'

'It seemed right to tell him. Do you… Do you think I shouldn't have?'

'Not at all. If your gut instinct told you to go ahead, then it did. But it is significant. You must feel, deep down, that he's important enough in your life for you to want him to know where you once were and where you're at now.'

'Maybe I just had a glass of wine too many, Tanya.'

'And maybe you're still in denial. Should I dust off my scrying ball?'

'Don't you dare!'

'Then stop looking so miserable. He bared his soul to you, too, and *he's* not full of regrets, is he?'

'He most certainly is. He came by the next morning and read me the riot act.'

Claudia relayed the conversation almost verbatim, finishing with a mournful, 'He doesn't trust me. And he missed meditation tonight. So did Millie.'

'I don't believe he doesn't trust you. I expect he was just angry at himself and took it out on you. C'mon, Claudia, you can read people better than this. What's the matter with you?'

'I'm out of sorts.'

'You're entitled to be out of sorts over the radio thing. But as for Jason… Do you think you could you be really falling for him?'

Claudia spluttered on her wine. 'Just because I admit he's attractive and has a nice smile – *when* he deigns to bestow it on anyone – and just because I confided in him after too much wine does *not* mean I'm falling for him!'

'If you say so, my lovely. If you say so.'

*

Seated in the radio station's tiny waiting room, Claudia was so nervous, she felt sick. The lemon balm tea she'd had before she came out had done no good at all.

Unable to sleep, she'd been up since five thirty, playing out different scenarios in her head, planning possible answers to questions and unexpected curveballs.

Sarah and Evelyn had insisted on giving up their day off to drive her there and back.

'I don't want you driving in a state,' Sarah had said. 'Do what you're told.'

Claudia was grateful to have them on either side of her now. Clutching the rose quartz around her neck, she closed her eyes.

Remember what Sarah said: You did this kind of thing all the time once.

That was in another lifetime. In her new life, she hadn't pictured doing this kind of thing at all. She'd envisaged owning her own business selling things she loved. She hadn't anticipated becoming embroiled in a feud that would threaten both her business and her peace of mind.

'Time to come through, Ms Bennett.' A young assistant beckoned to her. Sarah and Evelyn squeezed a hand each, and Claudia meekly followed.

Claudia had expected a quick chat with Ollie Barton before they launched into the interview – an opportunity to work out what he might ask. Instead, she was led straight into the tiny box-like studio, unceremoniously seated in the chair opposite him and handed headphones. As Tanya had suggested, he seemed determined to keep her on the back foot.

Ollie was in his late twenties at most, wearing a scruffy T-shirt and with a scruffy beard. He cast her a cursory smile. 'Just a couple of minutes till this track ends,' he told her. 'Everything okay?'

No, everything is not okay. I'm here against my will, and I may throw up over your consoles. 'Fine.'

'Thanks for coming in at such short notice.' The track he'd been playing ended, and he was back on air. 'So, after our fascinating interview last week with the owners of the newest enterprise in Porthsteren, Hester's Cauldron, today we welcome the owner of Healing Waves, established two years ago.'

Claudia didn't *feel* welcomed. She felt like she was in a hostile goldfish bowl.

Ollie gave a summary of the Hester's Cauldron interview, which did not put Claudia in a good light, and then… 'And now to Claudia Bennett. Thank you for joining us. Let's begin by finding out something about you and Healing Waves. What made you set up *your* business?'

Claudia took a deep breath. Carefully skating over her life before Porthsteren, she gave him a basic rundown.

'You'd class Healing Waves as a New Age shop?'

Claudia had the feeling he was digging her a trap, but she couldn't put her finger on how.

'In broad terms,' she answered cautiously. 'But I don't like to be pigeonholed. Healing Waves will be what I want it to be, and that might shift over time.'

'You don't like to be pigeonholed. And yet isn't that exactly what you've done with Hester's Cauldron?'

Claudia balked. 'I've done no such thing!'

'Amber and Raven would beg to differ. According to them, you've pigeonholed them as a tourist and teen trap.'

'That isn't accurate. I said they would *appeal* to tourists and to teens.'

'Why is that so terrible?'

Claudia gave him her best glare. 'I didn't say it was.'

'But you implied it, along with your many accusations.'

Many accusations? All Claudia wanted to do right now was vacate this hateful chair in this hateful little room and never look back.

She lifted her chin. 'Let's get one thing straight, Ollie, shall we? I have made no accusations *whatsoever*. I had a private conversation that was overheard.'

'Doesn't that amount to the same thing?'

'Hardly! A public accusation carries intent. A private conversation is just that.'

'Semantics.' He shrugged, and Claudia bet the listeners could picture it, even if they couldn't hear it. 'In these *private* conversations, you were heard calling the owners of Hester's Cauldron frauds. Is that true?'

'Not word for word, no. I was asked by someone *else* if I thought they were frauds.'

'What *did* you say, word for word?' His tone was sarcastic.

Helen Pollard

And that was where it all fell down, because Claudia hadn't mentally filed away her conversation with Jason verbatim. Even if she had, she doubted she'd dare repeat it on air.

Ollie stared at her, challenge in his eyes. Amber and Raven had done quite a job on him last week. She wouldn't get a fair hearing here. All she could work on was damage limitation.

Claudia looked him in the eye. 'I can't say, Ollie. Do *you* remember every word of every single chat you have with friends?'

'Point taken, Ms Bennett. But would it be fair to say we have the gist of these private conversations of yours?'

'No. It would be fair to say that I had concerns after I visited Hester's Cauldron, and I conveyed those concerns to a couple of friends.'

'And those friends conveyed them to their friends who conveyed them to their friends?'

'That's possible, but all I know as *fact* is that we were overheard by someone nearby.'

Ollie pushed on. 'And your concerns are…?'

'Merely that the ladies in the shop were handing out incorrect advice. I heard several instances of it, as did someone else I trust.'

'And you know better, presumably?'

'I know about the things that I sell – their history, their origins, their properties.'

'Does that matter?'

'Of course it matters!'

'Oh, come on, Ms Bennett. We're talking about trinkets. Gifts. Soap.'

'It matters to *me*,' Claudia said through gritted teeth.

'You don't like that I'm dissing what you sell, do you? And yet you were heard dissing what they sell at Hester's Cauldron. I gather that

Wicca and witchcraft are becoming very popular lately. Aren't you offending an awful lot of people?'

'Let me get this very, very clear, Ollie. I have absolutely *nothing* against witchcraft or Wicca.'

'That's interesting, because in the course of my research, I heard that some of the locals thought you were a witch when you first moved to Porthsteren, and you were forced to deny it.'

Research? He talked to Libby, more like. 'I wasn't forced to do anything. There were light-hearted rumours, so I thought it best that people were put straight. I was honest – I'm not a witch or Wiccan and never have been, but that's not because I have anything against it. My closest friend practises Wicca.'

'So you *don't* dislike what they're selling at Hester's Cauldron?'

How far should she go? 'I have no quibble with most of their stock, although I'm not personally keen on the ugly hag portrayal of witches. All I *said* was that people should give accurate advice if they're selling items that need to be understood by the buyer.'

'You've gone further than that. A teenager told Amber and Raven that you'd warned one of their friends.'

'All I said was that they should check their facts before buying anything they didn't understand. I doubt any sensible parent listening would quibble with *that* advice. Besides, Hester's Cauldron themselves have signs warning and daring their customers, all the way up the stairs and throughout their witchcraft section. You could argue that I was reiterating *that... if* you chose to.'

Ollie didn't seem to have an answer to that. 'You were also heard to say, and I quote, that you're "a paragon of virtue in comparison to the Hester's Cauldron gang".'

What the…? Panicked, Claudia dredged her memory. Did she say that? When? It took her a moment. *Ah.* To Sarah and Evelyn, when she was talking about offering Millie a Saturday job, and Sarah asked if Jason would object, and… Yes, she'd said it. In jest.

The microphone had stayed silent too long.

'That's been taken completely out of context,' she said firmly. 'The conversation – also private – was about something else entirely, someone else entirely, and it was merely a quip.'

'Merely a quip.' Ollie allowed a dramatic pause. 'As someone who moved to Porthsteren relatively recently to set up a business, you don't seem very supportive of two young people trying to do the same.'

Claudia *could* have pointed out she'd earned every penny she'd put into Healing Waves, not just borrowed it off a rich parent. She *could* have pointed out that she had to make Healing Waves work all year round, not just for six months a year. But that would only make her seem petty. She had to cut her losses.

'I will always welcome new businesses to Porthsteren, Ollie, and I wish the ladies at Hester's Cauldron every success in their venture. Indeed, I've expressed that view to numerous people although, oddly enough, *that* hasn't been reported, has it? It's a fascinating field they've chosen to specialise in, and I hope they enjoy learning more about their stock so they can help their customers make informed choices, just as I do at Healing Waves.'

Claudia took off her headphones and stood. For a moment, she thought he might inform his listeners that she was walking out – she could see him toying with it – but perhaps he decided that would make him look bad, too.

'Well, that's all we have time for. Thank you to Claudia Bennett, owner of Healing Waves. And now for some music…'

Claudia walked out without looking back. Sarah and Evelyn led her to the nearest café where they bought her mint tea and encouraged her to sip every few minutes.

'You did what you could, Claudia.' Evelyn patted her hand.

Claudia was still trembling. 'I made it worse.'

Sarah shook her head. 'No, honey. Not doing it at all would have done that. This way, you put what they said about you in context. You sounded firm and calm. If that's the best that could be done, you did it.'

Claudia sighed. 'It was a blur. I had it all rehearsed in my head, but I don't know if I said any of it. Perhaps I should listen to it.'

'Listen to it once only,' Sarah said firmly. 'Just for peace of mind. Then never again. Treat it as water under the bridge after that.'

'That's wise advice,' Claudia admitted.

'Comes with age,' Sarah grumbled, making Claudia smile for the first time that day. 'What will you do with yourself this afternoon?'

'Hide under my duvet and never come out?'

'Go for a long walk, Claudia,' Evelyn told her. 'Blow away the cobwebs. Paddle. You know the drill. We're away at a friend's in St Ives tonight, but phone us if you need to talk, okay?'

Claudia took their hands. 'I will. Thank you both.'

'You're welcome, honey.' Sarah stood. 'Let's get you home so you can do what Aunty Evie prescribed.'

*

Claudia did as she was told. The walk and the scenery helped. In a quiet cove, she drew a caricature of Ollie Barton and watched as the tide came in and washed him away. Then she went home and really did crawl under her duvet, her head pounding, her stomach growling with hunger but too nauseated to eat.

She managed to answer the phone to Tanya, who wanted to come over, but Claudia begged her not to. Tanya instructed her to eat some toast and even waited on the line while Claudia made some. When she could hear Claudia nibbling it, she reassured her that she'd done a sterling job in the interview, and now all they could do was wait and see.

Predictably, Claudia slept badly and was up early. Steeling herself, she listened to the interview. It wasn't as bad as she'd thought, but she resented that she'd had to do it at all, and she wasn't convinced she'd got her points across.

She dreaded opening up Healing Waves, and that dread was well-founded. Any locals who came in only wanted to talk about the interview, and Claudia thought she detected restrained frostiness in their manner – but perhaps she was becoming paranoid.

Closing the shop at the end of the day was an enormous relief. Upstairs, she fed Pudding, watched him shoot through his cat flap for a wander, and settled down with her favourite comfort food – a tub of Page Turner tomato soup.

She'd just finished it when Pudding shot back in, the cat flap clattering loudly enough to startle her and make her drop her spoon.

'Hey, Pudding. What's up?' Taking in the cat's bedraggled appearance, she reached down to pet him, then frowned. 'You're wet through! Is it raining?'

That cat hates the rain. Must've been caught out by a shower.

But when she crossed to the window, the sky was still blue. There was, however, an odd smell in the flat.

Claudia sniffed the hand she'd used to stroke her pet. Very strong, vaguely familiar. What was it? Crossing to where Pudding had sprawled across the doormat, tentatively thinking about washing himself but not as enthusiastic as usual, Claudia dropped to her knees and sniffed.

White spirit! How on earth…?

'Pudding! Don't you dare lick!'

She reached for her phone. Eight o'clock at night? Her sinking heart told her she'd get an answer-phone message giving her an emergency out-of-hours number for the vet, and she was right. She redialled. *Come on. Come on.* A polite woman answered, and Claudia babbled out her fears. The address the woman gave her to take her pet to was at least twenty miles away.

'Pudding! Don't *lick*!' Claudia shrieked at her panicked cat, who clearly didn't like the smell or taste of what was covering his fur.

Taking pity, the woman said, 'Wait a moment, dear. I'll bring the vet to the phone.'

The vet was kindly and gave her detailed advice which she scribbled down with a shaking hand. When he'd wished her luck and clicked off, Claudia looked at the list in despair. She needed help, but Sarah and Evelyn were away for the night, and Tanya was too far away.

She swallowed her pride and dialled.

Chapter Seventeen

When Millie answered her mobile, Jason could hear Claudia's panicked voice from across the room.

'Dad, it's Claudia. Yours isn't ringing. It's urgent!'

Picturing his own phone lying uncharged upstairs, Jason snatched Millie's from her. 'Claudia. Are you alright?'

Three minutes later, all he knew was that Claudia was hysterical but trying hard not to be, something had happened to Pudding, and she needed two extra pairs of hands.

The old Jason might have wasted precious time trying to get a straight answer out of her. But this newly-budding Jason allowed his gut instinct to kick in and tell him all that mattered was that they were needed right away. He spent all of five seconds thinking about the last time they'd spoken, when he'd treated her so badly. And then...

'Millie. Get something on your feet. I'll explain on the way.'

But as they sped down the hill and along the beach road, parking haphazardly outside Claudia's, he realised he didn't know enough to explain.

They raced up to the flat, where Claudia was holding Pudding tightly wrapped in a towel, her grip allowing him no room to move. Pudding didn't like it – his lip curled back, baring needle-like teeth.

Jason and Claudia shared a brief look, both acknowledging there were things to be said between them, before Claudia said, 'I've run the bath. Millie, can you fetch sunflower oil from the kitchen?'

As if that *makes everything clear.*

'On it.' It was a sign of Millie's faith in Claudia that she didn't blink at the request but simply did as she was told.

Jason shook his head. 'Claudia, I know you and Millie probably communicate by some kind of psychic phenomenon, but I need help. Care to explain?'

As Pudding strained against her hold on him, Claudia took a deep breath. 'He came in wet through. It's white spirit. I rang the vet, but I'd have to drive miles, and they said time is of the essence, and there's not much they can do that we can't. We need to bathe him and shampoo it off because it could burn him, then we have to coat him in oil to soothe his skin, then wash the excess oil off. Then if he licks his fur, it'll be oil and not the spirit, so it'll soothe his stomach if he's swallowed some.' Her eyes were shining wet, and her voice trembled. 'Jason, I can't *do* this on my own.'

His heart melting at her distress, Jason said, 'No. Of course not.'

He gave her what he hoped was a confident smile, but when he looked at Pudding, all confidence vanished. He might not know much about cats, but he did know they hated water. He doubted they liked to be slathered in cooking oil, either.

Pulling off his sweater, he followed Claudia into the bathroom, Millie trailing after them with the oil.

When Claudia unwrapped Pudding from the ruined towel and held him over the water, his love for his mistress went AWOL. He writhed and squirmed, murder in his eyes.

'Don't let him hover like that,' Jason said, sounding more authoritative than he felt. 'Just get him in.'

Claudia lowered the feline into the water, where he spat and twisted and clawed. A bright red scratch appeared on Claudia's arm before Jason could move in beside her to help hold the cat firm.

'Millie, use a jug to pour water over him while we hold him,' he said. 'Don't let the water get in his eyes if you can help it – his head isn't wet with the spirit, just his body.'

Millie did as she was told, but it only enraged the poor cat.

'I don't suppose you have any gardening gloves?' Jason asked Claudia in desperation.

'I don't have a garden, Jason.'

'I have an idea!' Millie shot off and returned a few moments later with two pairs of industrial-strength rubber gloves, helping them both pull them on and suffering a scratch or two herself in the process.

'Thanks. Right. Shampoo.' As they did their best to shampoo the cat, Jason grumbled, 'Why the hell couldn't you have a dog? They don't mind this kind of thing.'

He was rewarded with a nervous chuckle from Claudia as they worked, kneeling on the sopping bathroom floor side by side.

Millie washed off the shampoo with the jug, then they were onto the oil stage, Claudia smoothing it into the cat's soaking wet fur while Jason tried to hold him fast.

'Thanks for the gloves,' he said, casting a grateful glance at his daughter. 'Where did you find them?'

'The utility room at the back of the shop.'

Jason smiled, marvelling at his daughter's presence of mind.

They washed off the oil as best they could, the cat hissing and spitting, and Claudia ran a wide-toothed comb through Pudding's fur before wrapping him in the clean towel Millie handed her.

Pudding immediately calmed down, huddling into Claudia's arms, but there was no purring. Claudia carried him into the lounge, where she and Jason stared in amazement at the sheets and towels covering every upholstered surface.

'I didn't know where he'd want to sit, and I was worried he'd ruin your furniture with the oil,' Millie explained. 'I hope you don't mind me going into your bedroom to get them.'

Claudia beamed. 'Of course not. Thank you, Millie. You're a star!'

Millie smiled, pleased at the praise, and once more Jason marvelled at the sullen teenager he'd brought with him to Cornwall, usually reluctant to do anything she was asked to, dealing with tonight's situation so capably and calmly.

Claudia placed Pudding in his favourite armchair where he cowered for a moment, sodden and oily, before streaking past them and rattling his way through the bead curtains. When they went after him, he was nowhere to be seen.

Claudia looked under the bed. 'He's right at the back. It's cold back there. He's scared of us!' A sob caught in Claudia's throat as all three of them peered under the bed, Pudding's eyes shining mutinously out at them from the dark.

Jason couldn't bear Claudia's misery. *Bloody cat. Not that I can blame him.* Standing, he strode into the lounge and lit the fire.

'Dad, what are you doing? It's summer!'

'Find some tuna, Millie, and put some in Pudding's bowl.'

Jason's limited knowledge of cats stretched to them liking warmth and fish. He set Pudding's basket in front of the fire, then took the bowl of tuna Millie handed him.

In the bedroom, Claudia was still trying to coax her pet from his cold, dark hiding place.

'He'll come out when he's ready.' Jason set the tuna under the strands of beads so they'd hear him, then turned to Claudia. She looked shaken, and sick with worry. 'Don't you have some foul-tasting herbal tea to soothe healers of idiotic cats?' he asked brightly.

With a wobbly smile, Claudia took milk from the fridge. 'Hot chocolate with marshmallows?'

Millie clapped her hands, while Jason raised a surprised eyebrow. He noted it was goats' milk, but you couldn't have it all.

The milk was heating when they heard the rattle of the bead curtain. Jason pounced, lifting the startled Pudding into his arms and holding him close to his chest. Gently, he carried him to his basket, while Millie fetched the tuna and put it under his nose.

Accepting he was beaten, or at least deciding that tuna and a fire were a better bet than the coldest spot in the flat, Pudding deigned to nibble on the tuna and eventually, under Jason's careful coaxing, curled into his basket.

Jason's heart went out to the animal. He always looked a sight, what with his mottled colours, but now he just looked a mess. Jason knew cats were fastidious about grooming, but he couldn't see how Pudding would look up to much ever again with his fur in this state.

'Poor lad,' he murmured. 'You'll be okay. Claudia'll see to it.'

When he stood, his daughter and Claudia were staring at him. 'What?' he said defensively. 'He's been through the wringer. I can sympathise, can't I?'

'So it seems.' Claudia handed him his hot chocolate, which he sipped gratefully. A bit goaty, but just what they needed.

Millie pointed at them. 'You two are such a mess!'

She wasn't wrong. They were both bleeding, their clothes were drenched from Pudding's furious splashing, and Jason's T-shirt was ruined with oil from carrying him to the fire.

'I'll buy you a new shirt,' Claudia said miserably.

'You'll do no such thing. Friends help each other out. I never liked this one, anyway.'

Claudia glanced over at Millie. 'He thinks I'll get him something tie-dyed, doesn't he?'

'Yup.' They grinned at each other, their obvious companionship warming Jason's heart. It was good to see Millie smile, even at her dad's wardrobe misfortunes.

As they leaned against the kitchen counters, none of them wanting to go too near Pudding in case they spooked him, Millie disappeared in the direction of the bathroom, returning with cotton buds and a small bottle, and began to dab the liquid onto Claudia's wounds.

Jason turned up his nose. 'What's that? It stinks.'

'Tea-tree oil. You're next. Hold still. Cat scratches can be nasty.'

'You don't have to tell *me* that!' He glared at Claudia. 'Don't you have antiseptic cream like a normal person?'

'Tea-tree oil *is* a natural antiseptic, Jason. It'll go right into the scratches. Better than a cream.'

Jason couldn't argue with that, and it didn't sting as much as the liquid antiseptic he remembered his mother sloshing on his scraped knees as a boy.

'Great. Now I'm wet, oily *and* I stink.'

Claudia put down her mug, crossed over to him, laid a hand on one cheek and a kiss on the other. She did the same for Millie. 'I couldn't have managed without you both. Thank you. Pudding thanks you, too.'

Jason glanced at the traumatised cat. 'I doubt it, but we accept.' He finished his drink. 'We should go. He might settle better with just you here.'

He hesitated at the door. There was so much more to say – an apology from him for Monday, for certain – but he couldn't tackle that with his daughter in tow.

As they stepped outside, Claudia pulled Millie back and Jason heard her whisper, 'What's his chest size?'

Pretending he hadn't heard, he continued down the steps. Heaven knew what he'd end up with. But maybe he'd wear it anyway.

*

Jason called at Claudia's flat just after eight the following morning – too early, but he had to get to work long before she opened the shop, and there were things he'd wanted to do. Things he needed to say.

She opened the door dressed in yoga shorts and a vest tee, her hair held away from her face by a fabric band. The sight of her lightly tanned legs and sun-kissed shoulders sent a primal punch to his gut.

'Jason!'

'Hi. Sorry. I know it's early.'

'No problem. I just finished yoga. Come on in.'

'Thanks. How's the patient?'

Pudding was curled in his favourite armchair on an old fleece blanket. He still looked a dreadful mess, his fur clinging in some places and spiking in others, like a punk cat.

'Quiet. Not eating much.'

'Probably still has a gutful of oil from trying to clean his fur. You'll be tempting him with morsels of fresh fish and chicken, I imagine?'

'Yes.'

'Don't let him get too used to that,' Jason warned.

'Don't worry. We've already talked about it.'

Of course they have.

'I found the white spirit and disposed of it,' he told her. 'Decorators at a house over the road had left it near the bin, and the lid wasn't screwed on properly. I'm guessing Pudding brushed against it and knocked it over himself. I caught the builders just now and asked them to be more careful. They said they were sorry.' Jason bent to talk to the cat. 'Stay away from bins and toxic substances, mister. And I'm not sure you should be crossing that beach road. It gets busy.'

Pudding merely glared, but Claudia rewarded Jason with a warm smile. 'You're fond of him.'

'I wouldn't go that far. I just don't fancy going through a process like last night's again.'

Her lips twitched. 'Uh-huh.'

'Claudia…' *Get it done, Jason.* 'I owe you an apology over what I said on Monday. It's late, I know, but I was worried I'd only make things worse.' He sighed. 'It wasn't just about *what* I shared with you. The fact is, I haven't spoken so closely with anyone in years. Gemma and I lost that connection a long time ago, and my mates… You know what men are like. A chat down the pub about football and kids. Politics if you're feeling brave. We don't share our innermost feelings. After Sunday night, I felt uncomfortable, but I shouldn't have spoken to you like that.'

Claudia placed her hand on his, affecting his senses more than the light touch should.

'I was tired, so I may have been a bit quick to respond,' she admitted. 'But I wasn't uncomfortable about sharing with you. I trust you.' She allowed that small dig to sink in.

'I trust you, too. It wasn't my intention to suggest I didn't. I just wanted to be clear.' He sighed. 'And Claudia… Millie read about your interview on social media. She's listened to it. So have I.'

Claudia shoulders dropped. 'I didn't want to go on there, but…' She quickly summed up the last-minute invitation from Ollie Barton.

'You had no choice,' he agreed. 'And you handled it well, considering what he was trying to do.'

'Thanks. I just wish it would all die down.' Claudia sighed, and his heart went out to her. 'It could be worse. I could've had some solicitor's letter accusing me of slander instead.'

Jason cocked his head to one side. 'Yes. Interesting, isn't it, that they haven't done that.'

'I suppose it's all hearsay. They can't prove beyond a doubt *exactly* what was said and by whom.'

'Or they're worried that if they take an official step like that, they'd have to prove that any accusation of incompetence *is* slander and not the truth, which they'd struggle to do.' Glancing at his watch, with regret in his voice he said, 'I need to go.'

The careworn look on Claudia's face tugged at him, and without thinking, he bent to kiss her cheek.

Surprise replaced worry on her face. 'Thank you, Jason.' She pointed at her forlorn cat. 'For last night. For talking to the builders. For the apology. For caring about the Hester's thing.' As she saw him out, she gave him a warm smile of gratitude.

Walking to his car, that image imprinted on his brain, Jason wondered how on earth she remained unattached. Any man would be crazy not to want to do just about anything to be on the receiving end of a smile like that.

*

'Are people still on at you about that blasted interview?' Sarah asked when she popped round with spring vegetable soup.

Claudia sniffed at the soup in appreciation, then sighed at Sarah's question. 'Yes. And they're not buying anything.' She dropped her voice, glancing at her browsers. 'Thank goodness for the tourists!'

'How's Pudding?' Sarah pointed to the cat, curled in his basket behind the counter, where customers couldn't try to stroke him.

'Still traumatised.'

'I'd be traumatised, too, if you shoved me in a bath and covered me in shampoo and oil.'

Pudding looked up and gave her a woebegone expression.

'Sorry we were away last night, Claudia. You know we'd've come, otherwise.'

'I know. But it turned out okay.'

'Jason and Millie, your very own superheroes?'

'I guess.'

Sarah raised a speculative eyebrow. 'Hmm. It was one thing Jason helping last night in an emergency, but as for his follow-up activities this morning? Above and beyond the call of duty, if you ask me.'

Claudia smiled. 'I know. Especially since he's not a cat lover.'

'You sure it's the cat he's worried about, honey?'

'What do you mean?'

'You know what I mean.'

Ignoring her, Claudia said, 'I need to buy him a new shirt.'

'That's a pretty personal gift.'

'Not a gift – a replacement for the one he ruined. And I need to thank them both properly. Maybe dinner tomorrow night?'

'Isn't Millie going to her grandparents for most of half-term?'

Claudia slapped her forehead. 'My brain's mush after this week! Yes, she is – as soon as she finishes at Healing Waves tomorrow.'

Sarah's eyes took on a mischievous glint. 'Doesn't stop you having Jason round, does it?'

'On his own?'

'Why not? He might be lonely without Millie.'

'Ha! I should think he'd relish the peace and quiet.'

'Might relish dinner with you more. Like you said, you owe him, and not just for last night. Didn't you have dinner at *his* house last weekend?'

'Yes, although that was meant to be with Millie, too, but she went out.'

'So? You've survived one dinner alone with him. What makes you think you wouldn't survive another?'

Last time, we opened our hearts and souls to each other, and I'm not sure it was a good idea.

Sarah smirked. 'Think about it. I should get back.'

Claudia did think about it. She owed Jason thanks *and* a return dinner invitation. She could leave it until Millie was available. Or she could stop being a wuss and get on with it, instead of agonising all day.

She reached for her phone.

Hi. I was wondering if you fancy dinner here tomorrow night? As a thank you for helping with Pudding. And for the meal at yours last week. If you have time after driving Millie to Devon, that is?

Claudia refrained from adding a kiss as she would with any other friend – too much room for interpretation – and waited nervously for his reply. It took twenty-eight minutes.

A thank you isn't necessary, but dinner sounds good. Millie's grand-parents are meeting me halfway, so I should be back by six thirty or so. What time suits you?

Relieved at his straightforward acceptance, Claudia texted back a simple *Seven?*

Then she phoned Tanya. The last time they'd discussed Jason, he'd been pilloried for treating Claudia so badly. The least she could do was to tell her he'd apologised and redeemed himself with his help the previous night.

Tanya was beside herself over Pudding, so much so that she would have come to see the patient, but she was due to visit her parents for the weekend, a duty she limited to a few times a year. Much as they loved their daughter and were proud of her running her own business, they had never reconciled themselves to her extra-curricular activities as a witch.

When Claudia threw her dinner invitation to Jason into the conversation, Tanya was just like Sarah – speculative *and* mischievous.

The pair of them weren't helping with Claudia's misgivings at all.

*

'Looking forward to staying with your grandparents?' Claudia asked Millie as they restocked shelves during a quiet patch the following day. Millie was in the middle of unpacking colourful textile bags and passing them to Claudia to hang on hooks.

Their progress was hampered by Pudding trying to jump into the cardboard box, but as Claudia didn't want his still-oily fur anywhere near the goods, it was a battle of wills.

Millie laughed. 'You love your boxes, don't you, Pudding?'

'He spends half his time down here in boxes. The minute I unpack one, in he hops.' Claudia wagged a finger at the cat. 'No. You can have it when it's empty.' She glanced at Millie. 'So. Your grandparents?'

'I suppose I am. And it's for longer this time, so they can show me around and we can do stuff together.'

Claudia nodded in understanding. Days out and distractions might reduce the intensity.

Millie looked around to check that their one customer was out of earshot. 'Dad says you've been stressed about the radio thing. I'm sorry.'

'Thanks. *I'm* sorry if this nonsense makes it difficult for you working here, when you like going into Hester's Cauldron. Do you… go in there a lot?'

Subtle, Claudia.

'Yeah. It's on my way home.' Millie hesitated. 'By the way, has Dad said anything to you?'

'About what, specifically?'

Millie shifted uncomfortably. 'When Phoebe and Jessica came round this week, we'd bought something at Hester's, and I think Dad might've seen it when he came upstairs.'

Claudia kept her expression neutral. 'What was it?'

'A… a spell book.'

'No, he hasn't said anything. Were you spell-weaving?'

'Spell-weaving?'

'Casting spells.'

'Oh. No, we didn't get that far.'

What would Jason want me to say? Why didn't he warn me about this?

Because you've been distraught all week with one thing and another, and you weren't talking to each other so he didn't have chance.

'Will you, do you think?' Claudia asked carefully. 'Go further, I mean?'

Ugh, this is like some mother-daughter discussion about boys! How did I get landed with this?

Millie gave a casual shrug. 'Maybe. Some time. Amber and Raven said it'd be fun but that we'll need supplies…'

Which they sell, of course.

'So we'll need to save up more pocket money first.' Millie narrowed her eyes in that stubborn way that matched her father's. 'You can't tell Dad. Friends don't betray confidences. I won't forgive you, if you do.'

Well, this week just gets better and better.

What would Claudia do if this were her daughter? She'd have no qualms about her exploring alternative practices and spiritualities. But she *would* want to make sure she was safe and that her sources were reliable. Above all, she'd want her daughter to be open with her. Through his own stubbornness, that wasn't happening between Jason and Millie.

'Okay. Just don't go delving into things before you're ready, will you?'

'Don't worry. Amber and Raven said they can teach us.'

Oh no. 'They're practising witches?'

Millie frowned. 'They must be, or they wouldn't own a shop like that, would they?'

'I'm not sure the two necessarily go hand in hand, Millie.'

'How would *you* know?' And there it was – the anger, the stubbornness, the sense of betrayal that she'd confided something and look at where it had got her.

Claudia had to rescue this, fast. 'I don't know how skilled they are,' she said, hating every word. Tanya was convinced they dabbled at best and knew very little at worst when it came to the Wiccan side of their stock. Talking of Tanya… 'But my best friend's a witch, so I do know *something* about these things.'

Millie's eyes widened. 'Is that true, then? I thought you just invented it to shut that stupid Ollie Barton up.'

Ah. Jason hasn't mentioned Tanya to Millie yet, then.

Claudia sighed. She may have regained a few kudos with Millie, but she might have dug herself a deeper hole with Jason.

'Who is she?' Millie asked, enthralled. 'What kind of things does she do? What…?'

Four customers came through the door in quick succession, thankfully putting an end to the conversation for now. Claudia only had time to whisper, 'I wouldn't tell your dad I spoke to you about that, if I were you, Millie, or we'll *both* be in trouble.'

Chapter Eighteen

Jason had been surprised by Claudia's dinner invitation, especially since he knew that she knew that Millie would be away. After their last dinner together, he couldn't deny he felt some trepidation. But he could hardly refuse, and he'd do plenty of rattling around the house on his own over the next few days – not that he wasn't looking forward to that, for a little while anyway.

Since Jennifer and Harry had met him halfway to hand Millie over, he'd had time to get home and shower and change before setting out… making it seem like a proper date. Jason wasn't sure how he felt about that.

At Claudia's door, he was greeted by the smell of something delicious roasting and Claudia's only-just-there scent as she kissed his cheek in welcome. He followed her into the glow of the lamplight, taking in the small table under the window set for two, and lingering on the vision of Claudia in a long skirt of swirling sea blues and a simple white top that showed off her figure with its flowing lines.

Pulling himself together, he lifted the bottle he held in one hand and flowers in the other. 'I brought these. Consider the flowers a replacement for the ones I chucked over your DIY fire.'

Claudia smiled as she placed the flowers in a vase. 'Thank you. I'll arrange them later. And talking of replacements…' She handed him a tissue-wrapped parcel.

Knowing this must be the dreaded shirt replacement and expecting the worst, Jason was pleased to unwrap a simple collared T-shirt in a denim-blue fabric. 'It's soft.'

'Bamboo.'

He held it against himself. 'You needn't have. But I love it.' And he did, not least because there wasn't a speck of tie-dye in sight.

'Wine?'

'Please. I walked, so I don't have to be good.' When she looked amused, he hastily said, 'What's cooking?'

'Butternut squash.'

Who knew a vegetable could smell so good? 'I assume we're having another ban on the topic of Hester's Cauldron tonight?'

Claudia looked panicked for a moment, puzzling him, then said, 'That's a very good idea,' with some relief.

They chatted about Millie's progress at her Saturday job, and Jason was glad that Claudia found her useful. When Pudding sauntered through from the bedroom with a rattle of bead curtains, Jason was pleased to see that his fur looked a bit more like a feline's should.

'I thought he'd never look the same again,' Claudia confessed.

'He's a survivor, like his mistress,' Jason said, more to himself than to her, but she smiled. 'Can I help with the cooking?'

Claudia gestured at the tiny kitchen area. 'Not unless we want to injure each other. I would say "feel free to explore", but that'll only take you two minutes, and you've been here before.'

'I think every one of those times has been fraught at best and a crisis at worst. I'm happy to explore.'

While Claudia lifted the squash from the oven and turned to a pan on the hob, Jason wandered. Shells, bowls of colourful pebbles and sea glass, crystals. Only three photographs – Claudia with Tanya on the beach; Claudia with Sarah and Evelyn outside The Porthsteren Page Turner; and a selfie of Claudia and Millie making soap. It struck him what an honour it was for Claudia to display one of herself and his daughter when there were only three photos in the room.

A translucent statuette caught his eye, an interpretation of a female figure – no face, no details – with exaggerated curves, her arms stretched to meet in a circle over her head. Its simplicity appealed to his aesthetic senses. It was very Claudia.

'What's this?'

'A goddess. For channelling divine feminine energy.'

'Uh-huh.' Jason resisted the urge to shake his head. Apart from anything else, he didn't see why Claudia would need a prop for that. She exuded divine feminine energy without any help at all.

'You can channel yours, too,' she told him. 'Being male doesn't exclude you.'

'And I would want to do that why?'

'It would help you get in touch with your higher self.' Catching his doubtful expression, she said, 'That's not particularly mystical, Jason. It's about learning to trust your intuition, understanding yourself better, allowing yourself to be creative – which you already are in your work. And more playful – which you're not, nowadays.'

'Hmmph.' Jason touched the almost-transparent statue, feeling the cool, smooth surface. 'What's it made from?'

'Clear quartz.'

'Which is…?'

She smiled as she stirred. 'Do you really want to know?'

'Can you do it in a dozen words? My brain's already overloaded from channelling my divine feminine energy.'

Claudia laughed. 'Clear quartz has powerful healing properties. It can help with intention and protect against negativity.'

'I do like her,' he admitted.

'I'm sure she'll be pleased to know that. I'll tell her, next time we commune.' There was a wicked glint in her eyes, and Jason grinned.

He wandered nearer, to watch her cook. Her movements were graceful, confident, her hair glowing gold in the kitchen spotlights.

'How come you're not dating anyone?' he blurted out, mentally kicking himself the minute the words were out.

Staring at him in surprise, Claudia's lips curved. 'How do you know I'm not?' When his face fell, she laughed. 'Don't you think you'd've heard from Libby or Evelyn by now if I were?'

'In that case, crassly put thought it was, I'll repeat the question. How come you're not dating?'

'I've had offers.'

'I bet you have.' *Oh dear.* That had slipped out unbidden, too.

'But I didn't take any of them up. Partly because I didn't think it wise to get involved with a local while establishing myself in a new place, and partly because nobody tempted me enough.'

Do I tempt you enough?

'Wait. Are you saying you haven't dated anyone since your husband?' *Three years ago?*

'Does that surprise you?'

He thought about it. 'Yes and no.'

'Care to expand?'

Ah. 'No, because I know you think carefully about things – and there's probably an element of once bitten, twice shy. And yes, because you must've had men battering the door down.'

Claudia smiled, almost shyly. 'Thanks for the compliment, but not as many as you think. Even if men find me attractive, I scare them a little.' Deftly chopping green leaves, she turned the tables on him. 'How about you? Have you dated?'

Serves me right for prying.

'No,' he answered honestly. 'Although I was surprised at the interest I got, after Gemma died. It seems that becoming a widower gives you an edge, for some reason.'

'You weren't tempted to have an affair when you and Gemma grew apart?'

If anyone else had asked Jason that, he would've told them to mind their own business. He didn't mind Claudia asking.

'I didn't want to compound the problems we were having.'

'Not even after you found out she was having an affair?'

'I know some might think that would've been justified, but it wasn't long before she became ill and then... Well.'

Claudia reached into a cupboard for a spice jar. 'Sounds like your sex life's been in the doldrums for as long as mine, then.'

Jason almost dropped his wine glass. 'Er. Hmm. Yes. Sounds like it.'

She laughed. 'Don't worry, Jason. It was a comment, not a chat-up line.'

Did he *want* it to be a chat-up line? Perhaps a change of subject would be wise. 'You're very relaxed when you cook.'

'You're not?'

'I see it as a necessary chore. Millie complains that I'm not very flexible with recipes – I have to follow them to the letter. It's not intuitive for me. My daughter prefers to wing it, which involves a great deal of mess and rather mixed results.'

'I probably fall somewhere in between,' Claudia said. 'I use recipes for inspiration, but I like to play around and see where it takes me. As for being relaxed, I think you should enjoy doing something if you can.'

'Is that how you approach everything?'

'Other than the washing up. I hate that, and no amount of positive thinking will ever change it.'

He grinned at her honesty. Glancing at a pile of mail on her kitchen counter, he noticed an envelope addressed to *Ms C.R. Bennett.* 'What does the R stand for?'

Claudia added white wine to her pan. 'What R?'

'In your name. "C.R."'

'Oh. Rose.'

'Claudia Rose? I like that.'

'It's just a middle name. I never use it.'

'You should. It rolls off the tongue. Kind of exotic. Sumptuous. It suits you.'

Claudia gave him a startled look. 'You think I'm exotic and sumptuous?'

Jason blushed the brightest red he had in years. 'Well…'

Pudding saved him, choosing that moment to saunter over and let out a plaintive meow. Situating himself at Claudia's feet, he stared slavishly and unwaveringly up at her.

Mercifully distracted, Claudia sighed. 'Better feed him, or we'll get no peace.'

Jason glanced at the vegetable medley she'd been concocting. 'I gather he's not vegetarian, too?'

'Pudding loves me dearly, but even I know that would be a step too far. The advantage of me being vegetarian is that he doesn't beg for leftovers at the table. Doesn't stop him trying for an occasional treat, though.'

'You don't get birds and mice on the doorstep?'

'Rarely, nowadays. I did at first, but he seems to have grown out of it with age. Besides, I made it plain from the start that such gifts were unappreciated. We came to an arrangement.'

Jason was getting used to the way Claudia talked about the cat as though the two of them communicated fully. What did he know? They certainly had that way of looking into each other's eyes.

She turned her attention to the cat. 'How about the chicken scraps that Aunty Evelyn brought you yesterday?' She smiled at Jason. 'Pudding loves chicken. Watch this.'

When Claudia pulled on the fridge door, Pudding's ears pricked up like radar shields. As she took a plastic container out, a deep mew rumbled in his throat and he stood on his hind legs like a dog begging for a bone. When she took off the lid, his nose went mad, his whiskers twitching.

'Are you hoping it's chicken, Pudding?' Claudia teased.

The cat moved nearer to where she'd set the tub on the counter, stretching his front paws all the way up the cupboard doors. When she moved sideways with the tub towards his bowl, he scuttled sideways along the cupboard doors too, paw over paw, all the while making a terrible fuss and gazing up at her with pleading adoration in his eyes.

Jason grinned. He hadn't imagined Claudia would tease her pet like that. The thought entered his brain that if she teased *him* like that, he'd probably plead pathetically and gaze at her with adoration, too.

Ah, Jason, pull yourself together, man.

With that comical interlude over, Claudia was free to serve dinner at the tiny table in peace.

However experimentally Claudia approached her cooking, Jason couldn't complain at the result. The food on his plate was so tasty, he didn't even think about the lack of meat, and it was certainly colourful – roasted butternut squash, pine nuts, garlic, onion, wilted spinach, with sourdough bread and fresh butter.

'This is delicious,' he told her.

'Glad you like it. Not missing anything?'

'I may not be a vegetarian, Claudia, but that doesn't mean I spend every meal gnawing the flesh off animal bones. I eat chicken, fish, the occasional steak, but I wouldn't say I was a serial carnivore.'

'Good. I'd hate to think I was entertaining a caveman to dinner.'

Jason was equally keen on the dessert she served in small glass bowls. 'What's this? Home-made ice-cream?'

Claudia kept her face non-committal. 'Try it and see.'

Jason did. 'Mmmm. It goes well with the raspberries. Definitely bananas involved.'

'Because that's all it is. Bananas, blended then frozen.'

'Not even a *trace* of ice-cream?'

'Not even.'

Jason loaded up his spoon. 'I could get converted to these intuitive dishes of yours.'

'That's good, because I plan to have you round here more often.'

Jason's pulse skipped. 'That *is* good.' The rhythmic sound of the sea, the salty breeze through the open window, delicious home-cooked food, the company of an equally delicious-looking woman…? 'Great, in fact.'

*

Claudia was pleased with the way the evening had gone so far.

Jason was good company – and he had relaxed, as far as Jason ever relaxed. During the meal, they'd stuck to safe subjects like his new work project – converting a defunct old people's home into luxury apartments – and steered clear of controversial topics like the power of the moon or the ability of crystals to change the molecules around them. So far, so good… until they settled on the sofa with their wine.

'I've been thinking about Lee,' Jason said.

Claudia made a face. 'Do I detect an insightful comment on the horizon?'

'Only that he was an idiot.'

Claudia chuckled. 'Very insightful.'

Jason turned his body towards hers. 'Claudia, I'm sure you know this already, but I have to say it. You're beautiful, exactly the way you are. Lee was blind not to see it. I imagine he didn't appreciate your other qualities, either.'

Intrigued, Claudia asked, 'Which other qualities? My weirdness? My way-out-there practices you love so much?'

He smiled. 'Your kindness, your generosity, your compassion.'

'Praise indeed. Thank you. And no, Lee didn't appreciate that side of me. Or perhaps it was simply that he didn't bring those things out in me.'

It was disconcerting, Claudia thought, to feel so comfortable with someone who disagreed with or was suspicious about half of what went on in her head, but who was open to understanding her, if not her beliefs. Someone who appreciated her for who she was.

Tanya was right. She was attracted to him. More than that. She was developing feelings for him.

They had drifted nearer to each other, his legs turned towards hers, hers curled beneath her so she leaned in closer. The conversation faltered.

Jason frowned. 'Sorry, did you say something? I lost concentration for a moment.'

'No. I think we just ran out of conversation at the same time.'

He shook his head. 'I feel like you and I could never run out of conversation. But perhaps the time for conversation is over for this evening.'

Jason placed his wine glass on the coffee table, and Claudia had a sinking sensation at the thought that he might be leaving.

But his eyes, the palest blue of the sea on a winter's day, never left hers during the manoeuvre, and she couldn't tear her own gaze away. He wasn't leaving.

Anticipating him making a move to kiss her, the moment stretched out for too long.

He isn't going to make a move. So, it's down to me, is it? Do I want to?

Claudia deliberately slowed her breathing and tuned into her inner voice. She didn't have to try hard. It was screaming at her to stop worrying and take the initiative.

Jason spoke her name, low and soft. 'Claudia Rose.'

Her name, said that way, by him, was the only push she needed. Claudia leaned in, breathing in the light citrus scent of his skin, brushing her lips over his. For one brief moment, he remained passive, and she thought she'd made a mistake. And then his lips stirred under hers and his hands moved to her hair, his fingers in the wild curls. Time stretched out, seemingly infinite.

Pudding's head nudging against their legs brought the kiss to an end. They both laughed at the cat's mew of protest, but when Jason moved in to kiss her again, Claudia placed a hand against his chest.

'I don't want to go too fast, too soon, Jason. I don't think you do, either. We both need to be sure about this.'

Jason let out a long sigh. 'You're right. You always are.'

Claudia mouthed 'Sorry'.

'No, I'm grateful. I think.' He placed a hand on her cheek. 'I've wanted to kiss you for longer than I realised, Claudia Rose.'

'Me too. It's the same for me.'

He smiled that rare and fabulous smile of his. 'We have one thing in common, then. I should go. I need to clear my head.' When she frowned at that, he said, 'You may not be the witch they once thought you were around here, but you *have* got that enchantment thing down to a fine art.'

With a delighted laugh, Claudia followed him to the door.

Placing a feather-light kiss on her lips, Jason turned and went down the stairs. Claudia noticed he headed straight for the water's edge instead of walking along the road, and she smiled.

*

'Where the hell is everybody?' Claudia whispered to Sarah just before the meditation session was due to begin.

There were only four beside herself – Sarah and Evelyn, Jason (but no Millie, as she was still away at her grandparents'), and Libby. No Alice – and she rarely missed it.

'Beats me. It's half-term, so some of them could be on holiday.' Sarah frowned. 'That doesn't account for someone like Jenny, though – she won't go anywhere till the end of the season now. Too many tourists with salt-water-induced hair disasters to deal with.'

Claudia let out a breath. 'Do you think she's trying to avoid me? Distance herself, as a fellow Porthsteren business owner?'

'I haven't heard anything along those lines, honey,' Sarah soothed. 'And Libby's here, isn't she?'

'Probably more for the gossip than the meditation. Well, she'll be disappointed tonight. Not enough co-conspirators.' Claudia glanced at the clock. Five past eight already. 'Can't wait any longer, I suppose.'

She closed the door and began. But Claudia struggled to concentrate with the low attendance preying on her mind and Jason's presence in the room. She hadn't been able to get their kiss out of her mind since Saturday night, and she'd jumped every time her phone rang, making her feel like an awkward teenager. But he hadn't called. Then again, she hadn't called him, had she? Perhaps neither of them knew what to make of how the evening had ended... and that in itself justified her calling a halt to it when she did.

Claudia was so wrapped up in her thoughts, she almost didn't notice when the guided meditation ended. Her carefully-chosen track on the healing powers of forgiveness for oneself and others had been somewhat lost on such a small gathering.

At least Jason was amused by the subject matter. 'Shame you didn't have a bigger audience for it,' he said afterwards, his eyes twinkling.

Pleased there wasn't any awkwardness in his manner, she asked, 'How's Millie?'

'Fine. Jennifer and Harry are keeping her occupied.'

'Good.' *At least she won't be cooking up any ill-advised spells at their house.* 'How are you coping without her?'

'Loving the peace and quiet, but I know the novelty will wear off soon. I do miss her.'

Claudia nodded. 'Do you fancy coming to mine for a drink? I can't see this lot lasting more than five minutes.'

'I'd love to. Thanks.'

Her heart racing a little at the idea of being alone with him again, Claudia tidied away the tea mugs and kettle. Sarah and Evelyn were keen to get off home, and Libby took the hint. No doubt she had people to inform on how ill-attended Claudia's latest session had been.

*

In Claudia's flat, Jason gave Pudding a stroke then sat on the sofa while Claudia fetched a bottle of wine from the fridge. He picked up a book from the coffee table, read the blurb on the back, then flicked through it.

'You have a book with moon dates because…?'

'The moon is a very powerful thing.' Claudia handed him his wine and sat next to him. 'It pays to be attuned to the lunar cycles.'

'I'll take your word for it.'

She smiled, but Jason could see tired lines at her eyes and shadows beneath.

Concerned, he asked, 'Are you okay?'

'I'm fine.'

He gave her the well-practised look he gave Millie when he didn't believe her. 'Claudia, I'm not an acquaintance on the street who wants a glib answer, or Libby at the General Store demanding your life story when all you need is a bar of chocolate. I'll ask again. Are you okay?'

A shrug… and then her head was in her hands. She took a minute before straightening up, pushing curls from her face. 'No.'

'Tell me.'

'You saw for yourself – attendance tonight was rubbish.'

'You think it's to do with the Hester's debacle?'

'I can't see what else. People don't like unpleasantness. Gossip and tittle-tattle are one thing, but this has escalated. Airing dirty laundry on the radio, mud-slinging… Other business owners might worry it could damage Porthsteren. As for Healing Waves, I'm pulling in the tourists, but a lot of regulars are staying away.'

'It's summer. Perhaps they're busy.'

'It's never been like this before – takings are down compared with this time last year. The few regulars that do come in only want to gossip, not buy. Healing Waves should be a sanctuary, not a hotbed of bitchiness. All this adverse publicity…' Claudia sighed. 'I still think I was entitled to express my private opinion in a private conversation with people I trust, but I shouldn't have allowed it to be overheard. With Ollie Barton's help, Amber and Raven have made me look petty, snobby, and scathing about anything witchy or Wiccan… which is as far from the truth as it could be.'

Jason tried to soothe. 'You have a good, solid business in Healing Waves.'

'I thought I did. I was so proud of myself for building it from nothing. But you've seen how cleverly Hester's Cauldron is set out; how it entices. My self-confidence took a nose-dive the day I went in there.'

'Hester's is theme-driven, Claudia. A novelty. As are the owners. But Healing Waves is eclectic. It has a lasting appeal.' When this didn't cheer her up, he asked, 'Are you seriously worried about finances?'

'I sunk everything I had into Healing Waves. I make a comfortable living, but it wouldn't take much to destabilise that.' Claudia took a sip of wine, and he noticed the tremor in her hand. 'It's not just about money. Sarah and Evelyn have joked about retiring. What will I do, if they do? We're joined at the hip – people walk along the beach to visit *both* of us. What if the Page Turner becomes something incompatible with Healing Waves?' She sighed. 'I've put so much *effort* into this village, making friends, becoming a part of the community. I can't do it all again somewhere else, Jason. I did it once, and it took all of me. I can't… I can't lose everything and start again.'

Unable to find any words of comfort, Jason folded her in his arms, allowing her to sob. It was what she needed.

'Sorry,' she said when she'd finished, her teary eyes tugging at him.

'Don't be. You're entitled. And you need tea, not wine.'

He took her glass away and made chamomile for her. She needed distraction. But as he looked at her for inspiration, all he could see were those riotous curls around her slightly blotchy face.

Before he could stop himself, he'd blurted, 'Do you dye your hair?' *Ungentlemanly, Jason.* He made an apologetic face.

But Claudia laughed. 'Thank you for changing the subject. And as left-field as the question might be, I don't mind answering. No, I don't.'

Jason fingered her curls. 'But all those colours… It looks like you've spent a fortune on it.'

'Ha! The colours, maybe. The style, *if* you can call it that? Not so much.'

'I like it. It's…'

'A mess?'

'I was going to say natural. Unruly – in a sexy way.'

Claudia raised an eyebrow. 'Anything else you need to know about my womanly secrets?'

Jason could think of a few things, but if he was going to keep this decent… 'What perfume do you wear?' Her scent was light, tickling his senses without overpowering them.

'I make it myself.'

Of course you do. Heaven forbid that Claudia should do anything as conventional as wear shop-bought perfume.

'Jasmine with a hint of rose and a tinier hint of vanilla,' she told him.

'I like it.' *It's seductive. Exotic. Like you.*

She smiled. 'Another thing you like! I'm doing well tonight.'

Fed up with all this attention his mistress was getting from an interloper, Pudding jumped down from his armchair, strolled over, nudged their hands, then flopped on the carpet, playing cute. Stretching to a surprising length, he rolled onto his back, staring beseechingly up at Jason with amber eyes suspiciously like his mistress's.

Unable to resist, Jason dropped to his knees and reached out his hand.

'Don't be fooled by that look,' Claudia warned. 'Cats are different to dogs. You *think* he wants his tummy tickled, but believe me, he doesn't.'

Jason frowned. That wasn't the signal he was getting from the cat. Tentatively, he stroked Pudding's velvet-soft belly. Pudding purred for all of three seconds. And then Jason's hand and wrist were locked in a vice-like clamp by four paws and all available claws. Needle-like teeth helped the endeavour along.

'Aargh!' Jason tried to pull away, but the cat only rabbit-kicked with his back legs. 'Help!'

'Stop that! Bad cat!' Instantly by his side, Claudia distracted the cat with one hand while she pulled the fabric belt from her trousers with the other, then dangled it above the cat until he decided it might be more fun than Jason's flesh.

With a sigh of relief, Jason inspected the many pinprick dents on his forearm and hand.

'You're lucky he didn't play full on,' Claudia said. 'He was only being half-hearted. Taking pity on you as a newbie.'

'I'd hate to really rile him, then.'

'Did he draw blood?'

'A bit.'

'I did warn you.'

'You did. And I won't do it again.'

Claudia shot him a sympathetic smile. 'He fools everyone with that. He's hard to resist.'

As is his owner.

Claudia was still kneeling on the floor next to her pet, deftly managing the cat's playful tugs with the belt while holding Jason's gaze. The desire that flooded through him was so strong, it took his breath away.

He leaned over to kiss her, and there was no tentative exploration this time. His body was pushing him to *mean* the kiss.

Claudia didn't complain. Dropping the belt and leaving the cat to amuse himself, she dragged Jason back onto the sofa, barely breaking the kiss, then deepened it when they landed in an untidy heap among the cushions.

Jason's heart hadn't slowed since the cat's attack. If it sped up any more, paramedics might be required. He hadn't wanted, hadn't *needed* someone like this for so long. Not since…

Since never.

'I might need first aid,' he said when they finally broke apart. 'Or at least a blood pressure monitor.'

'We do seem to have chemistry.'

'They say opposites attract.'

She ran a finger over his lips. 'Does that bother you?'

'Right now, this minute? Not at all.' To prove it, he moved in for another kiss, which was just as spectacular as the last.

'Will it bother you in the future?' Claudia asked when he'd taken what he wanted.

'Hmm?' With his senses flooded, Jason could barely get his brain to function.

'About opposites attracting,' Claudia supplied helpfully, then smiled. 'Until you've thought about that, maybe we should leave things there. It's late, and you have work tomorrow.'

Work was a distant concept, but Jason stood. 'Okay. And sorry. You only invited me in for a drink. And I only meant to ask if you were okay.'

'And you did. And I told you I wasn't. And you comforted me, and then you distracted me – in a very nice way. It was exactly what I needed.'

'Happy to serve.'

She kissed him lightly and then he was out the door and down the steps, but he didn't go to his car straight away. He walked down to the water's edge. Throwing caution to the wind, he took off his shoes and allowed the night-cold waves to run over his feet, his heels sinking into the sand so he had to concentrate on keeping his balance… which was better than concentrating on Claudia.

Jason's system was swamped with sensations. Her scent; her soft lips moving on his, encouraging him to want more, to want *her*… Even in the early days with Gemma, he hadn't experienced that kind of desire. That had been a youthful, earnest passion.

It felt different with Claudia. Wiser. Deeper. Special.

When Jason finally fell into bed, he gave up on analysing his thoughts and allowed himself to think only of how it had *felt* to be with Claudia.

That night, his dreams were filled with how it might feel to make love with her in that magical flat of hers with its fairy lights and crystals and goddesses and bead curtains and cushions the colour of the sea.

Chapter Nineteen

Claudia was *so* looking forward to her day off. What with the storm and Millie's oracle cards and the dreadful Ollie Barton, it felt like she hadn't had much of one in weeks.

But first… Millie was due home tomorrow. That meant that tonight was the last of Jason's free evenings. Should she?

Her fingers tapped out the text as if of their own volition.

Do you fancy dinner at mine tonight?

While Claudia waited for his reply, she pulled on shorts and a T-shirt. She jumped when her phone pinged.

I do fancy it. And you. But you cooked last time. I should cook for you at mine.

That first part was a little racy. Claudia liked those little comments he made when she least expected them – he seemed so strait-laced the rest of the time. Not that his kisses had felt strait-laced last night…

No, that's okay. You have work today and I don't. Six thirty?
Six thirty is good. If you're sure?

I am.

With shopping to do and dinner to prepare, Claudia decided against too ambitious a day. Half an hour's drive later, she was setting herself up on Marazion beach with the spectacle of St Michael's Mount in view. It was early June now, and it would be busy, but since she'd been over to the island before, she was content to admire it rather than join the visitors queuing for boats across to the island or waiting for the tide to go out so they could safely walk the causeway. The sight of the castle on the rock was, as ever, impressive, and it put things into perspective, making Claudia's worries seem smaller.

This thing with Hester's Cauldron would die down. Nobody would have time for it once the summer tourists started really flooding in, and by the end of the season, hopefully everyone would have forgotten the unpleasantness. Hester's Cauldron would close for the winter, and Claudia would have her locals back.

As for Jason... Claudia didn't know *what* to feel about him. In a natural reflex, she pulled out her phone, checked she had a signal, and dialled Tanya.

'Hi. Can you take a quick break?' she asked.

'One of the benefits of being self-employed. Consider it done.'

'Did you have a good weekend at your parents'?'

Tanya made a disgruntled noise. 'Dad could only ask about my work, as usual – he can't cope with anything he doesn't approve of. Mum asked if I'd found a nice man yet, and when I said I didn't need to be defined by a man, thank you, she pointed out that I might fare better if I stopped playing with all this silly witch stuff. Do *you* think I enjoyed it?'

Claudia chuckled. 'There are advantages to my mother living across the Channel. I get away with just one winter visit a year.'

'Lucky you. How's Pudding?'

'He looks almost normal again.'

'Hester's?'

'Sick of the whole topic.'

'I'll ask no more. How about Jason?'

'Ah. That's what I wanted to talk to you about…'

Looking across at the island, Claudia filled Tanya in. Her thank-you-for-helping-me-with-the-cat dinner on Saturday and their kiss. Their post-meditation drink on Tuesday and another kiss. Her invitation for tonight.

'Good grief, Claudia! Can't I leave you in charge of your own life for just one weekend? My head's spinning!'

'So was mine after the kissing.'

'Oooh. That's quite a statement coming from a woman who's sworn off men for the past three years. I *said* you two had chemistry.'

'You did. And, as always, you were right. But there's still the rest, Tanya. He said something about opposites attracting, and I told him he ought to think about that. It's all moving a bit too fast.'

'*You're* the one who invited him to dinner twice in one week.'

'That's because Millie's away, so he's more relaxed.'

'And why exactly do you want him to be more relaxed?'

'I…'

Tanya laughed, low and throaty. 'I'll leave you to ponder on that.'

'I don't want you to leave me to ponder. I want you to tell me what to do.'

'You're a thirty-four-year-old woman, Claudia. I can't tell you what to do. But your intuition can. You've spent three years honing it. Try using it tonight. As for me, I've a website for a pop-up beach shack café to finish by tomorrow morning, so I'll have to love you and leave you, otherwise I'll be pulling an all-nighter.' Tanya allowed for a dramatic pause. 'As might you be. Good luck!'

Claudia glowered at her phone, then sat back and tried to enjoy the beach while thinking about what Tanya had said, calculating how much time to leave before starting back, and wondering which supermarket to call at. No way would she shop at Libby's and risk advertising the fact that she had a guest for dinner.

*

Shopping went well. Cooking went well. This time, Claudia chose something she could prepare in advance – soup followed by a salad. That way, they would be more relaxed.

And there was that word again.

For a moment, she dithered over what to wear, then told herself not to be ridiculous. She never wore anything that didn't make her feel good nowadays, so her turquoise midi-dress would do just as well as anything else.

When Jason first arrived, they exchanged a look that suggested they might be nervous but weren't about to admit it, but they soon settled into each other's company, drinking wine, eating, chatting. He told her about his parents who had moved to New Zealand a few years ago to join his brother there and Claudia explained her mother's propensity for swapping husbands with alarming regularity. Claudia spoke about her plans to try making her own candles when she had time in the winter to experiment, and her inability to provide online shopping while she was still a one-woman show – unless she wanted to work herself to death, which was hardly the point of her new start in Cornwall. Jason told her about his progress in his new job and how he hoped to set up his own practice one day.

And, inevitably, when they settled on the sofa after dinner, they kissed. Claudia allowed herself to enjoy his citrusy scent, the thrum of her escalating pulse... but finally broke off to ask him, 'Did you think about it?'

'Think about what? How the hell am I supposed to think about anything when you kiss me like that?'

Claudia couldn't help but laugh. 'About "opposites attracting", Jason. It's not necessarily a good thing, is it?'

'Feels good to me right now.' When he leaned in, she placed a hand firmly on his chest. He sighed. 'Alright. Yes, I thought about it, but I decided there wasn't an immediate or perfect answer and left it that. Can't *you* leave it at that?'

Claudia wasn't sure, but if Jason wanted to be carefree tonight – and he rarely got the chance – then maybe she should let him. When his lips met hers again and his hands began to roam across her back, down to her hips... well. It no longer seemed to matter.

Claudia responded with her own explorations, running her hands across his back, his chest. Needing to feel his skin, she moved her hands under his shirt to feel his muscles. With a sharp breath, Jason slid his hands up to brush the sides of her breasts then cup them through the summer-thin fabric of her dress.

Her breathing ragged, Claudia drew back from the longest kiss she had ever shared with anyone. 'We need a breather.'

'Yes.' Jason's breathing was as erratic as hers.

Claudia studied his face. They both knew where this was leading, surely? It couldn't follow any other course. They wanted each other. He wasn't often free to be alone with her.

Was he thinking along the same lines?

'Claudia, you're staring at me.' Jason placed his hand on her cheek. 'What is it?'

'I'm trying to work out what you're thinking.'

'All you have to do is ask. You're not psychic… Are you?'

Claudia smiled. 'No. Don't worry. So, what *are* you thinking?'

He kissed her lightly on the lips, then sat back, giving her a smouldering look. 'I wasn't thinking at all a moment ago. But if I *had* to say…? It's a mess in here.' He tapped his head. 'I'm thinking how good it is that we're friends now. How grateful I am for what you're doing for Millie. How much I hate that mermaid fantasy figure in your shop – which hasn't sold in the eight weeks I've known you, by the way, proving my point that it's hideous.'

Claudia let out a startled laugh… and registered the fact that he knew exactly how many weeks they'd known each other. That was significant, wasn't it?

'But mainly,' he went on, 'I'm thinking about how much I want to lead you through those irritating bead curtains of yours and make love to you.'

'Well, that was honest!' Watching his expression, Claudia said, 'I sense a "but".'

'Claudia, you know I haven't slept with anyone since Gemma.' He shook his head. 'I didn't want to bring my dead wife into this. What I'm trying to say… The truth is, I'm a little nervous. And I can't believe I admitted that. Now tell me what *you're* thinking.'

Oh dear. But it was only fair that he should be allowed to ask in return. And she should be honest. There was every chance she was about to sleep with him, after all.

'I want you, Jason. It feels right – you know me and my gut instinct. But I'm a little nervous, too. I haven't slept with anyone since Lee.' She smiled. 'Seems we're in the same boat.'

Piercing, pale blue eyes caught her up and refused to let her go. 'Maybe we should just throw ourselves in at the deep end.'

Claudia recognised his honesty and care for her… and desire, mirroring her own. 'Maybe we should.'

She brought her lips back to his. Perhaps it might have been better to skip the honesty, she thought, as their kiss only simmered. Perhaps it had taken some of the magic away. But honesty was *right* for the two of them.

With that thought, something in her shifted and settled. Her lips relaxed under his, and she moved closer until her breasts were pressed against his chest. When Jason deepened the kiss, rational thought left her altogether. The magic was still there, alright.

'Come with me.' Taking her hand, Jason pulled her off the sofa, batting the bead curtains aside with impatience. When he spotted the large pink crystal on her bedside cabinet, glistening under the fairy lights strung above her bed, he said, 'Even in here? Dare I ask what it is?'

'Rose quartz. It reduces stress and promotes healing. It's also associated with romance, although in my case, that isn't why it's here.'

Jason smiled. 'It suits tonight's purposes, at least.'

All talking stopped as he kissed her again, until every sense in her body was heightened, from her lips to her toes and all points in between.

'Too many clothes,' he grumbled as he tugged at her dress. When she was down to her underwear, Claudia started on his shirt, his jeans. Impatient, he helped her, then dragged her onto the bed.

For a brief moment, despite the soft glow from the fairy lights and a salt lamp on the shelf, Claudia felt too exposed, too vulnerable. And then his hands were on her body, exploring the curve of her breasts above her bra, her hips, her stomach, and she no longer felt vulnerable but wanted.

'You're so beautiful,' he murmured against her skin as his lips followed where his hands led. 'Like a wild-haired goddess.'

Claudia's lips curved. She was no goddess, but this man wanted her for *her*. With his touch driving her too far, too fast, she turned her attention on him, all nerves gone as her hands ran across his chest, down to his waist.

He pushed her hand away. 'Still too many clothes.' A logistical problem he solved for both of them in record time.

Skin to skin, they held each other for a moment as they absorbed the new sensations. And then the heat was back, her heart thudding against his, and they let it take them where it wanted.

Afterwards, they lay in the pink glow of the lamp, their hearts thumping, Jason's arm falling possessively across her chest, his face turned towards her.

Claudia was not inclined to speak. She had no idea what she would say. Jason appeared to feel the same, but there was no awkwardness. Their lovemaking had felt right. Lying together like this felt right.

She felt his breathing slow, his arm growing heavy across her body. Before he fell asleep, he whispered 'Claudia Rose' against her shoulder.

The way he said her name, the only man who used that name, and only at important moments, told her he felt it was right, too.

*

Jason was woken early by Claudia's living and breathing alarm clock – Pudding. The cat leaping onto the bed barely dented Jason's deep sleep, but when he felt paws batting at his eyelids, that brought him round quickly enough.

'Aargh!' He swatted at the cat, then figured he ought to be less combative with an animal that had so many claws near his eyeballs.

He needn't have worried. Now that Pudding had someone's attention, he was content to curl into the crook of Jason's arm, velvety soft fur against his bare chest, while Jason idly tickled between his ears and came round fully.

Claudia was still asleep, her hair spread across her pillow, golds and reds glinting in the early morning sun that sneaked through the slats of the wooden blinds. Her mouth was curved in a cat-like smile.

She was obviously used to her pet's morning habits and could ignore them. Perhaps Pudding had decided that if Jason had the effrontery to share her bed, he should learn what morning meant around here.

As Jason lay there, Claudia's shoulder against one arm, the purring cat under the other, the whoosh of the ocean a backdrop to his thoughts, the wind chimes jingling lightly in the breeze, he felt, for the first time in a long time, that life was looking up. Not because he'd broken a longer run than he would have liked of a sexless existence… although that wasn't negligible. Jason could have done that any time if he'd wanted to, but he wasn't looking for mechanical, loveless sex. He'd had enough of that with his wife, longing for their earlier days when it had meant something to them both.

Sex with Claudia had been worth the wait.

Pudding, on the other hand, obviously believed that waiting for something worth having was basically overrated. His gentle nips at Jason's hand hinted that breakfast was due. Not wanting to wake Claudia, Jason shifted Pudding, climbed carefully out of bed, pulled on his boxers, and cursed the rattle of the bead curtains as he padded barefoot into the kitchen.

'I don't know where she keeps your food,' he told the cat. Pudding responded by stalking to the appropriate cabinet and sitting at its door.

Jason gave the cat half a sachet and put the kettle on. When he'd made tea – Claudia would have to settle for normal, since he had no idea which of her many leaf teas was correct for mornings – he went back into the bedroom to find her just waking.

'Thanks.' She struggled into a sitting position, demurely dragging the sheet up to cover her breasts, and took the mug he handed her. 'I slept like the dead!'

Jason grinned. 'That might have been down to the mind-blowing sex.'

She spluttered out a laugh. 'You thought it was mind-blowing?'

'Er – yeah.' Doubt crossed his features. 'You didn't?'

'I don't think my mind had anything to do with it, frankly. My body, on the other hand…'

He groaned. 'Please don't mention your body. I'm having enough trouble controlling myself as it is.'

Glancing at her bedside clock, Claudia gave him a long look, her golden eyes teasing him from under long lashes. 'It's still early. Why worry about controlling yourself? I could miss my yoga. Do you have to be at work early?'

'No, but I need to go home and change, and I don't have my car.'

Claudia smiled. A siren smile. 'If I drive you home, will that give you enough time for some mind-blowing sex first?'

*

After he'd showered – if you could call it that, in Claudia's tiny cubicle – Jason glanced at his watch. At home, he'd have time to change, but a shave was five minutes he didn't have. Designer stubble, maybe?

Claudia grabbed her keys and they clattered down the steps from her flat. She was already heading to her car when Jason looked back to see a dog walker staring at Healing Waves. Jason moved nearer to see why.

'Claudia. Come back here.'

They stood side by side, gazing in dismay at the crudely spray-painted black symbols on the shop's white walls.

Pulling out his mobile, Jason phoned work to say he'd be late, claiming his car had a flat battery. He didn't feel like explaining that his new lover had evil symbols painted all over her property.

'What are they?' he asked when he'd ended the call.

Blinking back tears, Claudia pointed to each. 'That five-pointed star in a circle is a pentacle. It symbolises the four elements and spirit. The triple moon, you know from my necklace. That one over there is an Eye of Horus. It's for protection.' Claudia sighed. 'They're all associated with witchcraft.'

'For crying out loud!' Jason's dismay at the graffiti was overtaken by the thought that in two days' time, his daughter would be working within these walls. He hated the idea of Millie getting caught up in this stupid feud.

'None of these symbols are harmful,' Claudia told him, understanding his need for reassurance. 'So why paint them on my walls?'

'Oh, come on, Claudia. This *has* to be the work of those two from Hester's Cauldron.'

'I'm not sure about that.' Claudia drummed her fingers against her thigh, studying the wall. 'For a start, these symbols aren't remotely artistic, are they? The Hester's crew have an eye for presentation. These are rough and ready.'

'Covering their tracks.'

'And the symbols they've chosen are benign – nothing that screams "black magic", which you'd think would be the effect they'd want if they're out to damage my reputation.'

'We all know they don't know their subject very well.'

'But what do they stand to *gain*?'

'Making your life miserable? Casting you in a poor light?'

Claudia threw out her arms in frustration. 'But that doesn't work, does it? Think about it. They tout all things witchy over at Hester's Cauldron, while they've put me down as a sour, outdated New Ager. So why would they want to suggest *I'm* a witch?'

'Ollie Barton brought up those old rumours. Perhaps they're taking advantage.'

'But wouldn't that work *against* them? Make people intrigued about me again? Direct attention *away* from Hester's?'

Jason didn't have an answer to that. But if he couldn't deal with the theory, he could at least be practical. He took out his phone again.

'What are you doing?' she asked.

'Photographing the evidence. Phoning the police.'

'The police? Oh, Jason, no…'

He looked at her, incredulous. 'Claudia, you have malicious graffiti painted across your property. That's criminal damage! And your insurance company will expect you to report it.'

Claudia shook her head, fire-and-flame curls bouncing madly around her face. 'I'm leaving the insurance company out of this. After the storm damage, my premiums will already be sky-high. I can fix this myself.'

'That's your choice. But the police *will* have be told. You can't ignore this.' Seeing her pale face, he softened his tone. 'Do you have white paint that'll cover it?'

'Maybe.'

'Go and find it. We'll get to work as soon as the police have been.'

But by the time the police had attended, so had everyone in Porthsteren… along with local press photographers.

Jason knew Claudia didn't relish the attention. He wasn't too keen himself. Would people put two and two together and work out that he was there because he'd spent the night? He *could* have been out on an early walk and seen the damage and alerted her to it. Or she could have seen it first and phoned him for support. He hated the idea of asking her to cook up a plausible story with him. She was distraught enough already. And he didn't want her to be offended that he was so keen to cover up their... whatever it was.

In the end, Jason didn't have the heart to bring it up. Claudia would know not to say anything. She'd told him to trust her discretion once before, and he should do so now. Not that he had any opportunity to catch her alone as she did her best to run Healing Waves while juggling the police and the press and the casual bystanders.

Knowing it wasn't what Claudia wanted, Jason stopped short of voicing his opinion about the culprits to the police. Even though he itched to say something, she was right about there being no proof.

The police confirmed what Jason already suspected – the chances of catching anyone were minimal-to-none. There were no CCTV cameras at this end of the village, only at the harbour to protect the boats. Porthsteren rarely had trouble like this. Unless a kindly witness came forward...

Still, Jason was glad he'd called them. Such things should be reported. Something else might happen, and he didn't like *that* thought at all.

Sarah and Evelyn were in and out of the Page Turner all morning, bringing cups of tea as required, upset on Claudia's behalf.

'Good job you were here for her, Jason,' Sarah stated matter-of-factly when Claudia was out of earshot. He could have sworn he saw a glint of curiosity in her eyes, but if she had her suspicions, she was discreet enough not to say anything. 'Claudia never believed in gossip. And the one time… well. Now look.'

'But it *wasn't* gossip, was it?' Evelyn objected. 'She was chatting with friends, and it was overheard.'

Sarah sighed. 'The end result's the same, though, isn't it?' She turned to Jason. 'Claudia isn't into everything that Tanya is, but she does believe in "harming none". She doesn't like to hurt anyone's feelings. She worries about karmic retribution.' She pointed at the graffiti. 'And here it is.'

'What the hell are you talking about?' Jason asked her, lost.

'Claudia believes that if you voice something negative, you're sending negative energy out with it.' Sarah smiled. 'You know her – she tries to turn anything into a positive. Haven't you noticed that whenever she talked about Hester's, she countered everything negative with "I hope they do well" or whatever?'

'Well, whoever's in the karmic retribution office today has come down a bit hard on her, if you ask me,' Jason grumbled.

Claudia only managed to persuade him to go once he'd applied the first coat of paint, pointing out that it had to dry before the next coat, which she could do herself. As he left, he had to settle for giving her a supportive peck on the cheek. Too many onlookers. She mustered a weak smile, and he knew she understood. He could only hope that nobody noticed he was walking home to fetch his car.

As he drove to work, his stomach growling loudly at its lack of breakfast and no sight of lunch, Jason forced himself not to think about the morning's events… or about what had happened last night between him and Claudia. The roads were narrow and winding – dangerous, if you didn't keep your mind on the task. And once he'd reached the office and swallowed down a stale doughnut lurking in the mini-kitchen, he had to corral his mind so he didn't come across as a sleep-deprived idiot.

But by the end of the day, his brain was screaming at him to process things. And so, before the long drive to fetch Millie from the halfway point he'd agreed with Harry and Jennifer, he took a short stroll in a nearby park, barely registering his surroundings.

Claudia Rose. How that name suited her, suggesting mystique, a promise of something – some*one* – unusual. She was kind and generous. She could be infuriating. She was thoughtful. She had a fiery temper, on the rare occasion she unleashed it. She was vibrant and yet serene.

And she was beautiful.

Last night had been magical, if he was feeling lyrical about it. Any misgivings had disappeared as he was surrounded by her – her scent, her warmth. Claudia had given herself to him without any sense that she had given away any part of herself she didn't want to. Knowing what he did about her, that was touching, emotional… and it made their lovemaking meaningful.

Why should that worry him? He wasn't after a one-night stand or a short-lived fling. Something like that wouldn't be wise with a local, someone he couldn't avoid afterwards, someone so close to his daughter.

And there it was. Millie.

A one-night-stand his daughter didn't know about couldn't hurt her. A complicated relationship with someone she cared for could. Millie was in a difficult enough phase already. The idea of threatening their delicate status quo was unthinkable. Millie welcomed Jason and Claudia getting along, but how would she feel if she knew they had become involved? She might turn cartwheels. She might throw something at him. She might not speak to him, so he wouldn't know *how* she felt. What if he and Claudia became serious about each other?

Jason wasn't sure he was ready for serious. Serious led to commitment. Commitment was something he'd felt saddled with for years, from the moment his marriage began to fail to the death of his wife to the aftermath of becoming a single parent to a traumatised teenager.

He knew that Claudia would never stifle him, not knowingly – and being with her made him feel lighter, not heavier. Jason didn't *want* to regret his night with her. But his doubts and fears meant that, to some extent, he already did.

Chapter Twenty

When the ping of the doorbell heralded Tanya's arrival, Claudia was relieved. After the rubbish day she'd had – after its *very* promising start of early morning sex with Jason – her best friend's arrival was perfectly timed.

'You wanted to see me?' Tanya asked with a quirk of her lips.

'Did your crystal ball tell you that?'

'No. My intuition. And social media. Why didn't you call?'

When she folded Claudia in her arms, Claudia allowed the tears to fall. 'Because I knew you'd charge over here,' she mumbled.

'I would have.' Tanya pulled away. 'Will wine help?'

'Maybe. Here's my key. I'll just finish up here.'

'Fine. Gives me time with my favourite furry friend.'

When Claudia entered her flat soon after, two glasses of wine were already poured. Tanya and Pudding were lying together on the rug, gazing into each other's eyes, Tanya stroking his belly and Pudding making no attempt to stop her, his purr as loud as an engine.

Claudia shook her head. 'Why don't you get your own cat?'

'I'm a witch. A cat would be too obvious, don't you think?' Tanya moved to the sofa, much to Pudding's annoyance, picked up her wine and said, 'Tell me about Jason first. I was going to phone you tonight anyway, to find out what happened.'

'Oh. Ah.' *Was that less than twenty-four hours ago?*

Claudia told her. Not the intimate details, but the gist. When she'd finished, she asked anxiously, 'Do you think I made a mistake?'

'Not at all. We said to listen to your intuition, and you did.' Tanya smiled. 'Sounds like it paid off.'

Claudia's own smile was coy. 'It did. It was… different than with Lee.'

'I should hope so!'

'What I mean is…' Claudia grasped for the right words. 'I could tell Jason wanted *me*. Lee wanted my body, I think, not *all* of me. And even then, there were all the stipulations – preferring my body a certain way. It didn't feel like that with Jason.'

'So, not only great sex, but sex that meant something to you.' Tanya let out a dramatic sigh. 'I'm jealous.'

'Don't be. Just because *I* thought it meant something doesn't mean that Jason did. His life's more complicated than mine. He's fetching Millie back this evening.'

'You and Millie get on well. Surely that won't be a problem?'

'What I see as a problem and what Mr Volatile sees as a problem can be two different things.'

Tanya patted her hand. 'Well, I'm pleased you found someone you wanted to move forward with. You were right to take a break after Lee, but I'd've hated it go on *too* long. You should be with someone special.' Her green eyes turned dangerously cool. 'I hope Jason knows that.'

'I wouldn't know, would I? The morning's events scuppered any meaningful discussions, not that we'd've had a chance. We were already pushed for time, after…' She blushed, then sighed. 'Jason insisted on calling the police about the graffiti.'

'Quite right.'

'He also wanted to tell them he suspects Hester's Cauldron, but I wouldn't let him.'

'You don't suspect them?'

Claudia explained her theories, just as she had with Jason that morning.

Tanya mulled it over. 'I'm with you. Yes, they have something to gain by making your life difficult. But the symbols were ill-chosen – too benign. And they were crudely drawn by an amateur. Their shop displays prove they're not amateurs – artistically, anyway. And all this does is draw attention to you; get people speculating about you being a witch again.'

'Which is the last thing Jason wants, with Millie working at Healing Waves,' Claudia grumbled.

'Hopefully, he won't take it too seriously.' Tanya winced. 'And I can't believe I'm defending that narrow mind of his.'

'It'll only get narrower, because he doesn't know yet how much in awe his daughter is of the fact that I'm friends with a real witch.' Claudia huffed out a breath. 'Maybe I shouldn't have mentioned that in the radio interview.'

'You had a right to defend yourself, and that was as good a way as any.'

'Jason *also* doesn't yet know that Millie and her friends are saving up for supplies so they can try out spells from a book they bought at Hester's.'

'Ah.'

'Do you think I should tell him?'

'Did Millie ask you not to?'

'Yes.'

'Then you can't, can you?'

'I slept with him, Tanya. That changes things.'

'It changes a lot of things, but…' Tanya looked at her empty wine glass. 'I could do with another of those. Can I stay over?'

'Of course! You don't have to ask.'

'I do if Jason might come looking for a repeat performance.'

'He won't. Millie's back, remember?'

'Ah, yes. Millie.' Tanya refilled her glass. 'She has a right to experiment, Claudia. All you can do is gently guide her. I don't mind talking to her, if you think it might help.'

'I'm sure her father would love that!'

'Yes, well, he might have to choose, mightn't he? Unfettered experimentation versus structured guidance.'

'I'm not sure he even realises it's a problem, let alone that he's stuck between two choices he'd prefer not to have to make. Millie *thinks* he spotted the spell book, but he hasn't said anything to her or me. That makes me think he doesn't imagine they might actually use it.'

'Then it's down to you and me,' Tanya said firmly.

'Go behind his back, you mean?'

'Only until we find out how serious Millie is. I know that goes against the grain for you, Claudia, but Millie has you over a barrel. Besides, if this is only a brief whim, Jason need never know. Why cause unnecessary upset?'

Put like that, Claudia found it hard to argue. Millie would never forgive her if she blabbed. And Jason's blood pressure was probably already at a dangerous level.

'As for this evening…' Tanya delved into her copious bag. 'How about a protection spell? Then pizza.'

'Do they go together?'

'Well, they're not mutually exclusive.'

*

Jason and Claudia weren't the only ones upset about the graffiti. Millie had already found out about it by the time Jason fetched her the previous evening. Social media could be a pain sometimes – there was no escaping anything or protecting her.

'Are you worried about working there on Saturday?' he'd asked her on the drive home.

'No. Why would I be?'

If Millie hadn't figured it out for herself, Jason didn't want to be the one to point out that her situation was awkward – a customer at one establishment and an employee at the other. Perhaps she hadn't associated the damage with Amber and Raven. And since Claudia didn't agree with him and wouldn't want him to say anything, he had to keep his mouth shut on that score.

This morning, Millie insisted that they drive to Claudia's to help with the painting.

'She needs to concentrate on the shop,' Millie said. Jason couldn't argue with that, and since his daughter had got up unusually early for a teenager on school holidays to do it – and there was the other small matter of checking on how the woman he'd recently slept with was holding up – he agreed.

Claudia was already on her knees outside, beginning to slap on the second coat of paint.

Jason's stomach flipped when she turned and smiled, a streak of white paint highlighting a red curl. The graffiti, work and Millie's return had all snatched away any chance to discuss what had happened between them.

A text hadn't seemed adequate. *Thanks for the life-changing sex but I'm not sure a relationship is a good idea right now?* Hardly.

Looking at Claudia now, her cropped jeans and T-shirt clinging as she stood, her hair escaping its makeshift restraints, he wondered why on earth he *wouldn't* want a relationship with her.

'Did you have a good time in Devon?' she asked Millie.

'It was okay, thanks. We've come to paint. Then we have to do a supermarket shop. Then we'll come back late afternoon and do another coat.'

'That's very thoughtful of you.' Claudia turned to Jason. 'Off work?'

He jerked a thumb at his daughter. 'Too young to leave for an entire day. You know that old saying: *While the cat's away.*' At that, Claudia looked worried, prompting him to ask, 'Are you okay?'

'Hmm? Yes. Considering.' She smiled at Millie. 'You really want to paint?'

'Yep. So does Dad. Don't you, Dad?'

A sharp kick to Jason's shin had him saying, 'Absolutely', making Claudia laugh – something he was willing to get a bruise for.

'I'll order coffees to show my appreciation, then open up.'

Five minutes later, Evelyn came out with their drinks. 'Flat white for Jason. Mocha for Millie.' Indicating the wall, she said, 'Shame yesterday's coat wasn't enough to cover it properly.' She looked up at the clear sky. 'Good day for it to dry, though.'

'Yep. We'll do a final coat later.' Millie sipped her drink, glancing at the sign over the bookshop. 'That's a great name – The Porthsteren Page Turner.'

Evelyn smiled. 'Do you know how it came about?' When Millie shook her head, she said, 'Would you believe that my surname's Turner and Sarah's mother's maiden name was Page?'

Jason grinned. 'That's fantastic!'

'Serendipitous, certainly.' When Jason's gaze drifted to the sign over Claudia's, Evelyn said, 'Claudia came to Porthsteren to heal. The sea does that for her. And then there's the play on words – something coming at you in waves. In this case, Healing Waves.'

Just like Claudia, with me and Millie, Jason thought. *Every time we need her. Isn't it time I do something for her?*

That thought stayed with him all day, through the painting and the food shop and the putting away and the drive back to Healing Waves late in the afternoon. His brief conversation with Claudia cemented it.

'Good day?' he asked her, noting the worry lines.

'I, well…' She glanced over at Millie, busy prising the lid off the paint tin, oblivious. 'Quiet. Well, not quiet, but people only wanted to talk about the damage.' She sighed. 'Not many tourists, either. Maybe the half-covered graffiti put them off, or they'd seen the news. Who knows?'

'I'm sorry. I hope it picks up soon.' Jason kept his voice low. 'Claudia, we should talk about… You know.'

She nodded understanding, then jerked her head towards Millie. 'Yes, but some other time.' Then louder, 'Well, I'll leave you to it. Thank you.'

Jason's heart stuttered. Knowing she understood his situation meant a great deal.

And that was it for him. Her worry over her takings, the shock and hurt she had to absorb every time something like this happened… The storm was just an act of nature, but the accusations over gossip, the radio interviews, and now the graffiti? It was too much.

'Millie, I forgot something at the other end of the village,' he said. 'Can I leave you to it for ten minutes?'

'Sure.'

The drive only took him a couple of minutes.

The greeting he received was frosty. 'We didn't expect to see you in here.' The red-headed one raised an artificial brow. 'We gather you *disapprove* of Hester's Cauldron.'

That took him aback. He'd only been in here once.

The other girl joined her partner. 'You're the one who said we were frauds.'

Ah. That would explain the frostiness.

'And we know you're tight with the owner of *Healing* Waves.' She said 'healing' with a sneer. 'Miss Sweetness-and-Light. All of Porthsteren knows *she* disapproves of us even more.'

'That's what I came to speak to you about,' Jason said, desperate to get a handle on the conversation. He hadn't expected them to be so aggressive. He'd also expected the shop to be almost empty at this time of day, but it wasn't – although he saw no one he recognised, thank goodness.

He lowered his voice. 'You must be aware, surely, that it was *you* who made all this spiral?'

'We didn't ask Ms Bennett to diss us on the radio.'

'Claudia would never have spoken publicly if you hadn't pushed her into it.'

The redhead folded her arms, her stance confrontational. 'She'd *already* spoken publicly, hadn't she? Telling everyone what she thought.'

'No. She was overheard chatting to friends. There's a difference.'

'I don't see how, if those friends tell someone down the pub who tells the postman who tells Libby at the General Store.'

She was right, of course. But you'd have to keep your mouth permanently closed in a place like this to avoid it.

'That wasn't her intention,' Jason insisted. 'You've forced the issue and created this ridiculous feud.'

'I wouldn't call it ridiculous. I'd call it protecting our business interests.'

Jason gave her a knowing look. 'Any publicity is good publicity? You wanted everyone talking about Hester's Cauldron, and now they are?'

The dark-haired girl waved her hand around the store. 'It hasn't done any harm. How busy is Healing Waves right now?'

Don't rise to the bait, Jason. Say what you came to say and get out of here. 'Look, the reason I'm here—'

'Yes, why are you here? To protect your girlfriend?'

'Claudia and I are just friends.'

Another arched brow from the redhead. 'The kind of friends who leave each other's flats first thing in the morning?'

Ah.

Jason took a deep breath, marshalling his thoughts. 'I came to talk to you as two sensible, mature business owners, but since that's getting me nowhere, I'll just spit it out. What you're doing to Healing Waves has to stop. Verbal sparring is one thing. Physical damage is another. I suggest—'

'Stop right there.' The redhead held out a hand, palm facing him. 'We have no idea what you're talking about.'

'Oh, I think you do.'

'*If* you're referring to yesterday's incident, Raven and I have been nowhere near Healing Waves. I suggest you think very carefully before you throw accusations like that around. We have lawyers.'

Jason couldn't help himself. He'd heard their backstory from Evelyn on one of his visits to the Page Turner. '*Daddy's* lawyers?'

She gave him a long, cool stare. Jeez, these women were ice queens.

'Does it matter, as long as they're good at their job?' she said. 'Which they are, by the way. *Very.* Now, if you wouldn't mind, we have customers to serve. Don't hurry back.'

Beaten, Jason stepped outside and leaned his back against the cool stone wall of a nearby cottage.

Well done, Jason. Talk about how to make a bad situation worse.

He waited for his heartbeat to slow and his temper to fade, but that was too big an ask. How could a man who led meetings at work with competence and quiet authority, mediating between clients and contractors and authorities, be reduced to a blethering idiot by two twenty-somethings? The uncomfortable idea that he'd been unable to keep his emotions in check because this involved Claudia surfaced, but he ruthlessly buried it again.

Still, he wouldn't have had to go in there if Claudia would forget this rising-above-it-all stuff and allow him to talk to the police properly.

At Healing Waves, Millie had just finished painting, and Claudia was locking up.

'Where did you disappear off to?' she asked.

He couldn't face confessing. Claudia wouldn't approve, even if it was for her sake. Maybe she wouldn't find out…? *Yeah, right.*

'Nipped to the General Store. Ready to go, Millie?'

'Yep.' Millie stood and brushed off her jeans.

Claudia frowned. 'I can't tempt you to a cuppa?'

Jason could see that Millie wanted to, but he needed to go home and lick his wounds. 'Sorry. We have to get back.'

He saw the brief flicker of confusion and hurt on Claudia's face before she said, 'Okay. See you tomorrow, Millie. Thanks for painting.'

'Wasn't that a bit rude?' Millie challenged him as they climbed into the car.

'I have a banging headache. I need to get home. Take some painkillers.' *Lie down in a darkened room.*

'I'm sure Claudia would've had something that might help.'

'What, like weed-of-hedgerow tea?'

Millie spluttered out a laugh, then let him be.

As the car climbed the hill, Jason allowed his analytical mind to take over. He'd found out two things. One – those women were enjoying this debacle, or at least, they didn't mind the publicity. And two – they were denying responsibility for the vandalism at Healing Waves. Well, they would, wouldn't they? It didn't mean they weren't behind it. Who else had anything to gain from making Claudia's life difficult?

*

It was a good Saturday at Healing Waves. Claudia had Millie restocking shelves because they really did need restocking, rather than just to occupy the girl – a positive sign. She felt better with the graffiti covered up. And with more tourists than locals in the shop, there wasn't much idle gossip – a blessing, with Millie there.

In quieter moments, she chatted with Millie about Devon and asked, as casually as she could, whether she'd caught up with Phoebe and Jessica yet.

'Phoebe suggested a sleepover at hers tonight, with Jessica.' Millie waggled her phone. 'I messaged Dad, but he hasn't got back to me yet.'

Claudia's heart began to thud, loud and slow. If Millie went to Phoebe's…

Jason and I could spend the night together.

And Phoebe could have Millie dabbling in sorcery.

That, I can't do anything about. Jason, on the other hand…

When Jason called for Millie at three, his daughter immediately complained about his lack of reply.

'Sorry, kiddo. Didn't see it. What's up?'

When Millie explained, there was the briefest of looks between him and Claudia, before he said, 'No problem. It'll be good for you to catch up with them before school on Monday.'

Hustling Millie out, a wicked smile at his lips, he mimed a texting motion behind his back.

Claudia waited a couple of minutes, then took out her phone.

Mine at seven?

She was afraid he might take it to heart that she hadn't suggested his house. But she couldn't invite herself – and the truth was, she'd feel uncomfortable sleeping with him in the home he shared with Millie.

She needn't have worried. A simple *See you then* came back ten minutes later. Perhaps he felt the same way.

Claudia's euphoria at the turn of events did not last long, however. First, she had Alice to contend with, an anxious look on her pale face.

'Claudia. I saw all about the graffiti in the papers. I'm so sorry.'

'Don't worry, Alice – it was just one of those things. But thank you.' When Alice stood there fidgeting, Claudia said, 'Not out and about with George today?'

'Saturday afternoons, he's always at the Smugglers' Inn,' Alice said tightly. She glanced at her watch. 'Better go. He'll expect his tea promptly when he gets back. Anyway, I just wanted to say I'm sorry for your trouble.'

Claudia stared after her as she left the shop. *What a bizarre conversation.* It was good of Alice to stop by, she supposed. But as for the days of having your man's tea on the table when he got back from the pub... Hadn't that gone out with the ark?

At four, Evelyn bustled through from next door. 'Have you heard?'

'Heard what?'

'About Jason.'

Claudia's heart stopped. 'What? What's happened?'

Perhaps seeing that all the blood had drained from Claudia's face, Evelyn quickly said, 'Nothing like that. Sorry. I meant about Hester's.'

Heaving a huge sigh of relief, Claudia said, 'No. What about Hester's?'

Ten minutes later – breaking off when customers came in – Claudia was up to speed. She couldn't be sure how accurate Evelyn's version was, since it all depended on how many mouths it had passed through along the way, but the gist was bad enough.

'I'll kill him! I *told* him not to say anything! He just can't help himself, can he? I'll…'

'I'm sorry, Claudia.' Evelyn looked miserable. 'Sarah didn't want me to tell you. She said you and Jason are… close, but I said that was all the more reason for you to know.'

'You did the right thing, Evelyn. Thank you.'

*

'Have a good time. And behave,' Jason said as he dropped Millie off at Phoebe's.

And don't do anything with that stupid spell book I'm not supposed to know about… other than burn it. Because if it was yours and not Phoebe's, that's what I'd *be doing.*

Millie rolled her eyes. 'You always say that.'

'It's my job.'

As he drove back into Porthsteren, Jason persuaded himself that he and Claudia needed this opportunity to talk about what was going on between them. But if it led to where it did before… His body was clear on where it stood, but his mind remembered the doubts after last time.

And yet he couldn't ignore the way his pulse had quickened when Millie asked about the sleepover; the look Claudia had shot at him across the counter, a look filled with knowing and promise, a look he couldn't resist.

On the way, he bought flowers.

Over the top, Jason?

Don't care.

When Claudia opened the door, he barely got over the doorstep before she laid into him. He certainly didn't get a chance to hand over the bouquet.

'What were you playing at, going to Hester's Cauldron yesterday?'

Not the greeting he'd expected, but perhaps one he deserved.

Jason closed the door and placed the flowers on the nearest surface. His tone defensive, he said, 'I went to appeal to their better natures.'

'And?'

'They haven't got any.'

Claudia drummed her fingers on the small dining table by the door, setting his teeth on edge. 'More like you went in there firing off accusations and getting their backs up?'

'I only tried to do what was right, Claudia, and I won't apologise for it. Those women are behind the vandalism, and you know it. Just because you're too soft to say something doesn't mean I have to let them walk all over you.'

'I wouldn't use the word "soft".'

Her eyes narrowed dangerously, like a cat's about to pounce. If it was Pudding he was facing off against, Jason would have been seriously worried.

'I might use "planning a measured response after weighing all the facts and actually having proof",' she said.

'They needed a warning. That's all I went to deliver.'

'And did it work?'

'No,' he admitted.

'No. And from what I gather, as well as holding my business in smug contempt, they are now under the impression that I need to be protected by a man because I'm incapable of looking after myself.'

Jason shuffled, uncomfortable under her livid gaze. 'That would be accurate also.' He sighed. 'I cocked up. I admit it. Happy now?'

'Do I look it?' Her eyes flashed golden fire. 'Honourable intentions are all well and good, Jason, but you can't let your temper get the better of you like that. You need to learn to control your emotions better.'

'Oh, like you? Because I'm telling you now, Claudia, all that serenity crap of yours irritates the hell out of me sometimes. And for your information, I control my temper and emotions just fine when *you're* not in the equation!'

Jason wrenched open the door and started down the steps.

Chapter Twenty-One

Claudia wasn't sure whether to be disturbed by that last admission of his or whether to take it as a compliment. She did know she only had a split second to decide whether to leave it at that – Jason stomping off in a sulk, their evening ruined. She'd prepared a meal, despite what Evelyn had told her, although she hadn't known whether she'd serve it to him or dump it over his head.

Don't let him go like this.

'Jason!'

He was almost at the corner of the building. Claudia saw his hesitation, the determined steps continuing on his way, and her heart sank.

But then he stopped and turned. 'What?'

'Come back in.'

He stood, his chest heaving with temper, before retracing his steps and climbing the stairs. At the top, he declared, 'I'm not coming back in for another dose of that crap.'

'Okay.'

Stepping in, he picked up the abandoned flowers and thrust them at her with a gruff, 'For you.'

They spent the next ten minutes in awkward silence as Claudia opened wine, handed him a glass, fiddled with a pan on the stove, prepared a salad, sliced rustic brown bread.

Maybe I should have let him go.

Jason occupied himself by stroking Pudding with caution, as though the cat might attack him as viciously as his mistress had.

When Claudia had run out of small tasks to occupy her, from the safe distance of the kitchen she said, 'I'm sorry.'

'Me too. I made a mess of it.'

'Your heart was in the right place. I shouldn't have got so angry with you.'

Jason stood and cautiously approached. 'Well, like I said, your serenity can be overrated. And I know it's a cliché, but you *are* beautiful when you're angry.'

Her attempt at a smile wobbled, and then his lips were on hers. Gentle, inquisitive.

'We've had a rubbish couple of days,' he said. 'No chance to discuss anything. Sleeping together… I hadn't expected it. Not so soon, anyway.'

Claudia kept her eyes on his. 'Do you regret it?'

He gave her that half-smile, the upturn at one corner that she adored. 'Would I have come here, bearing flowers, if I did?'

Despite his words, Claudia saw the doubt in his eyes. It was understandable. As she'd said to Tanya, his life was complicated.

As though he could read her thoughts, he said, 'Let's just take it as it comes for now. Nobody else has to get involved at this stage.' He sighed. 'Although… Did your grapevine tell you that the Hester's women know I left here yesterday morning?'

'No.' Frowning, Claudia carried her pot of overcooked mushroom stroganoff to the table, leaving him to follow with bread and salad. 'That's not good.'

'Maybe the grapevine hasn't got that snippet. Or maybe Amber and Raven aren't sure of their facts and were just goading me.'

'What if they say something to Millie?'

Jason served himself salad. 'I might not like them, but I find it hard to imagine they'd ask a fourteen-year-old girl about her father sleeping with her employer.' He made a face. 'That sounds awful. Sorry.'

She laid a hand on his. 'No more apologies.'

'Then no more worrying, okay? Tell me more about… I don't know… your mother?'

'Ha! Don't get me started.'

Jason successfully distracted her throughout the meal, and by the time they had curled up on the sofa, Claudia had managed to relax. After he'd plied her with an extra glass of wine – 'Medicinal. Get it drunk.' – and put an arm around her as she sipped, his fingers playing with her hair, stress seemed a very distant thing.

Jason didn't say anything as he pulled her off the sofa and through the bead curtains, until… 'Your cat's in the bed.'

Pudding glared balefully at them from one eye, the other firmly shut, making the point that he *had* been fast asleep, thank you very much.

'He's not *in* the bed,' Claudia said. 'He's only allowed at the bottom of the bed on *top* of the covers.'

'Oh, well, that's alright then. What now? I don't think a spectator's going to improve my performance.'

Claudia smiled. 'You'll have to turf him off.'

'Why me?'

'Because you're the interloper.' Jason's expression told her he was reading too much into that statement. 'In *his* life, not mine,' she added hastily. 'Oh, for goodness' sake. I'll do it.'

She scooped the cat up, Pudding remaining in his sleepy coil as she transferred him to his favoured armchair.

'See? That wasn't so hard, was it?' she said as she went back through to the bedroom.

'If I'd've done it, I'd be in intensive care,' Jason grumbled. 'But thanks.'

'You're welcome. So, now we have the bed all to ourselves, what are you going to do about it?'

His wicked smile made Claudia's stomach flip. 'Plenty. I'm going to do plenty about it, Claudia Rose.'

*

It was just one of those things, Claudia told herself afterwards. A set of circumstances. Nobody's fault. Everyone trying to do their best.

Or it was universal payback – have a great time in the sack with Jason, and you'll pay some other way.

Millie popped into Healing Waves on the way home from school on Monday, excited to tell her news to someone she thought she could trust. She and Phoebe and Jessica had tried casting a spell at their sleepover on Saturday. Nothing terrible had happened, and they felt it had been semi-successful, although she stopped short of saying which spell exactly.

Perhaps Claudia should be pleased that Millie trusted her, but in these circumstances, she could have done without it. She also could have done without knowing that while all that was going on, she and the girl's father had been rolling around in bed together.

As Millie finished her tale, Tanya – taking a diversion on her way home from a meeting in Hayle – called into Healing Waves, and Claudia introduced them.

'You're the witch?' Millie asked, eyes wide.

'Yes, I'm the witch. Good to meet you, Millie. I've heard a lot about you.'

Millie glared at Claudia before turning back to Tanya. 'I haven't heard much about *you*.'

Tanya winked. 'That's because Claudia likes to keep me all to herself.'

'Millie, could you watch the counter for a minute?' Claudia asked. 'I have something I need to show Tanya out back.'

'No problem.'

Whispering in the utility room, Claudia told Tanya the latest news.

Tanya blew out a breath. 'Witchcraft is often self-taught, Claudia. Trial and error.'

'I understand that, but I doubt Jason would. He'd view it as silly nonsense at best and dangerous dabbling at worst.'

'Do you want me to have a chat with her? Make sure she understands?'

'Would you? Oh, but… Jason might not like that.'

'What, he might not like a knowledgeable person chatting to his daughter about her interests, instead of letting her play it by ear and spend all her pocket money at Hester's Cauldron?'

'Okay. You're right.' Although Claudia felt pretty sick about it.

Back in the shop, Tanya said, 'So, Millie, Claudia's a bit busy, but I'd kill for a mocha before I drive home. Are you up for one?'

Millie jumped at the chance, making Claudia smile.

She wasn't smiling an hour later. 'You offered to *teach* her? For goodness' sake!'

'It wasn't my intention. But she isn't daft, Claudia. We started out okay – her asking questions, me laying out some basic principles. But she soon twigged what you and I were up to. She made the point that if we're so worried, maybe I should teach her.'

Claudia was pale under her light tan. 'And you agreed? Just like that?'

'Not exactly. I told her I was willing, within limits, but *only* if her father agrees. And I made it clear that I won't take her word for that – I'd have to speak to Jason.'

'He is *not* going to be happy about this, Tanya!'

'Maybe not, but we've solved one of our problems, haven't we?'

'Have we?' As far as Claudia could see, they'd just created several more.

'If this is only a whim, Millie won't be brave enough to tackle Jason, and that'll make her realise she's not fully committed. She might still dabble, but that could've happened anyway. If she *is* serious about it, she's obliged to tell her father, thereby relieving you of the responsibility of keeping all this from him.'

A little colour came back into Claudia's cheeks – but only a little.

*

Up until Monday night, Jason *had* been riding on cloud nine. Or at least cloud eight-ish.

Saturday night and Sunday morning with Claudia had been nothing short of wonderful, despite their inauspicious start. He couldn't imagine how things would have been left between them if he'd stormed off. He hadn't liked her anger, but it was justified – he'd made a mess of things with Hester's Cauldron. That place had a lot to answer for, in his opinion. But her anger had passed, and so had their awkwardness.

The more time he spent with Claudia, the less he worried about where it might go. Perhaps taking a leaf out of her book, he wanted to relax and enjoy the journey. Millie was a potential problem, but at the moment, what they were doing shouldn't impact on her.

Work was slotting into place, too. After two months of feeling out of place and overwhelmed, he was finally getting to grips with his projects and his colleagues' personalities. The partners had called him in that morning to tell him they thought he was doing a good job – a huge relief. The idea of finding a new job, of uprooting Millie again, was unthinkable.

Millie had already begun cooking dinner when he got home – generally a sign that she wanted something. That was okay. Jason was in a magnanimous mood.

She made her play after dinner. And he couldn't believe what he was hearing.

'You want my permission for Tanya to teach you how to become a *witch*? You know how I feel about that sort of thing!'

As Millie wriggled in her seat, a distant part of Jason's brain registered how much she must want this, to risk asking when she knew what his reaction would be.

'Dad, calm down before you burst a blood vessel.' Millie's attempt at humour fell on stony ground. 'I know how you *used* to feel. But I thought, what with us spending more time with Claudia…'

Claudia again.

'You *know* I'm interested in this stuff.' Millie's chin wobbled. 'Since you don't approve of Hester's Cauldron, I thought this way was better. Have you even *met* Tanya?'

A tear fell, touching Jason's heart.

'Yes, I have.'

'And?'

'I liked her,' he admitted. 'But that doesn't mean I believe in everything she believes. It doesn't mean I want you to, either.'

Millie was crying in earnest now. 'I don't get to have my own interests? I don't get to grow up? I always have to do what you say?'

'Millie…'

But she was already heading for the stairs. The loud slam of her bedroom door spoke volumes about his parenting skills.

Damn Tanya. Damn Claudia.

He'd snatched his car keys from the kitchen counter and was out the door before he'd even thought it through.

*

Claudia was doing yoga when Jason pounded at her door. Even though she'd half-expected it, the wave of anger and resentment that rolled in with him was impressive.

Since she'd had her turn ranting at him on this very doorstep just the other night, she listened patiently as he raved about witchcraft and his daughter being exposed to bad influences.

Eventually, she waded in. 'Jason, you are *so* blinkered. Don't you think that Millie comes across "bad influences" every day at school? You can't control half of what she does, so the half you think you can, you go over the top about.'

'You think it's over the top for me to not want my daughter to be taught *witchcraft*?'

Claudia took a deep breath. If it wasn't for Millie, she'd call a halt to this conversation.

'I'll list a few points for you to mull over, okay? Then that's me done, because I'm getting tired of going around in circles with you. Are you willing to listen, at least, before you go away and ignore everything I say?'

Jason opened his mouth, then closed it again. Finally, he said, 'I'm listening.'

Claudia sighed. She was wasting her breath, but she would do this for Millie's sake. 'You're an intelligent man. You listened to Tanya at the Smugglers' Inn, and you couldn't object to what she said in an abstract sense, so please don't use words like "witch" and "witchcraft" in the kind of tone you're using. Surely that's beneath you by now?'

'Fair enough.' He shook his head. 'But we're talking about my daughter here.'

'Look, if Millie wanted to go to church on Sundays, would you stop her? If she took an interest in Buddhism, would you object? You need to put aside inbuilt prejudice from old storybooks, think about what Tanya told you, and ask yourself if Millie looking into Wicca is any worse than anything else that might catch her eye. If she learns new things, develops a healthy respect for nature and her environment, is that so terrible?'

'In theory, no. In practice…'

'If you think Tanya'll have Millie cooking up powdered bat's wing in a cauldron or dancing naked in the woods with a bunch of hedonists, then you already know that's total bollocks.' Claudia ignored his raised eyebrow at her rare colourful language. If it brought him up short, that was no bad thing. 'You know Tanya's decent and careful. She has no desire to influence Millie or inculcate her into anything dodgy. All she wants to do is balance out Millie's notions. You think Hester's Cauldron is a bad influence. You wish Millie didn't like it in there. But she finds those young women fascinating, Jason. They're attractive and wear exciting clothes and make-up. They're charismatic. They take time to talk to her.'

'Because they know a mug when they see one.'

'Maybe. Maybe not. But I *don't* think they're trying to instruct her in dark magic or sign her up to a coven.' When his expression remained stony, she said, 'If you're worried about that, then surely the sensible way to counteract it – because disapproval will only drive her in the opposite direction – is to have someone explain to Millie what Wicca is *really* about. Let her make her own mind up.'

Jason said nothing, but Claudia had thought she'd wasted her time with him before and yet he'd come around.

'Well, I'm done here.' She made ready to close the door. 'I'll only remind you that Tanya's a busy woman who lives a good distance away. She doesn't *need* to spend time with your daughter. She offered because she wants to help and she's qualified to do so, unlike Hester's Cauldron. Take your pick, or Millie will take hers.'

Jason's expression was mutinous. 'And I'll remind *you* that I'm Millie's father. I don't need you to explain her psychology to me, nor do I need your advice on how to handle my own daughter. You're not her mother, Claudia, so stop trying to take on that role and undermine mine.'

He might as well have slapped her face. Shocked, Claudia staggered back a step, turned and walked to her bedroom, leaving Jason to let himself out.

*

Claudia didn't feel like running meditation the following evening, but she couldn't cancel just because she felt out of sorts.

It didn't surprise her that Jason didn't come. It did surprise her that Millie turned up. She'd assumed Jason would forbid it or lock her in her bedroom or something equally draconian, in case Claudia set up a bubbling cauldron right there in the room above the Page Turner.

Claudia went through the motions for the next hour, but she knew her leadership had been flat.

So did Sarah. 'Everything okay, honey?' she asked over their cuppa.

'Fine.'

'You don't look fine.' Sarah glanced around to check where Millie was. 'Dare I lay a guess on Jason?'

'Pah,' was all Claudia could manage. 'That man infuriates me.'

'Evelyn used to drive me nuts at first,' Sarah told her. 'Still does, come to that. But that's often a sign of how much you care about someone.' When Claudia shook her head in denial, Sarah said, 'It's true. If you don't give a damn about someone – about what they do or think – then they can't irritate you, can they? Think about it.'

'I don't *want* to think about it,' Claudia grumbled. 'Anyway, who says I care about Jason?'

Sarah leaned in closer. 'I do. I know we're not supposed to know, and you have Tanya to talk to, but if you ever need me or Evie, we're always here for you.'

'Thank you.' Claudia hated the idea that Sarah might feel shut out. She should offer up *something*. 'The thing is, I need to take a step back with Millie.'

'At Jason's behest?'

'Yes.'

'But why?' Sarah frowned. 'Anything to do with Tanya and Millie huddled over their mochas at the Page Turner yesterday?'

If only that were all. 'Partly. Millie wants to get into Wicca. Tanya offered to set her on the right path. Better her than Hester's Cauldron.'

'Jason isn't keen, I take it?'

'Understatement of the year.'

'Someone could do with shaking some sense into that man, if you ask me. About you as well as Millie.' Sarah tutted. 'He isn't breaking up with you over this, is he?'

In other circumstances, Claudia might have smiled at Sarah knowing far more than she'd been told, but a pervading sadness flooded through her at her friend's perceptive words. 'I… I hadn't thought of it like that.' She'd thought of it as another row, another source of disagreement. But Jason had gone a step further with his comment about her trying to be Millie's mother. That still stung. 'I suppose I hadn't really thought of us being together,' she explained to Sarah. 'We weren't even dating, just catching time together, so as for breaking up…? Well. I hadn't thought of it like that.'

'And now *I've* made you think of it like that. I'm sorry, honey.'

'Don't be. Sometimes I need the obvious pointing out to me.'

Sarah smiled, but as Millie headed their way, she whispered, 'I have no idea how you'll take a step back from her, honey. That girl idolises you.'

As if *that* made Claudia feel any better.

*

When he'd dropped Millie off at meditation, Jason breathed a sigh of relief. That gave him over an hour. He drove home with a sense of purpose mixed with misgiving that made his stomach clench.

He'd agonised all day, to the point where he'd got little work done and irritated colleagues with his lack of attention. But his row with Millie the previous night had eclipsed everything else. His daughter had gone from not liking him much to not liking him at all.

Claudia didn't think much of him, either. He hoped, when she calmed down, that she understood he was only trying to protect his daughter; wanting her to share his own mindset. But that incessant explanatory style of hers, telling him why he was wrong and pointing out how unreasonable he was… It had made him so mad. He'd accused her of interfering. Of trying to be Millie's mother. He doubted she'd understand *that*. His thoughtless comment must have hurt her. He'd been way out of line.

Well, he would deal with the problem of Claudia later. Right now, Millie was his priority.

At home, he pulled out his phone, searched online for the number, then dialled. There was no guarantee she'd answer her business number so late, but self-employed people rarely clocked off at five.

'Tanya Webb. Can I help?'

Jason might have smiled at the surname if he hadn't been so nervous. 'Tanya, it's Jason.'

A long pause. 'What can I do for you?'

'Do you have time for a chat? Preferably online? Face-to-face would be better for me.' *So I can read your expression. See the nuances.*

'I suppose. I'll warn you now, though, I don't have any make-up on. And I'm in my pyjamas.'

'I can live with that.' The woman didn't need make-up, from what Jason remembered.

'I'd pop over there in person, but my broomstick's in for a service.'

Two minutes later, Tanya was there on his laptop screen, a guarded expression on her face. 'You gonna ball me out about Millie?'

Well, that's *straight to the point.*

'I was hoping to speak to you about Millie – not quite the same thing. She told me about your offer last night.'

'I'm guessing you're not keen. And no, I don't need my crystal ball for that.'

Jason sighed. She wasn't giving him much leeway here.

'The truth? No, I'm not. I was mad. I spoke to Claudia…'

'Oh? What did she say?'

Claudia hasn't spoken to Tanya about my outburst yet? Is that good or bad?

'That I was blinkered. That my stubbornness would only drive Millie in the wrong direction. That Millie has a right to explore new things. That you're only trying to guide her while she does.' *And a few more things besides, none of them complimentary.*

'That's quite a nutshell you summed it up in.' Tanya waited, then prompted him with, 'And?'

Jason blew out a long breath. 'Give me some good reasons to agree to this, Tanya, beyond the ones that Claudia already rammed down my throat.'

Tanya raised an eyebrow. 'Okay. Well, like I told you before, Wicca respects nature and the planet – values I assume you've instilled in your daughter. It's also to do with harming none. I can't imagine you have a problem with that, either.'

'No, but… You said something about believing in gods and goddesses?'

'Some do, some don't. Millie can choose. All she needs is an open mind.'

'As opposed to a closed one like mine?'

Tanya sighed. 'Alright, let's try this: Wicca is a very individual path – of learning, of self-development, of self-empowerment. It honours women all over the world; recognises past sacrifices. Surely that's as good a path as any for your daughter to follow, isn't it?'

The woman was so damned reasonable. And as Claudia had pointed out, she had nothing to gain by doing this.

'What about crystal balls? Spells?'

Tanya hesitated, as though knowing this was where she could lose him. 'Scrying is a way of going into a relaxed state that allows us to "see" more than when we're hyper-alert and too aware of everything around us. You let Millie do meditation, don't you?'

'I… Yes.'

'As for spell-weaving? That's about intent, partly – choosing a spell would help Millie think about what she wants or needs to manifest, which is a good thing.' She smiled reassurance. 'I promise you I'd lead her in gently; make sure she understands every stage. Not push her if she loses interest.'

Jason studied Tanya's earnest, elfin face. He might not share her beliefs, but he believed in her sincerity.

He broke the silence. 'Okay. I'll speak to Millie.'

The look of surprise on Tanya's face was blatant. 'You're doing the right thing, Jason. I'll be careful with her, I promise. Get her to call me.'

'Will do. Thanks, Tanya.'

Closing the connection, Jason sighed. He still had the problem of Claudia to deal with. Yes, he'd behaved badly, but he was tired of apologising. He'd already given in to Tanya. He couldn't face another major headache tonight.

Is that how you think of Claudia, Jason? As a problem? A headache? If you do, then perhaps a cooling-off period wouldn't go amiss.

Chapter Twenty-Two

Since she had to drive to Falmouth for an evening at Tanya's, Claudia had an excuse to spend her Wednesday off at one of her favourite places on the way there – Glendurgan Garden. Three valleys of exotic plants and trees leading down to the beach… The perfect place to lose herself, exploring, deliberately pushing all thoughts and worries from her mind and concentrating on her surroundings.

By the time she arrived at Tanya's, she'd found an equilibrium of sorts.

'Go out or stay in?' Tanya asked her.

After her day outdoors, Claudia found the idea of hunkering down in Tanya's tiny cottage claustrophobic. Besides, if they stayed in, Claudia would probably spend the evening crying. In public, she'd have to restrain herself.

'Can we go out?'

'There's a new place opened that does a few veggie dishes. Let's give it a try, shall we? *After* a glass of wine at the pub.'

Once they were seated in Tanya's local, busy for midweek, Tanya asked, 'Any news from the police?'

'No. I doubt there will be. If anyone had seen anything, they'd have come forward by now.'

'I'm sorry, Claudia. Now, about Jason…'

Assuming she was after the latest rundown, Claudia told her about their row over Millie, ending with his accusation that she was trying to be the girl's mother.

'I can't believe he said that!' Tanya was livid. 'He's an arse. Just wait till I speak to him again!'

'Don't you dare. He'll think I've asked you to turn him into a toad or something.'

'No need. He already *is* a toad.'

'That's unkind to amphibians.' Claudia frowned. 'Wait. What do you mean, "speak to him *again*"?'

Tanya sighed. 'It's a long story. Let's get to the restaurant, shall we? Or we won't get a table.'

Claudia followed Tanya through the streets of Falmouth, admired the Moroccan-influenced décor of the restaurant and ordered a lentil burger.

'What do you mean by "again"?' she repeated. The suspense was killing her.

'Jason called me last night,' Tanya admitted. 'He got my number from my website.'

'*What?* Why?'

'He agreed to me meeting up with Millie.'

'*What?*' Knocking her water glass, Claudia carefully mopped up the spill.

'Could you find a different response, Claudia? I'm going to get bored with that one soon.'

'But I don't understand!'

Over the meal, which Claudia barely tasted, Tanya filled her in. While they talked, Claudia realised that Tanya looked a little stunned at the turn of events herself.

'Well, that's good, I suppose,' Claudia finally said, pushing her plate away.

Tanya frowned at her lack of enthusiasm. 'I'd've said it was quite a result. Millie phoned me earlier, and we agreed a date.'

'So why hasn't Jason let *me* know?' Claudia asked.

'Maybe he hasn't got round to it yet.' But Tanya didn't seem convinced.

Claudia thanked the waiter for her mint tea and sipped. 'Or maybe, even if he's done a U-turn on Millie seeing you, it doesn't mean a U-turn over what he said to me.'

Thin-lipped, Tanya said, 'I would've challenged him about that, if I'd known. He only told me he'd spoken to you and that you'd been rather... strident.'

Claudia sipped her tea again, hoping it would settle her stomach, but it made no difference. 'Could we go? I need fresh air.'

Slipping off their shoes, they walked back to Tanya's along Gyllyngvase beach. The fresh air was downright chilly now, but Claudia didn't care.

'What will you do about Millie?' Tanya asked.

'Jason made it clear he doesn't want me so involved with her. The fact that he agreed to her seeing you doesn't alter that.'

'You can't drop Millie like that.'

'No, but I can back off. I'll have to work with her on Saturdays as usual, but there'll be no more giving advice, no heart-to-hearts, nothing beyond chatty conversation.'

'Do you think you can do that at this stage?'

Claudia's lips set in a hard line. 'I can try.'

'What about Jason?'

'What about him?'

When Claudia swiped at a tear, Tanya tutted. 'You're in a relationship with him, Claudia. You slept together. More than once.'

'I don't think he sees it as a relationship. Just because he gave in to the attraction between us doesn't mean he wants to deal with the consequences.'

'You think he regrets getting involved?'

'Honestly? Yes. Involvement with any woman would affect Millie, but he's ended up with one who has wacky ideas he can't cope with and doesn't want his daughter exposed to.'

'That's bollocks!' Tanya snapped. 'He might have thought of you that way at first, but not now. I know it's been like pulling teeth with him every step of the way, and he doesn't always agree with you, but he does respect you.'

'I'm not sure that matters.' Claudia sighed. 'The fact is, he's happy to have sex with me, but he doesn't want me to get ideas above my station when it comes to his daughter.'

'I'm not sure that's quite fair…' Tanya began.

'You're *defending* him?'

'No. I'm trying to understand him.'

'Well, good luck with that.'

*

Waking way too early and unable to get back to sleep, Claudia left a note for Tanya and set off home. If she was back at Healing Waves by seven, she might even have time to make a batch of soap – although she'd have to bring Pudding down to sit and watch. He never liked her overnighting at Tanya's. Too little attention. Too little food.

As she drove, she thought about Jason. He'd spoken to Tanya but not had the grace to tell her? To explain himself or apologise?

That was disappointing. And it hurt. She'd shared so much of herself with him. Her past, her body, her hopes and fears – all given freely. And all, as far as she could see, thrown back in her face.

The sight of the police car outside her building made her heart stop. The Porthsteren Page Turner or Healing Waves? Her gut told her the latter. Parking crookedly next to the patrol car, she rushed to the front of the building.

Her shop window was shattered, glass spread across the terrace in front and sprinkled copiously within – over her window display, in and among her goods.

'Ms Bennett?' It was the same young police officer who'd attended the previous week. His familiar face was small consolation to Claudia. 'We've been trying to reach you for the past hour.'

'I'm sorry. I was staying with a friend. I think my mobile's on silent.' *Stop babbling, Claudia.* 'When did this happen?'

'Someone over the road heard the noise and came to investigate about…' The officer glanced at his watch. 'An hour and a half ago.'

'Five thirty in the *morning*?'

'The perpetrator obviously didn't want to be seen. Not long after that, you'd get dog walkers, joggers.'

'Perpetrator?'

He pointed into the ruined display. Three large rocks from the beach, perhaps picked up just yards away, lay among the rubble.

Claudia sank to the ground, her head in her hands. 'Oh no.'

The policeman kindly crouched so that he was at her level. 'Ms Bennett, do you have any idea why you're being targeted like this?'

'Targeted?'

If her parroting his every word annoyed him, he didn't show it. 'The graffiti could just have been wanton vandalism – although the symbols suggest otherwise. But now this? I'll ask you again. Do you know who could be targeting you?'

'I can tell you who.'

Jason had rounded the corner like a hurricane… and he was the last person Claudia felt able to cope with right now.

'Jason, what…?'

'I was on my way to an early site meeting. Saw the police car.' He looked over at the damage, then back at her. 'Are you alright?' He stopped short of wrapping his arms around her, although she sensed he wanted to.

Well, he can keep his arms to himself.

'Yes. I was at Tanya's.'

'We met last time,' the officer said. 'Mr Craig, isn't it? You were saying?'

Recognising what he was about to do, Claudia murmured a warning. 'Jason…'

But he gave her that stubborn look she knew meant he wouldn't be shifted. 'I have my suspicions.'

Claudia glared at him. 'Suspicions aren't proof, Jason. That's how poor Hester was hounded out of here, remember?'

'We're not talking about an old healing woman.' Both of them ignored the poor police officer, lost at the reference to the Moon legend. 'We're talking about two melodramatic and vindictive young women.'

Claudia shook her head. 'Bad-mouthing me is one thing. Damaging my reputation to improve theirs? Maybe. But serious vandalism… I can't believe they'd go this far.'

'I can.'

'So you're going to chase them up into the hills with a pitchfork?'

At this, the young officer looked alarmed. 'Er. Ms Bennett, Mr Craig…?'

Jason turned back to him. 'There's been acrimony between Hester's Cauldron and Healing Waves.'

At this, the officer gave him an enquiring look. 'Would you care to explain, sir?'

Jason did. Claudia wasn't at all keen on his commandeering attitude or his strategy with the police, but she was impressed by the swift yet careful way he summed up the series of problems with Amber and Raven. To her surprise, he ended by reiterating that although it had been very unpleasant, he had no proof that they would go this far – he merely felt it might be a lead worth following.

Claudia only hoped the police officer assumed that Jason doing all the talking despite her being the owner was down to her being upset rather than incapable of speaking for herself.

When he'd left, she turned to Jason, saying in a clipped voice, 'You need to get to work.'

'Looks like I'm taking the day off.'

'You said you had an early site meeting.'

'Too late now. Another colleague's there. He can handle it.' He took out his phone and walked towards the beach as he spoke.

When he came back, she said, 'Let me guess. Millie has flu? You sprained your ankle? The car's got a flat tyre?'

'I told them a friend has an emergency.'

Oh. That made it so much harder to tell him what a pig he'd been this week.

He gave her a knowing look. 'I assume you're mad at me on two counts. Firstly, for overriding you with the police. That had to be done, and you know it.'

Claudia gave a small nod. She accepted that. The damage was more serious this time. For the sake of her business, she couldn't allow the situation to escalate.

Jason placed a hand on his chest. 'Secondly, what I said on Monday? I apologise wholeheartedly. It was uncalled for.'

Claudia opened her mouth to respond, but as she glanced around, she saw that they were beginning to get an audience of walkers and joggers. It was like being in a goldfish bowl. And when Sarah and Evelyn came around the corner...

'We can discuss it later,' he said quietly. 'Let's just deal with this for now.'

'You can't—'

'I'm a grown man. I can do what I like. And you can't do this on your own.'

And so followed another day where Healing Waves was closed and business was lost. More phone calls – to the insurance company, to the emergency glaziers, and to Tanya, who offered to come over but changed her mind when she heard Jason was already there.

Meddling matchmaker.

Jason was invaluable with the clearing up, taking on the bulk of the glass removal, sweeping and vacuuming, while Claudia judged what stock might be safe to keep. As Sarah and Evelyn had found after the storm, anything nearest the front of the shop had to go – it was unsafe to sell. What if someone used her soap and cut themselves on a slither of glass? Or rummaged in a cloth bag they'd bought and sliced a finger?

All the while, she pushed to the back of her mind what this would do to her insurance premiums.

Sarah or Evelyn appeared at regular intervals with hot drinks and snacks to keep them going, and when, by five-ish, they had done the best they could and the window was boarded up, Jason called things to a halt.

He'd been right – she couldn't have done all this alone, or certainly not as quickly. The fact that he'd risked disapproval at work and let others down in order to help her, with no hesitation whatsoever, went a long way to make up for his recent misdemeanours.

'Smugglers' Inn to eat?' he asked.

Claudia hesitated. This morning, she'd still been so disappointed in him, and now they might be going to the pub together? 'What about Millie?'

'She's at Jessica's. I'm picking her up at nine thirty.'

Exhausted, Claudia went up to her flat to feed Pudding, then allowed him to drive her to the pub and buy her a glass of wine. But it soon became apparent that they wouldn't get any peace, what with locals coming over to commiserate and gossip about who might have done such a thing. Claudia wondered how much they were gossiping about her and Jason sitting together, too. Word must have got around that he'd spent the entire day helping her. With Millie to think of, that wasn't good.

After twenty minutes, she whispered, 'Beans on toast at my place instead?'

Jason smiled in relief. 'Perfect.'

After they'd eaten their simple supper, Jason made decaff tea. 'Are you okay?' he asked.

Claudia sighed as she stroked her much-neglected cat, his expression making it clear that he didn't appreciate not having her full attention more often.

'It's yet another setback, isn't it? It costs me time and money while I'm closed, then while I restock. Tourists don't come to Healing Waves because they *need* something – they come because they like the look of the place. It won't attract them over the next few days.'

'I know. Look, about telling the police, if it wasn't the Hester's gang, then nothing's lost – the police having a word with them might make them think twice about disrespecting you in future. And if it was them, even if it can't be proved, they'll stop there.'

'You're right.'

Jason cupped his ear with a hand. 'I'm sorry?'

Claudia gave him a look. 'I said, you're right.'

'Okay. I won't gloat.' When she slapped his arm, his expression became serious again. 'Claudia, I *am* sorry about the other night. You've done a lot for Millie. What I said about trying to be her mother… It wasn't fair.'

Claudia merely nodded. It was good that Jason wanted to apologise, but what he'd said still smarted, so she turned to the main reason they'd argued – Millie's burgeoning interest in Wicca. 'Tanya told me you'd agreed to her helping Millie.'

'Yes. A lot of what you said made sense, once I'd calmed down.'

'It goes against the grain for you.'

'Yes.'

Claudia placed a hand on his. 'You're a good man, Jason.'

He shook his head, lacing his fingers in hers. 'I just want to do what's best for my daughter.'

Claudia *could* have said he had a habit of going about that the wrong way. That he rubbed his daughter and everyone else up the wrong way while he was at it. But she reminded herself that he'd gone totally against his own feelings to allow Millie to see Tanya. That was no small thing. As for continuing to allow his daughter to blame him for divorcing her mother, keeping Gemma's affair to himself for the sake of Gemma's memory… How painful must that be, keeping it locked inside like that? Absorbing Millie's anger and frustration day after day?

'You're a good man,' she repeated.

He managed a small smile. 'Sometimes I wish I wasn't. It might hurt less.'

Claudia leaned in and brushed her lips against his. He needed a distraction. An outlet for all that stress and tension he held inside.

'You don't have to be good with me,' she murmured against his mouth. 'Would that help?'

Returning the kiss, he nipped her bottom lip lightly with his teeth, then sighed. 'I'm sure I could be very bad with you if I tried, Claudia Rose.'

Her heart thumping, she took his hand. 'Let's find out, shall we?'

As she led him to the bedroom, for a panicked moment she hoped he hadn't misconstrued what she had in mind. There were no whips or handcuffs in her wardrobe. What she *could* offer him was to let down her barriers more. To encourage him to let down his. No restrictions between them; just allowing themselves to be how they wanted to be. No rational thought.

As she unbuttoned his shirt, he glanced apologetically at his watch. 'I only have an hour.'

'Then we'd better make the most of it.'

*

Jason barely slept that night. He had no idea what was happening – whether his life was going pear-shaped or finally looking up; whether his relationship with Claudia was a great idea or a terrible one; whether his relationship with Millie was improving or worsening. Every day turned the previous day on its head.

Claudia was the main cause of his wakefulness tonight, though. They were drawn to each other like magnets, yet they had nothing in common. He didn't believe a quarter of what she believed in. He didn't like that he seemed to spend half his time apologising, yet there was always a good reason to. She brought out the best in him… after she'd brought out the worst in him. After what she'd been through today, so soon after the storm damage, he'd wanted to wrap her in cotton wool and make sure it never happened again. At the same time, he'd wanted to throttle her for her reticence with the police. He simply wasn't in control with her.

As for their one precious hour of lovemaking, control hadn't played much of a part in *that*. When she'd led him through the bead curtains… One look from those golden eyes could turn him on. As for that full mouth waiting for him to kiss her, the floaty clothes clinging to curves he already knew could drive him mad, and a bed only inches away…? He'd been lost.

Jason had thought they'd given themselves freely to each other before, but he'd been wrong. There'd been so much farther for them to go – in desire, in sensation, in raw need. His body still throbbed with it.

Did amazing sex justify them being together? *Were* they together? He hadn't even admitted to his own daughter that they were involved. Millie idolised Claudia. If it was important, why hadn't he told her?

Because I don't know how I feel yet, other than bewitched. I need to know if it's something before I drag Millie into whatever it is. I told Claudia I want to do what's best for my daughter, and that will always come first.

*

Claudia spent Friday still closed, replacing soap, restocking, reordering.

Jason didn't call, but he texted. That was okay – he had work to catch up on after losing a day helping her.

The glaziers had replaced her window by Friday teatime, and Claudia could not have been more grateful. She couldn't afford to lose Saturday business. Texting Millie to say she was still needed after all, she stared at the new glass and the empty display space. A window display meant working all evening. With a sigh, she texted Tanya who, on standby all day, offered to drive over to help.

Claudia *had* thought things couldn't get any worse. That was until a fifty-ish man in a sharp suit stalked into Healing Waves, his latent aggression unmistakable.

He looked around with disdain. 'Ms Bennett?'

'Yes?'

'Thomas Barker. Amber's father.'

This can't be good.

'How do you do?' Claudia held out a hand that was pointedly ignored.

'I would do better, Ms Bennett, if you and your boyfriend ceased waging your campaign against my daughter and her business partner.'

What? Talk about being wrapped around his daughter's little finger!

Claudia did her utmost to sound calm, although her heart was racing. 'I assure you, Mr Barker, there is no campaign. Perhaps Amber and Raven haven't provided you with a full account of events.'

'Are you saying that my daughter lied to me?'

Very probably. 'I'm saying there are two sides to every story.'

'Think what you like, Ms Bennett, but you can't accuse my offspring of criminal damage without consequences and set the police onto them with no proof whatsoever.'

'I did nothing of the kind.'

'That's not the way I see it. And by the way, I suggest you rein in your boyfriend and ask him to refrain from making accusations on their premises in front of their customers.'

Claudia's mouth set in a thin line. 'Already done. For that, and *only* that, I apologise.'

The man's eyes narrowed to vicious slits. 'I shall be visiting the police tomorrow to say much the same. But rest assured, Ms Bennett, the next time I have to come down from London, I will bring a highly qualified and very expensive solicitor with me. I suggest you think about that.'

When he'd gone, Claudia sat, head in hands. Was she ever going to wake up from this nightmare?

Tanya arrived to rescue her sanity. Insisting on wine as they worked, she listened to Claudia's tales of woe, now numerous.

'I hate people throwing their weight around like that!' she said of Amber's father. 'Who does he think he is?'

'Does it matter? If he has clout, then he has clout. I don't intend to get on the wrong side of him, if I can help it.'

'What about Jason?'

'I don't think he'll pull a stunt like that again – storming in there. He knows how I felt about it.'

'Are you mad at him for telling the police about the feud yesterday?'

'No. He was right to. It's not his fault it backfired.'

'But why was he here at all?'

As they worked, stringing fairy lights through large shells and crystals, Claudia filled Tanya in on Jason passing by, missing work to help her clear up, his apology, the kindly but claustrophobic nature of the pub. The beans on toast.

'Very exotic! And then you had hot, dusty sex, right?'

'Right.'

Tanya's mouth fell open. 'Crikey! I was being sarcastic!' When Claudia sighed, she said, 'What's that for?'

'I don't think it was a good idea.'

'Since when was hot, dusty sex not a good idea?'

'It's less the sex and more the man. We argue... We kiss. We argue... We have sex. We argue... We have even better sex.' Claudia had thought about that a lot since Jason had left her in bed the night before. 'I mean, what's the point?'

'Apart from the fact that the sex gets better every time you fall out?' Tanya sat back on her heels, her green eyes on Claudia, unwavering. 'The *point* is, you're in love with him.'

Claudia stared at her. 'No, no, no. We're attracted to each other. We're friends, *when* he's not yelling at me. And we're great in bed together. That doesn't mean I'm in love with him.'

Tanya gave her a sad smile. 'Been too busy to listen to that intuition of yours lately?'

'My intuition works just fine, thank you.'

'Didn't say it didn't. Just said you haven't been listening.'

Claudia thought about that later. Half the night, in fact. By morning, she still couldn't decide whether Tanya was right or stark raving mad. Claudia was so wound up about everything that was going on in her life, she just didn't know.

If Tanya was right – and Claudia wasn't admitting she was – then the main problem was Millie. Jason wanted to keep their relationship from her for now, but that couldn't last forever. And despite his apology, Claudia couldn't forget what he'd said about her trying to be Millie's mother. She knew it had been said in anger… But if she *was* in love with him, would that make her behave like that towards Millie even more, in Jason's eyes?

And so, when Millie came to work, Claudia found herself doing just as she'd planned before Jason's apology – keeping a polite distance, watching every word, judging which topics were safe and which to steer away from. It wasn't easy, but it was necessary – at least until Claudia decided whether Jason's apology was enough for her… although she had a feeling the sex would have led him to assume it was.

Perhaps sensing Claudia's mood, Millie became quiet towards the end of her shift.

At three, Claudia saw her out onto the terrace. 'Is your dad coming for you?'

'Yes. He said he'd wait on the road for me.' Millie frowned. 'Is everything alright, Claudia?'

'I'm just a bit tired.'

'Only I was wondering, can we make more soap some time?'

Ah. 'Sorry, but I have to pick my times on the spur of the moment in the summer because I'm so busy. Maybe when things quieten down a bit.'

Claudia hated the disappointment on Millie's face, watching her sadly as the girl rounded the side of the building, but she was determined. Jason had made his position clear, apology or no. Until he could wholeheartedly accept Claudia's friendship with his daughter, Claudia couldn't see how to avoid Millie getting a little hurt.

Sarah, who'd been wiping tables on the terrace, came over before Claudia went back inside. 'I overheard that little exchange. Millie sounded confused. Is this really necessary, Claudia? I thought you and Jason were getting on okay now. He helped you all day after the window got smashed, and I heard you were in the pub together.'

'Yes, but that doesn't change this thing with Millie, does it? I can't keep on going against his wishes, Sarah. I've been doing that for weeks now. Up until recently, I got away with it, but…'

'If this is about the Wicca thing, that wasn't even your doing!' Sarah said hotly. 'It's just a teenager's natural curiosity and that blasted Hester's Cauldron.'

'I know. And Jason sees that now. He's agreed that Millie can meet with Tanya.'

'So what's the problem?'

'I think he feels that if Millie wasn't under my influence, it might not have happened. And of course, her accessing Tanya *is* through me.'

'So you're still going to hold Millie at arm's length?'

'It's what Jason wants, even if he tries to pretend it's not.'

Sarah huffed, ignoring a customer trying to grab her attention. 'After all you've done for that girl! Millie's come along in leaps and bounds since the day she set foot in Healing Waves, and I defy anyone to say otherwise.' With that, she stormed off to find out what her impatient customer wanted.

Back inside Healing Waves, Claudia hated that Sarah had her doubting her strategy. It didn't help when she found Millie's mobile phone under the counter.

Damn. I'll have to take that up there, if she doesn't realise she's left it. So much for keeping my distance!

Chapter Twenty-Three

'I *hate* you!'

Jason's face turned ashen. 'That's a strong thing to say, isn't it?'

'No. It's about right. Why would you *do* that?'

Jason floundered. He'd picked Millie up from Healing Waves, got home, asked her how her day had gone. She'd told him she'd left her mobile behind. He'd asked if she wanted to go back for it. She'd said no thank you, she'd already *tried* that.

They were barely over the doorstep before she'd launched into him, telling him how distant Claudia had been with her all day; how she'd overheard Claudia and Sarah talking, from the side of the building when she'd doubled back for her phone – something about keeping her at arm's length because Jason wanted it.

Jason was struggling to process it. He'd apologised to Claudia, hadn't he? Even if that wasn't enough, he wasn't sure why she'd take it out on Millie when they were so fond of each other. As his daughter stared him down, he wracked his brain. He'd said it before, too, he supposed – about not liking her influencing his daughter. But that was ages ago, before they got to know each other. Before they… well…

'Millie, about Claudia…'

'Oh, we all know what you think of Claudia!'

'I don't think you do,' Jason said carefully, his mind flooding with images of him tumbling with a golden-haired goddess on her bed behind bead curtains, her wild curls spread across the pillow as he made love to her.

But Millie had more to say. 'You think she's bonkers. You don't like anything she sells, anything she does, anything she believes in.'

'That's *enough*! It's true that I wasn't keen at first, but I've given way on a great many things for your sake *and* for Claudia's. I've listened. I've tried to understand. Don't I get *any* credit?'

'Why should you? Do you give *her* any?'

If only you knew. 'Of course I do.'

'Then why would you tell her to stay away from me? Can't you see how much she's helped me?'

Millie's anger came at him like a wall. Shakily, Jason said, 'I didn't tell her to stay away. I...'

I told her to stop trying to be your mother.

'It doesn't matter, does it?' Millie ranted. 'She doesn't want to be my friend any more. Thanks a lot, Dad. I'm off to get ready for Jessica's.' She stormed out, the pounding of her boots up the stairs accentuating her fury.

Jason sank down at the breakfast bar, his elbows on the polished granite, his head in his hands. All his high hopes for a new start where they could move on from Gemma's death, where Millie would make new friends and take an interest in school and deal with her grief and lose some of that damned *anger* that wore them both down to shadows of themselves...

And now look at where they were, all because of an overheard conversation. *Again.* Millie already blamed him for everything from wanting to divorce her mother to the sun not shining on a morning, and now this.

Thanks, Claudia. Thanks a lot.

When he drove Millie to Jessica's half an hour later, he pointed out that she still didn't have her mobile. She told him he was welcome to retrieve it for her, since Claudia didn't want *her* around more than necessary.

Jason decided that wasn't an option he could face right now.

Back home, he didn't fancy dinner. It would only sit like cement in his stomach. Instead, he mooched aimlessly around the house, knowing that Millie was probably spending the evening telling her friends what a bastard he was.

When the doorbell rang at nine, he was busy burning toast. Millie had her own key, so why not just let herself in?

Tossing the burned toast in the bin, his stomach growling at the delay for the one calming item it fancied, he padded to the door.

Claudia stood on his doorstep, her hair scraped away from her face in an attempt at a ponytail. She looked pale.

'I brought this. Millie left it.' She handed him the mobile. 'And we need to talk.'

He hesitated, then moved aside for her to enter. She stood in the kitchen, sniffing the air.

'Burned toast,' he explained curtly. 'Take a seat.'

'It's not a social call.' But she perched on a bar stool.

Jason's heart sank. He'd never heard her so business-like. He tried for something positive. 'I'm glad you got Healing Waves reopened so soon. Did the police follow up on Hester's Cauldron?'

'Yes. And in response, I had a lovely visit from Amber's father, threatening me with legal action.'

Jason ran a hand through his hair. 'Jeez, Claudia. I'm sorry.'

'Don't apologise. It had to be done. But I do need you to stay out of it now. Leave it to the police.'

'Did they get anywhere?'

'The officer who spoke to us on Thursday came by this afternoon. They don't believe it was Hester's. They had a visit from Amber's father, too, but I think it only got their backs up. They told him they were entitled to make enquiries on such a serious matter and would not be swayed from their duty… although they also told him he had nothing more to worry about.'

'It's a mess.'

'Yes.' Claudia looked around. 'Millie told me she was going out tonight. Is she back yet?'

'No, but she's due any time.'

'Then I'll be quick. Tanya phoned me. Millie cancelled their meet-up.'

Jason's heart sank. 'When?'

'Late this afternoon.'

After my daughter told me she hates me.

'I didn't ask her to,' he said defensively. 'Did she tell Tanya why?'

'She said it was too much hassle arguing with you about everything. Tanya reminded her that they had your permission, but Millie said she knew you hadn't really wanted to give it. Tanya said to let her know if she changed her mind.'

Jason sighed. 'I'm sorry.'

'Are you? I don't think so.'

'Don't tell me what I think.'

'You didn't give permission with your whole heart, Jason. Millie knew that.'

'No, I didn't give permission with my whole heart!' he snapped. 'I was coerced into it – by you, by Millie, by Tanya. I didn't stand much of a chance, did I? That doesn't mean I'm not sorry that Millie cancelled.'

Claudia shook her head. 'You've made a mistake. It would've been better for Millie to do it this way. Who knows what she might do instead?'

Still raw from his scene with Millie, Jason didn't fancy another bout of being told what a crap parent he was. 'Don't tell me about making mistakes. You made a pretty big one yourself.'

Claudia frowned. 'What mistake?'

'Millie overheard your little conversation with Sarah this afternoon.' Satisfied when she looked crestfallen, Jason rubbed it in. 'Won't you *ever* learn to check who's around before you speak? Don't you think that gossip has already caused enough trouble around here?'

'It wasn't gossip. It was a conversation expressing genuine concern for your daughter. Sarah's worried about her. I was trying to explain.'

'Explain what? How I'm the big bad wolf? I didn't ask you to unfriend my own daughter!'

'I have *not* unfriended her. I know you disapprove of me getting too involved. You reminded me I'm not her *mother*. Funnily enough, I took that to mean you wanted me to spend less time with her. I was trying to back away, as kindly as I could.'

'I've apologised for what I said, so don't keep throwing it back at me. I'm tired of being the bad guy, Claudia. I'm tired of being blamed when I don't give in over things I don't agree with. And I'm tired of being blamed for wanting some control over what you fill my daughter's head with!'

She looked at him, shocked. 'You make it sound like I deliberately inveigled my way into your lives just so I could experiment with all my wild ideas on Millie. That is *so* unfair! I wasn't looking to befriend a difficult fourteen-year-old. *She* was drawn to *me*. That was hardly my fault. I did the best I could with the situation.'

A noise in the hall made her stop. Worried, Jason held up a hand and went to check, but there was nobody there.

When he came back in and shook his head, Claudia went on, 'I like Millie. I've enjoyed watching her drop that defensive armour bit by bit, so we could see the real girl underneath. I won't apologise for wanting to help her.' She sighed. 'But you and me, Jason? We've been on this merry-go-round ever since we met. You don't like something, I explain it, you grudgingly accept it… Rinse and repeat. Well, you know what? I'm done with that.'

Claudia proved her point by stalking out into the hall, slamming the front door, climbing into her car and backing out of his drive like a banshee.

Back in the kitchen, Jason didn't even want toast now. He didn't like that his apology had been tossed back in his face – he'd thought that Claudia's compassion for his situation and their lovemaking the other night meant it had been accepted.

He knew there had been other instances where he'd expressed doubt about her ways and his desire to protect Millie, but he wasn't happy that she'd made Millie miserable by being so distant with her – or that she'd discussed it with Sarah *and* allowed it to be overheard.

He sat for a while, his stomach roiling, then glanced at his watch. He'd told Millie to be back by nine. It was nine thirty. Texting her was no use, since her phone was staring at him from the kitchen counter.

His brain told him to leave it a while longer. His gut told him he couldn't. He phoned Jessica's landline – something he was now glad he'd insisted on Millie providing – and explained.

'But we dropped her off about a quarter of an hour ago!' Jessica's mother said. 'I watched her let herself in. Are you sure she didn't go straight up to her room?'

'I'll check. Thank you. I'll get back to you.'

Jason did check, but he knew in his gut that Millie wasn't in the house. As he searched every room to be sure, his mind raced. While he and Claudia were talking, they'd heard a noise in the hall, but no one was there. Had Millie come in, then left again? Had she heard anything? And if so, *what* had she heard?

He phoned the first person he thought of – Claudia.

*

'No, Jason, she's not with me, but… Will you listen? Just meet me at the beach. We'll start there.'

Claudia clicked off her phone, threw on trainers, sent an apologetic look at Pudding who'd been unceremoniously turfed off her lap, dashed down the steps from her flat and out onto the beach.

She had no idea where Millie might be, but the beach was as good a place as any to look. Jogging along, Claudia was glad of the street lamps dotted along the beach road that cast pools of light across the sand.

She spotted Millie at the rock where they had sat together the day Claudia taught her to listen to the waves, just as she heard a screech of brakes on the road above. Jason must have seen her jogging along and stopped to join her.

They converged on Millie together. Millie was immediately subjected to a fierce hug from Jason, followed by a tirade along the lines of what the hell did she think she was playing at and did she realise anything could have happened…? All to be expected, but not helpful, as far as Claudia could see.

Laying a hand on Jason's arm to quiet him, Claudia said to Millie, 'Perhaps you could wait in the car? Let me speak to your dad for a minute.'

Millie gave her a searing look that made Claudia wince before stomping off, tears and mascara streaming down her face. She'd heard something she shouldn't have, that was for sure.

Jason rounded on Claudia. 'Do you *mind?* I was in the middle of...'

'Yelling at her? How helpful do you think that is?'

'My daughter went missing in the dark without her phone, Claudia. I have a right to yell. She needs to understand...'

'Jason, Millie did *not* go missing! She left the house for some breathing space because she was upset. You wouldn't have been worried if she'd been walking home from a friend's house, would you?'

'No, because I would've known where she was, and besides, I would've picked her up at this time of night. She could have gone anywhere. Anything could have happened.'

'But she didn't, and it didn't. She was here at the beach, the first place we looked, and not for long. She wasn't in any danger. It's well-lit here. There are people outside the pub and dog walkers on the beach. Porthsteren's a safe place. You're overreacting.'

'*Overreacting?*' He shook his head. 'You think you're so clever, don't you? Knowing where she'd be.'

'I didn't know. I just guessed.'

But Jason wasn't in a listening mood. 'Have you *any* idea how sick this made me feel? The sheer *dread* that something might have happened to my daughter?'

'Of course I have!'

His face was cold with fury. 'No. You don't. You really don't, Claudia. You've never had kids. You have *no idea* what it's like!'

And with that, he stormed off to join Millie in the car.

Claudia stood in the same spot until she saw his lights fading up the hill, then flopped down on the sand, ignoring the damp seeping through her jeans, hugging her knees to her chest.

Jason may as well have punched her. He knew how much she'd wanted a family; how it had all gone wrong for her. He was the only person in Cornwall apart from Tanya that she'd told. To have her confidences, her heartache, thrown in her face like that, when he knew how much it meant to her... She didn't care how distraught he was. He'd crossed a red line, and she couldn't see how they could ever come back from that.

When Sarah had asked her whether Jason was breaking up with her over Millie, Claudia hadn't known how to answer.

She knew now. Whatever relationship she and Jason might have had simply couldn't survive when one person could be so thoughtless with the other's feelings – no matter what the circumstances.

*

Jason and Millie drove home in silence, but when she tried to disappear off to her room, he grabbed her arm. 'No way, young lady.'

She glared at him. 'Oh. Sorry. Haven't you finished shouting at me yet?'

No, I bloody well haven't. But Claudia's words were still ringing in his ears. 'I won't shout. Come and have some tea.'

To his surprise, Millie followed him into the kitchen and waited silently while he filled the kettle and made decaff – a small nod to Claudia. He was tired. He didn't need caffeine keeping him awake all night.

He handed a mug to Millie. 'Tell me why you ran off.' When Millie remained mutinously quiet, he said, 'Tell me what you heard.'

At that, the tears began to fall again. 'That Claudia hadn't wanted to befriend a *difficult* teenager. That it wasn't her fault I wanted to spend time with her. That she was dealing with the *situation* as best she could.'

Jason sighed and sipped his tea. It burned his tongue, so he added more milk. 'That was a small part of a bigger conversation, Millie. You heard the worst part. It's out of context.'

'I heard what I heard, Dad! You can't put that in context.'

'Yes, I can. Claudia said those things in her own defence, because I'd suggested she was taking over with you. What you didn't hear was what she said afterwards – about how much she likes you.' He frowned, trying to remember Claudia's exact words, but he couldn't. 'About seeing you get better since you came down here. She's enjoyed being a part of that.' He watched his daughter struggling with emotion. 'C'mon. Drink some tea.'

When Millie tried, the combination of that and the tears only made her hiccup.

'Please don't blame Claudia, Millie.' *Blame me. Might as well. You blame me for everything else.* 'What she was saying, if either of us tried to listen, was that she might not have been looking to befriend us, but she's very glad she did. You, anyway.'

Most certainly not me. Not now.

*

Despite her exhaustion, as soon as she closed Healing Waves the next day, Claudia made the drive to Falmouth to pour out her frustration and misery to Tanya.

'I'm tired of excusing his speak-before-you-think attitude. I'm tired of making allowances for what he's been through; for his difficulties raising Millie on his own. I'm entitled to be spoken to in a civil manner by a man who's supposed to care for me, surely?'

'Yes.' Tanya sighed. 'I know we're all prone to saying the wrong thing, but Jason does have a particular talent for it.'

'I'm not talking about the odd *faux pas* here, Tanya. He crossed *so* many red lines last night.'

'He touched a nerve, that's all. He won't realise how much having a family mattered to you.'

'Tanya, I told him I left my husband because he wouldn't have a family with me; because he was trying to cheat me out of having one. How hard can it be for Jason to work out that my chances are getting slimmer? That I'd have to start all over again; find someone interested in a family – someone who hasn't already been there, done that and doesn't want to do it all again?' Claudia fought back tears. 'I won't hook up with someone just to have children. I need to be with the *right* man. I know a family might not happen for me. I don't need it thrown in my face by someone I thought I was close to.'

'He'd had a scare,' Tanya soothed. 'He said it in the heat of the moment.'

'Jason has more heat-of-the-moment moments than any man I've ever met, and I'm tired of being the brunt of them.'

'But isn't that what attracts you to him, too?' Tanya asked her bluntly. 'His fire? His ability to express emotion?' She swirled her wine in the glass. 'Lee was a cold fish in comparison.'

'That isn't the point.'

'Then what is the point, beyond him being thoughtless and saying the wrong thing?'

Claudia sighed. 'He doesn't trust me with his daughter. He never has. Oh, he's occasionally indulged my attempts to help, but he considers it playing at best and interference at worst. He'll always put Millie first.'

'Yes. He will.'

Claudia stared at Tanya, shocked. 'That's harsh.'

Tanya gave her a sad smile. 'Claudia, Jason will always be a father first and foremost, before he can be anything with or for you.'

'I know that. And that's the way it *should* be.' Claudia's voice hitched. 'But it's hard to know I'd always be second best.'

'Not *be* second best. Just come second in a clinch, maybe. Jason knows how much you've done for Millie. You sold yourself short once, with Lee. Don't ever do it again.'

'Huh. Who needs positive affirmations when they have a friend like you?'

'I'm only saying what Jason should say but hasn't. He cares about you, Claudia, but he's been putting his daughter first for so long, he doesn't know how to release the stranglehold that has him in.'

*

Even though Jason had smoothed things over with Millie a little – she was at least talking to him in monosyllables – she still spent most of Sunday in her room.

He spent the day out on the decking, staring out to sea, running over his conversation with Claudia on the beach, trying to justify what he'd said. Some of it, he could; some of it, he couldn't. The parts he couldn't... He might as well have his lips sewn together so this never happened again because, once more, he'd gone too far. Would she accept yet another apology, or had he run out of credits?

Only one way to find out.

But when he took an evening walk down the hill and along the beach, Claudia's lights were off, and the only answer to his knock was Pudding shooting through the cat flap to rub his head against Jason's legs and mew loudly, hoping an extra food delivery had appeared.

'Can't help you, mate,' Jason said, tickling his ears. 'No access.' *To the flat or your mistress.* 'At least she's still talking to you. Probably won't talk to me ever again.'

That thought depressed Jason more than he could say, haunting him through waking patches in the night and following him into his working day.

When Tanya phoned him not long after he'd got to work, he was in the middle of a convoluted discussion with a colleague, but when he saw the caller display, he immediately said, 'Sorry, I have to take this' and went outside.

Tanya was not complimentary. When Jason managed to get a word in edgeways, he pointed out that he'd tried to see Claudia last night but she'd obviously been busy slinging insults at him in Falmouth.

'Then you'd better try again. And don't mess it up!' And to make sure he didn't, Tanya provided him with a long list of what had upset Claudia and how to put it right. By the end of the call, his head was spinning.

He'd be lucky if it was still on his shoulders by the time Claudia finished with him.

Chapter Twenty-Four

'Ms Bennett. Good morning.'

'Morning, Officer. Can I get you some tea?'

No customers in the shop at the moment, thank goodness. Police presence probably isn't good for business.

The policeman looked at the jar of leaves Claudia held up and said, 'Er. No, thanks. Just had coffee. I brought this. It's addressed to you, but it was left at the police station by a distraught woman with a disturbing story. Would you mind opening it, please?'

'Distraught woman?' Claudia asked, panicked. 'What distraught woman?'

'Alice Walters.'

'*Alice?*' She snatched the envelope from him. 'You didn't read it?'

'It is addressed to you, miss.'

With shaking fingers, Claudia opened the letter.

Dear Claudia

By the time you read this, I will be on my way to… a long way away. I want to thank you for all you've done for me. I know I haven't always been good company. But you were always kind. I admired you for making a new start, opening your shop in Porthsteren, away

from whatever life it was you wanted to leave. Well, it's my turn
to do the same. I know you suspected George of things – things he
didn't do. But I'm so sorry for what he did do, on account of me.
The police will explain.

Alice

The officer waited patiently before asking, 'May I read it now?'

'Please.' Claudia handed it over. When he'd folded it back into the
envelope, she said, 'Tell me.'

'Alice called at the station this morning. She'd waited until her
husband went to work. She had a suitcase. She was leaving him. She
told us he'd caused the damage to your shop.'

Claudia stared at him. '*George* did those things? But why on earth…?'

'She told us he'd never approved of her frequenting your shop or
your other wotsits – workshops, meditation.'

'I knew that. But that's just disapproval.'

'It went much deeper than that, Ms Bennett. He thought you were
a bad influence. Lately, he felt that Alice had changed. And then, a
couple of weeks ago, he found her journal. She told us she bought the
notebook here.'

So Alice was *writing a journal, after all.*

'He read it. There was a lot about how much she liked your shop;
how much she enjoyed the meditations. Towards the end, she wrote
about wanting to leave him.'

'Oh no.'

'He burned it. Threw out everything he could find that she'd bought
from you – crystals and the like. In his mind, everything began to go
wrong when you came to Porthsteren. He decided you needed to be

scared away or put out of business. He'd hoped the symbols would turn people against you. When they didn't work, he had to go further.'

'You've spoken to him, then?'

'Yes. We picked him up at work. He confessed straight away – he was so angry when we told him his wife had left and reported him, it all came pouring out.'

Claudia sat down, her legs numb. 'I don't believe it! So when Alice came to you, she already knew?'

'More or less. She'd found the black spray-paint can in his shed. It was new and they had no other use for it. The morning the window was smashed, he'd told her that work had texted to call him in early, but she checked his phone later, and there was no text.'

The blood drained from Claudia's face. How could someone local, someone she knew, hate her so much? Blame her for so much?

'Ms Bennett?' The officer's voice seemed far away. 'Ms Bennett. Head down, please.' When she didn't respond, he simply pushed her head to her knees.

'Is there anyone I can call?' he asked her when some colour had returned to her cheeks.

'Next door. Sarah or Evelyn. Please.'

When he returned with Evelyn, she clucked and fussed and made the poor man repeat his tale, while brewing Claudia peppermint tea.

'Well, I should go,' he said when he was sure Claudia would be okay. 'Can I keep the note?'

'Yes. Thank you for everything.'

'You're welcome.'

'What a nice young man,' Evelyn said as he left. 'And such a terrible story!'

'Yes.' *One that will be all around Porthsteren by the end of the day.*

Evelyn hugged her tight. 'Will you be alright, Claudia? Shouldn't you close up for a while?'

At that, Claudia gritted her teeth. 'Can't afford to. This place has been closed too many days this year already. I'll be okay.'

'But you'll phone Tanya?'

'Yes.'

'And Jason?'

'No.'

'Oh. Okay. Well, call us if you need *any*thing.'

'I will. Thank you.'

Claudia got through the day in a haze, keeping herself busy, Sarah or Evelyn popping in once an hour to check she hadn't fainted on the floor, and Tanya phoning twice more after Claudia had delivered her initial report.

By the time she got up to her flat, all she could think about was yoga. All Pudding could think about was dinner, so she saw to him before changing, putting on some South American flute music and settling down on her yoga mat.

The loud knock on the door did not please her. Nor did seeing Jason on her doorstep.

'What do *you* want?'

'Good evening to you, too.'

'I'm not in the mood to play games, Jason. I've had a crap day. Just say what you want to say, then go.'

'Can I at least come inside? Or do you want everyone to get a bulletin tomorrow morning from Libby at the General Store who got it from the harbour master who got it from that woman walking her dog on the beach?' He pointed to a prancing Cocker Spaniel and its owner, down on the sand.

'Fine.' Claudia stood aside to let him pass. 'Tea?'

'Will it have arsenic in it?'

'Who knows?'

'Then I'll pass, thank you.'

If he was waiting for an invitation to sit, he would be waiting a very long time. 'Well?'

'Tanya phoned me today. Twice.'

Claudia closed her eyes as she tried to subdue the boiling sensation in her arteries. Opening them again, she said, 'She shouldn't have done that.'

'Yes, she should. The second call was to tell me the latest about Healing Waves. I'm sorry, Claudia. I know you must be miserable about it.'

'Yes.' She shot him a challenging look. 'Will you be popping into Hester's Cauldron to apologise to them?'

'Er. No. Best not, I think.'

'Hmmph. And the other call Tanya made to you without my permission?'

'That was to tell me that I'm a stubborn bastard. She was right about that. But she thought I wouldn't apologise without being pushed, and she was wrong about *that*. I came by last night, but you weren't here.'

'Oh, you're apologising? I'm sorry. I must've missed it.'

Jason took a deep breath. 'Look, I appreciate you might not want to make this easy for me, Claudia Rose, but if you make it impossible, then I'll go, and we'll be at loggerheads forever and a day.'

It wasn't his logic that softened her, but his use of her full name.

'Okay.' She sat and indicated that he should, too, noting that he chose the seat farthest from both her and Pudding, as though he didn't fancy being injured by either of them.

'What I said was unacceptable. I was fraught and emotional, and I said things I shouldn't have. I apologise.' He glared at her. 'You didn't miss *that*, right?'

'I heard. I'm not sure it changes anything, though.'

Jason sighed. 'What I said was over the top. I know how much you've done for Millie. And I know she opens up to you in a way that she won't with me.'

It wasn't surprising he might resent her for that, at least, Claudia thought.

'She misses her mother,' she said. 'But I'm a poor substitute for Gemma, I'm afraid.'

Jason's Adam's apple bobbed. 'No, you're not, but nobody's trying to substitute Gemma here. That's not possible. What's important is that Millie has someone in her life who understands her and is happy to spend time with her. Someone who accepts her for who she is.' He looked down at his hands. 'I don't want our differences, the things I said the other night, to come between you and Millie.'

If Claudia had felt bad before, she felt a darned sight worse now. She'd thought he'd come to apologise for the hurtful things he'd said, but that was just an excuse for him to grovel for his daughter's sake.

Claudia walked to the door, indicating they were done, leaving Jason no choice but to stand and follow, a puzzled expression on his face.

'Don't worry, Jason. I would never deliberately hurt Millie because of what's going on between us. If I know you sanction her spending time with me, then that's what matters. If you and I disagree in the future, we'll have to find a way around that without Millie playing piggy-in-the-middle, but this will do for now.' She gave him a small, tight smile. 'Goodnight, Jason.' And without waiting for whatever he was going to say – because he could only make things worse – she closed the door with a firm click.

There was a moment's silence, and then she heard the tap of his feet on the metal stairs. Leaning against the door, she sank down to the floor, her head in her hands. When Pudding, his instinct for upset keen, padded over, clambered into her lap and rubbed his mottled face against hers, the floodgates opened.

*

'Jason Craig, you are such an idiot! What is *wrong* with you?'

It seemed that Claudia had phoned her best friend the previous night to report on Jason's latest misdemeanours and to tell her off for contacting Jason in the first place.

And so Tanya had phoned him at work again – his colleagues must think he was having some wild affair – to tell him she had an afternoon meeting twenty minutes from Penzance, and she expected him to meet her after work or else. When he pointed out that that would make him late home to Millie, she uttered a string of swear words he wouldn't have thought she knew and told him the child would probably live through the ordeal.

Peering at his arm now, wondering if it would bruise, Jason took a look around the café to see if anyone had seen him being punched by a skinny, five-foot-three blonde.

'I did what you told me to,' he insisted.

'No, you didn't. You made things worse.' Tanya shook her head, muttering to herself, 'How could you *possibly* have made things worse?'

Jason took a gulp of his tea – too weak – and said, 'I followed your instructions to the letter, Tanya. I went to apologise – which I did well to manage at all, since she was so damned confrontational.'

'Hmm. I wonder why?' Tanya murmured.

'Then I said a bunch of other stuff, and… It all went wrong.'

'Okay, Jason, think carefully about exactly what you said and how you said it, because what I got from Claudia isn't what I'm getting from you.' Tanya rolled her eyes. 'You two are on different planets to each other, you know that?'

'Very probably. Okay, tell me what I said that I didn't think I said.'

'You apologised for what you said the other night on the beach.'

'Yes. But she said being sorry didn't change things.' Jason frowned in concentration. 'So then I told her I thought she was good for Millie. She said something about Gemma, and I told her nobody expected her to stand in for Gemma. Was that it?'

'No, that was okay, in the context.' Running out of patience, Tanya said, 'You told her you didn't want your differences to come between her and Millie.'

'Was that so terrible?'

'No, but…' Tanya pulled at her short blonde hair as though she wanted to tear it out at the roots. 'Don't you think she might have wanted to hear that you wanted to put your differences aside for the sake of you as a *couple*? Not just for your daughter's sake?'

'I thought that was implied.'

'It wasn't.'

'Well, I *might* have got into that, but I was down the stairs before my arse was clear of the doorway. I don't understand why she was so mad.'

Taking pity on him, Tanya placed a hand on his across the café table. 'She wasn't mad. She was disappointed. Claudia knows you'll always put your daughter before her. But she was beginning to hope she might at least come a very close second. Last night, you put Millie first. Again.'

'But that wasn't what I meant! I mean, I did, but there was more to say.'

'Yes, there was.' Tanya smiled sadly. 'And you didn't apologise for the one unforgivable thing you'd said, did you?'

'About her not being a mother,' he admitted quietly. Tanya was right – it had been unforgivable, after Claudia had opened her heart and soul to him about her hopes of having a family being dashed by that selfish bastard of an ex of hers. 'I suppose I was trying to ease myself in – you know, start with the general, then move onto the specific. But I never got the chance.'

'If you decide to try again, Jason, put *her* first. Just this once. Make her feel like she really matters to you.' Tanya glanced at her watch. 'You need to get back to Millie.'

Jason left the café with her. 'Thanks, Tanya, for what you're trying to do.'

'You're welcome. But bear in mind that if Claudia finds out I'm meddling again, she'll kill me.'

Jason smiled. 'Suits me. I don't want her thinking I need help from a witch to run my love life.'

Startling him, Tanya reached out to touch his face. 'You said it. *Finally!*'

Jason's brows knitted together. 'Said what?'

'Think about it.'

Walking to his car, he muttered, 'What did I say? Why do these women expect me to remember the exact wording I used all the time? All I said was that I shouldn't need a witch to run my love life for me... *love*. Ah.'

Climbing into his car, Jason sat for a moment. 'Love life' was just an expression, wasn't it? He wasn't, was he? In love with Claudia? He dropped his head to the steering wheel and banged it a couple of times in the hope of working out what the hell was going on in there. A passer-by stared at him, concerned.

He started the car. Whether he was in love with her was a moot point. Firstly, he doubted Claudia wanted him to be. Secondly, Millie might not want him to be, either. And even if she claimed not to mind, there were too many fireworks and variables to drag his daughter into this.

Jason drove back to Porthsteren in a daze not suitable for rush-hour traffic and winding roads. When he got home, Millie had made pasta. Again. He was going to start looking like fusilli at this rate.

When they'd eaten – or both pushed it around their plates for a while – he decided there was one matter he *could* do something about.

'Millie, I've been talking to Tanya.' *Perfectly true.* 'We both think you should reconsider learning from her.' *Also true, even if that's not what we talked about.*

Millie's shoulders slumped. 'I told you, I changed my mind.'

Jason hoisted himself from the bar stool and carried the dishes to the sink. 'For the wrong reasons.'

'You told Claudia you'd been forced into agreeing.'

He caught her gaze and held it. 'I said a lot of things I shouldn't have.'

'You honestly don't mind if I phone Tanya?'

'Honestly.' And this time, Jason meant it. although it occurred to him that he ought to text Tanya to forewarn her. 'I'd leave it till tomorrow, if I were you, or you'll be late for meditation. I'll give you a lift.'

'You're not coming?'

I'm not welcome until I've tried apologising again. And I can't do that in a room full of people hoping to find some Zen. 'Not tonight. I have work to do.'

'Okay.' Millie pounded upstairs to get ready, leaving Jason to grab his phone and send the witch a text.

*

Late Sunday afternoon was Millie's first date for Wicca lessons. Tanya had agreed to drive all the way to their house so that Jason would feel comfortable with it – a generous gesture.

Jason wasn't sure he'd ever feel comfortable with it, but he did feel settled about it, and that would have to do.

He still hadn't been to see Claudia. On Wednesday, he'd had Millie to pick up after drama, and as she'd been in a chatty mood with him for a change – perhaps because he was being supportive about the Wicca thing – he hadn't felt he could abscond for a 'walk'. On Thursday, he'd had a late meeting with a client. He knew that on Friday Claudia and Tanya were spending the evening together, because Tanya had texted to tell him. She'd also told him to pull his finger out, and she'd made it graphically clear from where. Saturday, Millie was working at Healing Waves, and since it was Claudia's busiest day, he didn't think it would be the best timing.

And so here he was on Sunday afternoon, drinking tea out on the decking, procrastinating.

'Dad, are you okay?' Millie came and sat down in the other chair.

'Fine. Shouldn't you be getting ready for Tanya?'

'Nothing to get ready.' Millie stayed there, quietly studying him.

'What is it?' he asked.

'When are you going to tell Claudia that you love her?'

Jason sloshed tea all over his feet. '*What?*'

Millie rolled her eyes. 'C'mon, Dad. Everybody knows it but her. I do. Tanya does.'

'Has Tanya been talking to you about me and Claudia?' *I'll kill her!*

'No, but I mentioned to her that Claudia seemed down yesterday, and Tanya said she was worried, too.' Millie drew her knees up to her chest, watching the spilled tea trickle into the cracks between the decking. 'Claudia puts on a bright face, but…'

'She's had a lot to deal with, Millie. The damage to the shop, not so long after the storm in the spring. And it's a long, busy season. She can't be expected to be on top of the world all the time.'

Millie gave him a look. 'Dad, I'm fourteen, not four. I know there was *something* going on between you two.'

He looked at her for a long while, then nodded, beaten. 'You knew, huh?

'Yup.' She grinned that cheeky grin she used to send his way as a little girl. He hadn't realised how much he'd missed it. It sent a pang to his heart.

'Millie, Claudia and I don't see eye to eye on…'

'On just about everything. Yeah. Got that. Hasn't stopped you falling in love with her, though, has it?'

Jeez. He couldn't believe he was having this conversation with his teenage daughter. 'No.'

'I *knew* it!' Millie leapt to her feet and did a victory dance.

'Alright, smartarse, that's enough.'

Laughing, she plopped down onto the decking by his side. 'Why won't you tell her?'

Jason heaved a sigh. 'It's complicated.'

'Because of me?' Millie asked, serious now.

Oh, dear lord. How could he tell her yes, because of her? He opened his mouth, but nothing useful transferred from his brain to his tongue.

Millie turned to him, her eyes appealing directly to him. 'I don't want you to not be happy because of me. If you two like each other, you should do something about it.'

'I could never be unhappy because of you, Millie.' Jason sighed. 'But... What about Mum?'

Tears welled in her eyes. 'Mum's gone. And you weren't happy with her. With each other, I should say.' When Jason raised an eyebrow at that, she said, 'I've been unfair on you. I knew that, deep down, but with Mum dying...'

'I know.'

Millie took his hand in hers, a gesture that caused tears to well up in *his* eyes. She hadn't held his hand in so long.

'Mum wouldn't have wanted you to carry on being unhappy, Dad. You were getting divorced anyway. You would've found someone else eventually.'

'It's not just that.' Jason squeezed Millie's hand. Took a deep breath. He could be honest with his own daughter, couldn't he? '*If* Claudia wants anything to do with me – which she may not, because I've made an awful mess of it so far – we have no idea how it'll go. If it works out badly, that might hurt you as well as me and her. It'd be hard for you to be friends with her if she's not talking to me. Or friends with me if you side with her, which is far more likely.'

'It might *not* go badly.'

'It's too early to know that. But even if it went well...'

Realisation dawned on Millie's face. 'We might all end up living together, you might even marry her, and then she'd be my stepmother?'

'It's... a very distant possibility.'

'Why is that a bad thing?'

'It's not a bad thing. But it is a *big* thing. I don't expect you to accept a replacement for your mum.'

'Dad, I think Claudia's great. And I wouldn't see her as a replacement for Mum. She'd be... Well, she'd be Claudia.'

Jason looked into his daughter's eyes. She'd come such a long way, these past months.

He sighed. 'I think we're jumping the gun a bit. Claudia's not even speaking to me.'

'Only because you're not saying the right things.'

He rolled his eyes. 'I'm surrounded by know-it-all women. You're all driving me mad.'

Millie grinned. 'But in a good way, right?'

He reached out to ruffle her already-scruffy hair. 'Yeah. Right.'

The doorbell put an end to their discussion.

'That'll be Tanya.'

Millie jumped to her feet and raced off to answer it while Jason sat there, stunned.

I was only going to go and see her to apologise, and now I might be telling Claudia I love her? How did that happen?

When Tanya came through to admire the view, he jumped to his feet. 'Hi. Bye. I have to go.'

'But Jason…'

As he grabbed his car keys, he heard Millie say in a low voice, 'Don't stop him. He's on a mission.'

Chapter Twenty-Five

Claudia had only just closed the shop, climbed the stairs with weary bones, plonked herself down on the sofa and picked up her cat when there was a pounding on the door.

With a sigh, she shifted Pudding and hoisted herself back to her feet.

It was Jason. With a determined look on his face.

Just what I need.

'Claudia Rose, we need to talk. And this time, you're going to let me say what I need to say, and you're not going to jump down my throat or pick on my choice of words or twist the meaning into something else.'

Claudia arched an imperious eyebrow, although his forceful tone meant she wasn't as confident as she appeared. 'Must be important. Should I be worried?' she asked.

'Depends on how you take it, but it *is* important. Could we sit down? Less confrontational that way.'

Claudia almost smiled at the way he'd switched from his rehearsed forceful opening to that nervous request.

'Fine by me. I'm sick of confrontation myself.'

She made for the sofa, curling her legs beneath her in a deliberately casual pose. Expecting Jason to choose the armchair, she was startled when he sat beside her and took her hand in his. The familiar warmth from his fingers flooded through her, setting her skin humming, as though her hand was telling the rest of her that they had come home.

This is too hard.

'Claudia. This animosity between us? We're better than that. It has to stop.'

'I couldn't agree more.'

He nodded, seemingly satisfied with his opening gambit. 'I can't always subscribe to the things you believe in, but I appreciate that they matter to you.'

'Thank you. That'll help where Millie's concerned.'

'This conversation isn't about Millie. Well, not in that sense, anyway.' Jason squeezed her hand. 'You've done so much for her, and I haven't thanked you anywhere near enough. I've ranted and railed a fair bit, but I haven't shown enough gratitude. She's happier, more positive than she's been in a long time. She's dealing with her grief; accepting it as a part of herself. That's down to you. I couldn't get anywhere with her.'

'That's because she blamed you for what went wrong between you and Gemma.'

'I think you've helped her with that too, in a roundabout way. She's finally cutting me some slack. I put that down to your influence on her. And I mean influence in a *good* way. You're an incredible woman.'

Startled by the compliment, Claudia shook her head. 'I'm not. I've just had longer at this new start thing than you. Thank you for saying that about Millie, though. I appreciate it.'

'That isn't all I came to say, and you're not kicking me out halfway through this time.' Jason's serious expression worried her. 'I want to talk about the future.'

Her heart sank. Had he decided that Porthsteren wasn't right for him and Millie?

'Claudia, you and I are like chalk and cheese.'

She sighed. She knew that. He didn't need to rub it in. 'What are you saying?'

'I'm saying I'm in love with you.'

'*What?*'

'I should have said it sooner, but I was in denial and out of touch with myself or whatever label you want to put on it. I'm not in denial any more.' He waited for a long moment. 'Please say something.'

But Claudia was speechless, her heart beginning to work its way back up from her feet, juddering like a faulty elevator. She'd expected another half-assed attempt at an apology. Another blazing row. She hadn't expected him to take her hand in his and tell her he was in love with her. Closing her eyes, she tried to tune out the million thoughts and feelings vying for dominance; tried to tune into the quiet voice within.

Tell him you love him.

I can't. There are too many obstacles, too many things we can't reconcile, too many...

Tell him you love him.

But a bigger voice drowned it out. The hurtful things he'd said were still too strong.

Jason read her mind. 'Claudia, what I said to you about you not knowing what it's like to be a mother was unforgivable.' He stood to pace the room. 'I *know* you wanted a family with Lee. And I know that you couldn't take up with any old someone just to fulfil that dream. You're right to do that. You deserve to be with someone who'll cherish you and respect your dreams.' He smiled. 'I'm sure I fall short of what you need in so many ways, but...' He stopped pacing and frowned. 'You haven't said anything since I told you I love you.' He swallowed. 'I guess you're telling me in the kindest way possible all

I need to know.' Nodding sadly, he said, 'Well. Thanks for listening. I appreciate it.'

Tell him you love him.

Claudia stood. 'That's it? I don't get *my* say?'

'But you were just sitting there…'

'You had a chance to think about what *you* wanted to say before you got here, didn't you? Aren't I allowed a little thinking time?'

'I…'

She shook her head. 'Doesn't matter. I don't need it.'

'Ah.' His face fell.

'Don't assume that because I don't need long to think means I won't say anything good.'

His expression was anguished. 'Then could you just get on with it? This is killing me!'

She smiled. 'Jason, you are the most infuriating man I've ever met, and that's saying something. You don't look before you leap, you're opinionated, your tolerance levels are woeful, and your temper needs taming.'

'Er. Thanks?'

'You're also the least selfish father I've ever come across. You put your own wellbeing way below your daughter's – and don't tell me that's only natural, because I can't imagine there are many who'd take the punch on the chin that you took over Gemma's affair for the sake of their daughter's memories. Under that gruff exterior, you have the kindest heart. And…'

The hope on his face was endearing.

Time to put him out of his misery.

'Maybe we could find a way to muddle along together.'

Tell him you love him.

'I love you.'

There. That wasn't so hard, was it?

Jason stood for a moment, disbelief on his face. And then he was across the room, folding her in his arms and squeezing her so tight she couldn't breathe, but she didn't care. Being in his arms was so right. For a moment, she absorbed the joy. And then that tricky little thing called reality reinstated its hold, and she pulled away.

'What about Millie?' she asked.

'It was Millie who sent me here. She knew I was in love with you before I knew it myself.'

Startled, Claudia laughed. 'She doesn't mind?'

'She's thrilled. She loves you. She hasn't said that yet, but I know she does. Not in the way she loved Gemma, but in a new Millie-Claudia way. It won't be easy. You should understand what you're letting yourself in for...'

'You haven't told me yet *what* I'm letting myself in for. Are we officially dating now?'

'*Dating?*' Jason gave her a puzzled look. 'Claudia, I only ever told two women I loved them before you. The first was a girl called Rebecca. I was sixteen and we were... Well, let's say some kind of endearment was required as a form of persuasion. It wasn't a long-lived relationship. The second was Gemma, and I married her.' He smiled. 'I'm sure dating will be involved at first, but I want so much more than that. I want us to have a *life* together.' His brow furrowed. 'And since the three of us and that demonic cat of yours won't fit into this so-called flat, that would mean you relocating to our place.'

Claudia's jaw dropped. 'You're asking me to move in with you?'

'Is... Is that a problem?'

Claudia grabbed a fistful of curls as she processed the idea. 'We've known each other for, what, three months? One minute we can't be in the same room without picking a fight, the next you're saying you're in love with me, and the next we're living together. Isn't that kind of fast?'

He gently unravelled her fingers from the hair she was tugging at and held her hands down at her sides. 'Claudia Rose, if there's one thing I've learned over the past couple of years, it's that tomorrow's never certain. I don't want to waste any of our tomorrows.'

Tell him yes.

Claudia passed a hand over her stomach to quiet her infamous gut instinct. This was too big to race into. If it was only about her and Jason, they could live with the consequences, but there was Millie to consider, whether Millie herself thought it was a good idea or not.

Letting go of Jason's hands, she moved away to drop back down on the sofa. 'Everything inside me wants to say yes, Jason, but if Millie got hurt…'

He crossed the room to kneel at her feet and took her hands again. 'Millie wants us to try. I told you, she adores you. I know you want a family of your own, but—'

'That doesn't matter,' Claudia cut in. 'I love Millie, you know I do. Having a family of my own is something I parcelled away in the attic of my mind a while ago.'

'Claudia, let me *finish*, will you?' Jason held her gaze. 'You can still have a family of your own.'

It took a moment for her to compute what he'd said. Another for it to sink in. 'You want to have a child with me?'

Jason took a deep breath. 'I know I'm looking ahead too far. I know we don't know each other well enough yet, and we need to see if we can live together without killing each other first. But I don't want that to be a deal-breaker for you.'

Ah. A sweetener.

When she said nothing, Jason said, 'I thought that would make you happy.'

Claudia took a juddering breath. 'Jason, you shouldn't consider starting another family just to keep me on board. I love you. I'd like us to be together. But a baby, when you already have a teenager? That's not a promise you should feel obligated to make.'

He shook his head and smiled. 'I'm no martyr. If I didn't want to start over, I wouldn't offer – even if I thought it was what you wanted. But I'm *so* in love with you. You'd be a wonderful mother. For you to be the mother of our child, if that happens for us? I'd be a lucky man.'

Claudia looked into his face for the longest time.

He means it.

Jason gave her no more persuasive words or pleading looks, but waited patiently, his eyes never leaving hers.

He means it. Tell him yes.

'Claudia, this suspense is no good for my heart.'

'In that case… Yes.'

He buried his face in her hair. 'I won't mess this up. I promise.'

'I know you won't. I won't let you.'

His kiss was long and sweet. When they pulled away, he rested his forehead against hers and murmured, 'Claudia Rose'.

They both jumped when Pudding leapt up between them.

'Aww, are you feeling left out, baby boy?'

Jason rolled his eyes. 'I presume that if I take you, I have to take the cat?'

'Yup.'

Claudia jumped again as a movement caught her eye. 'We have visitors.'

Jason spun his head around, and they both stared at the two faces at the window beside the door. Tanya and Millie.

'You'd better come in!' Claudia yelled.

They didn't need to be asked twice, bundling untidily through the door.

'How long have you been there?' Claudia asked.

Tanya shrugged apologetically. 'Only a couple of minutes.'

'How much did you see?' Jason asked.

'Just kissing.' Millie made a face. 'Gross.'

Jason stood and went over to his daughter, ruffling her hair. 'Better get used to it, kiddo. It was your idea.'

As Millie high-fived Tanya, Jason looked from one victorious face to the other. 'Aren't you two supposed to be casting spells or stirring cauldrons or whatever it is you conned me into allowing? You're not supposed to be interfering in my love life.'

Tanya grinned. 'So, you *are* admitting you have a love life?'

Jason reached for Claudia's hand, his pale blue eyes open and honest, melting any reserve Claudia might have still had and flooding her heart with hope.

'I believe I have the love *of* my life,' he said quietly, then reached for Millie with his other hand, clasping hers tightly in his. 'The other love of my life, anyway.'

Claudia smiled as she looked from him to Millie. She could settle for that. A man who loved her for who she was. A girl who had flourished under her friendship. The possibility of her own child to complete their family. Yes, she could settle for that.

She reached for Millie's other hand so they were joined in a circle of three.

A Letter from Helen

Dear reader,

Thank you for choosing *The Little Shop in Cornwall*. I hope you enjoyed reading about Claudia, Jason and Millie (and Pudding!) as much as I enjoyed creating their story.

To keep up to date with the latest news on my new releases, just click on the link below to sign up for a newsletter:

www.bookouture.com/helen-pollard

As you may have guessed, Porthsteren isn't a real place, but if you've been to Cornwall, I'm sure you will have visited wonderful coastal villages just like it – the kind of places that make you want to pack up all your worldly possessions and do exactly what Claudia did and make one of them your home. I love creating imaginary places for my books – the only problem is, I have to keep reminding myself that they're not real after all!

Developing my characters is like having imaginary friends in my head, the minor characters as well as the main players – it can get rather crowded in there! But there's always room for a cheeky pet, and Pudding fit the bill for this story perfectly.

Knowing that my books give readers a brief escape to somewhere sunny and picturesque, allowing them to lose themselves in my characters' lives for a while and stop worrying about their own, means a great deal to me.

If you enjoyed the read, I would love it if you could take the time to leave a review. It makes so much difference to know that readers have enjoyed my book and what they liked about it… and of course, it might encourage others to buy it and share that enjoyment! You can find me on Facebook and Twitter.

Thank you!
Helen x

 HelenPollardWrites
helenpollard147

Acknowledgements

As ever, a huge thank you to my publisher Bookouture for allowing me to bring my stories to life and get them out into the world. The entire team deserve praise, but very special thanks go to my editor Cara Chimirri for her support, her confidence in my writing and her love of my story. Thanks also to Claire Bord for her support, to Peta Nightingale for her unerring patience, and to Kim Nash and Noelle Holten for the publicity magic they weave.

My dear husband is a long-suffering soul. I can only hope I never find the end to his endless patience! I couldn't have done this without him.

A debt of gratitude goes to our current feline friend Cleo and her two predecessors. Many of their characteristics helped me to write Pudding with an equal helping of love and tongue-in-cheek.

A special shout-out to my writing friends, Authors on the Edge. Our meet-ups in Hebden Bridge always leave me energised and understood – never an easy task!

And finally, to the book-loving community at large – fellow writers, bloggers and of course all you readers out there – thank you. You make it all worthwhile.

Printed in Great Britain
by Amazon